INTO THE FLAMES

James Delargy was born and raised in Ireland and lived in South Africa, Australia and Scotland before ending up in semi-rural England where he now lives. He incorporates this diverse knowledge of towns, cities, landscapes and cultures picked up on his travels into his writing. His first novel, 55, was published in 2019 and has been sold to over twenty territories to date. It was followed in 2021 by the standalone thriller *Vanished*.

𝕏 @jdelargyauthor
jamesdelargy.com

Also by James Delargy

Vanished
55

INTO THE FLAMES

James Delargy

**SIMON &
SCHUSTER**

London · New York · Sydney · Toronto · New Delhi

First published in Great Britain by Simon & Schuster UK Ltd, 2024

The right of James Delargy to be identified as author
of this work has been asserted in accordance with the
Copyright, Designs and Patents Act, 1988.

1 3 5 7 9 10 8 6 4 2

Simon & Schuster UK Ltd
1st Floor
222 Gray's Inn Road
London WC1X 8HB

Simon & Schuster: Celebrating 100 Years of Publishing in 2024

Simon & Schuster Australia, Sydney
Simon & Schuster India, New Delhi

www.simonandschuster.co.uk
www.simonandschuster.com.au
www.simonandschuster.co.in

A CIP catalogue record for this book
is available from the British Library

Paperback ISBN: 978-1-3985-2514-6
Trade Paperback ISBN: 978-1-3985-2516-0
eBook ISBN: 978-1-3985-2515-3
Audio ISBN: 978-1-3985-2517-7

Typeset in Sabon by M Rules

Printed and Bound in the UK using 100% Renewable
Electricity at CPI Group (UK) Ltd

MIX
Paper | Supporting
responsible forestry
FSC C171272

To Harps. My World.

One

January 20 – 09.00 – Wind direction NE – Surface speed 35km/h

2 hours since North Rislake evacuation

South Rislake status = Amber (Prepare for possible evacuation)

The snarl ripped through the dry trees, the devil cracking its knuckles as it incinerated even the fresh growth. The fire closed in on the town, relentless, ripping, burning – destroying everything in its path. The houses at the edge of Caldicott would be first to meet this insatiable beast. Twenty-two hours since the initial report and the front had already spread to almost unmanageable levels. A combination of strong prevailing winds and the ferocity of the flames. Ten trucks from two zones, McLindon and Doory, meeting the run. One hundred and fifty men and growing working in shifts around the clock. Volunteers mixed in with the pros. Soot-plastered faces, skin scorched

1

by the heat. Burns and blisters and the distant baying of animals caught in the flames. Hell on earth was about to visit Rislake. And it wasn't leaving until it devoured everything, until it brought the town back to base elements and memories of what once existed.

Already the walls of the white house on Caldicott feel the heat approach, the paint cracking, the edges of the timber curling into foetal balls. Hiding even though there is nowhere to hide, the windowpanes quivering, shaking at the thought of what awaits, reflecting the quiet suburban street shrouded in black smoke, the edges like a mirage.

But people were prepared. Procedures and plans enforced, counterattacks at the ready for this annual threat, an evacuation of the north side of town called for two hours ago.

The evacuation had done its job. The houses are empty. Or they should be. But in the white house on top of the hill there is a body. It lies silent between the hallway and the main room, a pool of blood crusted to the floorboards that had once been home and will soon be cinders. A body alone and helpless to resist the flames. The fire had not taken them from this earth, but it soon would.

Two

Detective Sergeant Alex Kennard had no one but himself to blame for being caught up in this. In his late thirties, he was at the stage of life where he was afforded neither the empathy of youthful inexperience, nor the sympathy of elder incapacity. You were meant to know what you were doing. His golden age. That perfect mix of years of experience in the job combined with muscular cohesion. But the grey in his hair and the layer of fat that clung to every muscle hinted that maybe his golden age had passed him by. Blink and you'll miss it. Maybe it had come and gone with the botched hostage incident in Parramatta. The whole reason he was here in the Blue Mountains, hailed by his old boss, and Ann, his wife, as a new start. But five months later Katoomba was a place that already bored Kennard, his working days filled with trivial complaints, stolen cats, petty theft and the occasional booze-induced assault. He didn't like being idle. His brain didn't like it. It brought up matters that were best left locked away. Parramatta for one, and the disastrous home-warming barbeque last week too. It had been designed to help him integrate into the new station and forge some connections. He had been reluctant to host but was coaxed into it by Ann. An informal gathering. Some beers and a barbie on a lazy Sunday. Loose tongues that led to a jibe from DS Simon Uptill that cut too close to the bone and instigated a punch that he couldn't take back.

The barbeque had been another of his attempts to make the town feel like home which had gone awry, only adding to his feeling of being adrift and unconnected. This was not Sydney, surrounded by asphalt and people and an endless choice of food, events and entertainment. Katoomba and the countryside was not home.

Neither was Rislake but he had been off-duty and at a loose end when he heard the call and volunteered to help police the evacuation of the town about a half-hour to the west of his new home, a place thankfully not in the path of the bushfire.

Ann wouldn't miss him. Tonight was bridge night, so she would dash from her part-time job at the accountants to an evening that Kennard knew he wouldn't be welcome at. Not after last time. The chucked hand and the subsequent chucked table. He'd offered to pay for the repairs but had been asked to leave instead. Fuck 'em. He'd only gone in the first place because Ann did. She could go on her own. Rislake might take his mind off it. If nothing else, it would be a blast from the past, returning to the small town where he'd spent six consecutive years holidaying with his parents and older brother when he was a young boy. Four weeks of fresh air before returning to Sydney. A break from the city, back to nature, high in the rich mountain green.

He was curious about the place. He hadn't been back

for twenty-five years and was excited to see what had changed about the town. And the people. Maybe snap a couple of pictures to show his parents next time he was in the city. One last look before it became cinder. Ashes to ashes. Quite appropriate given that Rislake had been something of a religious town in his youth, sporting a large Methodist community and church that his parents had made him go to every Sunday. Something that might, possibly, have been part of the tenancy agreement for renting their holiday home, but which his parents had never confessed to.

A thousand metres up in the mountains, Rislake had been born on land that swept like a rollercoaster with great dips and rises that obscured part of the town from view, helped by the mountain blue gums that provided shade from the sun in the summer and broke through whatever snow fell in the winter.

As he approached there was a noticeable pressure in the air, a sense of impending doom, a whiff of a landscape being torched. He had no idea what he would face or how he would react. Already the crowded traffic had him on edge, his head felt dull, his hands shaking on the wheel as his mind flashed back to Parramatta six months ago, rushing to the courtyard of the washed-out apartment block. Rhian Thorpe, holding his mum hostage, his dad's gun pressed to her head. All over a stupid computer that she had thrown out. One that the boy had obsessed over.

As the superior officer on scene, Kennard had taken charge, trying to talk Rhian down, but the teenager was having none of it, the crowd too big, the loss of face too great. The crowd had refused to disperse, baying Rhian on, their camera phones raised, filming instead of helping. Wanting to witness the action rather than be part of it. Voyeurism at its worst, Kennard's authority useless against the desire to capture the events unfolding.

He had turned back from another futile attempt to get the crowd to move on to find the gun pointed not at the mother but at him. The finality of a barrel almost within reach as the mob pushed and jostled, capturing his indecision and Rhian's determination on camera. But the focus of the gun soon switched again. In the absence of a dissenting voice the boy had made a decision. Kennard had dashed forward but Rhian was too fast, the bullet brutal. After that there was nothing Kennard could do. Amidst the screams, Rhian's blood and the now fleeing crowd he had backed away. His colleagues had asked what he was doing but Kennard didn't know. He only knew that he had been so close but now he needed to be far away.

Even now crowds still freaked him out. Even after six months of counselling, talking, listening, breathing. Rislake would be the test.

Exiting the highway was easy. The smart people were leaving town, not entering it, the beeping horns providing a soundtrack to the impending sense of doom that manifested itself in the orange glow that hung in the distance, northeast of the town. The invading army about to raze everything to the ground. An army that would take no prisoners.

Kennard aimed for the Incident Control Centre. It was being run out of the school classrooms, the gym repurposed to provide shelter for those residents who had been temporarily – and possibly soon permanently – removed from their homes. The operations room had been set up in the chemistry lab, its windows looking out towards the fire, which gave it the air of a war room with a front-row view of the action it was orchestrating. The communications operators had set up on some of the broad desks, laptops, phones and a bevy of equipment circling them. As Kennard stood there wondering what he should be doing, people and reports flitted in and out, uniformed officers from all branches manning radios and running the latest satellite weather data to try to predict paths and the ETA of those paths. Kennard soaked in the buzz of the room, his fingers twitching, his eyes drawn to any and all movement. He tried to convince himself that there was no danger here but the feeling was hard to shake. He wanted to boost. Straight out of there, straight back to Katoomba and his empty house. It was a cowardice which brought a coiled anger that manifested easily these days, one he tried hard to subdue.

More people came and went, voices raised, dashed and panicked. Kennard felt himself start to sweat, his skin prickling, rubbing his forefinger on the inside of his thumb. Trying to count the calluses. A coping mechanism. But it didn't work. Giving in to his nerves, he headed outside into the car park still cursing his spinelessness, as an angered cry came from the edge of the cordon that had been placed on the main road outside the front of the school, which marked the start of the 'no-go' zone. Keeping people on the safe side of town. Safe for now at least.

JAMES DELARGY

A squat man was grappling with a couple of officers who were preventing him from crossing the barricade of cones and marked Chrysler police cars. It was two against one, but the fight was evened up by the sheer ferocity and determination of the attempted interloper. The man was shorter than average, his face a bundle of features all battling one another for superiority, like a Mr Potato Head doll. He was striking but not handsome, late twenties with a shaved head that glistened with sweat.

Kennard kept his distance until the two officers had an arm each restraining the man. His bulging eyes looked as if they were trying to breach the cordon of their own accord.

'Why the fuck aren't you out there looking for Trace?' he cried, white jabs of spittle flying from his lips like sea foam.

'We need you to calm down,' said one officer as Kennard approached, his hat knocked to the asphalt and slowly turning grey with ash drifting from the dull sky overhead. Kennard flashed his badge.

'His wife is missing,' one of the officers explained.

'Not my wife,' said the man. 'His.' He flicked a glance over his shoulder towards another man who was slumped by one of the squad cars at the barricade, his head in his hands.

'Who is he?' asked Kennard.

'Russell Hilmeyer.'

The name caused Kennard to stop in his tracks. Rislake was a trip down memory lane, but he hadn't expected to find any familiar landmarks.

Kennard had only been a seasonal visitor and five years older, but even as a child Russell Hilmeyer was the talk of the town. A star of the local under-10 footy team, a brute of a seven-year-old, he was already being scouted by some of the bigger teams and towns, his future career bandied around even then. The fame had gotten him bullied by kids up to three years older, but he had been able to defend himself. The kids around eleven or twelve could have taken him if they tried, but none of them dared in case they came away bested.

But Russell Hilmeyer was no brute now. He didn't move, hunched over like a pile of dirty washing in his full firefighting gear, fluorescent yellow trousers and jacket with an orange sash over each shoulder.

'We wanna go look for her,' said the stocky guy, his battle with the officers ended.

'And who are you?' asked Kennard.

'Joel Anselmo.'

'Right, Joel, come with me.'

Kennard exited the school gates and approached Russell, who stood up as he reached him. He had turned into the man Kennard would have expected. He was a decent chunk over six foot and athletic, muscles that were being slowly decayed by his thirties but that for the moment held their own. His blue eyes pierced the soot that stained his skin.

'Your wife is missing?' asked Kennard.

Russell shook his head. There seemed to be no tears, but they could easily have evaporated away in the heat. 'She's not missing. You know her, Joel. She could be off painting.' Russell's words sounded like classic denial to Kennard, disbelieving them as soon as they were uttered.

'Come on, Russ,' said Joel.

'When and where did you last see her?' asked Kennard.

'There!'

Russell pointed in the direction of the far side of town, the side that now boasted a magnificent and horrific backdrop of orange and red that coloured the horizon and sky until the upper layer of dark grey smoke and ash took over. There was something majestic about how threatening it was. How small it made him feel. As if he was watching the end of the world approach.

'But not since Tuesday. I've been away. Working.'

'Has anyone . . . ?'

'No one we've asked,' said Joel, panicked.

'Her mobile?'

'Tried it,' said Russell, shaking his head, fear tightening his expression. 'It's either off or out of signal. Not unusual around here or unusual for her if she's painting. Hopefully somewhere far away from here.'

Two of the local constables joined the commotion. The older officer with the wattled neck spoke. His face was cragged but his voice sympathetic, as if talking to a close friend. 'They're re-checking the school again, Russell, mate.'

'We've already checked. She's not there,' said Joel.

Kennard turned to Russell. 'Where do you live?'

'Caldicott.'

Kennard had heard the name mentioned in the command room. It was a road on the northwest of town scheduled to be first in line to meet the merciless front of the fire.

The older officer interrupted. 'I know you heard Bairstow's orders, Russ.'

At this, Russell went quiet, not meeting anyone's eyes. Kennard understood immediately what had been said. Going out there was too risky. Stay put. For now.

Joel interrupted, turning to Kennard. 'Ten minutes. That's all. Just us. We're not rookies.'

'I'm sorry, Mr Anselmo. I have no authority here,' said Kennard, the words bitter on his tongue. Where *did* he have authority anymore?

The plea from Joel was heartfelt and it was also not directed at Kennard. At Kennard's shoulder appeared a tall man in an orange helmet. The white dash across it marked him out as Bairstow, the Group Captain, a man Kennard had last seen ordering a retreat from Leersby, another battle line left to the enemy.

'Sorry, Russell, I can confirm that Tracey is missing.' His voice was firm, unrelenting.

Russell picked his head up to meet the words, but it was Joel who spoke. 'You have to let us go in, Captain.'

Bairstow shook his head. He sported a beard that softened a hard, beaten face. 'We don't know for sure that she's there and I can't divert a truck to support you at present. The best we can do is drive it back and force a window.'

'That might be too late,' Joel said.

'Have you called everyone that she might be with?' asked Kennard.

'Everyone,' said Joel.

Once again Russell turned his eyes to the ground, lost in misery.

After Bairstow left with Joel in tow, Kennard stayed with Russell who had slumped against one of the barricades. If nothing else, he was capable of providing support to a man whose wife was missing.

'Been a while since I was here.'

He got no response from Russell, who merely stared into the distance towards his house. One that he might never get to see again.

Kennard continued. 'My parents dragged me up here summers as a teenager. Much changed? Benny's Ice Cream parlour still around?' He hoped to form some sort of connection with Russell. Get him talking and try to dilute his worries. But there was no getting inside, Russell a brick wall.

'I knew you when you were younger. Well, I knew of you. Everyone did. On the footy field.'

Russell raised his head, then clambered to his feet, favouring his left leg. Age creeping up on him. Kennard knew the pain well. The look on Russell's face was sour, as if Kennard had disgusted him. 'Long time ago,' he said, and moved along to the next car in front of the barricade and took a seat again.

Just then Joel returned, shuffling towards Russell, furtive in his movements. He glanced over at Kennard, then crouched beside Russell. From his pocket he produced a set of keys.

'Savo's PC,' said Joel. 'We go now.'

'Where?' asked Russell, finally looking at his friend.

'Your house.'

'She's not going to still be there? Is she? She'll be some-where else,' said Russell, forlorn hope crippling the words.

'Better we know,' said Joel. 'Then we try elsewhere.'

Russell paused, considering his friend's request and then nodded. Grabbing Joel's offered hand, he clambered to his feet. Something that didn't look easy in the heavy fireproof trousers and jacket.

Russell looked over at Kennard, narrowing his eyes in antipathy. 'Not gonna dob us in, are ya?'

Kennard looked at both the men, desperation written on their faces. He was faced with a choice. One that he had to make quickly. He wasn't going to dob them in. But he also wasn't going to stand idly by.

'I'm coming with.'

Russell shook his head. 'You aren't a firefighter. You don't belong there.'

'Better that he's with us than against us,' said Joel.

Russell flashed a glare towards Kennard that spilled over with downright menace. One that warned he wasn't going to tolerate any bullshit. Kennard felt like one of those eleven-year-olds – older, more experienced, but intimidated as hell.

'Just don't get under our feet. You've no idea what we'll face out there,' said Russell.

Three

Tracey – Before

Tracey Tredwell had always dreamed of living in a house on a hill. Up above it all. Not a mansion or a castle (those dreams had been tempered early on), just a place she could call her own that wasn't on a floodplain like her childhood home. It had been built in a nook by a stream, the dirty water from the Fevertree Mill making it stink to high heaven. On a good day. Then, three times a year, no more and no less, the rains would come and cause the stream to burst its banks, covering their garden in a grey foam that sat on top of the grass and refused to budge. A nasty foam that killed the grass, bleached the colour out of her jeans and turned her trainers off-white, like they had been soured.

Her mum had explained it was the residue of whatever chemical they used in the mill, to treat the paper and make it white. Everyone wanted their toilet paper to be a uniform colour. No one wanted to imagine that they were wiping their arse with paper that someone else had used. Which made sense. But having to accommodate other people's luxury at the expense of her own was frustrating and stayed with Tracey.

The stink got everywhere. The house, the car, the wardrobes, the food. It meant she and her younger sister Karen having to endure the endless taunts of the other kids. The Deadwells. Smelly Deadwell. The NotSmellWells. The list was endless. And the taunts might have lasted for the rest of her school years, if it hadn't been for two things. One was the fact that, when she turned thirteen, she blossomed into what her dad's friends had called 'a head-turner'. Men began to look at her like she was something to be captured, like the trout they always boasted about hauling in but no one ever saw. What it meant was that no longer were she and Karen — who rode her coattails — known as the Deadwells.

She was just coming to terms with this new power when the second thing happened. They moved. From Fevertree down to the Blue Mountains, trading one outpost for another, this time a beaten-up farm on the outskirts of Rislake.

Fourteen was a hard time to move. To start all over again. Especially when it felt like they'd gone back to square one, this time the taunts aimed at her mum and dad for buying the place from Corey Gannerson. Her dad had rushed the sale through, scuppering the plans of some of the local church elders to purchase it, a few extra grand shoved under the table for an immediate sale. Plenty thought that Gannerson signed the papers even though he didn't know what he was agreeing to, but he did – his vision was just coloured by the greens and oranges of the cash pushed his way. Dad could be ruthless like that. Taking what he wanted, moving them if he desired, his way the only way. Tracey could see the family trait in her and her sister.

The church elders, backed by others, whipped the town into a frenzy, putting Gannerson at the head, stating that Dad had made him sign while under the influence.

The case never made it to court. Gannerson did as he was going to and pickled his liver within a year. They found him wedged in one of the flooded storm pipes, floating alongside the empty bottles. It was a horrible way to go, but one that Tracey often returned to. If she was ever going to go out by her own hand, drinking herself to death on some decent grog would be her choice. Champagne. Absinthe. Some of the Winston cocktails they boasted about in Melbourne.

The Gannerson farm wasn't built on a floodplain, but on rocky ground on the west side of town. A farmhouse, a couple of sheds and fields out the back, beyond which was nothing but wilderness for miles. Her sister had taken to that well, her sense of adventure teased, helping Mum and Dad fix the place up. But Tracey wanted more than that. She wanted fame, and not in a celebrity television way. She wanted to be the artist rather than the model, despite her looks; for respect, for people to see past her beauty. And Russell Hilmeyer did.

Everyone in school wanted Russell. The tall, tanned, toned footy star with a smile that was slightly bent out of shape but all the more radiant for it. He was going to be the next big thing. Hands like spades. A leap like a kangaroo and an arse in shorts that even her mum drooled over. And her mum didn't even like football. Never tuned into a game in her life when they were living in Queensland. She couldn't name a single team, the Brisbane Lions the name of a zoo exhibit for all she knew.

Despite all the competition – and there was a lot of competition – Tracey won first prize, rapidly dumping Liam Gaffney, whom she had stolen off her sister originally, and becoming Russell's girlfriend, which brought her a taste of fame, adoration and hatred. The dark side of being in the public eye. Whispers about what she did for Russell to keep him happy, things that might make her mother blush, or jealous.

They got married at eighteen, the reception afterwards paid for by the Methodist church Russell's parents were prominent members of; sandwiches, vol-au-vents and cakes of all colours and sizes laid out on fold-up tables in the school car park. Their wedding had all the trappings of a town celebration rather than a personal one. For back then, Russell *was* the town, the great hope, the star.

Three months into the marriage and she got her big house on the hill. On Caldicott, on the northeast edge of town. It came with a big mortgage but an even bigger future. The first of many houses, she hoped. Here, Sydney, Bali, LA.

Just six months later it was all in ruins. Russell got injured. Hope turned to despair turned to pity. He needed to find work and so did she. Footy was meant to be his life, so he hadn't tried hard in school. His parents were long gone, off to some African country she had never heard of to bring the locals the word of Jesus Christ. A permanent mission, their calling. They'd left a few months after she and Russell got married and had only been back a couple of times in what had now been twenty years; a solemn reunion with their boy, blessings offered, a simple celebration in the church before they were off again. There was apparently no one worth saving in Australia.

But they had worked hard, her and Russell. They scraped along like so many people did. He worked odd jobs, as did she, fitting her painting around shifts in the souvenir shop in town, listening to the creak of the wood of the house on the hill as it spoke to her, the calls of the kookaburras out back, the restless cicadas and insects whispering. Those days she enjoyed, cut adrift and alone to paint.

She was so isolated sometimes when Russell was out overnight firefighting or on a removals job that she'd often wonder how long it would take for someone to realize if she ever disappeared. But then her eyes would drift back to the current painting, and she'd find herself lost in it again. There was nothing wrong with being lost time and again.

Four

They nabbed the spare gear from one of the standby trucks. Russell looked Kennard over briefly and picked out the fit like an off-the-cuff tailor. Kennard was half-way between the two in height at six foot, but similar to Russell's weight. Too much food and not enough exercise. They kept watch as he slipped what they called the bunker gear on. Russell had guessed well; the synthetic fabric trousers and Kevlar jacket fitted snugly. Kennard pulled on the steel-toe-capped boots with the puncture-resistant midsoles and listened to his heart thud as he drew the protective hood over his head. In the full kit the entire world seemed to shrink; just him against what lay ahead. Maybe this was how every firefighter felt when they went into battle. Them against the flames. He drew on the goggles. If nothing else, they would help disguise him for the next part of their plan. Finally, Joel passed him a white helmet with a grey dash, the nameplate blank. The unknown firefighter.

They made their way to the PC, the Personnel Carrier. 'I'll drive,' said Joel.

'You'll need the keys for that,' said Russell, dangling them from his fingers.

Joel patted at his pockets. Russell had obviously swiped the keys when Joel had helped him up, Joel's wistful look betraying that this was a party piece Russell had performed many times.

'Not having you drive,' said Russell, spite in the words. 'Useless bastard's failed the pro driving exam twice, haven't you?'

'Dunlap had it in for me, you know that.'

Russell laughed, dismissing his friend's complaints, clearly the alpha of the two. Joel was left seething at being bested but trying to disguise it.

They slipped into the red 4x4 easily. Everyone was too busy elsewhere to notice. Though it looked sturdy, Kennard couldn't help but feel less than protected in it, surrounded by windows that would surely crack in the intense heat of a bushfire. He felt his breathing begin to stutter, nerves on the rise as Russell pulled out of the schoolyard. Instead of turning towards the roadblock, however, he drove in the opposite direction.

A minute later they took a sharp left turn down a dirt alley behind a row of houses, straight towards the other side of town and the fire, having skirted the roadblock entirely. Russell navigated the alley with the confidence of a local, but Kennard also realized that he might have been confusing confidence with panic. They had, in effect, hijacked an emergency vehicle for their own ends. And he had not only looked the other way but agreed to join in the escapade. It was for a good reason, he reminded himself.

Russell's wife was missing and despite one nagging feeling that he was stepping into a situation beyond his current comprehension, he had another nagging feeling. That he needed to find her. Make sure she was safe. For her sake and his own. Proof that he could step up to the mark when needed.

Swinging out of the alley, they found themselves at the lower end of Rislake, down in the hollow where the river – when there was enough water – cut the town in half.

As they climbed the hill, a hush lay over the north side of the town. Everyone had been evacuated, apart from Russell's wife, and as the sky grew darker and Kennard peered between the front seats, he became acutely aware that there was a chance that this was a fool's errand. He was putting himself in danger and Tracey might be safe, somewhere else entirely.

They traversed another unfamiliar street. Out the front and sides of the truck, a gloom was descending quickly, as if they were driving towards twilight. Counter to this burgeoning gloom, the temperature inside the Personnel Carrier began to increase. It had been prickly to begin with, but the heat had intensified immeasurably ever since they'd started up the rise. It felt as though they were heading directly into the centre of the inferno and Kennard didn't know much, but he did know that driving straight towards a bushfire was not a smart idea. There was a reason fires like this were attacked from the flanks and not from the front. One wrong move and it could overwhelm them in an instant.

From underneath them came a sudden tacking sound.

He recognized it: the asphalt and bitumen being ripped up from the road as they drove, the heat leaving its mark on everything. Ash fell from the sky, parted by the wipers that Russell had switched on.

'I'm taking Ditton,' said Russell.

'Goura's quicker,' said Joel.

'You think I don't know that?' spat Russell. Joel looked admonished as Russell continued. 'Just that I don't trust that new surface. Likely to come up in the heat.'

Joel didn't respond, accepting the decision. There was no talking inside the cab after that. Nothing needed to be said. Their goal was obvious. Get to Caldicott Road. Get to Russell's house. Find Tracey Hilmeyer.

The silence allowed Kennard to concentrate on what he was doing. The foolishness of it. His nerves increased. He clamped his hands to his legs to try to calm them. He was doing this to prove himself – and possibly save a life – but it was a careless and risky venture. As an officer with nearly ten years of service under his belt, he should have known better. He doubted that Bairstow would ever question a serious police investigation, so why did Kennard feel entitled to question his decision not to enter a part of town under threat from a raging bushfire? Was his desire to make amends for Parramatta misjudged? Whatever it was, it was too late now to turn back. He was along for the ride into hell.

Russell hitched the next left. Too fast and too sharp, the 4x4 drifting sideways as if the road was slick with oil. There was a collective gasp from all three of them, the kerb approaching fast. The vehicle caught itself, pitching onto two wheels and narrowly avoiding going over on its roof, before righting itself with a loud pop that startled Kennard.

Russell steered to a halt. 'Bugger.'

'What is it?' asked Kennard.

'Tyres. Think I've fucked them.'

Russell's comment was interrupted by another set of distant pops. Car tyres exploding in the heat like kernels of popcorn.

'How much further?'

'Couple-a hundred metres,' said Russell.

Kennard could see the look of fear in his eyes in their rear-view mirror and sweat edged around his goggles. The degree of heat had become extremely uncomfortable. It wasn't something that could be solved by turning up the air con or rolling down the window. He could almost smell his flesh stewing in the heavy bunker gear.

He looked out the front window. Up ahead the road ran dead straight, the houses towered over by a blanket of sinister red, like a bloody hand about to strike. All Kennard could think of was the Nick Cave song, and how he wished he could be sitting by a pool sipping a whisky and coke and listening to the bare passion of *The Boatman's Call* on repeat.

'Let's keep going,' said Joel.

'It's fucked,' said Russell, worry held deep in the lines around his eyes.

'We have to.'

'We go on, we might not get back.'

A realization that caused Joel to pause.

Russell continued. 'She's not there. She wouldn't be. We've nothing that valuable to save.'

No one moved; brinkmanship, fear in all eyes. Kennard felt his heart flutter in relief. He had come to the edge, but Russell hadn't forced him to jump over. This was enough. There was courage in his actions. He had shown that to himself at least. There was a long way to go with the others, his former friends and colleagues, the press and, of course, public opinion after the shit around Rhian Thorpe. Even Ann was pissed with him over punching Uptill last week. Something that would have been deemed out of character. Before Parramatta. Now this. Out of the frying pan and into the flames. He had done enough, hadn't he?

'So, what now?' asked Joel.

The smart move was to hightail it out of there on three wheels or however many were left. But the smoke clogged brain cells, as well as eyes and noses. They were so close. Just a few hundred metres and they would have an answer.

'I'm going to go,' said Kennard. He turned to Joel. 'Call for backup.'

'What are you—?' asked Russell.

His question was interrupted by the searing heat as Kennard opened his door. It was like sticking his head into an oven, suffocating in its intensity, no off switch, no relief.

His exit was announced by another pop, a lone car up ahead lurching towards the ground as if giving up the ghost. Another one lost to the flames.

Joel grabbed the CB and started to radio in their position, calling for a pumper and identifying three occupants in attendance: himself, Russell and another. Joel didn't even know his name. Allowing Kennard the horrible realization that they wouldn't be able to identify him if he died here.

He tried to put it out of his mind. He squeezed his hands into fists and began to walk. It was madness, the heat causing his skin to tingle, the asphalt waxy beneath his feet.

Gritting his teeth, he forced the pace, his gloved hand up to shield his face from the worst of the heat and failing to help. This was a stupid idea. Of all the ideas he'd ever had, this was probably the most fucking stupid. And he'd had plenty of stupid fucking ideas.

The road continued slightly uphill; this side of town was nowhere near as hilly as the main street but, given the intensity of the heat, it was like climbing a mountain.

Houses passed by on the right and left. Even from a distance Kennard could see paint peeling off them, stray embers floating on the breeze looking for a home. Plastic toys had been left behind to melt into indistinguishable, grotesque shapes, swings and deckchairs waiting to be mauled in the fire. Stuff deemed expendable. Yet Kennard was here. He wasn't expendable. To himself if no one else.

With fifty metres to go, a hand found his shoulder, pulling him back. He turned to find Russell by his side.

'We need to go,' said Russell, breathing rapidly.

'It's so close.'

'I know. But we can't.' There was pain in Russell's eyes, glancing first at Kennard and then at the white house at the top of the hill.

'You want to, I want to. So, let's do it,' said Kennard.

'I don't want to have to explain how you burned to a crisp out here,' said Russell, forthright. 'Bad enough that we took the PC.'

Russell's words rang true, but something told Kennard not to stop. Taking a searing hot breath of air through his mask, he made for the house.

The heat seemed to goad him on, daring him into battle as if frying the common-sense circuits in his brain. The protective gear that he had donned helped shield him against most of it, but nothing could stop it entirely. He could feel the sweat prickle on his skin, boiling underneath his clothes. He had read about adventurers to the Poles developing a crazed, almost siege mentality against the cold. This is what it felt like. It called to him. *Come and see. Prove you're a man.*

He reached the front door of the two-storey house. The wooden façade was intact, paint peeling and curling from the wood, the grass of the poorly kept garden turning crispy underfoot. He stood to his full height, squeezed his eyes shut for a moment and prepared to enter. Somewhere nearby he heard glass shattering. A warning to go no further. Kennard ignored it and stepped inside.

The front hall was sparse, a few pictures adorning the walls, the wallpaper curling like a paperbark tree, a simple wooden staircase opposite the living room leading straight up to the landing above, the timber beginning to warp with the heat. Like outside, the thermostat had been cranked up to boiling.

And there, in the hallway, surrounded by a pool of dried blood, was Tracey Hilmeyer.

Five

For a moment, Kennard just stopped. As if some form of rigor mortis had taken over. He hadn't expected to find Tracey Hilmeyer. He wasn't sure what he'd expected to find. Probably just an empty house, in which case he would have retreated down the hill as fast as he could to face whatever questions the GC, Senior Sergeant and his own DSS had. Haskell would probably order another round of counselling. Or just lock him up and throw away the key.

But here was Tracey, in a pool of blood. He felt his own blood pressure rise. The crippling heat seemed to increase the pressure of everything. He felt like he was about to burst out of his clothes like some value-brand Incredible Hulk, the familiar signs of stress, exacerbated in this heat.

He refocused on where he was. The feeling persisted that he was in over his head but there was no time to question himself. Make a first assessment and get out of there. The sheer amount of blood wasn't a good sign. Nor was the blue, washed-out tinge of her skin and lips. Inching down the hallway, he made it to her body.

Kneeling carefully, he touched her hand with the back of his. The skin was warm. His hopes rose briefly but were soon dashed by the lack of pulse and thick stench of decay in the air. Accelerated, no doubt, because of the heat. Tracey was dead.

Kennard stood up. A wave of dizziness threatened to topple him. He scolded himself to focus. Get a grip. This wasn't his first dead body, although reconfirming that to himself didn't help.

A few deep breaths helped the dizziness pass and he tried to clear space in his clogged brain to make a few mental notes. The situation was urgent now. First of all, Tracey Hilmeyer's body was situated in the hallway. At the foot of the stairs, her head facing the living room. As if she was possibly heading for the front door but never made it.

A sudden blast of heat behind caused him to tense up. The fire was upon them. But when he turned, he saw the front door had opened, allowing heated air to flood in. Russell Hilmeyer had finally made it home. In the distance, Kennard could see the flashing lights of a fire truck making its way towards them through the falling ash like the last days of Pompeii.

Russell locked eyes with Kennard.

'We have to . . .' he started, impatient. Then he saw the body of his wife.

Realizing what was going to happen, Kennard advanced down the hallway to meet Russell in the middle. He was no match for Russell, who bypassed him entirely, a natural swiftness to his sidestep that, despite his slight limp, Kennard was unprepared for.

Regaining his balance, Kennard shouted after him. 'Don't touch her!'

But it was too late. Russell was kneeling beside his wife, holding her across his lap.

'Trace? Trace? Wake up!'

Kennard could make out the keening in his voice, the bitter end of their marriage. 'Til death do us part come tragically correct.

'She's dead,' said Kennard. He put his hand on Russell's quivering shoulder, trying to get him to step away from his wife. Russell shrugged it off and glared at him.

'I need to examine her,' said Kennard, making a second attempt to ease Russell away.

Outside, over the distant roar of the approaching fire and intermittent cracks of shattering glass, there was a hiss of airbrakes. About twenty metres from the front of the house a massive red-and-white fire truck had come to a halt. Through the gloom, Kennard could see about ten firefighters disembark in full gear and work their way around its sides, detaching hoses and turning spigots with an air of controlled alarm. None of them wanted to be here. They had given up on this part of the town. They had decided to live to fight another day. Loss of property was regretful but recoverable. Loss of life wasn't. It invited questions. But Kennard couldn't distance himself from this decision. He knew he had helped drag them all into this.

'What happened?' asked Russell, looking up at him like a child asking a parent for answers while holding a poor, dead creature in his hands.

'That's what I need to find out,' said Kennard, gathering as much sympathy in his voice as he could, given the suffocating heat. But Russell already had a theory.

'Those stairs. She was always running down them. When we built the house, I knew that they were too steep, but that's what she wanted. And when she wanted something, I usually got it for her.'

Kennard nodded. He needed Russell out of there. *He* needed to get out of there.

'Can you back away from her for me, Russell?'

Russell looked down at his wife, dead in his arms.

'This is my wife!' he yelled, plaintively.

Kennard pursed his lips tight. Offering another expression of sympathy. 'I need—'

Russell's eyes flared. The pupils almost seemed to burn red, though Kennard knew that was impossible. It was just the damned fire playing tricks. He tried again. 'We need to get her out of here. Before she . . .'

Russell didn't say 'burns up', but Kennard knew that was what was on his mind. Hard not to be in this heat.

'You got a body camera?' asked Kennard.

Russell looked at him blankly.

'To photograph the scene.'

Russell shook his head.

'Can you ask your colleagues out there for me?' asked Kennard, swivelling to turn his back towards the rear of the house and finding that it helped alleviate some of the raw power of the fire, albeit to a miniscule degree. Though even the smallest relief right now was welcome.

'I don't want her photographed. Not . . . like this.'

Russell looked at the door. Then his wife. 'We have to move her.' The doleful pleading in his eyes was persuasive, but behind it was a look that unnerved Kennard. Sheer determination. A willingness to do anything for his wife.

'We will, but first we need to get photos. In situ. For—'

'We have to get her out. This place is going to collapse, you stupid bastard.'

Kennard couldn't disagree. If coming here was stupid in the first place, staying here was worse. But he wanted the pictures. Parramatta had taught him that his memory could be questioned. Photographs couldn't.

'I don't want the last abiding memory of her on this earth to be this. I don't want people to know she died falling down the stairs.'

'She didn't fall down the stairs, Russell.'

Russell froze. 'What do you mean?'

While Russell had been lamenting his wife's tragic death, Kennard had been scanning the scene. The amount of blood located around Tracey's head could indeed indicate a nasty fall. But there was no blood on any of the steps. And, most importantly, the blood splatter he had detected was directed towards the front door rather than towards the living room like it should have been to be consistent with a fall down the stairs. And if she didn't fall, that raised some questions, to which he didn't have much time to come up with answers.

'This is a crime scene. I believe your wife was murdered,' said Kennard, knowing that the delivery was brutal but hoping that it would shock Russell into letting her go.

'Murdered? But who would—?' Russell continued to hold onto Tracey's body.

'That's what I want to find out,' said Kennard.

Gripping a stunned Russell under the armpit with a tenderness that was at odds with the life-threatening situation, Kennard managed to pull him up. His presence, and Russell's, had disturbed the scene, but he could still get something from it. He was sure of it. He just needed a camera.

Six

January 20 – 10.00 – Wind direction NE – Surface speed 32km/h

3 hours since North Rislake evacuation

South Rislake status = Amber (Prepare for possible evacuation)

Kennard ushered Russell outside. Into a frenzy. Hoses had been rigged and aimed towards the back of the house, the firefighters jolting as the water spat out of the nozzles. Other firefighters darted here and there, crossing among the whipped smoke, there and gone in an instant, each shadowy figure causing Kennard to pause, his grip on Russell Hilmeyer his only anchor.

Suddenly that anchor broke free, and Russell disappeared off into the smoke. Kennard grabbed the next firey along, a young woman who shook her head and pushed him out of the way when he asked for a camera, her feet spread, right foot back, left foot forward to maintain her balance.

Kennard glanced around for another option. To his side he could see Russell, Joel and another firefighter nod at each other and make for the house. He knew what was happening. Russell was going to try to retrieve his wife's body. He couldn't let that happen. Despite his nerves protesting the intervention and possible conflict, he stepped forward to block them.

'You can't move her,' he shouted at the three of them.

'I have to,' said Russell, leading the group. There was no doubt in his voice.

Kennard realized that there would be no persuading Russell, so he aimed his pleas towards Joel and the other fighter.

'I think she's been murdered. I need someone to call Incident Control and get them to send a forensics team. And I need a camera.'

Joel swallowed hard. Russell obviously hadn't informed them of this development. 'Murdered? Trace? You're sure?'

Kennard nodded. Sweat seeped down his face. 'It looks like it.'

Joel looked panicked all of a sudden, unwilling to meet Kennard's eye.

A hand shot out. The third guy had ripped the body camera off his chest and handed it to Kennard.

'Here you go! This will record and feed back to HQ.'

Kennard nodded thanks then looked at Joel and Russell. 'I need you two to help save the house. Or keep the corridor to the house open. For Tracey.'

Kennard didn't think he needed to instil how important

this was, but he tried to inject gravitas into a voice and throat stinging in the dry air.

'I don't want to leave her,' said Russell.

'You're not leaving her. You're protecting her,' said Kennard.

'Too late,' said Russell, despondent.

Kennard asked Joel to call Incident Control and get a forensics team – ideally a Forensics Services Group rather than a SOCO team for experience – out here. He returned to the house, alone, with only a mute Tracey Hilmeyer for company. Holding the camera and keeping it as steady as possible, he moved through the hallway recording the scene. The space glowed red from the lights, as if the walls, the floor, the pictures were on fire already. He recorded the position of the body and what he had discovered on entry. Following protocol. And trying not to scream in fear as he heard the crack of another pane of glass, the roar of the fire replaced by the crash of water on the walls of the house, rattling the planks as if the Big Bad Wolf was trying to blow it down.

Over the sound of the fire and the hoses came the cries of the firefighters outside. An order for the lines to be moved, trying to counter the perpetual movement of the blaze. A bushfire was unthinking and unfeeling, but also persistent and insidiously smart. Drop your guard and it would drop you.

Kennard wanted to leave. He had recorded the scene. Forensics would do the rest. But they wouldn't be here for God knows how long. Preparing himself, he rolled Tracey's body over. At the back of her head, just below the crown, there was a bloodied gap where the skull had been deformed. Obviously violently. And not by a fall down the stairs. This looked to have been a single blow.

Kennard tried to compose himself. His heart was beating so hard it was all he could hear. He tried to swallow but all moisture had been sucked from his body, his tongue firmly lodged against the top of his mouth. Coughing to free it, he swung around to try to locate any murder weapon but found nothing in the vicinity that seemed immediately capable of causing such damage. No pokers by the fireplace, no baseball bats, no 2x4s covered in blood. A more thorough search was needed.

Time ticked on, his heart beating out the seconds, his brain screaming that he should leave. That no amount of daring was going to bring Tracey back.

Kennard finally stumbled outside. His clothing almost seemed to slosh with sweat, as if he were liquefying inside the suit. He spotted Russell and Joel supporting parallel lines.

'Did you call it in?' he asked Joel.

Joel nodded. 'They'd better hurry.'

'I know.'

'I don't think you do,' said Russell. 'This is blowing strong.'

'What can I do?' asked Kennard.

With a shove, Russell handed him the line. 'Hold this. Feed when necessary. Move when necessary. Follow Spike in front.'

The canvas line was heavy, rigid in his hands. Suddenly it pulled, jerking him forward. In front of him the firefighter moved, the nameplate on the back of the white helmet adorned with the name Spike. Kennard stumbled forward but his focus was not on Spike. It was on Russell, watching as he made for his house a third time. Kennard had the photos now, but he didn't want the scene disturbed further. He went to drop the line, but Russell turned away from the house and towards the truck, slumping against it, holding his head in his hands.

Kennard returned to duty. As Spike took a step, so did he. As he did, he looked up. Behind the house the fiery glow seemed to have intensified, flames licking higher and higher, the heat ever more oppressive. It looked as if the sun was going to rise from the horizon for the second time that day. But there was no ozone layer, no clouds and no millions of miles to protect them from its raw power.

Kennard stuck with Spike for what seemed like a lifetime but was likely no more than ten minutes. His nerves were shot, still trying to come to terms with the series of macho choices that had led him here. It had been hard enough to keep himself together when he was only feeling the heat inside the house. But with the monster in full view, all he wanted to do was run and hide.

Help arrived soon after in an unusual and pissed-off fashion. Bairstow, the orange helmet with the white stripe, striding into view.

He had a number of reasons to be hacked off, including the hijacking of an official fire vehicle, the insubordination of two of his men, the risk to life and the fact that he had been proven wrong when they'd found Tracey's body. Kennard knew that Joel and Russell would get it in the neck worse than he would. If it came to it, Kennard would vouch for them. Claim that it was all his idea and they merely provided access and kept him safe. He'd take them for a long, cold schooner after. Out of gratitude and because the beer might loosen a few tongues.

As it turned out Bairstow gave him nothing but a scowl, moving past him and straight to giving orders to the crews on site, his voice loud and remorseless as if he hated every last one of them. Anger issues, maybe. Kennard knew all about those. Punching DS Uptill at the barbie last week being a prime example. Because punching a colleague was still very much frowned upon, even if the arsehole deserved it.

The last time she had spoken to him, Ann had suggested seeing a counsellor again. Parramatta had obviously struck deep into his core. How could it not? Memory wasn't like a blank disk that could be wiped or rebooted. Shit was held on file for ever, no matter how ruinous to his mental health. Ann was giving him space to consider it, but in this choking bushfire there was no space to breathe, let alone think of anything else but the immediate.

Tracey Hilmeyer. And who had killed her.

Seven

Bairstow gave the order for the second truck to get into position as Kennard watched from beside the first. The thick smoke had dulled the red glow, but the flames were closing in quickly, approaching from the northwest. With his brief stint at firefighting finished, he had contacted his own boss, DSS Haskell, and given her a short rundown of the situation. A female victim called Tracey Hilmeyer with a fatal head wound that should be treated as suspicious. The crime scene under imminent threat of destruction.

'I'll get someone out to you. Hold tight.' There was unease in Haskell's voice.

'What do you mean, "hold tight"? I've got this,' said Kennard, shouting into his phone so he could be heard over the noise. If he knew Haskell, that smarmy bludger Uptill would be her first choice to take the case. The firefighters had called in relief and Uptill would be called in to relieve Kennard.

'I make the decisions, DS Kennard. Forensics are on their way.'

'That's it?'

'*Hold tight*, DS Kennard.'

With that, Haskell was gone. She had been uneasy with him ever since he'd joined her station – the broken and shamed Sydney cop dumped on her doorstep. The barbeque last week was meant to have built bridges with his new colleagues, but it had done the complete opposite.

Forensics were just over an hour in arriving, the three of them looking as on edge as Kennard felt, dressed as firefighters in ill-fitting blue helmets. Kennard met them at the front door of the Hilmeyer house.

'Lyle Andrews, SOCO,' said the man in the lead, only his brown eyes and the dark skin around them visible. They made a move to enter. Kennard followed.

'Where are the rest of you?' asked Kennard.

The last in line spoke. Female, stocky, a raspy voice that suggested she was a smoker. Which might come in handy out here, lungs used to the choking air. 'Be grateful you have us, mate. There's a bushfire going on, if you hadn't noticed.'

With that the team set to work, Andrews directing the other two to photograph the scene.

'I've already done the Spielberg bit,' said Kennard.

'We have this,' said Andrews. Giving Kennard the big Fuck Off, which was fair enough. He was about to head outside when Andrews called him back.

'You want to help?'

It was a question that Kennard wasn't given time to answer. 'There's a Personnel Carrier parked down the road. It has an extra kit bag we couldn't carry. Bring it.'

Mission accepted, Kennard weaved his way past the trucks, relieved to be moving away from the fire. He located the PC, parked neatly parallel to the kerb as if on a routine call-out. In the back he found the satchel and slung it over his shoulder. It weighed a good forty kilos and made the slog back up the hill that little bit more torturous. He had just about made it to the top when a hand grabbed his shoulder and spun him around so fast he almost fell over.

'What's happening? Is Trace out?'

Russell was standing in front of him, his helmet and hood off, sandy hair jutting out at unnatural angles, cheeks stained with soot.

'The forensics team are in there now.'

'I need to see her.'

'You will. Later.' Kennard left out the 'for identification' part. 'Right now you've a job to do.'

Joel was standing behind, still in full gear. 'You gotta leave them to it, Russell.'

'I don't gotta do anything,' said Russell, glaring at his friend before dropping his head and returning to his shelter behind the main tanker, shielded from the direct heat. Kennard continued on.

He didn't get far. Bairstow beckoned him over. Kennard braced for a telling-off. Instead, he got a blunt assessment.

'You've got half an hour.'

'Tell that to Forensics,' said Kennard.

'You called them in, you tell 'em. They've half an hour. I don't want our escape route closed off. Right now, the winds are in our favour. But a slight change and we're fucked. So, half an hour and we're pulling back.'

Kennard understood what he was saying. Their avenue of retreat was all-important. Like the supply line for an army. Keep it open or risk starving. Of food in that case – of oxygen in theirs.

He made his way back into the house and informed Andrews, who didn't hold back with his 'Fuck', though there seemed to be some relief mixed with the disappointment.

Given the tight deadline, Kennard stuck with them, learning that the body was decaying more rapidly than normal, the cells, blood and organs breaking down and putrefying, though that was easy to tell given the stench in the air. He also learned that their bosses had been reluctant to send them out here, risking their lives for a dead person. Corners were being cut to try to gather as much information as possible, as they attempted to do their jobs in an environment they hadn't been trained to deal with. Kennard could only admire them for standing up to the challenge. All too quickly Bairstow appeared at the door with the five-minute warning. Time to move the body.

As Forensics finally rescued Tracey Hilmeyer from her house, transporting her to the makeshift PC hearse in a heavy-duty bag, Kennard talked to Andrews.

'Murder?' asked Kennard.

'Looks like it. The blunt-force trauma looks pre-mortem. Doesn't look like it came from a fall. We'll get more detail during the autopsy.'

'The blood spatter?'

'The body had been moved. Probably soon after death given the pattern and pool of blood around the victim's head.'

'Got a time of death?'

'Hard to be exact given the conditions, but I think it was at least twenty-four hours ago.'

Eight

The removal of Tracey's body caused a stir even among the battle-hardened firefighters, the break in concentration allowing the hoses to try to kick for freedom before being wrestled under control again. Kennard followed the body bag, the surreal funeral procession making its way out of the would-be crematorium for a trip to the morgue.

As Tracey's body was being loaded into the back of the Personnel Carrier, he took the opportunity to speak with Bairstow, Russell and Joel milling close by.

'Can you save the house?' asked Kennard.

'Let it burn,' said Russell. 'I don't want it saved. I'm never going to set foot inside it again.'

'Come on, mate. It's your house,' said Joel.

'Mine and Trace's house. If she's not there, I'm not either.'

Kennard could see the reflection of the approaching fire glowing red in Russell's eyes. He was adamant that the house should burn. His reasoning was sound. The grieving husband who didn't want the memories of what he had seen. But the hard fact was that Tracey had been murdered, so he might have an alternative reason: the total destruction of any evidence that remained. For without anyone else in the picture at the moment, Russell Hilmeyer had to be the prime suspect. Kennard knew that it was a sad truth that over half of the women who were murdered were killed by their husbands, partners or other relatives.

'I want it saved. It's a crime scene in a murder investigation,' said Kennard, tensing up, hands curling into fists again, ready for a battle. Another remnant of Parramatta. On edge at the slightest cue. Wary.

'Ain't gonna happen,' said Bairstow.

'If you need more resources, I can get them,' said Kennard, not knowing if he could.

'I'm not throwing more people into harm's way.'

The lights on the PC carrying Tracey's body lit up, carrying across the ashy gloom.

'I want to go with her,' pleaded Russell.

'You're needed here,' said Kennard, looking to Bairstow for support.

Bairstow nodded, weary already. Not needing this drama on top of everything else. 'All hands to the pump, Hilmeyer. And I don't want any more vehicles doing a runner, you hear?'

'You'll be called for formal identification when they're ready,' said Kennard to Russell, trying to appease him.

Russell stared at the PC, itching to make a dash for it but the vehicle swung around sharply, the engine straining, tyres *tack-tack-tack*ing as they lifted the asphalt. Kennard watched Russell bow his head, refusing to watch his wife leave as Joel followed the vehicle's progress all the way, his eyes narrowed almost as if he were fighting back tears.

With the PC gone, Bairstow pulled in a woman in a similar orange helmet but with two extra white stripes along the crown, like go-faster stripes. The nameplate said Mirza and Kennard guessed she was his deputy.

'Retreat to the other side of Caldicott. We'll use the road as a firebreak. Fell any overhanging trees you consider a risk.'

So that was it. 148 Caldicott was going to burn. Kennard followed the logic. Using the street as a firebreak gave them the best chance at containment considering the wild bush stretching out for miles behind the house.

'Could you not bulldoze behind it? Create a firebreak there?' asked Kennard. He had seen this technique used on the news before.

Bairstow turned his head, lips twisted in thought. 'If we had another couple of hours. And crucially: a bulldozer,' he said, dismissing Kennard before returning to making plans with his colleague. Station points. What to call in. What to use. Hosing down the road to prevent dragging up all the asphalt and making it inaccessible. Kennard stepped into Bairstow's line of sight.

'I'm ordering you to try and save the house.' Kennard hadn't wanted to start a dick-swinging contest, but felt he had no choice. 'This is a murder investigation, which means I am in charge of the scene. I want all attempts made to save it.'

Bairstow glared at him. Mirza too. Kennard knew what he was asking for was a tall task. He watched both of them study him, eyes fierce behind their Perspex helmet shields. The barrier didn't temper the glares.

'My *strong* advice is to abandon it,' said Bairstow.

'Mine too,' added Mirza.

'Noted,' said Kennard. 'But I'm in charge. Save it.'

Bairstow shook his head slowly, disgusted. 'You're taking the heat for this.'

The words made Kennard's stomach curl, but he held his nerve.

'It could put a number of other properties under threat. And if any of my people are injured, I'll haul you over what's left of this place after and bury you.'

Bairstow growled like he meant it. Hard enough that Kennard considered backing down. But he needed the house. He needed evidence.

'So, what do we do?' he asked.

'That's our job. You do yours,' said Bairstow bluntly. 'And right now, your job is to stay out of our way.'

'Can I have Forensics back in?'

'Not until I clear it as safe. You have authority over the dead body. I have authority over the live ones and making sure they stay that way.'

'So, you'll let me know.'

'First thing,' Bairstow said sarcastically.

Kennard bit his tongue. He didn't like being belittled. It had happened too many times in the past few months. But he needed Bairstow and his crew to save that house. He didn't want to prioritize the dead over the living, but even the dead deserved answers.

Nine

Kennard waited behind the pumper, shielded from the worst of the heat. The first part had been done. Body recovered. House – and any evidence – saved. For now. He called DSS Haskell, ready to fight his corner. It rang. The wait let his thoughts dwell on the fire, the people and their proximity, causing more sweat to trickle down his face, his heart beating a quick rhythm in his chest. His fear grew, roiling in his stomach. He knew what was on the other side of the pumper. Yet, to his surprise, he wanted to stay.

Haskell answered. He informed her of the situation. The short version. The body had been recovered. His call on saving the house. Taking charge of the scene.

There was a pause. 'Right-o. You take the lead, Kennard.' Her disappointment at having no other immediate option oozed from the receiver.

'That's it?' Kennard had been expecting more of a battle.

'What did you want? A royal blessing?'

'Where's Uptill?'

'You don't need to know where DS Uptill is, DS Kennard.

48

You just concentrate on not making me regret this. You're skating on thin ice after last week's boxing match. I don't need officers that stir shit or are incapable of doing their duty.'

And there it was. What she was gunning for. An excuse to kick him off the team.

'But I'm not leaving you up there on your own. I'm sending someone.'

Someone else was good. It should be a two-person case. But who had he not pissed off at the barbeque?

'Who?' asked Kennard. The list was small and unpleasant: Sancho, DePaul, Hoskins. All in Uptill's corner.

'Head in the game, DS Kennard. Just focus on what needs to be done.'

The first thing he needed to do was catch a PC back to the Incident Control Centre at the school. Russell and Joel rode the same vehicle, Russell complaining about being denied permission to accompany his wife's body to the morgue. Again, Kennard explained patiently that Forensics had to be allowed space to do their job. Without outside interference.

'You're treating me like a suspect.'

Kennard wasn't going to deny it. He couldn't. He had been looking forward to the welcome ride away from the frontline. He needed distance from the inferno, time to think and time to bask in the relative cool. But with Russell in the same vehicle the journey was awkward, any relief constricted.

His instincts – and, if he was honest, a touch of anger –

cut in. 'Where have you been in the last forty-eight hours?'
he asked.

Russell twisted around in the front seat to look at
him. His face, unburdened by the fireproof balaclava and
helmet, curled into a sneer. Gone was the handsome man.
In his place was a man with an expression that forced
Kennard to be on guard, a fury embodied by the curl of
wrinkles across the tops of his cheeks.

Russell glanced towards Joel, who was sitting beside
Kennard in the back. 'Told you, he thinks I'm a suspect.'

'Everyone is until we rule them out.'

'Everyone?' asked Joel, uncomfortable.

'I wasn't here,' said Russell sharply.

'Where were you?'

Russell squeezed his eyes tight and shook his head. 'Can
you quit with the questions?'

'I can't do that, Russell. I'm trying to find out who
might have seen her last.'

'Not me. Told you. I was out of town most of Tuesday
and all Wednesday. Working.'

'Give the bloke some space,' spat Joel towards Kennard.

'It's a simple question.'

'Yeah, for someone who hasn't just held his dead wife in
his arms, mate,' Joel retorted, nothing friendly or matey
in his tone.

Kennard wasn't going to back down. Russell might have
been grieving, but, as the husband, the quicker Kennard
could rule him out the better.

'What was your relationship like? Were you and her
getting on okay?'

'Getting on ...? What do you mean by that?' Russell wrestled in his seat like he wanted to climb over it and grab him by the throat, causing Kennard to flinch. A display of unbridled anger that suggested a man capable of violence.

'Have a fuckin' heart,' Joel said to Kennard, eyes pinched, anger seeping through.

Russell took a deep breath through his nose, teeth clenched. 'He'll find out anyway. It's been tough. The last year.'

'Mate—' said Joel, in what seemed to be an attempt to shut his friend up.

'It's a small town. Someone will run their mouth,' Russell offered as the PC climbed the hill on the south side of town. The safe side. 'She hadn't been doing well. Not since she lost it last year.'

Kennard was intrigued. 'Lost what?'

Russell glanced out the window, colourful houses passing by on a street Kennard vaguely remembered from his youth.

'The gallery.'

'What ...?'

'An art gallery. It wasn't like the Googleheim or anything, but it was hers,' said Russell.

Kennard caught the mistake, but Russell's downcast expression hinted it was more ignorance than a joke.

Russell continued. 'I thought she could cope, but it got to her.'

'She's been through a lot,' added Joel.

'Like you know half,' said Russell, anger flashing at his friend.

Joel seemed to want to say something back, but he held his tongue.

'Okay, so if you were out of town for the last forty-eight hours, when was the last time you saw your wife?' asked Kennard, boiling like a cabbage in the bunker gear.

'Tuesday morning,' said Russell, resigned. 'She was watching daytime soaps. I didn't even say goodbye.'

The tears that had been threatening to spill finally arrived, no baking heat to dry them up this time. Kennard had managed to break a grieving man. He felt no pride in it, but the questions needed to be asked. He paused to let Russell gather himself. Long enough for the PC to make it back to the schoolyard.

Kennard got out. He would try to tease more answers out of Russell inside. Maybe even buy him coffee. One thing a school would have was plenty of rooms to talk privately in.

But Russell didn't exit the PC. Nodding to the driver, a guy with a flattened parrot-blue mohawk, he said, 'Marshie, take us back.'

The driver looked at his passengers, wide-eyed, unsure.

'You heard him, Marshie,' said Joel, locking the doors.

'Russell, I need to talk to you,' said Kennard.

The PC pulled away with a squeak of the tyres, hard rubber on hard asphalt. Kennard watched them leave and wondered whether he should go after them. This was a bushfire that threatened an entire town after all. All hands were needed to fight it. Even Russell's.

What he needed to do was contact Bairstow and ask him to prevent Russell, or anyone else for that matter, from entering the crime scene. Rushing inside the school, he headed to the chemistry lab and approached a woman with platinum blonde hair who was working on a bank of laptops. A nametag attached to her plain light-blue blouse identified her as Lenka.

She started a little as Kennard suddenly loomed over her, but the momentary discomfort quickly gave way to a smile.

'How can I—?' she began.

'I need to get through to the GC.'

'Which one?'

'Bairstow. Over on Caldicott.'

A couple of clicks and Kennard was patched through. Bairstow growled and complained but promised that he would post someone on the door to prevent Russell from attempting to enter his own house before abruptly hanging up.

'Do you want to sit down?'

There was worry on Lenka's face. Kennard realized he was leaning on the table, arched over, reviewing the situation.

'I'll be fine.' He smiled weakly.

'Make sure of it.'

Thanking her, he retired to the crowded school hall. He paused at the door, steeling himself, assessing the throng, assessing the danger. It took him straight back.

Ten

Parramatta – Six months ago

Kennard was second on the scene, having left the bakery across the street to follow Ces Nannup and Lisa Marker inside an apartment block opposite. Instinct told him something big was happening. It was the way Ces and Lisa had entered, no pause for backup, no time to waste. Something urgent.

He caught up with them inside the lobby. Lisa looked surprised to see him. She was a few years younger than Kennard, which still made her a good deal older than Ces. She was the experienced partner, quicker with her wit than with her legs but a solid mentor to the younger man.

'D-branch are quick these days!' she said.

'I was in the area,' said Kennard, not mentioning the bakery. 'What have we got?'

'Hostage situation. Mum and son,' said Ces. He was a recent addition to the team, three years deep in-state on the edge of the bush and recently transferred to the city. He was eager, if a little raw. Kennard shouldn't have been surprised that he had lunged at the first sign of action.

Out the back of the dreary apartment block they found chaos. A standoff between a crowd and a couple of people huddled by the large, communal bins. The crowd were armed with phones, aiming them at something Kennard couldn't make out with all the people in the way.

'Can everyone get back, please?' he shouted.

Barely anyone in the crowd acknowledged him, unwilling to give up their prime shooting spots.

He turned to Ces. 'See if you can't get backup down here now.'

Ces nodded. 'You two okay?'

'We'll see. Don't go far.'

With that, Ces was off. There was a hunger in the crowd. Thirty people were gathered around like seagulls waiting to move in on a meal. Kennard and Marker started to push through it.

'Police, coming through.'

They were met with insults, phones directed at them now as much as at what was going on in front. Recording it all.

As they pushed past the front row, the incident presented itself. Almost corralled by the giant wheeled bins, a teenage boy was standing behind a woman, a gun held near her head. A son holding his mother hostage.

Kennard took a step into the courtyard, out into the open. He approached the boy and his terrified mother carefully, each step taking him a little closer, tension rising in his bones. The boy stared at him, then back towards the crowd, who were baying for something, anything, to happen.

'Just drop the weapon, son.'

'Who are you?' asked the boy, the question spat in Kennard's direction.

'I'm Detective Sergeant Kennard. Alex.'

'A fucking jack,' said the boy, tensing up a little more, wary of the authorities.

'What's your name?'

'Rhian,' said the boy, almost reluctantly. As if not wanting to associate himself with these acts.

Kennard attempted a half-smile. 'Why don't you put the gun down, Rhian? Let your mum go and let's talk.'

As soon as the boy dropped the gun and released the hostage, the bulk of his job would be done. Danger averted, only the pieces to sweep up.

Behind him the unsolicited advice from the crowd continued. 'Bro's gonna shoot!' 'Take him out!' 'Don't trust the feds!'

Through it all he could hear Marker trying to disperse the swarm, but this was essential viewing. The 'I was there' moment, cameras at the ready.

Kennard tried to forget about the audience. He focused on Rhian. The boy's eyes were red, twitching in panic or high on something. Maybe both. They seemed to be pleading for Kennard to stop this. A recognition that he had gone too far but didn't know how to back out of it. A teenager who even in this moment didn't want to lose face, unsure of where he was or what he was doing. The needle balancing on its tip, free to swing either way.

Kennard heard a commotion behind him. Marker crying out. He glanced over his shoulder to see a large man with a shaved head standing over his fallen colleague.

'You okay there, Lisa?' asked Kennard.

'That was assault,' growled the man, his phone aimed squarely at Marker. As powerful a weapon as the boy's gun, if not quite as immediate. 'I'm within my rights to stream this.'

'This is a police matter,' said Marker, scrambling to her feet.

'Tell that to my subscribers.'

'You all have to leave,' said Kennard.

'Not while I'm earning off this. I'm within my rights to stay. Public place, mate.'

Kennard glanced at Marker. He wanted to arrest the man. From the blushed red overwhelming her face, she wanted to arrest him as well. But now wasn't a good time. Controlling the crowd with only two of them was difficult enough. There were too many variables. Not least Rhian and the gun.

Kennard took another few shuffled steps. He was within ten metres of them now. Still too far.

'Rhian? How about you let your mother go, son.'

This set Rhian off. 'Son? You ain't my dad.'

Kennard put his hand up, an apology. But also a break-through. 'I only want to sort this all out.'

'You sort it out by getting this bitch to relax.'

Rhian was seething now, the gun tapping against his mum's head. She yelped in response, staring mutely at Kennard, urging him to fix this. Makeup oozed from the corners of her eyes, dark rivers of fear etched on her face.

'Just put the gun down and we will.'

'Nah. No deal.'

'We can solve this, Rhian.'

'You gonna get me a new computer? Bitch dumped it in one of these bins. In pieces.'

'That's easy to solve. We—' started Kennard.

'Two grand it cost me. And she's bitching over a few hundred.'

'My credit card,' said Mrs Thorpe, her voice trembling then falling off. As if she knew she shouldn't defend herself but had been unable to resist.

'I'm sure we can sort it out. No one's pressing charges, Rhian,' said Kennard.

His mother nodded eagerly, playing the game now, her green dress shimmering as she moved. Dispel the danger now, sort the details out later.

Behind him he heard more agitation. Kennard glanced back to see the man with the shaved head still arguing with Marker.

He turned back to find the gun pointed at him. Aimed at his chest. Kennard froze. Words failed him, as if he had been shot already and all the air taken from his lungs. He tried to regain his composure, tried to reassure himself that the boy didn't want to shoot. That he only wanted attention. That he only wanted to be heard.

'What's going to happen now?' asked Rhian.

'What do you mean?'

'What will happen to me?'

'It will all be sorted.'

'Bullshit.'

'I swear to you, Rhian. No one's been injured. Just put the gun—'

'It's all over now.'

'Nothing's all over.'

'It is. This'll be everywhere now. Viral.'

'It won't.'

'Don't bullshit me. I know this shit better than you, grandad.'

Kennard couldn't argue with him there, his online presence restricted to a few social media sites that he had signed up to but never used.

He risked a glance over his shoulder. More uniforms were appearing on the scene, but the crowd wasn't going away easily, the man with the shaved head seeking a definitive conclusion to his live-action drama. One which Kennard couldn't let happen.

He turned back to Rhian, but the gun was no longer pointed at Kennard. Rhian had turned it on himself.

Kennard met the boy's eyes. Tears streamed from them like they did from his mum's, all hope gone. A path taken that he felt he couldn't recover from.

Kennard darted forward just as the mother screamed. The gunshot drowned everything out. Too loud and too brutal, crashing around the concrete and metal bins as if looking for a home.

Rhian Thorpe slumped to the ground, his mother screaming, the arm that had been restraining her now slack, her son's blood speckled across one side of her face.

Kennard stood there. He couldn't quite believe what had happened. All the visual cues were present, but there was no sense in them. He had just one resounding thought, louder than the screams and ringing in his ears: that he had failed.

Involuntarily he backed away, not feeling his feet or legs, almost as if mother and boy were slipping away from him. With the finality of the gunshot the will of the crowd had changed. Nobody was urging Rhian to shoot now; they were screaming and running for the way out. Looking for somewhere safe to process what they had been calling for but had never expected to happen. Kennard had been so close. Close enough to reach out and touch the gun if he'd dared. Maybe that was what Rhian had been looking for. Kennard to take the power from his hands rather than give it up. But that choice was too far away now. In another world. Mother and boy continued to slide further from his mind. He heard Ces ask what he was doing but there was no answer. He didn't know. Sirens erupted in the background, the screams of the crowd and the instructions from Marker and others white noise that swallowed him up in confusion. Only one thing was clear. The boy was dead.

The investigation was watered down, assurances given that there was nothing Kennard could have done, but it could not hide the fact that he had failed. There were witnesses; there was video evidence. There was a dead boy. A grieving mother. Lives ruined.

In the days and weeks that followed, the thought of quitting followed him everywhere. In bed, watching TV, even to the dunny. But the police force was all he knew. What had once been natural for him got lost somewhere between his brain and his muscles. He began to second-guess every decision, not trusting his instincts like he once had, instincts that had served him well in the past. Ann wondered if a change of pace might help. His boss thought the same. So, he was shuffled off to the Blue Mountains where the pace of life was deemed more suitable to his 'talents'. Where he could seek solace in petty thefts and domestics. Enjoy the views and the quiet life, Sydney remaining beyond the trees, somewhere a long way below. Stick him up in the same clouds that had dulled his senses. Clouds that were fluffy and obscured everything. There could be nothing damaging in the clouds.

Eleven

'You sure you're all right?'

Kennard looked at the mug of tea that had been thrust in front of him. Light brown, milky, the hand slim and tanned, almost the same colour as the drink.

He blinked hard, washing Parramatta from his mind. He found himself leaning against the wall by the edge of the school gym hall, the smell of tea and desperation in the air.

The mug was being held by the woman from the operations room. Lenka.

'You looked like you had broken down,' she smiled.

'I pretty much had,' he said, to a look of confusion.

Again, she nudged the tea at him. 'It was for someone else, but you look as if you need it more.'

Kennard took it. Nodded his thanks.

Lenka looked out across the room. 'What do you make of it?'

Kennard looked at the gym. It had been set up as temporary living quarters, camp beds lined up neatly across the floor, people milling around looking for food or company, the hall bustling and noisy. It looked like most of the residents had remained in town. Their houses, possessions, lives and loves were all here. For the moment at least.

'Kind of makes you glad you don't live here,' said Lenka. 'I know that's harsh and all but . . .'

'That is harsh,' said Kennard, smiling.

She grinned. 'And that's brutally honest.'

'I'm a cop.' The words a reminder almost as much to himself as to her.

'Do what we can,' she said.

'Do what we can,' he replied.

'Right, I better be . . .' She flicked her head back towards the corridor and the chemistry lab.

'Stay safe,' said Kennard.

'You too, Detective.'

With that she was off. Kennard watched her leave, her brief kindness filling him with something that had been lacking recently. Hope.

Looking around the gym, he tried to spot a familiar face, one that he might recognize from childhood. He aimed himself at an elderly group huddled in the corner talking among themselves. If Kennard had learned one thing over his years in the force, it was that if you want a witness, or simply to find out gossip, ask the elderly. They were unlikely to be engrossed in their phones, their heads instead up and alert for danger, paying attention to their environment.

He approached the group, six men and women who eyed him with caution. All were dressed in their Sunday best as if they had stepped out of some 1950s magazine article, no impending apocalypse about to interrupt their yearning to be properly attired on all occasions. There was no one he recognized from Sunday mornings spent in the narrow church at the foot of Main Street, where all the oldest buildings in town were clustered together, bordering the meandering stream that swelled into a river when it rained. Introducing himself, he got names and addresses, a lecture about his lack of hygiene and a pat on the back for tackling the fire.

The six seemed to have been led by hair hierarchy – a hair-archy, Kennard chuckled to himself, earning a glare from the most talkative member, Mina Forrester, a bow around her head that accented what looked to be a particularly spectacular bouffant wig.

'Did they find her?' enquired a man with a severe bowl haircut, when Kennard asked about Tracey. His question was abruptly answered by Mina.

'Of course they haven't, Roger. I'm guessing she's missing. Or dead?'

'Why do you say that, Mina?' asked Derek, her second in command, his mullet made ever more powerful with age, whisking around behind him like straw caught in the wind.

'Because the detective wouldn't be asking otherwise.'

There was a collective 'Ah' from the group, as if they had solved the case.

'In fact,' continued Mina, 'I think she might be dead.'

She stated it like a fortune teller would, leading, looking for the answer that matched her assumption.

'I'm just trying to pin down her movements,' said Kennard. 'When did you last see her?'

Mina nodded and looked around her group as if divining for answers.

'Last Thursday,' said Derek.

'Friday for me. At the *supermarché*,' smiled a woman with hair as pink as her face, fair-skinned and out in the sun too long.

'That's supermarket,' confirmed Mina.

'Thanks for that,' said Kennard. 'Anything more recent?'

'Monday afternoon. In that tourist shop she worked in. Rislake Souvenirs. On Main Street. Not the most original branding,' sighed Mina, to mumbled agreement.

'Open at strange times too,' added Derek.

'Closed most lunches,' said Roger.

Kennard leaned in. 'Any reason why?'

'We didn't go in, so we wouldn't know why,' said Mina, answering for the group.

There was nothing else forthcoming, a couple of anecdotes about Tracey previously owning an art gallery in town and taking up residence in the pub most nights was the best that he got from others in the room.

So far no one, aside from Russell, had seen her in person since Monday afternoon, when she had locked up the shop and presumably gone home. Where she had then been murdered.

Twelve

Tracey – Before

On most days, she refused to look out the front window for the memories it brought. But a job was a job, and she was good at it, selling all manner of crap to tourists with more money than sense. So good, in fact, she was able to pick out the timewasters now, those pretending they were in to buy something, pointing at things and going *ooooh* and *aaaaah* as if she'd invited them in to critique the piece. Trying to look as if they were making up their minds on it. Showboating, for some unfathomable reason.

She'd never understood why people loved souvenirs. They were catnip to tourists. It was almost as if they didn't trust their eyes or their memories and so they needed to bring back items that jogged their memory, trinkets that confirmed that they'd had a good time.

Her parents had been the same, but instead of souvenirs they'd collected ornaments. As though by filling the shelves they could prove to themselves that they had lived a full life. Tracey could see the point of a painting but, aside from a few exceptions, not so much an ornament. Ornaments only gathered dust, whereas paintings offered a constant source of beauty, brushstrokes here and there, personal touches that awaited discovery on every viewing.

At least it was the start of summer. It meant that the shop would be busy, a sustained flow of people in and out. Different people. Opportunities to capture them. She preferred spontaneous rather than posed for the most part, and over the last year she had picked up a basic conversational understanding of French, Spanish and German, which helped. Others like Japanese and Chinese remained out of her reach, but she tried her best. It had surprised her how accommodating people could be when asked, when she explained what she wanted. A smile and a swish of her long blonde hair helped. Hard to refuse.

Noon was fast coming when trade tailed off for lunch. The one thing that all nationalities had in common was the need for food. The last bus had come by twenty minutes ago, Dazza shepherding his tour into the shop in return for some beer money every week from Tony Steyn, Tracey's boss. It had been a profitable group. She'd sold a Chinese couple a digeridoo that would present a logistical nightmare to get back home, three boomerangs and a painting of a sunset to a German man who had gone as beet red as the painting itself when Tracey had explained that it was hers. A nothing painting really, one she did to sell for some extra money, not her passion. Aside from that, it was the usual mix of Rislake-labelled tat, stuffed kangaroos and koalas. Called cute by people who had obviously never met the razor-clawed bastards in real life.

There had been no one worth paying special interest to. Disappointing but not unusual. With nothing to do, she braved a glance outside, refusing to allow her eyes to drift across the street. A few tourists dressed in colonial khaki floated past, peering around as they climbed the hill, as if Rislake was one giant theme park that they had been dropped into. She supposed it was amazing in its way. There was beauty in the untouched nature of the shopfronts, resisting the changing times, a frontier look of wooden verandas and intricate cast-iron pillars which held wonder for visitors used to sharp edges and sleek stone.

A couple of her old schoolmates and drinking buddies passed by locked in conversation. The last few years she had drifted away from Sharon Evert and Louisa Montgomery. Shazza had gone by the way of permanently hassled motherhood and Lou had married into the church and become a resident do-gooder rather than the rebel she once was, popping out children like they were going out of fashion. Three so far. As if on command. Tracey supposed that was the most Christian thing she could do to support the church: deliver as many God-fearing ankle-biters as she could. After all, if you can't beat them, outnumber them. In the last few years Tracey had started to feel the urge to join that group. As a mother, not a Christian; she had enough on her plate already. But her body was telling her it was time. That the clock was ticking.

Winnie and Harald tottered by. Her erstwhile neighbours. As ever, they couldn't help but sneak a glance inside, keeping a watchful eye on everything that occurred in town like self-appointed Stasi. The wave she offered back sent them scurrying off, their matching shirts announcing that they were headed for the bowling club situated at the top of the hill. The only flat land that wasn't outside of town.

Sergeant Gary Reinhold passed by the other way, waddling down the hill. She had never seen him attempt to go uphill, one of his constables always on call to give him a ride from Chrissy's Bar'N'Grill a couple of doors down. 'Sinner's Cave' as the Methodists called it. Bottomless coffee and topless staff, though Sandy Christobal's breasts almost dunked into the schooners she served nowadays.

Tracey had brought her own lunch with her, as she usually did. She wasn't of a mind to leave the shop. She would throw up the 'Out for Lunch' sign and relax out back. Maybe sneak a smoke to help mellow her out. She had a new batch to try out. Tony was unlikely to pop in. He rarely did. Tracey got the impression that he avoided her as much as possible because he couldn't give her more hours behind the counter. He was under significant pressure to employ the wider family, bound by an unwritten nepotism rule that had been enforced upon him when he'd taken over. Tracey had told him that Tick, his German Shepherd, may as well get a couple of afternoons on the rota. That it would have likely sold more than some of the other dipsticks in the family who were more interested in their phones than peddling souvenirs.

But Friday was her shift. The start of the weekend. A day of painting tomorrow. Somewhere remote and quiet maybe. Just her, her paint and her brushes.

Thirteen

January 20 – 13.00 – Wind direction NE – Surface speed 30km/h

6 hours since North Rislake evacuation

South Rislake status = Amber (Prepare for possible evacuation)

Kennard contacted HQ in Katoomba. The bushfire threatening the Hilmeyer house added an obvious motive for Tracey's death. He got through to the main desk.

He bathed in the soothing tendrils of the soft English lilt that responded.

'How can I help you, DS Kennard?'

He could picture the permanently rosy cheeks of the middle-aged woman that the voice belonged to, but her name eluded him. Worse still, she recognized him.

'I need a background check on some insurance policies. Life and house insurance and anything else you can dig up on a Russell and Tracey Hilmeyer, 148 Caldicott Road, Rislake.'

'I can do that. I'll get back to you as soon as possible.'

'Thanks,' said Kennard, cutting the call.

He returned to the main hall. He felt like a vampire trawling the room for victims to suck information from.

It felt strange interviewing people on the hoof. Normally there was an address to visit when tracking down witnesses. A home or place of work. A glimpse into their personal life that offered some framing to their answers. A clue as to who they were. A foundation. But everyone here was the same. Nervous bundles of energy worried about their houses, their belongings and their future. Most of them knew Tracey Hilmeyer. No one had a bad word to say. A lot of 'likeable's. A few 'talented's. More than a few 'gorgeous'es. Artistic without the snobby side of it. Or at least until the last year, when she had fallen off the radar a little it seemed.

He nabbed a family who were trying to discreetly make their way through a packet of Tim-Tams as if they were contraband. As they sent their three small kids off to play hide and seek around the stage at the far end of the hall, Kennard got speaking to them.

They were shocked at the news of Tracey Hilmeyer's demise. He kept her apparent murder out of the conversation for now.

The wife, Sharon Evert, spoke first, the stress of the whole situation rife in her voice as she picked at a cardigan ripe with bobbles. 'It was a shame about that gallery.'

With his wife setting the ball rolling, her husband, an older man with grey hair and a severe expression that hadn't changed since Kennard had joined them, spoke up too. 'Not that you ever went in, Shaz.'

'I know, but a bit of culture. Local culture.'

'So, she was talented?' asked Kennard.

The husband shrugged.

'Don't ask Dave, the only culture he knows is Vegemite.'

'What happened to the gallery?' asked Kennard. It was something that many people had mentioned without going into details.

'Economics,' said Sharon.

'No one has the money,' said Dave bluntly. 'Not around here. Everyone's on their arse.'

Sharon rolled her eyes. 'It's a shame though.'

'Did you know her well?'

'Classmates. Many years ago. Used to be pretty tight, then this lump of piss happened,' she said, nodding towards her husband.

'You didn't keep in touch?'

'Not regular. Seen her in the pub a few times, like you do everyone.'

'She was well-liked,' said Dave.

'Because everyone fancied the pants off her,' said Sharon. 'Still did mostly.'

'Not this one,' said Dave. 'She was nowhere near as pretty as you.'

'You gotta say that. Otherwise, I snag this last Tim-Tam,' smiled Sharon.

Kennard left them to their friendly argument. He was

considering his next move when a figure appeared alongside him.

'DS Kennard.' Kennard flinched at the voice then swung around to find a small, neatly manicured hand thrust towards him.

DSS Haskell's choice of partner might have been a compromise but was still heavily weighted in her favour. DS Georgina Layton, a year into the role and very much a PBN. A Paint-By-Numbers officer. Competent, pleasant and helpful. Deliberate to the point of seeming aloof. More politician than policewoman, her plans and strategies all mapped out beforehand. She knew the people to talk to, what to say and what to do. As if she had been coached. An officer who was more concerned about not making a mistake than excelling or showing initiative. The mindset he had seen in rookie officers. Don't stick your toe in the sea in case a shark comes and rips it off. She hadn't attended his BBQ last week. Over a personal matter. Apparently.

'Are you up to speed?' asked Kennard, shaking her hand. It was bird-like, engulfed by his meaty paw.

Layton glanced around to make sure that they couldn't be overheard. Good practice. 'Tracey Hilmeyer. Thirty-two years old. Found in her home approximately 09:50 hours today. The DS in attendance, DS Alex Kennard, suspects foul play.'

So, she had the basics. Which, to be fair, was all anyone had.

Layton paused, dragging a small blue inhaler from her pocket and taking a hit from it, ceding the floor to Kennard.

He took up the gauntlet. 'Next steps are to find out when Tracey was last seen alive. The husband, Russell Hilmeyer, claims to have seen her on Tuesday morning. I have a few sightings on Monday afternoon at Rislake Souvenirs, the shop she worked in. Initial forensics indicate that she was likely dead for at least twenty-four hours.'

'Leaving a gap of twenty-four hours where she wasn't seen.'

'Exactly. Russell Hilmeyer claims to have been out of town on Tuesday and Wednesday, which we'll need to check out.'

DS Layton pulled a tablet from her bag and slid it in front of Kennard.

'This is a photo we have of Tracey Hilmeyer. From her social media.'

The photo was chalk and cheese from the sight Kennard had faced. Dave Evert had been right. When alive, Tracey Hilmeyer would have turned heads. Dyed blonde hair, chestnut-coloured eyes, a few signs of the wear and tear of life, but she looked younger than her thirty-two years. For certain, death didn't do her justice.

'Any signs of sexual assault?' asked Layton.

'None immediately obvious. She was fully clothed, nothing out of place. But at present we are prevented from searching the premises thoroughly.'

'Domestic issue?'

'The husband admits Tracey had been troubled and withdrawn in the past year.'

'Any reason?'

'Looks like it was a failed business venture. An art gallery.'

'So how was she missed during the evac?'

'Chance. Seems that she took herself off-grid sometimes. To paint.'

'Anyone immediately obvious for the attack?'

'No one's had a bad word to say about her.'

'Even the husband?'

'What are you thinking?' asked Kennard.

'A crime of passion.'

'We can't rule it out.'

'And the husband's whereabouts at present?'

'He's out fighting the bushfire. What we need to find out is why in the initial evacuation stocktake Tracey was included in the count.'

Exiting the school, they crossed the top of Main Street. Despite the lingering threat it was doing a roaring trade, raking money in before it all went up in flames. The very definition of a Fire Sale. The quaint independent stores that drew in the visiting tourists looked brighter than Kennard remembered. He recalled beige shopfronts and everything washed in sepia. Dull window displays and a sedate pace of life, the train station perched at the top of the town as if getting out of Rislake was something you should aspire to, the lights and opportunities of Sydney at the end of the line. But not now; now there was colour everywhere, not least the orange to the northwest. Like the geography of the land, life in this town was like a rollercoaster. Peaks and troughs. Drought to flood to fire.

Taking a deep breath, he skirted the edge of the bustle, allowing space, watching everyone who passed him by, eyes keened for movement.

'You okay?' she asked.

While his eyes were scanning the crowd, Layton was watching him. Closely.

'Why does everyone keep asking me that?'

'I guess because you look like a kangaroo in headlights.'

'Just taking it all in,' said Kennard, trying to compose himself. Already Layton was getting on his nerves. Which wasn't a good sign. Haskell had sent her here for a reason. Probably to spy on him. Make sure that he didn't fuck up.

He was distracted by an elderly couple at a cash machine. It was spitting out notes like colourful tickertape.

'You okay?' he asked them, all the time looking at Layton, forcing home the point.

They both turned to Kennard with a smile. They were dressed in matching tops adorned with a set of black bowls in a nest of green overlaid by 'RBC', Rislake Bowling Club presumably, and both sported a shock of white hair set into neat perms that almost seemed to have grown in sync, perched on the tops of their heads like candyfloss.

'Yes, dear, but thank you for asking.'

As the machine continued to whirr colours like a rainbow, the pair kept their eyes fixed on him. Kennard noted no suspicion in them. Here was a stranger distracting them from what looked to be a thousand bucks or more – maybe their life savings – sitting in the mouth of the machine, and yet they were both giving him their undivided attention.

He nodded at the cash. 'You'll need a security detail for all that.'

They laughed. The woman reached out and touched his arm. Kennard didn't mean to flinch, even need to flinch, but he did. The old woman didn't seem to pay attention to it. 'Oh, everyone's much too busy. What with this bush-fire. That's why we want to get our money out. In case it all burns up.'

Kennard had no answer to this. It was cute, inexorably dumb, but an all-too-real threat for this pleasant elderly couple.

'Are you from around here?' asked Layton.

The woman pointed towards the north side of town. The danger zone. 'Caldicott Road.'

Kennard's ears perked up at that. 'So, you know Tracey and Russell Hilmeyer?'

The pleasant smile faltered. 'We're neighbours. Winnie Thompson.'

'And I'm Harald. Thompson,' said Harald, promptly, as if he didn't want to be left out.

Kennard picked up on the change of mood. 'Close neighbours?'

Husband looked at wife, who raised her eyebrows in response. Kennard didn't push for an answer. He knew one was coming. He could sense their urge to talk.

'Used to be,' said Winnie, sighing.

'What happened?'

'Last year happened,' said Harald, pointing at the large hearing aid wedged above his ear. 'See this? Didn't need this with the noise from their place. You could hear them from Botany Bay.'

'Music?' asked Layton, sensing a story too.

'Music, talking, shouting. Get on her wrong side and that woman could start a row in heaven.'

'Maybe now she'll get the chance to,' said Winnie, the words vicious from her sweet mouth.

'So, you know she's dead?' asked Layton.

'Bill Knighton told us.'

'And he is?'

'Oh, just Bill. He probably heard from one of his buddies working the line. They call him the Ears of God around here.' At this she chuckled.

'Can you tell me when you last saw the Hilmeyers?'

Winnie turned her attention back to Kennard. 'I saw Russell leaving on Tuesday morning. And her ...' She looked at her husband, who was deep in thought.

'Saw her Tuesday afternoon,' he said.

'Time?'

'I'd say around 5pm. Heading into her house.'

'And at no point after that?'

Both thought about it. 'No.'

At least that narrowed the window during which Tracey's whereabouts were unknown to after 5pm on Tuesday afternoon. But Winnie wasn't finished.

'But we did hear shouting coming from over there on Tuesday night.'

Kennard perked up. 'An argument?'

'Yes.'

'With?'

'I dunno.'

'Russell Hilmeyer?' asked Kennard.

Winnie shrugged her shoulders.

'Did you hear what was said?'

Both husband and wife shook their heads this time.

'Could you identify the voice? Male? Female?'

'Male.'

'But you don't know if it was her husband?'

There was a moment of silent deliberation between them before the couple shrugged in unison.

So, Tracey had been in an argument around the approximate time of her death. That was something. It also seemed to indicate that she might have known her killer.

'About twenty minutes after the shouting I heard a car pull away. Quickly,' said Winnie.

'Did you see it?' asked Layton.

Winnie shook her head.

'A licence plate? A description? Colour? Make?'

'No, sorry, I need my glasses for anything past a few metres,' she said, wincing in apology.

'Okay,' said Kennard, sharing a nod with Layton. 'I'll need you both to make a formal statement.'

'Now?' asked Harald. 'We've a match starting in forty-five minutes.'

'I think they'll understand,' said Kennard.

'You don't know the bowling association very well, do you, Detective?' said Winnie. 'They don't take kindly to tardiness.'

'Or scruffiness,' added Harald.

Or that a bushfire was rapidly approaching the town, thought Kennard.

'I promise we'll be as quick as possible,' said Layton, flashing them a smile.

While he and Layton accompanied the reluctant and newly cash-rich couple to the local police station perched at the top of the hill near the school, Kennard had time to think.

Who could Tracey have been arguing with? Instincts and logic said her husband. He would have had access to the house and had already stated that they had argued on previous occasions. But Harald and Winnie couldn't identify the voice. Then there was the vehicle that had left rapidly a little while after the argument ended. Without a description or a licence plate it could have been anyone. Who was driving it? And did they murder Tracey Hilmeyer?

Fourteen

Kennard entered Rislake police station behind Layton and the husband-and-wife bowling team. At first glance the station was nothing to write home about: breeze-block walls covered in plasterboard, posters tacked haphazardly around a bland greyness to the cabinets and desks, nothing remarkable about the place aside from the tinsel hanging from the tops of the posterboards and a fully decorated plastic Christmas tree in the corner. Apparently, no one had told them that Christmas was four weeks gone, and it signalled that the sergeant didn't care too much for appearances.

Winnie and Harald took a seat by the front desk, making themselves comfortable, as if it was their own home. By the end of the day, it might well be. Kennard watched Layton flash her badge at a pair of local cops who each sported a look of stressed bewilderment, one staring at a mass of red lights on his computer screen indicating incoming calls and the other neck-deep in paperwork. Kennard left them to take a statement from the elderly couple and asked for the sergeant.

A distracted finger pointed them towards a small plasterboard office that jutted out into the main room. The blind on the window was pulled down. Kennard knocked and entered.

To the side of an untidy desk sat a large man on a small armchair, feet up and reading through files. He was wedged in tight, his stomach bulging up over the arms of the chair.

The sergeant introduced himself as Reinhold. He didn't seem at all fazed by Kennard and Layton's presence; in fact, he seemed glad that there was someone else to take up the slack. Sweat rolled down his closely shaved skull but it was a false indicator of exertion. Only his hand moved, to shake Layton's then Kennard's.

'Ah, so you're the Kennard they're slagging off,' said Reinhold, keeping hold of his hand.

'What do you mean?'

'The one putting Caldicott and Floral Drive under threat.'

'It's a crime scene.'

'We might have another if that fire destroys more folks' properties out there.'

Kennard let the warning pass. 'Tell me how Tracey Hilmeyer was missed.'

'What do you mean "missed"?' Reinhold held his stare. 'I sent the boys out to roust the area.'

'Which involved?'

'Couple of vehicles, couple of megaphones.'

'That's it?'

'That's all we've got.'

'No door to door?' asked Layton.

Reinhold laughed. Short and dry. 'There are only six of us, Detective Sergeant, and plenty a' ground to cover. Plus, we can only advise people to evacuate; we can't insist.'

There was no malice in the words, no defensive posturing, everything done with the minimum of fuss.

'A rollcall was taken. Everyone north, from Caldicott to Angel Pass, was accounted for.'

'Not everyone,' noted Kennard.

There was a slight dip of the sweaty, rotund skull in acknowledgement. 'Not everyone.'

'So why didn't you go back and check? Why did you assume Tracey was out?' asked Layton.

'For a very simple reason. Her red Mazda is parked on Main Street. Caldicott is a good twenty-five to thirty-minute walk. Our belief was that she drove to town upon evacuation. No one informed us any different.'

A case of Tracey falling through the cracks. It was a failure in procedure that would be investigated later. By someone further up the ladder than Kennard and Layton.

'So why is her car parked on Main Street?' asked Kennard.

Reinhold shrugged. 'It's parked outside the shop she worked at.'

'Rislake Souvenirs.'

'That's the one.'

'And no one checked inside the house?'

'Or the shop,' added Layton.

Reinhold shrugged. 'Look, we stuffed up.'

'Too right.'

'But don't come around throwing blame,' said Reinhold, finally displaying some frustration. 'Tracey was well-liked around here, so don't go upsetting folk.'

'I think they'll be upset enough given she's dead,' said Kennard, realizing immediately that it was too strong.

Reinhold settled back into the chair, shaking his head. 'That's the type of comment I want to avoid, Detective.'

'What can you tell us about her?' asked Layton, trying to smooth the waters.

'Don't think she was particularly happy.'

'What do you mean?'

'She used to be. Used to be the life and soul, singing in the Hockney, drinking in the Imperial. She was big into promoting art to kids, teaching the odd class in the schools on painting. Nothing permanent, no money in the budget for that. But been seeing her around less and less.'

'Since the gallery failed,' said Kennard.

'Can't say it failed, mate. She gave it a good go,' said Reinhold. 'Put herself out there. Never had much trouble with her. Good woman. Pretty Sheila, too.'

'What about her family?' asked Layton.

Reinhold laughed, taking a gulp of something from a water bottle. 'Parents are long gone. Died back in the mid-nineties. Car crash. Battled a semi coming down from Hartley. Nasty one. They were picking pieces up for days. Probably still some out there.'

Kennard felt himself turn against Reinhold, seemingly dismissive of a tragedy. He recognized the signs, his anger building, his index finger twitching against the base of his thumb.

'Why the laugh?' asked Kennard. He could feel Layton's eyes on him, watching, judging.

Reinhold nestled back in his seat again, the leather creaking under his sweaty mass.

'She has – had – a sister, Detective. But you wouldn't have wanted them in the same room. Karen Tredwell, Karen Lautahahi now. Lives in the Gannerson place. Poolmaroo, out west of town.'

'So, the sisters weren't close?'

Reinhold laughed and looked into the distance.

'As close as I am to making the Olympic sprint squad. In fact, if causing each other grief was an Olympic sport, they were that good they'd have been accused of doping.'

'Is Karen around?'

'Dunno. I got an officer heading out there now to break the bad news, then check out Tracey's car.'

'We'll check the car,' said Layton.

Fifteen

'Why did you volunteer to check the car?' started Kennard, as he grabbed a scalding cup of coffee from the machine in the breakroom and waited for Layton to do the same.

'Best way to know someone is to study where they spend a lot of their time. And as we can't get to the house . . .'

Kennard had already made a call to Bairstow, checking in to see whether it was possible for them to return to the Hilmeyer house. It was a no. And he couldn't provide an estimated time. Kennard hoped that he wasn't stalling through malice. It might have been that Bairstow simply had Kennard's well-being in mind, but he doubted it.

With both Lenka and HQ briefed to patch through any go-ahead calls from Bairstow straight to his mobile, they set off to find Tracey's red Mazda.

It didn't take long. The steep slope allowed them to look down over the scene. The gridlock remained, as did the crowd. Despite the northern half of the town being evacuated, the population seemed to have quadrupled in the last twenty-four hours, the street a slow-moving fun-fair ride which blasted out a car horn every few seconds.

Honk if you want to go slower. There was no sense of panic, but Kennard could pick up the urgency that flirted between terror and excitement. Camera crews filmed and interviewed, nabbing passers-by for a moment of glory. Shopkeepers tried to hawk their goods. People exchanged tales of woe. He studied the orange glow in the distance and wondered if it was getting any closer. It was obviously not an immediate threat to the south of town otherwise the crowd would quickly disperse. But the flickers of red in the orange warned that the threat wasn't going away anytime soon. One shift in the prevailing winds and the nervous excitement could turn to a deathly silence. On the street there were four red vehicles: two SUVs, one ute, and, halfway down the hill, parked at an acute angle to the kerb, a 2005 Mazda 3.

'Good to go?' asked Layton.

'After you.'

Kennard hated using Layton as a shield. It felt cowardly, but he followed as she carved through what the press had dubbed 'fire-tourists'. Men and women, some even dragging terrified children with them, walking with their phones out in front of them like zombies as they tried to capture the last death throes of a town.

It took five minutes of jostling to get to the Mazda, the only saving grace being that he wasn't centre of attention, Layton bearing the glares and insults as they wove their way through. His first impression of the car was that it needed some love, the hubcaps cracked, a myriad of scratches and dents across the panels. Well-used, nearly twenty years old.

JAMES DELARGY

Minus a set of keys, Kennard got ready to crack the lock. He had come prepared, having stolen a wooden doorstop and metal cane from a set of blinds in the station. They could bill him for them should the building survive the inferno.

His phone buzzed. Layton's too. She flicked her head at him. 'HQ,' she said and moved down a side alley to take the call. Leaving Kennard alone. Among an ever-shifting crowd. The sweats started immediately, an enormous weight suddenly pressing down on him. He took a deep breath and turned towards the car, trying to ignore the reflection of the crowd in the window. He concentrated on what he had to do. Holding the doorstop at the top of the pane, he wriggled it into the rubber join, working it up and down with a *pluck-pluck-pluck* before feeling it catch the upper edge and give him purchase. Using his weight, he pushed down on the window, being careful not to push too hard and shatter the glass. He wanted the car and any evidence inside to remain as undisturbed as possible.

'Hey! He's trying to break into that car!'

Kennard turned to find a woman with huge, hooped earrings pointing at him.

'I'm a police officer,' said Kennard, pressing on with the break-in.

'Bullshit you are.'

Kennard sucked in another breath, his lungs tight. 'Why the hell would I break into a car in the middle of a packed street?' he asked, turning the question onto her, his anger rising.

'You're using plain sight as a distraction. I've heard of that before.'

'Then explain why I'm still trying to open it?'

The woman shrugged. The slow-moving crowd had stopped around them, temporarily distracted from their phones. They closed in on Kennard. He felt his blood pumping, his body throbbing as if stung.

'Let's see your badge.'

'He's a cop.' Kennard recognized the voice. Joel, watching on. On a break from the front, it seemed.

'Let him show us.'

The baying from the crowd continued. Kennard's eyes danced from the woman with the earrings to the man who had sidled up next to her, a phone turned from the fire towards him, the new source of wonder.

His mind flashed back to Parramatta, the phones held up above the crowd's heads like antennae, capturing weakness.

'You okay?'

The voice interrupted. Layton. To his rescue.

'Yeah. Just . . .' Kennard didn't want to get into how the crowd had upset him. '. . . wanting to get this done. Pronto.'

'Says he's a jack,' said one man in a muscle shirt. Talking to Layton.

Layton flashed her silver badge with the soaring wedge-tailed eagle on it. 'He is. Now back up,' she said sternly, offering no chance of confusion.

The man obeyed. As did the woman with the hooped earrings. Joel remained among the crowd, watching on in silence as others cooed with curiosity.

With Layton watching his back, Kennard returned to the window, the pane forced down a couple of inches. He thrust the metal rod in, searching for the top of the lock and failing. The pressure of having a crowd watching his every move.

'Need some . . . ?' asked Layton.

'I've got it,' said Kennard, sweat forming droplets on his skin, breathing hard, catching a whiff of her perfume in the process. Understated, as expected.

He tried again to hook the lock, his tongue poking out the side of his mouth.

'What was the call about?' he asked.

'The insurance searches. All came up negative. The policy on the house lapsed eighteen months ago, and no life insurance has ever been taken out on either spouse. Under either name or that address.'

Kennard took a deep breath. He supposed it would have been too easy. And stupid of Russell to have taken out a policy recently and then killed his wife.

'So, he's not going to gain anything from his wife dying or the house burning down,' he said.

'No. Rules out financial gain as a motive.'

And just like that, Kennard's top motive, a husband out to profit from his wife's death, had gone up in flames.

He did find some success with the car, though. The rod's wire found the top of the lock, which popped up. Entry gained. He didn't dare open it with all this pedestrian traffic around, however. He needed space.

He looked at Layton, who read his mind, rapidly putting a cordon in place on the busy pavement, displaying a relaxed authority. Measured and competent.

Sliding on one of the pairs of latex gloves he habitually kept in his pocket, Kennard opened the door and scanned inside. It was a mess – discarded wrappers and glossy magazines scattered across the seats and piling up in the footwell. The air was pungent, a squashed sample pouch of No.7 perfume leaking on the floor, masking the funk of the rotten apple cores, banana skins and moulding yoghurt. Whoever she was when she was alive, Tracey was not tidy.

Easing open the glove compartment, Kennard twisted himself forward to look. Inside, an unsteady truce held, the compartment full to the brim, almost seeming to quiver on the edge of collapse. Packets of tissues, used tubes of hand cream and little white bottles. Pills. Codoxamol and Febridol. Opioids. Kennard had come across them often in Sydney, usually abused – Codo the more powerful, though Feb would do the job well enough. Most were empty. All were expired and Kennard strongly suspected that none would have been used to treat the depression people had hinted at. He would have to talk to her doctor.

There was one other thing of note. Tucked neatly into the logbook he found a series of photographs, headshots of men of all different ages and races, some posed for, others taken naturally or even surreptitiously. It was so unexpected that it threw Kennard for a moment. There seemed to be no reason for the photos, which had been kept pristine in the logbook rather than strewn around the car like everything else. Did they suggest an affair? Many affairs? No one in town had mentioned it, but maybe he hadn't been asking the right questions.

He exited the car. Layton was explaining to the crowd that this was a routine check of an abandoned car, trying to keep the fuss to a minimum. Of course, it was much more than that. The pills needed to be tested, and he also wanted to check for traces of blood, DNA or anything else of significance.

He was about to address Layton when his phone rang. It was Bairstow, the Group Captain. He was barking over the hiss of background noise.

'You want in, Detective? Then you'd better haul your arse over here now.'

Sixteen

January 20 – 14.10 – Wind direction NE – Surface speed 27km/h

7 hours since North Rislake evacuation

South Rislake status = Amber/Yellow (Prepare for possible evacuation)

Kennard held the phone to his ear and stared into the distance, towards the darkening orange tint on the horizon.

'Who was that?' asked Layton, firmly maintaining the cordon around them.

A glance at the crowd confirmed that Joel was no longer spectating. Good. Kennard didn't want him to get wind of the news and relay it back to his mate.

'Bairstow. The GC.'

'We got the okay?'

'Yep.'

'Want me to go?' she asked.

Kennard turned away from her and towards the Mazda.

It was simply a distraction, space to allow him to think. Away from the eyes of the crowd. He knew what awaited him on Caldicott and he didn't know if he could face it again. Even the thought scared him. But ... he couldn't shake off the other fact. The case intrigued him.

He turned to Layton. 'We can't both go and leave the car unattended. And Bairstow will only allow one of us in. I don't want to push it. Besides, I've been there before, I know what I'm looking for,' he lied, the words coming out rootless, unattached to any of his better senses.

Layton wore a look of frustration at being shunted to the side.

'I'll get you up there later,' Kennard assured her, but her expression warned that she knew he was talking bollocks. That there might not be a later. 'Get Andrews or another team on to Tracey's car. See if they can pick up any evidence. And check out those bottles of pills. We need to know what condition they might be alleviating. Or not.'

With that, he charged up the hill, aiming for the school again and relieved to be away from the crowd and Layton's glare. It was only as he passed the waiting fire trucks, vehicles and soot-covered firefighters in the schoolyard that it really hit him: that he would have to return to the hell that was Caldicott.

After donning the bunker gear once again in the locker room, something that took him twice as long as the crew he was hitching a lift with, he rode the pumper truck all the way back. Under the mass of layers his skin prickled, with the rise in temperature as well as his burgeoning nerves. His stomach lurched as they crossed the dip in the valley and climbed the hill towards Caldicott once again.

As he sat in the back, Kennard had the sense that he was heading towards his destiny. The thought made his guts squirm. Destiny was so final. The end of the journey, the darkness closing in, smoke drifting across the windscreen and enveloping the entire vehicle, ready to whisk it off to somewhere it would never return from. The talk in the cab between the firefighters was muted. They were discussing the slight change in wind direction. He couldn't tell by the tone if it was welcome or whether it just added another complication, another factor to be accounted for. The tension he felt seemed to be shared among the passengers, which didn't make him feel any better. They were supposed to be the experts here. So, if they were nervous, then he supposed he was right to be shit-scared.

The pumper broke through the pall of smoke, the Hilmeyer house appearing in the distance through the gloom. Immediately he could see that the fire crews were winning the battle to save it, at least for the moment. The flames had been pushed back. The heat and residual terror remained, but their power was nowhere near as crippling as before. Kennard reminded himself not to get complacent. The fire was as malevolent as ever. That victory might only be temporary.

Bairstow met him straight off the truck.

'You're getting a chaperone,' he said, sans pleasantries.

'Why?'

'I don't want you staring at the floor while the roof caves in. One of my deputies, Mirza, will make sure the structural integrity of the building is sound. If she says get the fuck out, you get the fuck out. Understood?'

That sounded just fine to Kennard. Best not to fuck with the people who knew how to keep him alive.

'Don't send Mirza. I'll do it.'

Right behind Kennard was a weary-looking Russell Hilmeyer.

Bairstow paused. Kennard couldn't believe that he was even considering it.

'No, Russell,' said Bairstow. 'You're rotated out, right now. Get back to base.'

'But I know the house. The layout, the—' said Russell, not giving up.

'You sit this one out, Hilmeyer,' said Bairstow, his stare unwavering. Russell paused, then reluctantly nodded, his GC a commanding presence, assured, something Kennard could only admire.

Bairstow turned back to Kennard. 'Mirza's waiting at the front door. She's been fully briefed,' he added pointedly.

Kennard made his way to the house. Hoses cracked off the exterior, pressurized streams of water that seemed to be doing little but delaying the inevitable, a plaster over the ever-growing cracks.

Mirza was outside the front door. She was petite even in the thick layers of uniform and distinctive orange helmet. He was pretty sure that if he got into trouble, she wasn't carrying him out. A good reminder not to take a false step.

As they were about to step inside, she repeated pretty much word for word what Bairstow had said, her voice straining against the roar of the wind and spit of the hoses.

Kennard nodded agreement, eager to get inside. He had no idea how much time he might have. They had been somewhat lucky in that the prevailing winds had died down some, meaning the fire had a little less reach. But they were still in danger of the flames sweeping around and cutting their escape off or blasting straight for the house.

He followed Mirza inside. The hallway looked oddly empty minus Tracey's body, only the halo of blood remaining. If she was flustered by the scene, Mirza didn't show it, scanning the walls and roof for any tell-tale cracks or disturbance.

As she reached the entrance to the living room she turned and looked at Kennard. 'What are you waiting for?'

'Is it safe?'

'I'll let you know when it isn't. You do your job, Detective, and I'll do mine.'

Kennard pointed towards the living room. Mirza stepped carefully around the dried blood and into the main room. As she busied herself checking out the architecture, Kennard scanned the room's contents. Nothing looked out of place. Beige curtains that glowed orange with speckled red and blue masked the scene of chaos outside. He flicked on his torch to counter the lack of proper light. On the far side of the room a sofa and two chairs faced a television bolted securely to the wall. A small book table and lamp perched beside an armchair. Two bookcases that were half-empty stared back at him, a layer of ash beginning to form on them and all the other available surfaces.

He could feel the butterflies rising in his stomach. Every ounce of his being wanted the murder weapon to be here. Recover it, log it, test it. If they could only find whatever it was, wherever it was, it would at least provide him with an answer to an urgent question: was it a random attack or something more planned? If planned, it was probably by someone Tracey knew. Kennard felt the rush. The one that excitement and danger always brought. Incomparable to anything else. The chance to find and handle a weapon that had taken a human life was an awe-inspiring thing. Such power and such desperation in one inanimate object. What had driven someone to murder Tracey Hilmeyer? The need to know grew as desperate for oxygen as the bushfire itself.

He made it across to the bookcase and scanned the shelves. There were a few books and ornaments that he checked for blood stains, but he found nothing with sufficient heft to do the damage caused to Tracey's skull; no pokers or instruments by the fireplace, no golf clubs or heavy-bottomed lamps. The living room looked clean of possibilities. Which didn't discount that something might have been removed after the fact.

He tried the kitchen next. It was as chaotic as Tracey's car had been, dirty dishes stacked in the sink like a precarious Jenga tower and a general untidiness that hinted at someone too busy or too depressed to clean.

Mirza's silence again cleared his entry. He divided the room into sectors and set about checking the cupboards and drawers, even behind the fridge. There was a broom, but a quick check determined that the handle was too light to have caused any major damage. The microwave and other small kitchen appliances lacked blood stains or were too awkward to wield.

Leaving the kitchen, they moved down a narrow hallway between it and the living room. A door at the end led to the adjoining garage. The heat was much more intense here, the thin walls offering little protection against the fire. Mirza held her hand up, asking over the radio for the garage to be dowsed as a precaution.

Kennard took heed of the warning and hurried over to check the toolboxes, picking through the tyre irons, crowbar and power tools, and around the floor and the workbench for something that fitted the blunt implement profile.

Mirza's radio hissed a two-minute warning. Moving back through, they made for upstairs, carefully treading using the far edge of the steps to minimize contamination, though he had pretty much ruled out Russell's suggestion of a fall.

Three bedrooms fed off a landing that contained only a small table with a decidedly plain vase of withered flowers. With Mirza's nod, he tried the main bedroom first. Only one side of the bed looked slept in. He thought back to Russell's alibi that he had been out of town since Tuesday. Initial indications seemed to confirm this, although being married, he knew how bed spread worked. Many times he had woken up perched on the edge of the bed at the point of tumbling to the floor.

Of the other two rooms, one was clearly for storage,

clothes and a pair of dining chairs perched on top of the unmade bed, the space sporting the musty smell of disuse.

The last room upstairs was a makeshift gym. Kennard scanned the equipment. Weight bars, dumbbells, kettle-bells – there were plenty of potential weapons here.

The radio hissed. Kennard knew what the order would be but continued searching as Mirza confirmed it.

'Time to go,' said Mirza.

'Just a little longer.'

'No. Next door has flashed, caught alight,' she clarified. 'We need to get out now.'

'I need to bag and lift this,' said Kennard. 'Call in some help.'

Mirza glanced around. 'You bag it, we'll carry it.'

'But you won't—'

'Bag it.'

So Kennard did, and then watched as Mirza defied her size and waddled downstairs in front of him carrying two bags in each hand, the free weights and the dumbbells. It was an impressive feat, her balance secure as she navigated the bottom of the stairs. Kennard followed with the weight bar. They made it outside to find flames rising from the angled roof of the similar two-storey structure next door, a blown-out window resembling an open-mouthed scream.

Kennard found himself panting as he hauled the bar to the PC Mirza had called. He was struggling for breath, but she looked barely flustered. He had underestimated her. He suspected he had not been the first.

Before he left the scene, Kennard approached Bairstow,

who was getting the low-down from Mirza. Although he had identified lots of possible weapons and escaped the house uninjured, the lack of any obvious bloodstains had left him feeling downcast.

'Thanks,' said Kennard, looking at Mirza. 'But I need to search the house again. In more detail. I need to take it apart.'

Mirza responded. 'I think the fire will do that for you.'

Bairstow spoke up. 'You've had your chance, Detective.'

'I need to get in there.'

'Yeah. Well, the fire has broken through to the next three houses. It's threatening homes that should have been safe. We have to ensure it doesn't snowball before we can even contemplate allowing you to return. Go back to town.'

Seventeen

The PC navigated the same dusky, smoky streets, bubbling asphalt and immediate horror on the way back, but knowing that he was moving away from the fire let Kennard relax for a moment, relinquish control. Something that he now found hard to do. Ever since . . .

The many therapists he had seen had given him 'methods' and 'tools' to deal with the memories, to help him relax. The process felt a little like grieving, making sense of what had happened and then developing the means to deal with it. The academic solutions. His colleagues, including Lisa and Ces, proposed other solutions, which mostly involved him snapping out of it. That it wasn't his fault. That he'd tried his best.

The problem was that even seeing Lisa and Ces brought it all back with a terrifying crash every time, like a levee had broken. All of the memories returned with a savage intent to destroy whatever shoots of recovery he had planted. Instantly and catastrophically. And after the flood it was a slow process for his mind to drain the thoughts away. His therapists insisted that recovery could only ever be slow and steady. What he had been through was not something that could be rebounded from quickly, no matter what his colleagues thought.

One thing had been quick. The internal investigation. Behind closed doors, they hadn't blamed him. The inquiry had found that he had tried his best to resolve the situation, to get Rhian Thorpe to drop the weapon and release his mother, but the professional investigation was merely one part of the whole process. The other part had taken place in public, and here he had personally shouldered a generous portion of the blame, his photo adorning every newspaper in the country, the videos of his stunned reaction played over and over online. There was some sympathy, but it was outweighed by the condemnation of those wondering how he could be allowed to remain on the force.

It was something that Kennard wondered himself. He knew that the journalists and activists were only seeing in binary, in terms of right and wrong; failing to understand that in the moment everything was grey, and every move had a drastic consequence. There were no replays. There were no second chances. Your mistakes were your own. And these days, extremely public. But it didn't make his failure to act any less wrong.

He had replayed the incident countless times over the past six months. If he could have moved quicker, if he could have said something different to make Rhian drop the gun. If he could have ushered the crowd away sooner, even though they had already been on site and filming long before he arrived.

He had been getting there, however – to what he called the base camp of acceptance, acclimatising to what had happened and finding himself in a place where, gradually, it didn't eat away at him all day, every day.

Time had allowed him to cope with the memory. It didn't cripple him as it had before. There were still days where he sat at the kitchen table staring into the distance as if catatonic, shut down for repairs, and on these occasions, he let the thoughts take over. He let them bite hard. He let them wound him. For as much as he wanted to totally forget that day, he wanted to be sure it never happened again.

The bags of evidence shifted forward on the seat, nudging his arm, as the PC came to a stop in the schoolyard, reverting Kennard back to the present and the job he had to do. He made a quick call to Forensics to arrange to take the gym equipment away for examination, and then asked HQ what the latest was with Tracey's body and the analysis of her car. He was informed that both examinations were still ongoing, and that Layton was still at the car with the Forensics officers.

He was tempted to join her, but across the yard he saw someone he wanted to talk to.

Russell lifted his head sharply from the trough basin set up on a table near the trucks, water cascading off his face, his eyes blinking, hair plastered back. Some soot remained despite the wash. Kennard assumed his appearance was the same if not worse, any notion of respectability out the window for now.

'What do you want?' asked Russell upon seeing Kennard, weary, spitting out the words.

Even with his face mostly clean, he looked a mess, his eyes heavy and red. Maybe from the effects of the smoke, or from having allowed himself a private moment to grieve.

'Just wondering how you're coping,' said Kennard, aiming for sincerity. Though Russell was a person of interest, he had just lost his wife after all.

'How do you think? I want to mourn. But I don't have time to be upset,' Russell said bluntly.

'Are you going for a rest now?'

'I don't think that's even possible.'

'Is Joel keeping an eye on you?'

'Joel,' he said, rolling his eyes. 'I don't need a mozzie always buzzing in my ear.'

'I thought you were friends?' asked Kennard, intrigued about the malice in Russell's tone.

'We are,' said Russell. 'Just sometimes he's a bit full-on. Always was. Ask those girls from Geven.'

'What girls?'

Russell shook his head. 'Forget it.'

'I'm going to find out anyway,' said Kennard, washing his hands in the basin.

'Nothing. Just Joel going full Joel. Clinging onto girlfriends like they owe him something. Stalking them, phoning them, hassling them. I kinda know what they're on about now,' said Russell, drying his face with an already black towel. 'Did you find anything in the house?'

Kennard pulled his hands from the trough and studied

him closely. Hard to tell if he was asking the question out of curiosity or fear. Some of the fire had bled from his eyes but the intensity remained.

'I have some leads,' he replied, keeping it vague.

Russell raised his eyebrows, looking for more details, but Kennard kept quiet. Russell didn't look particularly worried, but that didn't mean anything. Maybe because he knew that the murder weapon had already been disposed of elsewhere.

'We found your wife's car.'

'Where?'

'Main Street. What drugs was Tracey taking, Russell?'

Russell's open expression clenched shut, his eyes squeezed tight as if the question had pained him. It was followed by a long sigh. 'What *wasn't* she taking? Anti-depressants, anti-anxiety meds, beta blockers. Painkillers for crippling migraines. She had a lot of issues.'

'What kind of issues?'

'Depression. And not the oh-so-sad kind. Proper depression.' Kennard didn't know what the difference was between depression and *proper* depression, but let it go. 'From losing the gallery. It was what she lived for,' Russell continued, his eyes drawn from Kennard back across town. 'Once it went it was kind of like she was at a loose end: going out less, painting more, which leaked into our marriage. She took that job in the souvenir shop, but it barely paid. Then she had to listen to that sister of hers lord it over her any chance she got.'

'And you tried to help?'

There was a flash of anger. 'Of course I tried to help.

I was out there trying to earn money. Trying to improve our lives. Keep us afloat.'

'So, she was on her own a lot?'

Russell nodded. 'I think she was embarrassed at failing. Herself, me, even the town.'

Kennard knew the feeling.

'And the times she did paint, she would often take herself off on her own,' added Russell.

'What about friends?' asked Kennard, trying to tease the information out of him. More carrot, less stick. For now.

'Lots of friends. But some friends only want to know you when you're happy.'

'Male friends?'

Russell frowned. 'What are you getting at, Detective?'

Kennard found it hard to read from Russell's expression if he knew about the photos or not. He changed the subject. 'A lot of the pills I found had expired.'

Russell shrugged. 'I'm not surprised. She stashed them around the house. She took so many she tended to forget things. Either that or she didn't care to remember.'

'These weren't antidepressants.'

'They weren't?' frowned Russell. 'What were they?'

'Opioids.'

Russell looked lost.

'Was she in pain?' Kennard asked.

'Migraines. But she had codeine for those. I thought.'

'Nothing else?'

'No,' said Russell sharply.

'None of the bottles we found had a prescription label.'

107

'She might have torn them off. You know, in frustration.'

But to Kennard there seemed to be too many to be via prescription only. He wondered if Tracey had gone further afield to purchase them and concealed it from her husband.

'Do you know anyone who might have been supplying her? Through other channels?'

Russell paused. He casually wiped his face with a towel and then shook his head slowly. 'No. She was trying,' he continued. 'She had the job. As much as I know it hurt her, selling that rubbish. She just needed to help herself a little too. Make some easy choices.' His head dropped. As if he was struggling to contain his emotions.

'How do you mean?'

'Nothing. I'm just tired. Emotional,' he said, making it sound like a disease.

Russell was acting like the devoted husband, but even though they had ruled out the financial motive regarding insurance, Kennard had a hunch that he wasn't telling the whole truth. 'You said you were out of town last night.'

'Yeah,' he sighed, as if each question was taking a toll on him. 'On a furniture-removal job. I was only back this morning.'

'An overnight furniture-removal job?'

Russell breathed out hard, his jaw clenched. 'It finished late. I had a few stubbies after and didn't fancy driving home. I stayed at Joel's. Maybe if I hadn't ...' He tailed off, lost in thoughts of what might have been.

'But you didn't go home this morning either.'

'No. I passed by, but the call was already out about the bushfire.'

'You didn't go in?'

'Trace's car wasn't there so I assumed she was in town. Working. Or sheltering. Or off painting.'

'But you didn't check?'

Russell closed his eyes and shook his head. 'No. With the fire headed straight for our place I thought it best to have a home to come back to. I don't have any insurance, Detective. If it takes the house all I'll have is a crippling mortgage. And a pile of ash.'

Kennard nodded. 'And no life insurance cover on your wife either.'

'No,' said Russell, his eyes narrowed. 'Why? What's that supposed to mean?'

'It means we've checked.'

'Couldn't afford house insurance. And life insurance? We were both still young. We were trying to be happy.'

'I have a witness that said they heard raised voices coming from your house on Tuesday night.'

Russell tilted his head, either confused or suspicious of what Kennard was telling him.

'Between whom?'

Kennard didn't respond.

'Well, it wasn't me. I was in Sydney Tuesday night. On a job.'

'Can your whereabouts be corroborated?'

'Do they need to be?' asked Russell with growing suspicion.

'It would help if we could confirm your alibi.'

'I was doing some security work.'

'For whom?'

A pause. 'Kingsley Musa. A friend of mine.'

'And yesterday's furniture job?'

'For a couple moving to Geven. About forty minutes southwest of here.'

'Name?'

'Chang. If you need first names, I don't know. Go with Mr and Mrs.'

They would have to be checked out but, for now, Russell Hilmeyer had the guts of an alibi for both nights.

'Has anything unusual happened over the last few weeks or months?'

Russell looked at him oddly. 'This is Rislake. You said you'd been here before. Nothing happened back then, nothing happens now.'

'You know what I mean, Mr Hilmeyer. Had Tracey been acting strangely?' asked Kennard, digging.

Russell looked off into the distance in the direction of his house, the orange glow staining the edges of the grey sky.

'With the pills ... of course she was acting strangely. Happy, sad, nervous. Each day was like rolling one of those Bingo things ... tombolas. Take your pick.'

'Any particular incidents that you can recall?'

Russell twisted his mouth to the side and sighed deeply, as if not wanting to speak ill of the dead. 'She did say that she thought someone had broken into the house about a week ago.'

'Broken in? What made her think that?' asked Kennard, sensing a clue.

'There was an ornament missing from the bookcase.'

'What ornament?'

Russell squinted, trying to remember. 'A glass thing. Blue and gold. Something her parents gave her before they died.'

'And you weren't worried about that?'

'You've been in our house. We don't have much to steal. I was more worried about Trace. I thought she'd just misplaced it. Moved it and forgot about it. She was pretty mixed up, Detective.' There was a pained longing on his face. Kennard could feel the hurt, the man trying to protect her memory in his own mind. Not an unreasonable position for a recently bereaved husband to take, but one that wasn't helpful for an investigation.

'So, there was no break-in?'

'I couldn't find any evidence of it, no broken windows or latches, no signs of forced entry.'

'So, it wasn't reported?'

'There was nothing to report. We didn't need the cops out there. I think you can appreciate why. Though maybe . . . maybe I should have.'

Russell grabbed one of the plastic classroom chairs that had been brought out into the yard and collapsed into it. He cast a pathetic figure, singed and beaten, cursing himself for his failings. Kennard sympathized. But he couldn't help but think that Russell was holding something back. Just a hunch, nothing that he could pin a case on as yet, but he was sure there was something the other man wasn't prepared to reveal.

Eighteen

Kennard put in a call to Katoomba for someone to check out Russell's alibis ASAP. Then, finally giving in to his hunger, he found a sandwich place off Main Street, nestled in an alley behind a shopfront. He was moving up the long queue when he got a call from Haskell.

'If you're looking for a breakthrough, you'll have to give us more time,' said Kennard.

'That's why I'm calling. I'm taking you off the case. DS Uptill will transfer his Stokoe assault case to you and join DS Layton there to run the investigation.'

There he was. Uptill. The innocent victim by all accounts. Flattened by the ticking time bomb that was Alex Kennard.

'Why the change of heart?' asked Kennard.

'It's what I'm paid for, DS Kennard.'

'I thought you were paid to solve crimes. I want to stay on.'

'Do I have to remind you who is in charge, DS Kennard?'

'I think you might,' Kennard bit back, unable to hold his tongue.

'Honestly, I don't think you're ready for something of this magnitude.'

'Of all the DSs you have, I'm the most experienced. More than bloody Uptill.'

There was silence from the other end of the phone.

'I need detectives I can *trust*.'

'And how am I expected to do prove that to you if you won't give me a chance?'

Kennard didn't like begging, but he knew that Haskell responded to people showing a bit of grit.

There was a loud sigh from the other end. 'Forty-eight hours. Earn my trust.'

Kennard was about to complain that it wasn't long enough but decided not to. They probably had less than twenty-four hours in Rislake if the fire kept up.

Haskell had just hung up when Layton joined him, flashing her badge to quiet the complaints from the people waiting in line.

'You look like you've been in the wars,' she said.

'That bad?'

'It looks like you had a fight with a mascara brush and lost. What about the house? Find anything?'

'Maybe,' said Kennard, eyeing the sparse choice of food behind the glass and trying to decide if he wanted a croissant that was flaking into dust or a sandwich that he still wasn't convinced wasn't a faded plastic replica. 'Lots of potential murder weapons but no visible traces of blood.'

'So, either the murder weapon was removed from the house, or was on the murderer's person when they entered

113

and left? Meaning we can't rule out a crime of passion or premeditation?'

'No.'

They were up next. The owner's face glowed as red as the sky, as if she was hiding the rest of the sandwiches in her puffy cheeks.

'Tuna sanger,' said Kennard before she could ask. He would have to risk it. 'Want anything?' he asked Layton.

She shook her head. 'A nice old dear came out and fed all of us. She was interested in what we were looking for.'

'And what did you find?'

'More photos of men.'

'Headshots?'

'All of them.'

'Do we know why Tracey had them?'

'Still a mystery. Some were posed, some not. Almost like she was looking for someone in particular.' They made their way to a space along the window facing out onto the alley. In the distance the unnerving red-orange glow still dominated the skyline like the end of the world was coming.

'Anything else?' Kennard asked as he bit into his sandwich.

'More rubbish in the backseat. Painting materials in the boot. And as for the tablets, a lot of the painkillers were two or three years out of date. But there was definitely hash in one of the bottles.'

'Forensics told you that so soon?'

'My nose told me that.'

'Did your nose tell you what kind?' asked Kennard, raising his eyebrows.

Layton's look said *pull the other one*. 'Not my scene.'

'What is your scene?'

'Not your barbeque anyway.'

Kennard wasn't sure if this was an insult, but she was smiling.

'You want to talk about it?' she asked.

'Christ, no,' he said.

'You can if you want.'

'Good to know.' He didn't want to get into it. Not now. Not with a colleague he barely knew.

Layton returned to the subject. 'Forensics are checking the residue to determine more details.'

Kennard had downed most of the sandwich already, his dry mouth schlocking through the tuna mayo. He had forgotten to order anything to drink but he wasn't going to queue up again. As he fought for saliva, Layton continued.

'I've got feelers out for local hash routes, local dealers.'

'Good. Our priority now is to nail down Russell's alibis.' He relayed what Russell had told him about the furniture removal, security gig, Tracey's hard-luck story and the possible break-in.

'You believe him?'

'We'll see if the alibis check out. He seems cut up about the whole thing but until we can cross him off for sure, there's a big question mark beside his name.'

'Speaking of question marks beside names,' said Layton, staring at him.

Kennard looked at her. Though her brown eyes should

have been alluring, they seemed cold and calculating. She was young – twenty-six – and inexperienced, but held herself with self-assuredness, an underlying sense of authority. He wondered if she had ever been truly tested; whether her stress points had ever been picked and poked at until self-doubt ate away at her. He felt ashamed that right at this moment he wanted to see her undoubted confidence shaken.

'Is Haskell keeping you on this?' she asked.

Kennard frowned. Why would Layton be asking? Unless she knew in advance. Unless she was the one telling Haskell to boot him off the case. He decided not to kick up mud. Yet.

'She is. I'm the most experienced detective she has.'

'Even after—?'

'After what?' Kennard felt his muscles tense for an argument. 'Last week?'

'Not last week. Simon Uptill's been asking to be hit. I mean Parramatta. The whole reason you're kicking around up here.'

Kennard licked his lips. They felt dry. He blamed the tuna sanger but knew it wasn't that. 'I'm still here, aren't I?' he snarled.

She stared at him. 'Well, no running off on your own, then. We're in this together. You might not like me, but I don't really care.'

'Who said I didn't like you?' asked Kennard.

Layton raised an eyebrow. 'Just an impression. Don't get me wrong, though. I'm not here to make friends.'

'Why are you here, then?' Haskell had seen fit to post

her. With him. For a reason he had yet to pinpoint. It wasn't because Haskell didn't like Layton: they were two peas in a pod, ambitious to the point of being blunt. It was a lazy stereotype, one he hated himself for promoting and which was prevalent among other older male officers, especially in Sydney. Crusty jacks bitching when a female officer dared show ambition. As if it was wrong. As if the blokes wouldn't step on their granny for a promotion and the wage rise.

'I'm here to solve this. With you, DS Kennard.'

It was a clumsy attempt to forge a partnership, but Kennard decided to accept it at face value. For now. He had alienated enough people recently without adding another to the list.

They came to an agreement in silence, Kennard finishing his sandwich as Layton scribbled something into her notepad.

If she could keep him on the straight and narrow, they might just make a good team. After all, teammates didn't have to like each other, they just had to win.

This thought was interrupted by the buzzing of his phone. A text from HQ. It was a number for Kingsley Musa.

Out the back of the sandwich place and among the welcome shade of a coolabah tree, they made the call.

It was immediately obvious that Mr Musa was less than thrilled to hear from them. There was an aggressiveness in his tone that made it clear he thought the police were hassling him.

'Sir, do you know a Russell Hilmeyer?' asked Layton, cutting through his varied complaints.

'Yeah. Why?'

'Does he work for you?'

There was a clicking of tongue on teeth before they got an answer.

'Russell has worked for me, yeah.'

'This Tuesday? In Sydney?'

'Tuesday? I don't know. I'd have to check the job sheet.'

'We can wait.'

'You'll have to. I'm at the spa. Try me tomorrow,' said Musa, and hung up.

Kennard looked at Layton. Musa's obtuseness was like a red rag. He clenched his jaw tight.

'What are you thinking?' asked Layton.

'That I quite fancy a spa day.'

Nineteen

January 20 – 15.30 – Wind direction NE – Surface speed 26km/h

8.5 hours since North Rislake evacuation

South Rislake status = Amber/Yellow (Prepare for possible evacuation)

The drive to Puremount was pleasant, the air not choked with smoke and dust, the azure sky offering no indication of the horror behind them.

On the way, they got word from Geven that Bill and Xiu Chang had confirmed that a person matching Russell Hilmeyer's name and description had indeed helped transport furniture from their old house in Sydney to their new one yesterday – Wednesday 19 January. Another couple that had relocated from the city to the mountains. Kennard could only hope that their move was for happier reasons than his own.

They had also confirmed that Russell had arrived at

8am on the dot in Mornington and had been working until gone 8.30 that evening, only out of their sight for a couple of hours over lunch. This lunch was in turn attested by the owner of the local boozer, who stated that Russell had been there for well over an hour, shooting a few racks of pool and paying by card if they needed to be doubly sure.

This all left Kennard in a bad mood by the time they reached Puremount Spa. A mood he quickly transferred onto Kingsley Musa as he and Layton escorted the overweight middle-aged man out of the luxurious complex, inciting a commotion that disrupted the peaceful lavender-scented atmosphere that infused the faux marble walls, Musa's protests interrupting the soothing muzak playing over the internal sound system.

They drove Musa, now half-dressed in a bad suit, to his office, which was located in a sparse-looking industrial park on the outskirts of the town. His stomach bulged at the waist of his trousers, and he held his face like he had caught a fly in his mouth and was wondering whether to swallow or spit.

'This is harassment, you know?' he said as they arrived, casting his eyes around the empty car park as if searching for an audience.

Kennard recognized the show. He had met plenty of people in Musa's line of work who made a public spectacle of not cooperating with the police before rolling over to have their tummies tickled in private. Not this time, however. Kingsley's hatred towards them seemed to continue even after they were secluded inside his small office. Sleek brown cabinets lined the walls, a poster board with a giant map of Sydney and the surrounds was tacked up on one side of the space and dotted with pin marks, and used coffee mugs populated every surface. The whole place was cheap and nasty.

'You couldn't have waited an hour? Or two?'

'This is a murder investigation, Mr Musa,' said Layton. 'It's urgent.'

'You try running a small business, Miss. That's urgency.'

'It's Detective. And how about you just show us the job sheet.'

Kingsley grunted and tapped noisily at the keyboard. He spun the monitor around, fast enough for the bearings to crack in anger. On the screen was a simple spreadsheet. He typed Russell's name in the search bar. A number of jobs appeared but nothing dated in the last two weeks.

'See? Nothing. Waste of fucking time. And a hot stone massage.'

Kennard's hand twitched. He badly wanted to massage a hot stone into Kingsley himself. With speed and force. He tried to resist the rage.

'What was the last job he did for you?' asked Layton.

Kingsley sighed loudly as he scanned the screen. 'A private party in Sydney. Sixteen days ago.'

'So, not this Tuesday?'

'So, you can't read or listen? Fuckin' easy to become a detective these days, isn't it?'

'Answer the question, Mr Musa.'

Kingsley Musa sighed again. 'No. Not according to my records.'

'And how accurate are they?' asked Kennard.

Kingsley seemed to take this personally. 'Very. I run a tight ship. I pay my taxes. I need to know where my people are.'

'Does Mr Hilmeyer work for you often?'

'When he can. Sometimes a job clashes with a shift at the fire station, but he lets me know in advance.'

'So why hasn't he been working for you for two weeks?' asked Layton.

Kingsley looked away, mouth curling up into his full cheeks. He sported the look of a man who wasn't sure if he should talk or not, obviously weighing up the pros and cons.

'Just tell us, Mr Musa.'

'Will it help you lot piss off?'

'The quicker you answer, the quicker you can get back to your pedicure,' said Kennard.

'Hot stone massage,' mumbled Kingsley, his shoulders tense.

He obviously needed it, if stress was such a big part of his life. Kennard guessed it probably helped. If he wasn't being dragged forcefully from it by a pair of cops.

'The last job was a private party in Mount Druitt. There was an incident.'

'What kind of incident?'

'I don't know all the details—'

Which, as Kennard knew, was code for *I don't want to either snitch or implicate myself.*

122

'Tell us what you *do* know,' said Kennard. He would let it play out. Put the squeeze on later if needed. They could always drag Kingsley towards Rislake station and the bushfire and see how obtuse he was then.

'There was an argument between someone who was there and someone who shouldn't have been there. That's what I heard.'

'So, a fight? Was someone hurt?' asked Layton.

'No. Nothing like that. I *heard* ...' said Kingsley, emphasizing the word, 'Russell stepped in and prevented it from escalating.'

'Escalating? You mean knives, clubs, firearms?' asked Layton.

Kingsley shrugged. He wasn't going to divulge that.

'Did he seem spooked by it?' asked Kennard, wondering if weapons or organized crime were involved. If you needed security for a party, then it meant you expected trouble.

'I didn't get that impression.'

'Who arranged the party? Who paid for the security?'

'I won't tell you the names of my clients,' said Kingsley, typing clunkily on the keyboard before tilting his head towards the screen.

Kennard and Layton bent down to read the details. A party on 6 January. The name listed as 'Devon'.

'Surname?' asked Layton.

Kingsley shook his head. 'Paid in cash, before you ask.'

'Anyone else work the shift?'

'No, just Russell. They only wanted one. Probably to sub for someone on their own crew.'

'So, you sent your best?'

'The best available.'

'How did you hear about the incident?' asked Layton.

'Best to have open ears in this business, Detective,' said Kingsley, glancing at her. 'To know who has the money, who pays up, who doesn't and who has a rep for bringing aggro.'

'Could anyone else have employed him?' asked Layton. 'For the last two weeks?'

'I don't own him.'

'Do you *know* anyone who might have employed him?'

Kingsley paused, looking at both of them as if weighing up how helpful he should be. Weighing up what would get the cops out of there with the least damage to his reputation.

'It's a small market up here in the Blue. But down in the city . . .' He shrugged. '. . . tens, hundreds.'

'Could you ask around?' asked Layton.

Kingsley laughed. 'I could. But I won't. Not my job, is it?'

'A word would be appreciated.'

'I've two I can give you for free,' said Kingsley, grinning. 'Look, he could have been employed by anyone. Especially if it was cash in hand. Muscle work.'

'Meaning?'

'Security. Bouncing. Enforcement. That kind of stuff.'

'Collecting debts?' asked Kennard.

'You're the detective, not me.'

'That the kind of thing he does for you, is it?'

Kingsley laughed. 'I run legit. If I was mixed up in that, would I be in a shithole like this?'

'No, but I might be treating myself to spa days.'

'It was a gift from my wife. For my fortieth. Go inter-rogate her.'

'We just might,' said Kennard.

As they made it back to the car, in the huge, empty lot, they both leaned over the roof.

'What do you think?' asked Layton.

'He's a character.'

She lifted her chin. 'A liar?'

'I'm not entirely convinced by the whole business re-corded on one spreadsheet story.'

'I doubt he would have volunteered the muscle info if he was into it himself though.'

'No. He only volunteered information that didn't in-criminate him,' said Kennard.

'It definitely blows Russell's alibi out of the water for Tuesday.'

'That's for sure.'

'Maybe Russell was head-hunted to do some muscle work? Maybe he impressed whoever this Devon guy is,' said Layton.

'Giving him reason to lie about his alibi for Tuesday night?'

'Yeah. But there is, of course, the more obvious reason why Mr Hilmeyer was lying to us.'

Kennard nodded. Their prime suspect was a liar, that much was clear. But something nagged at him. Russell must have recognized the flimsiness of his alibi. He must have known that it wouldn't hold up against the briefest of searches. Was it the slip of a man under pressure? Because he was in over his head in some kind of illegal business? Or because he had murdered his wife, Tracey? No matter what it was, the end result was that Russell Hilmeyer had some explaining to do.

Twenty

Re-entering Rislake, Kennard found heavy traffic like before: the sensible folk heading out, the crazies heading in, fire tourists, thrill-seekers and relatives looking to help ship their kin to safety. Only a tight grip on the steering wheel prevented his nerves from taking over, his eyes fixed on the road.

'You all right?'

Layton's voice broke the spell, and Kennard forced himself to blink.

'Fine,' he said, a little too vehemently.

'It's okay if you're not.'

'I know what I am, Georgina,' he said, turning to look at her. He saw sympathy dull her face, a look he had grown used to and which he detested. 'We've a lot of shit to get through, let's concentrate on that.' The one sure way Kennard had found to defeat the terror: bury himself in work.

'I'll dig around the security angle,' said Layton. 'See what I can find out about this Devon guy and the incident in Mount Druitt. I'm worried that our Mr Musa is trying to direct us to where he wants us to look.'

'You mean not at him.'

'Or the nature of his business. You keep an eye on Russell for now, nab him for questions if possible.'

Kennard nodded, concentrating on the road and using the hard shoulder to circumvent the traffic, ignoring the honked horns.

'You want to help me?' asked Kennard, looking at Layton.

'I do.' The sympathy remained on her face.

'Then stick your head out the window and make a siren noise,' said Kennard, laughing, freeing some of the tension in him.

Layton laughed too. 'And there was me thinking you didn't want to draw attention to yourself.'

'Too late for that now,' said Kennard as an angry motorist gave him the finger as they passed.

Dropping Layton at the station, he made for the school. Outside it the chaos had lulled, people becoming a little more battle-hardened to the situation, shock coagulating into resolve. More power to them, thought Kennard. They would need plenty of it.

He entered the makeshift operations room in the chemistry lab. A third operator had been added to the bank, but he homed in on Lenka, easy to spot, her blonde hair like a beacon. She smiled when she saw him.

'Back again, Detective?'

'For my sins. Though I need a favour.'

'Hit me.'

'Can you give me Russell Hilmeyer's location?'

'Sure.' A few taps of the mouse and she had an answer. 'Angelton Road.'

'On the frontline?'

'Yeah. All hands on deck. The fire bridged the road.'

'And that's bad, I take it?'

Lenka nodded. 'Very.'

With her switchboard lit up, Kennard left her to take another urgent call, keen not to outstay his welcome. He was grateful for the help. In the past he had often found that even other emergency forces were suspicious of the police. It was obvious why. He had the power to take away a person's liberty. He was a future threat. Other first responders dealt with the past, the aftermath of something catastrophic. There to help in times of trouble. The cops were more than likely there to add to it.

He stepped outside for some thinking time and fresh air, or as fresh as it was going to be. It sat tepid in his lungs, blowing from the northwest, dry and scorching with the distinct flavour of destruction. He walked around to the footy field that had morphed into an overflow car park, vehicles parked in a discordant fashion, old and new alike: shiny SUVs, battered utes, old souped-up Holdens that reminded him of his youth. Overhead, the distant drone of an aeroplane distracted him, possibly a waterbomber carrying flame retardant to battle the blaze but obscured by the thick plumes of smoke.

As Kennard's gaze returned to ground level, he spotted someone he recognized sitting underneath a large tallowwood tree, close to the field. Joel Anselmo. Alone. Asleep.

Russell might be out of reach at present, but Joel might have some insight into his friend's state of mind.

'Mr Anselmo?

Joel's eyes flicked open, wide and frightened. Immediately on the back foot. The perfect opportunity to get some truthful answers.

'Russell Hilmeyer. How long have you known him?'

Joel tried to blink the weariness from his eyes, but they looked heavy.

'Hillsy? A few years—'

'He stayed at yours last night.'

Joel's face dropped. Shock that Kennard knew this.

'Yeah, we had a few. He didn't want to drive.' The answer was half-stammered, even reluctant. Not wanting to rat anyone out. Including himself. It confirmed Russell's alibi, for last night at least. But Kennard wanted more.

'What do you know about him? And Tracey?'

'Good people. Great people. Hillsy's a good mate. You can't get me to say anything bad about him.'

'I'm not asking you to. And her?'

'Trace was a star. When she was well. People flocked to her. She had this presence, you know? An energy. A sparkle when she spoke about painting and art and design and other shit like that.'

'But not in the last year or so?'

'Don't go raking all that up. How would you feel if you lost your dream?'

Kennard knew exactly. He could understand why Tracey might have retreated into her shell, embarrassed, frustrated, angry at the world. 'You were never over at their house?'

'Their house?' said Joel, suddenly nervous. 'No.'

'Any reason?'

'I don't think either of them can cook. Could cook.'

'Russell didn't mention anything more about their home life?'

Joel shook his head. 'He's a bloke. Blokes don't talk about things like that down the station or down the pub.'

Kennard wondered if that was the real reason, or if Russell was afraid of exposing their problems, Tracey's issues. If he'd been keeping them firmly under the rug.

He continued. 'I hear he did some work on the side too. Security.'

Joel was silent for a moment, weighing up his answer. 'Look, I don't want to say anything.'

'You haven't yet. You're only confirming what I know,' said Kennard. 'You seem anxious, Mr Anselmo.'

'I'm not . . . I was asleep and you—'

'So, Russell did some security work on the side?'

'Yeah.'

'For a guy called Kingsley Musa?'

Joel's eyes raised for a second in thought. 'I think so.'

'Has he worked for him in the last couple of weeks?'

'I dunno. Maybe. I'm not his . . .'

'His what?'

'His . . . keeper. Hillsy lets you know what he wants you to know.'

'So, he's secretive?'

'Everyone has secrets, Detective.'

'Has there been anything out of the ordinary going on with him in the last couple of weeks?'

'Like?'

'Odd behaviour. Anger. Depression.'

'Look, I know what you're getting at, mate, but there's no way he killed Trace,' said Joel insistently, but averting his eyes from Kennard's, out across the temporary car park, as he spoke.

'I didn't say he did.'

'Well, I'm just saying. No way. And I don't like these questions.' There was a grit in Joel now, a darkness around his eyes, his stocky body almost forming a shell.

'So, they loved each other?'

'Yeah. Bloody oath, they did.'

'They never argued? Raised voices? Raised fists?'

'Look . . . I don't . . . I think I should have a lawyer.'

'Why, what have you done?'

The weary eyes flashed alert, wide awake now. 'Nothing. You asked about the last few weeks, right? Russell asked me to cover a couple of his shifts. And switch a training night with him. And before you ask, I dunno why, I just took the extra work. But he seemed excited about something. More than usual. I thought he might have won some money on the horses or something.'

'Was he a big gambler?'

'Used to be. Got himself in trouble a few times, he told me. Owed people money.'

'How serious?'

Joel shrugged. 'Serious enough. Few grand, maybe more. Said Tracey tore strips from him last time over it.'

'But not now?'

'Nah, all in the past. Now it's something to pass the time while on call. Horses, footy, soccer, whatever happens to be going.'

'Big money?'

At this Joel laughed sharply. 'No. Maybe ten bucks on a knocktaker at Randwick.'

'A knocktaker?'

'A certainty.' He paused. 'That never comes in.'

'So, he never said what it was that had him in such a good mood?'

'No.'

'Can you hazard a guess?'

Joel shrugged. 'Your guess is as good as mine.'

'But you would say that he's been happier than usual.'

Joel seemed to take a moment to think about it.

'Yeah. Happiest I've seen him in a long time. And now this . . .'

'Do you think he's at risk of hurting himself?'

Joel stared at Kennard. A yes and Kennard might think of raising it, getting Russell taken off shift.

Eventually Joel laughed. 'He's out there fighting a bushfire. What do you think? We're all at risk of hurting ourselves. Now, can I get some sleep, Detective? I'm back out in an hour.'

Kennard thanked him and left him sitting underneath the tree, fully awake now, probably wondering if he had put his friend in the shit.

So, Russell had seemed happy. Kennard wondered when he could last say the same. There had been a time, before the crushing weight of expectation, when he had been happy – his twenties, maybe, working his way up the ranks while Ann studied to be a solicitor, debating the major topics of the day over dinner.

Now any debates seemed to turn into arguments. And not just with his wife. Last week's fight with Uptill – though it wasn't really a fight, given he had thrown the only punch – churned over and over in his head.

'*Quick to cover up, quick to shoot. Or* not *in your case. What's another dead bogan, eh, Kennard?*'

The jibe about Parramatta had sent him over the top. It was probably a joke, on reflection, but with an edge – as there ever was with Uptill. He was marking his territory, making it clear that Kennard, the city cop, wasn't going to come in and take seniority. It was the usual internal politics bullshit that he had dealt with for years, but this time it had been one remark too many.

Ann had wanted him to apologize, but even the thought of an apology caught in the back of his throat like the bitter smoke on the horizon, not quite formed and hard to budge. It was the plastic toy in the garden of the house in Caldicott, twisted out of shape. A mockery of what it should be. Ugly. Unsightly. Unwanted.

Twenty-One

Weaving through the cars, Kennard found himself at the bike shed, rows and rows of security bars dented and chipped from use and abuse, graffiti tagging the curved roof, stray bike locks awaiting their owners.

He wondered what had perked Russell up in the last few weeks and whether he was still on Angelton right now. The thought nagged at him that Russell had made his way to 148 Caldicott Road and was disposing of the weapon, which only made him want to go out there again. But by forcing Bairstow to try to save the Hilmeyer house he had put others in danger, and if that knowledge was made public, he would be the one that needed saving. He had no choice but to trust the Group Captain to keep all his crew in line, even if the man so obviously disliked him. Just like he had to trust that Layton was getting the information they needed on Kingsley's business and the mysterious Devon. That HQ was working on identifying the drug routes in the area. And the forensics technicians were narrowing down possibilities for the weapon that killed Tracey. He was only part of the network. And he didn't want to be the weak link. Not again. But all he had for now were rumours he couldn't substantiate, and people lied; facts didn't.

Kennard slid his phone out of the pocket of his trousers. The incessant heat blowing in from the northwest had dried the sweat, though the subsequent staining made the fabric look like an old watercolour left to rot in the damp. He needed a shower and a change of clothes. He needed a lot of things. None of which he was likely to get anytime soon.

What he did have was pressure to solve the case in a hurry. Forty-eight hours according to Haskell, but he doubted he had even that long. There was no guarantee that the town, the townspeople, or the killer would be around tomorrow. He needed an idea of what type of murder weapon he should be looking for. He wanted to go back to the house. He realized that his sense of panic was unreasonably wrapped up in its fate. As if a part of him was going to be burned into non-existence should he fail.

He stared at the phone. It was only a quarter to five, though it seemed much later in the smoky gloom. Right now, Ann would be packing up and heading for bridge. He sensed that she was glad to be free of him for a few hours, not having to worry if he was okay. It still amazed him that, whereas he could be stiff and awkward, she was like a chameleon, able to fit in anywhere, be it boozy police dinners with salty language and no boundaries, or bridge club evenings, all penguin suits and sparkly dresses. She was always sure in her own skin, unlike him – he was usually too uptight, thinking too much about fitting in to actually fit in. Even now she was trying to settle into her new life, and yet here he was, still running, still using work to avoid the issue. It was an addiction that masked the fear, and he wondered if it was also fear that had led Tracey to the bottom of numerous bottles of pills.

Ann's phone rang five times and went to voicemail. He listened to his wife's clipped message and left a message saying he hoped she was fine, and that bridge went well. It wasn't a two-way communication, but it was better than nothing. Afterwards, some level of calm returned, and he knew what to do next. In his mind, he had made this case his salvation. A personal quest. To find justice for Tracey.

'Sneaking a smoke?'

He looked up. Layton was standing at the edge of the bike shed.

'This takes me back,' she added, looking around.

'Not that many years, I'd suspect.'

'Not as many as you.'

'How did you find me?'

'Why? Were you hiding?'

'No,' said Kennard, a little too adamantly.

'Someone spotted you out here. Wanted to tell you that Kingsley Musa checks out. Came here from Sudan as a refugee when he was four. Lived in Bankstown before moving to Puremount. Founded his own business in security management four years ago. He's got ten people working for him on and off, depending on demand. Company has a turnover of three hundred grand. Profit of about forty.'

'So, small enough that he could keep everything in-house to keep overheads low.'

'Yeah. No criminal record either. Not even a hint of wrongdoing.'

'Good work.'

Layton stayed silent. Kennard wondered if he had come across as condescending. She was the same rank as him after all.

'Anything on our mysterious Devon?' he asked.

'No leads. But HQ is working on it. So, what now?'

Kennard felt the pressure not to sit on his hands, to force the issue and question Russell properly.

Twenty-Two

January 20 – 16.55 – Wind direction NE – Surface speed 26km/h

10 hours since North Rislake evacuation

South Rislake status = Amber/Yellow (Prepare for possible evacuation)

The Incident Control room was still a hive of activity. It put Kennard on edge, but he sucked it up, asking Lenka to issue an urgent request to speak to Bairstow.

He was about to retreat to the back of the room when Layton pointed at the screen, dots flickering on a map.

'What's that?' she asked.

Lenka looked up at her. 'Our PASS system.'

Layton shook her head in confusion, which saved Kennard doing the same.

'Each of the attending firefighters wears a PASS transmitter on their person. It allows us to track their movements.'

139

'And you need that?' asked Layton.

'The last thing we want is someone running dark around town, never mind someone without training or experience,' she said. 'It's been hard enough to clear the area as it is. You won't believe how many folks are too stubborn to leave their property to the mercy of the flames.'

'It's everything they have. You can't blame them,' said Layton, an unexpected bitterness in her tone.

'I'm not,' said Lenka, glancing at Kennard for an explanation of the outburst. He didn't have one. 'It's why Bairstow allowed a few that weren't in immediate danger to return and collect some valuables.'

'We could do the same at the Hilmeyer house,' said Kennard.

'I'm not sleep-deprived yet,' said Lenka as she flashed him a toothy smile. 'That's the GC's call.'

'And there's nothing from him?' asked Kennard.

Lenka glanced at the screen and shook her head. It felt like a deliberate ploy from Bairstow. A show of who was really in charge. Kennard was tempted to repeat his previous infraction and borrow one of the PCs, but he held off. He was already neck-deep in a hole he had dug, so he and Layton took a seat at the back of the classroom like rebellious children and stared into the distance at the fire.

'I have to ask *you* this time,' said Kennard.

'Ask me what?'

'Are you okay?'

'Yeah. Fine. Why?'

'You just snapped there.'

'I didn't snap,' said Layton, snapping back. She shook

her head. 'Ever experienced one of these before?' she asked, as a firefighter dashed into the room and handed one of the operators a sooty sheet of paper.

'No. Never been this close to one. You?'

'Yeah. My uncle's place in Gilgandra. 2013. Where I grew up.'

Kennard could see that there was a story behind this but let her continue.

'It came fast. Much faster than this. There was nothing we could do to stop it and no reason, according to the government, to save my uncle's place. Here, you have Sydney, the trees, the scenery, the tourist dollar. My uncle had nothing of worth. Apparently. We were left to mostly fight it ourselves. We had to drag my aunt away kicking and screaming, calling us every name under the sun. We watched the flames swallow it in the rear-view. Another couple of minutes and ...' She shuddered, her eyes squeezed shut. 'It was everything they had.'

Kennard could see that it had affected her greatly. It gave him a glimpse of the real Layton.

'Plus, it left me with this.'

She pulled the blue rescue inhaler from her pocket.

Kennard frowned. 'Are you okay working—'

'In a bushfire?' she finished. 'I can manage it. Intermittent asthma, they call it. It's mild.'

'Not out there, it isn't. I got as close as I want to,' said Kennard.

'Look, if you want to hang back, it's no problem. I can go in alone. Plenty to do here. You've been through enough too.'

Her eyes hinted at sincerity, but she was trying to turn the tables and he didn't need to be babied.

'I can manage,' he said.

'Make sure you do.' The hurt in her eyes had returned to something cold and calculating. A threat to keep it together. Shit happens and you have to get through it. It left Kennard wondering which was the true Layton; the one offering the poignant story about her uncle's farm, or the overbearing partner.

He was happy when Lenka swivelled in her seat and interrupted them. 'Group Captain Bairstow for you.' Official name. Official business.

'I'm not signing off on the Hilmeyer place,' said Bairstow immediately, his words bellowed over the roar of the onrushing fire.

'Fine, but we need to speak with Russell Hilmeyer urgently,' said Kennard, shouting back, which caused most of the people in the room to glare at him, raising his self-consciousness past comfortable levels.

'You don't have to shout, Detective,' shouted Bairstow. 'I can hear you just fine. *You're* not in the middle of a bushfire.'

'We need to talk to him urgently. Either you send him out or we come get him.'

'Don't!' said Bairstow, adamant. 'You want him that much I'll send him out with the next tanker.'

'When?'

'When it runs out.'

'Got an estimated time?'

'Way things are going, twenty minutes to half an hour. Anything else?'

'As soon as you can,' said Kennard, settling for appeasement.

'Good-o. Now put Stipowski on again.'

Kennard looked at Lenka, who pointed to herself and slipped the headphones back on. He watched as she logged some details before hanging up.

'Give them twenty minutes. They'll pull up here and drop Hilmeyer off.'

Even a twenty-minute wait was frustrating, but at least they wouldn't have to interview Russell in the middle of the carnage, where they would have been at a disadvantage. Out here they were in their element. Kennard's confidence grew. They had this. They would get the truth about where Russell had been on Tuesday night. And what he had been doing.

'I reckon we wait out of sight. Let him relax before nabbing him,' said Layton, whispering.

Another idea occurred to Kennard.

'Officer Stipowski?'

Lenka smiled at him, her lips warm and full even without lipstick. 'Lenka is fine.'

'Can you show us where Russell Hilmeyer is now?'

'Sure.' Lenka inputted an alphanumeric ident number into the computer. One of the many dots turned blue. It didn't move.

'That him?'

'It is. Looks like he's on Waverley.'

From the road markings on the computerized map, Kennard made out that Waverley was a side street off Caldicott. Russell was probably only about a hundred metres away from his house. He studied the dot intently. If it moved towards the house, they would know. He pictured Russell aiming a hose at the flames, fighting the kick; imagined himself feeding the hose behind, his eyes locked on the target.

He lost track of time, staring at the stationary blue dot like he had been hypnotized. It stayed constant and unwavering, oddly relaxing in its way. At some point a grey dot approached the blue dot, and they stayed together for a few seconds before the blue dot began to move. Kennard tensed up, knocked from his stupor. It was entirely possible that in the last couple of hours Russell had taken the opportunity to sneak back to his house to destroy evidence, but Kennard didn't think so. If he was going to do it, now was the time. He had been summoned from the frontline, meaning this might be his last chance.

The blue dot made its way along Waverley, turning left towards Caldicott. Kennard felt his breath catch in his lungs. If Russell did bolt for his house, then what? There was nothing he could really do except accuse him after. After the damage had been done.

The blue dot stopped at the corner of Waverley and Caldicott before being joined by other, grey, dots. Then suddenly they were on the move, faster than was possible on foot, moving away from Caldicott, away from the flames and back towards the south side of town. Kennard let himself relax, but only for a moment. He had some tough questions for Russell Hilmeyer.

Twenty-Three

The tanker pulled up in the yard five minutes later and Russell, along with four other firefighters in matching white helmets, disembarked. There was a brief, resigned farewell between them – a camaraderie gained from having made it back alive and in one piece. As they parted ways Kennard and Layton made themselves known. The look on Russell's face suggested a weary disgust. That he had exchanged one warzone for another.

'Do I get a moment's peace?' asked Russell.

'We need to talk to you about Tuesday night,' said Layton.

Expecting some sort of resistance, all they got was a shrug of the shoulders.

They led him into an empty classroom – Grade 7, according to the homemade sign above the whiteboard. This would have to do as an interview suite. Nothing was permanent in Rislake at the moment. Everything and everyone had to make do.

Layton offered Russell a seat and calmly informed him that anything he said could be later used as evidence.

'You weren't working security for Mr Musa on Tuesday night, were you?' said Kennard, patrolling the front of the classroom like a teacher.

Russell's gaze flashed back and forth between him and Layton. Kennard was anticipating defensiveness. He didn't get it.

'No, I wasn't.'

'So, where were you?'

'Doing a job for a friend.'

'Which friend?'

Russell stared out the window, this side of the school facing away from the approaching inferno. Outside, cars lay strewn across the footy field, the rolling smoke creating a false impression of a gentle mist, dulling the blue sky in the distance.

Layton spoke up. 'Devon?'

The speed with which Russell turned in his seat was enough to confirm that they were correct.

'We just need a surname,' she added.

'Don't have one.'

'Not much of a friend, then, is he?' said Kennard.

Russell licked his lips. They looked dry and cracked, after being exposed to the heat of the bushfire.

Kennard pushed. 'And what do you do for this Devon?'

'Odd jobs,' said Russell. 'Off-the-books jobs.'

'Muscle jobs?'

Russell stayed quiet.

'Can you give us an example?' asked Layton.

Russell paused for a moment, returning his gaze to the window again. 'Nothing illegal.'

'We didn't say it was,' frowned Kennard.

'I mean, just some bodyguard stuff. Looking after things.'

'Why does your friend Devon need a bodyguard?' asked Layton.

'Why not?' said Russell. 'Have you seen some of the whackas out there?'

'So why did you lie?'

'I told you. It's off the books, cash in hand. Money for the house. For us. For Tracey.'

Russell stared at the floor. He looked so small in the school chair, a child once again. Kennard wondered what he would have given to go back to that time. All the promise he once had.

While waiting for Russell Hilmeyer to return from the front, he and Layton had pulled everything they could find on him. To get a better feel for the man. It turned out that the kid Kennard had known as a star in the underage teams had graduated up the ranks. By fourteen he had been scouted and by eighteen he was well entrenched in the Swans youth teams, with many coaches predicting he would become a dominating centre half-forward or full-forward depending on any further growth spurts.

Accompanying one of the articles they'd found was a grainy black-and-white photo of Russell taking a towering mark over the back of a defender, hands outstretched to grab the ball, knee firmly entrenched in the overpowered defender's upper back. A majestic photo of a majestic player.

JAMES DELARGY

Then, during a reserve team game against the Greater Western Sydney Giants, Russell had taken a mark and landed just as a half-back was shoved over by a team-mate. The collision blew out his knee, leaving what was described in the article as a 'grisly aftermath'. There was immediate surgery and twenty-four months of rehab, but the knee was never the same. Russell drifted out of the team, out of the league and out of the sport entirely. It was a sad case of what could have been.

'You got contact details for this Devon?' asked Layton.

Russell nodded.

'And he can provide you with an alibi for Tuesday night?'

Russell spoke without lifting his head. 'Was that when Tracey ...' He tailed off, seemingly unable to muster the words.

Kennard looked at Layton. Her focus was on Russell.

Russell kept his head bowed. 'It wasn't me, I'm telling you.'

'You might be telling us, Mr Hilmeyer, but some of what you have already told us has been bullshit,' said Kennard, letting his anger flow.

Russell raised his head then. There was no fury in his eyes, rather an abject look of dismay, caught and not knowing which way to turn.

'It's the truth.'

'We'll see.'

'Anyway, I'm not the only one you should be looking at.'

'Don't worry, Mr Hilmeyer, we're checking all angles,' said Layton.

'Including her sister? They were always bickering. Over the farm, and the animals. And the complaints.'

'What complaints?'

'Trace made complaints against Karen. About the treatment of the animals. About the conditions on the farm. I told her to leave it, not to press them. Karen and Alvin are ... Let's just say I didn't trust them not to do something stupid. They're weird.'

'How do you mean?' asked Layton.

'It's culty out there – they're obsessed with saving money, oil, glass bottles, even their piss, everything done down to the last cent. And Karen's threatened Trace before. Over the land and the house. Trace wanted to sell it, but Karen couldn't afford to buy it. They even came to blows over it. Nothing spectacular, just half-punches and scratches – more for show than anything. They barely talked before then and they certainly didn't after. They just kept their distance. But I know Karen was angry about the complaints and I reckon she knew who had made them. And Alvin, I promise you, would have backed her up all the way.'

Kennard wondered if it was another attempt at deflecting attention. He pulled Layton to the side.

'What do you think?' he asked quietly.

'He lied about where he was on Tuesday. That's enough for us to hold him for questioning.'

'Agreed.'

While Layton kept Russell distracted by running over the main points of his story again for consistency, Kennard sneaked out of the room to speak to Haskell.

'DS Kennard. What have you got?'

Haskell was to the point, her speech as swift as the action she desired in her officers. Decisive and planned. It was why she had sent Layton – a mini version of herself guiding Kennard through this. The stabilizers for the wobbly cyclist. Or maybe she was there to shove him off the bike entirely.

'We have our main suspect, Russell Hilmeyer, with an unconfirmed alibi on the apparent night of his wife's death.' Kennard knew that Haskell wanted to interrupt, so quickly added, 'After he lied about said alibi originally.'

'Enough grounds to hold?' she asked.

'We think so.'

'Do you think this new alibi will stack up?'

'It needs checking out. But given that he lied the first time—'

'I'm told he's a firefighter,' interrupted Haskell.

'He is.'

'And we don't have a murder weapon as yet? Or a witness?'

'No, but—'

'Is he a flight risk?'

This threw Kennard off-guard. He had expected Haskell to jump at the chance to pull Russell in. It was the safest option. Hold him while they got all their ducks in a row.

'He might be now that his original alibi's been blown.'

'But he could have attempted to run at any point today, is that right?'

'He could have, but—'

'Even you must see the position I'm in, DS Kennard.

Detaining a serving firefighter in the middle of an ongoing bushfire event. If the arrest is seen to cost lives, it will look bad. For *us*.' She emphasized the 'us'. Kennard pictured himself being held by his collar over the edge of the kerb as the No. 87 bus came roaring into view.

'It might have already cost one life,' he noted.

'Which we could not prevent.'

Always there in the aftermath, thought Kennard.

'What do we have in terms of surveillance?' asked Haskell.

'Apart from standing beside him as he fights the fire?'

'Correct.'

Kennard thought back to Lenka and the PASS system. 'We can track him via transmitter. I've seen it in action. It works.'

'Very good, then. Watch him and we'll review after we check this new alibi.'

Haskell hung up, the decision final. Full stop. No point arguing. But Kennard had other ideas. He looked towards the chemistry lab. An idea formed, but he would need Lenka's help.

When he reached the lab, Lenka was still at her computer, sipping coffee.

'Lenka? If I suspected Russell Hilmeyer of suffering from excessive smoke inhalation, who would I speak to?'

Her smile turned to a frown. 'The medic. Dr Bailey. Is he showing—?'

'I sensed he was struggling to take a breath,' lied Kennard. 'But you know what they're like. He wants to get back out there.'

151

'I can call Dr Bailey now.'

'Please.'

It might not buy them much time, but maybe it would be enough.

Twenty-Four

Kennard called Layton out of the classroom to fill her in. A few stressed locals shuffled past, looking restless, ungrounded – almost like zombies.

'Haskell's not buying it. She's wary of the optics of holding a firefighter at this time.'

'Even though he lied to us?'

Kennard was pleased at the hint of exasperation in her voice, that maybe she wasn't just Haskell's stooge.

'We'll just have to prove her wrong. Meanwhile, I'm going to stall any attempt by Russell to get back to the scene.'

'How?'

'There'll be a doctor along soon to give him a check-up.'

Layton's face dropped. 'I guess you telling me means I'm on babysitting duty.'

Kennard flashed her a sympathetic, thin-lipped smile. 'I'm going to give Forensics a nudge.'

Pestering Professor Kirsten Matumbo for answers wasn't usually Kennard's MO, but he didn't have time to sit back and wait. He needed to know the style, shape and make of murder weapon they were looking for in case he got the call that the Hilmeyer house was accessible again.

'What can you tell me?' he asked, over a crackling line, avoiding any pleasantries.

'I could tell you to fuck off and wait 'til I cross my t's, but I'm guessing that isn't going to fly,' said Professor Matumbo, with an easy-going chuckle; a woman at ease in visceral elements that made even the hardiest officer blanch.

'Time pressures,' said Kennard.

'We all have those.'

'And a rising temperature.'

There was a brief silence, which Kirsten broke with a laugh. 'Is that all the foreplay for today?'

'I'm a married man.'

'Aren't they all,' she chuckled again. 'Right, main points. Cause of death was indeed blunt-force trauma. The angle of the wound suggests the trajectory was from above.'

'So, someone tall?' This very much ruled in Russell.

'Not especially. The victim was one-six-four in height, so pretty much anyone taller than that. Plus, she may well have been stooped over for all the evidence shows us.'

'Anything more on the weapon itself?' said Kennard, tucking himself under the stairs in the corridor, out of earshot.

'Metal. We detected microscopic pieces embedded in the wound. Chromium and vanadium. Alloy steel. Possibly a work tool.'

'Which doesn't narrow it down a lot, but it's something.'

'I'll take that as a thank you for all the hard work.'

'Sorry, I mean, thank you, Professor.'

'No worries.'

'Find anything else?'

'The blood pattern from the photos and from the wound indicates that although she was found facing the door, she had been facing the living area at the time of attack.'

'So, she was moved post-mortem?'

'There are no indications from the photos – and bear in mind I'm only working from those and Andrews' report – that she moved herself; no handprints on the floor or smearing that I would expect to be present if that were the case, though I'd like to see the scene first-hand.'

It was a response that only made Kennard more determined to save the house.

'As for the toxicology, we got it fast-tracked.'

The line went quiet then, and Kennard wondered if they'd been cut off. The fire had started taking down communication towers in its rampage, so comms were becoming frustratingly intermittent.

'Hello?' he asked.

'I'm waiting for the thanks,' said Kirsten.

'Thanks,' said Kennard, smiling. This was how Professor Matumbo was. She loved winding people up, always keen to inject humour wherever possible, which was probably necessary in her line of work.

'Such a gentleman,' she said, before continuing. 'A lot of urine was lost through the combined effects of being

155

expelled after death and evaporation given the elevated temperature of the site. But we were able to detect a significant level of cannabis and alcohol in what was left, as well as in her blood.'

The cannabis matched what Layton had found in the car, Kennard thought.

'There were also trace levels of codeine, but it disappears from the system after twenty-four to forty-eight hours.'

'We believe that she was taking Febridol and Codoxamol.'

'That could account for it.'

'What about any antidepressants?'

'The report notes the presence of selective serotonin reuptake inhibitors, or SSRIs. At around 15 per cent.'

'Which means?'

Kirsten took a deep breath. For Kennard this was code that he needed to listen carefully, otherwise he would be lost.

'SSRIs generally have a half-life of about one day. That means that for every day that passes without taking the medication, the level in the blood falls by 50 per cent. So, after one day, the level is reduced to 50 per cent of the original level, after two days to 25 per cent, after three days to 12.5 per cent, and so on.'

'So, it had been nearly three days since she had taken an SSRI?'

'Yes, but three days before her death, not before she was found. Her body would have stopped processing the inhibitor upon death.'

'And time of death was?'

'The best estimate we can give is similar to what the field officer gave you. The increased temperature upsets things greatly, especially since we don't know how long she had been dead before the increase in temperature.'

'So, we're looking at Tuesday?'

'Late Tuesday. Approximately thirty-six to forty-eight hours before discovery.'

So, Tracey had stopped taking the antidepressants a few days before her death. Was she feeling happier or had she just forgotten? Joel had told him that Russell had also been feeling happier in the last few weeks. Was it a coincidence?

He had one more question.

'In your opinion, could the codeine or SSRIs have been a factor in her death?'

'They might have been a factor in her condition prior to death, but they were not the cause. It was the blunt object solely that caused her death.'

'Thank you.'

'I'm glad you're happy,' said Kirsten. 'And there was one other thing.'

'What?'

Kennard could practically hear her smiling over the phone. She'd saved the juiciest for last.

'The victim was pregnant. About seven weeks along.'

Twenty-Five

Tracey – Before

January 13

The 'Customers Only' toilet, wedged under the stairs, was the last place Tracey Hilmeyer thought she would be when she found out she was pregnant. Her mind was a melange of emotions. First, she swore. Out loud. Then she shook her head. Why now? Why after all these years? Could this really be true? But the blue cross didn't lie. Not the first, nor the second. She wondered how she was going to tell the father. *If* she was going to tell the father.

Russell would be happy. They had talked about this day for years, but it had never happened for them. The subject had driven a wedge between them – and between her and his parents on their infrequent visits. It was always their first question, framed as an accusation: Why wasn't she pregnant? When were they going to have children? As if she – or Russell – could simply snap their fingers and make it so.

Russell was the father. Or at least he would be. She tried to think back. It had been just over three weeks since her period should have arrived. The cramps and build-up and familiar anticipation had never happened. It usually came like clockwork. If clocks worked by a process of pain, blood and tears.

But was he the actual father? There had also been that night out in Sydney. She'd been invited by Jase Litchfield and Shingala Abonwela, two old friends from Fevertree, unconnected to Rislake. They'd been reunited on social media, and had made a spur-of-the-moment decision to meet up. She'd thought it would help her forget about Rislake for a while. Acting before thinking, that was Tracey.

Russell had been away that day. On call or on a job, she didn't know. Like with most things, his whereabouts were left vague so that she didn't ask too many questions and he didn't have to answer too many.

The date had come around fast. December 6. The clock had ticked slowly all day, the decision as to whether she should go meet them looming over her. She was in one minute and out the next. The antidepressants and Codo had levelled her out some, but the level was akin to sailing a raft in the middle of an ocean. All she could really do was cling on as it bobbed up and down. Weed helped take the edge off and so she had spent that afternoon smoking and watching television, the words and colours meaning little to her.

By eight o'clock the Codo was wearing off. Her tolerance was rising, which was a problem. Her supply chain was getting more difficult to manage, and she had a debt building that eventually there would be only one way out of.

She paced the house once more. She decided to go to Sydney. Fuck it.

The drive was terrifying. The road closed in on her from both sides, concrete walls and rock, her vision tunnelling, car headlights blinding her, trucks with more eyes than the spiders that haunted her dreams, and single-beamed motorbikes, each beam piercing her soul. Her parents had lost their lives on this road. And she was going to join them. Ten years later. Back when they died, she was twenty-two and already living on Caldicott. She had moved out and moved on. Though she was only fifteen minutes away from her parents' place, she had rarely returned, her sister bearing the brunt of the caring duties when they fell crook. Karen was never going to ask for her help and Tracey didn't want to see her parents like that – slowly deteriorating as if they had decided to give up together. Which they had, in the end. No one had ever found out where they were heading when they had the accident. The car had been aimed towards Katoomba, but on Pike's Turn it had veered across the road into the path of an oncoming semi. There was only one winner in that fight.

The curtain of mountains swept open and Sydney appeared. Lights, people, a thumping energy that drew her in. Jase and Shingala and a party in Mount Druitt. Tracey found herself lost in the magic. The sights and the sounds. Champagne, vodka and everything else in between. Some Codo and an E to bring her to the next level. People and faces flexing in and out. Shingala introducing her to Devon King. The night turning into a blur.

Twenty-Six

January 20 – 17.58 – Wind direction NE – Surface speed 23km/h

11 hours since North Rislake evacuation

South Rislake status = Amber/Yellow (Prepare for possible evacuation)

Given the news that Tracey was pregnant at the time of her death and on unlicensed opiates, Kennard wanted to call in on her doctor. A quick search got the name and address. Another business perched on top of the hill overlooking the town, where all the professionals seemed to gather in their ivory towers.

Kennard entered the classroom just as outside the window Russell Hilmeyer was leaving on a PC, heading back to the front. Hurrying back out, he joined Layton just inside the main entrance to the school. She shook her head.

'Good try.' She gave him a wry smile. 'But I couldn't

hold him. Ten minutes and Bailey signed him off as ship-shape. Decided it was nothing that a good rest wouldn't solve.'

'One doctor can't help us, but another might,' said Kennard, before explaining to Layton what Kirsten had discovered.

They found the surgery in a smart red-brick building about a hundred metres from the school, the car park currently half-occupied by response vehicles.

Dr Whitehead was late middle-aged and soft-spoken, his mannerisms delicate and precise. He offered them both a comfy leather couch, as if preparing them for bad news. His bedside manner was immaculate, probably honed over a good thirty years as a GP. The certificates of graduation on the desk and walls attested to that.

Refusing all offers of tea, biscuits and a check-up – Kennard guessed he must have looked gravely ill – they asked the doctor if he had been aware that Tracey Hilmeyer was pregnant. Kennard was wondering if the pregnancy might have been the reason Russell had seemed happier and why Tracey had stopped taking her medication.

'This is news to me, Detective,' said the doctor, looking shocked.

Kennard frowned and glanced at Layton. 'You seem surprised.'

'I am indeed.'

His movements remained delicate even as he turned to his computer and tapped a few buttons, the keystrokes like whispers.

JAMES DELARGY

'Any particular reason for that?' Perhaps Tracey had confided in him that she and Russell were having marital difficulties, Kennard thought.

'I'm sure you are aware of confidentiality, Detectives.'

Kennard was about to butt in that this was regarding catching a murderer, but Layton spoke first, offering Dr Whitehead a smile. 'We appreciate that, Doctor, but there are time pressures on this.'

The doctor gave a leisurely blink, unpressured. He sighed. 'She and Russell had been trying to conceive for a number of years but there had been no progress,' he clarified.

'But they were still trying?' asked Layton.

The doctor nodded, his shock of grey hair floating back and forth, giving him an air of wisdom that probably helped earn the confidence of his patients.

'So, there were no problems in the bedroom?'

The doctor smiled and tilted his head. 'None that were intimated to me.'

'Was there a reason she was struggling to get pregnant?'

'None that could be verified. They both blamed each other. Russell wouldn't agree to a sperm check.'

'In case it insulted his masculinity,' said Layton.

'It's been tough for them. The last year. Ripe for arguments.'

'Arguments that turned physical?'

'She had bruises. Sometimes. On her arms.'

'Domestic violence?' asked Layton, leaning forward.

'I don't know for sure, but after thirty years working in the business, I know the signs. Though Tracey always seemed as if she could give as good as she got.'

164

'Which makes it okay, does it?' asked Layton, her nostrils flared in anger.

'No,' said the doctor, backtracking. 'I'm just saying that Tracey had a temper too. I witnessed it, on occasion, in the pub. Her and Russ getting rowdy. But she was a looker so she could get away with it.'

Kennard watched Layton try to temper a black flash of anger and stepped in. 'Any drug problems? Alcohol problems?'

The doctor shook his head.

'How often did she come and see you?'

'Once a month. Very regular.'

'For her prescription?'

The doctor nodded. 'And for someone to talk to.'

'What was her prescription?' asked Kennard.

'Fluoxetine. 30mg.' Antidepressants. A medium dose. Only a little higher than what Kennard had been on himself. The ones he kept forgetting to take.

'Does Russell Hilmeyer come to see you, too?'

The doctor glanced at the screen. 'Hydrocodone. For his knee.'

'What about Codoxamol? Or Febridol?'

'No. Why do you ask, Detective?'

Doctor Whitehouse seemed to be oblivious to Tracey's painkiller use, which made Kennard wonder how competent he was. Maybe he was just putting in the hours before a comfortable retirement. What it did mean was that Tracey Hilmeyer had been acquiring pills by other means.

'Do you think there's a chance somebody else got Tracey Hilmeyer pregnant?'

The doctor smiled. 'There are limits to my knowledge, Detective. But, as I said, Tracey Hilmeyer was a pretty woman. All I can tell you is that it wasn't me.'

They left the doctor's, heading to the low wall that led on to the pavement.

'So, Tracey got pregnant out of the blue,' said Layton. 'After they'd been trying for years.'

'Do the photos suggest Russell wasn't the father? That Tracey was sourcing goods by other means?'

That earned Kennard a raised eyebrow. He knew it was crass. And it might not have even been true. It would certainly never stand up in court.

'If Tracey told him that she was pregnant and that he wasn't the father, it could definitely be motive for Russell to kill her,' said Layton, checking her phone.

'And it sounds like there had been some violence before.'

'We need that alibi confirmed. And speaking of alibis . . .' Layton passed over her phone and spoke as Kennard read.

'We have a list of potential Devons. HQ is trying to whittle down who has the finances to fund that kind of party and where in Mount Druitt it might have been held.'

'How long?'

'There are four officers working on it, but I don't know.'

'Pressure them whatever way you can.'

'Will do.'

Despite himself, Kennard found that he was beginning to enjoy working as a team, particularly the feeling that he wasn't ploughing through this on his own.

Layton sighed and looked across town to the oncoming mass of orange. 'You know, the longer I'm here, the more it feels like I'm back in Gilgandra. Helpless as the fire advances.'

'We just need to get something that sticks with Haskell. You know she'll want it to be as tightly wrapped as that bun of hers.'

Layton smiled. 'That poor tortured hair.'

'Let's get her something she can't deny and then we can get out of here,' said Kennard, making for the street.

Twenty-Seven

With the team still hunting down the mysterious Devon, Layton and Kennard agreed to stop to eat. Which was harder than it should have been, even though the crowd on Main Street had thinned, the oncoming dusk highlighting the threat beyond. The two pubs, the Imperial and the Hockney, were chock-a-block, and the few restaurants that remained open were heaving with people enjoying what might be their last supper in Rislake.

The other option was the dive near the bottom of the hill, Chrissy's Bar'N'Grill, complete with a topless barmaid and questionable décor, both grown weary with age.

Tracey's Mazda had been hauled away from outside the souvenir shop for further investigation, and the space remained empty, police tape straggled in the gutter. Behind it stood the shop Tracey worked in, which had a CLOSED sign on the door but a light on inside.

Kennard didn't even need to ask. Layton was already stepping forward and rapping loudly on the door.

It was answered by a tall, broad-shouldered man who looked like a front-row with his stocky build and cauliflower ears. He introduced himself as Tony Steyn and didn't even ask why they were there, only what had taken them so long.

'Are you the owner?' asked Layton, looking around the shop.

Kennard did too and saw that it was dominated by shelves which were packed with local, regional and national goods; lots of greens and yellows, a main wall full of boomerangs and artwork and another section dominated by a series of didgeridoos angled into what looked like a tepee. Upon first glance there was nothing unusual or unique about it, nothing that he hadn't seen in a hundred other souvenir shops from Perth to Darwin to Hobart.

'I am,' Tony confirmed.

'Can I ask what you are doing here?' asked Layton.

Tony looked around. 'Trying to save what I can.'

On the floor were four boxes piled high with crystals and opals, the expensive stuff. A couple of digeridoos lay roughly taped together on the floor.

'Tracey Hilmeyer worked here, didn't she?'

'Couple of days a week. Best I could give her. Lots of hungry mouths to feed.'

'Was she a good worker?' asked Layton.

'Good? She was great. Better than the other bludgers I'm forced to employ.'

'In what way?'

'She brought in money like it fell off a tree. It was like witchcraft. She's the only reason this place stays open in the off-season. Could flog a lion to a zebra, could Trace,' said Steyn, smiling, almost in disbelief. 'Word is she was murdered? It's a shame. She was a very pretty woman.'

Kennard frowned at the comment. 'What was your relationship to her, Mr Steyn?'

'Mine?' he laughed. 'I employed her.'

'Did it ever get personal between you two?' The muscular rugby player might have been Tracey's type. The boss and the employee.

Tony gave another full-bodied laugh.

'I think my boyfriend would disapprove, Detective. About as much as I would. I deal with enough shit talk as it is in a small town.'

'But you didn't care that she was closing up at lunch?'

'I told you, she raked in enough I could put up with her closing up at lunch the odd time or having that sister of hers pop in.'

'Her sister?'

'Yeah, Karen. I caught them arguing on Monday. I don't make a point of coming around often but I needed to know if Tracey could cover the Thursday as Alfie, my cousin, can't make his shift. Court appearance.'

'What about?' asked Kennard.

'Some teenage boy shit.'

'I mean Tracey and her sister. What were they arguing about?'

Tony shrugged his shoulders. 'Photos. Or a photo.'

'Of what?' asked Layton, looking at Kennard.

'I don't know, only she asked if there were any more. I left them to it. You don't want to get in the way of Karen Lautahahi.'

'Is it okay if we look around?'

'As long as it's okay that I pack some of this stuff.'

With that, Kennard and Layton began to search the shop. As Kennard looked at the cluttered shelves, his mind drifted to Tracey's car, the expired pills and the hash. What if Tracey had taken advantage of the footfall of customers to sell drugs? In many ways tourists were the ideal customers. They might not always be seeking souvenirs, but they always wanted a good time. That's why they were on holiday after all. It might even explain her elevated sales figures. Some hash or painkillers complete with a crap souvenir to hide it in. He made a mental note to check back with HQ if Rislake Souvenirs had ever been red flagged as a front for selling drugs.

He scanned the counter and the till, noting a little curtained-off area behind them. A good place to do business. Skirting around, he gently pulled the beige curtains back. It was a small room not much bigger than a broom cupboard, with sets of keys on a narrow rack on the wall, some glossy magazines similar to those found in Tracey's car and a stack of yellowed paperback novels. A large fan was bolted to the top corner which would do nothing other than keep the warm air circulating. On one side was a locked waist-high cabinet that contained more souvenirs. The expensive stuff, guessed Kennard, the cheap tat stored in cardboard boxes underneath the display tables.

Out back was a walled yard with a double gate at the rear. Underneath a rigged awning were a swinging porch seat and a cracked leather armchair that had seen better centuries. There was a small table with an ashtray, a couple of empty beer bottles and some roach butts scattered around. Everything needed for a satisfying lunch.

It was Layton who spotted it as they passed back through the shop. Above the counter and in a corner that had once held a security camera was a plain cardboard box. Kennard brought it down. Inside were more photos. More men. Profile shots. But underneath those was something more intriguing. Paintings. Portraits, good ones as far as he could tell, full of honest, broad brushstrokes which seemed to hold nothing back, capturing a rich sense of the subjects.

Kennard studied the top one. It was of a Pacific Islander, the face impassive, stern, meaning business. Shoulders as wide as Tony Steyn's.

'That looks like Alvin Lautahahi,' said Tony, passing by with another loaded box.

'Are you sure?' asked Kennard.

'I could spot Alvin from a mile away.'

Her sister's husband. Was this what Karen had been complaining about on Monday? The photo and the painting? Had Karen been suspicious of something?

Twenty-Eight

January 20 – 18.53 – Wind direction NE – Surface speed 23km/h

12 hours since North Rislake evacuation

South Rislake status = Amber/Yellow (Prepare for possible evacuation)

Tony Steyn was still packing when Kennard left the store. Layton had exited a couple of minutes before to make a call. As he reached the pavement she hung up.

'Nothing on our Devon yet,' she said.

'Right.'

'Still wanting dinner?'

'What do you think?'

'I think it's hard to judge with you, Kennard.'

Dinner had been pushed to the back of Kennard's mind. 'I think we take the chance to go visit Tracey's sister. Find out what exactly they were arguing about on Monday.'

Karen Lautahahi's farm was fifteen minutes away, west

of town, the red sky to the north a warning that time was running out.

'What did you think of the paintings?' asked Layton as she drove. She had beaten Kennard up the hill and to the car. Again.

'Different.'

'A good different?'

'I thought so.'

'A bit too different for me. If I showed up to get a portrait done, I'd want it a little more obvious that it was me.'

'It was certainly obvious that it was Alvin. To Tony Steyn anyway,' said Kennard. 'Looks like Tracey's hobby was painting men. Portraits. Headshots.'

'Head only?'

Kennard looked across at Layton, who was smiling.

'You think that was why Karen was there?' she continued. 'Making sure that nothing was going on between her sister and her husband? You think it was a personal thing?'

'That painting looked personal. It took time, love, dedication.'

'Enough for Karen to murder her sister, though?'

That thought hung in the air as they approached the farm. The house was a little more ramshackle than most of the others in the neighbourhood, which said a lot given the state of them. Work had clearly been put in to patch it up, but the varied environment and the onslaught of time were defeating it, weeds climbing for the windows as if seeking shelter inside.

As they pulled up, a frumpy woman in jeans and a

striped top poked her head out from around the side of the building. She took a momentary glance behind her, then around the yard before she edged her way towards them.

Kennard got out to meet her, dragging his badge from his pocket. Her stride immediately slowed, as if she'd realized her mistake.

'DS Alex Kennard and DS Georgina Layton,' he said. 'Are you—?'

'What do you want?'

Kennard felt the power in the tone hit him. 'Just your name. For now.'

The woman held her distance, looking them both over. 'Karen Lautahahi,' she finally said.

There was little resemblance to her sister, only the vaguest hint of the high, angled cheekbones and strong chin, as if Karen had been the rough cut of the diamond that Tracey had been shaped from. The before and after. Her hair was bunched up in a mess that sat strewn across the back of her head like a bird's nest.

'You're Tracey Hilmeyer's sister?' asked Layton.

'Last time I checked,' said Karen coldly.

'And when was that?'

'When was what?'

'The last time you checked?'

Karen looked a touch confused by the question, her eyebrows arching towards the bridge of her thin nose. 'I don't understand.'

Kennard looked at his partner, who spoke. 'Has anyone informed you about your sister, Mrs Lautahahi?'

'Informed? Tracey? Nah,' said Karen, her eyebrows remaining fixed in a frown. 'What's she done?'

Kennard gritted his teeth. So much for Reinhold sending someone. Another task lost in the chaos.

'Nothing, Mrs Lautahahi,' said Layton.

'Which brings you out here because . . . ? If you're trying to get us to move 'cause of the bushfire, then you're shit outta luck. We haven't fought for all this just to give up. So, we're not moving unless you can get half a dozen trucks to move the animals and find them a place to graze.'

'We're not here about that.'

Karen paused, her frown deepening. 'Right. If this is about Alvin, then we have the papers. You try and lock him up and you'll get what the last guy did. You can't deny him rights now.' Her suspicion had reached red alert.

As if summoned by his name, a large man of Fijian descent who matched the man in the painting appeared from around the corner with three kids in tow, their hands dirty as if they had been digging in the mud. The children, aged between four and eight if Kennard was to guess, wore the same suspicious mien as their parents. He looked away. He had never known what exactly to do with kids, even his own nephews and nieces, leaving Ann to do most of the heavy lifting.

'I think we should speak alone, Mrs Lautahahi.' Layton leaned forward to try to indicate the seriousness of the matter. Karen picked up on it.

'Alv, take the kids around back. Check the cows have enough water in the trough.'

Husband and wife shared a look. Kennard knew it

well; Ann, too, was skilled at little flicks of her hands and shoulders, gestures that said, *I've got this.*

Karen waited until Alvin and the children were out of earshot.

'What do you need to tell me, Detective?' she said, the furrow of her eyebrows slackening.

'I am very sorry to inform you that we found your sister's body this morning.'

Kennard waited for the intake of breath, the shocked gasp, or a backward step in stunned denial, but there was nothing. Instead, Karen peered over their shoulders, either calculating something or calmly processing the dreadful information. Finally, she exhaled.

'Christ!' she said softly and blessed herself. 'Never thought she would OD. You hear about it, but ...' She tailed off, her pity stifled by bluntness.

'So, you knew she took drugs,' said Layton.

'The happy pills. Yeah. In my opinion she needed a higher dose.'

'So, she wasn't happy?' asked Kennard.

'I don't know about that, officer. What she needed were pills to make her see sense.'

'About?'

'This place. She owned half of it, you know? Half this house, half this land. Not that she did anything with it, but she wouldn't let us farm or even graze on her half. So it went to waste. Because of her pettiness. It's hard enough scratching a living out here, never mind with one hand tied behind our backs.'

Kennard found himself shocked at the callousness.

At how easily her sister's death had been dismissed. He had never really got along with his own brother, but he at least made sure that they called each other every few months to catch up, to check that their parents down in Sydney were still in full working order sailing their little cabin cruiser around the bays in their retirement. If his brother were to pass away suddenly, he would at least offer some regret.

Karen seemed to read this in his expression. 'I'm obviously sorry she's dead and all, but I have more pressing concerns, Detective. You see that big orange thing there in the distance? We might not have much, but I don't want it all turning to ash. It already seriously spooked my animals last night.'

'The firefighters are doing everything they can,' said Layton, injecting some badly needed empathy into the conversation.

'They can do all they want, but you can't stop a bushfire. It either burns out or burns down.'

With this, Karen set off for the farmhouse, clearly more concerned about her farm than her sister's death. Kennard decided to provide her with one final detail. One he was sure would shock her into some form of grief.

He stepped inside the kitchen after her. 'We believe that your sister was murdered, Mrs Lautahahi.'

But Karen Lautahahi stayed remarkably stolid. All but for a tensing of the left eye. A tiny chink in her armour.

'Murdered? Are you sure?' she asked. Kennard noticed her gulp after she asked the questions.

'We are.'

'So have you come here to tell me or question me?'

Kennard frowned. It was an odd response, to believe that they were out there to question her.

'We thought you had been informed,' said Layton.

'Riiiight,' said Karen, elongating the word. 'Any ideas on who murdered her then?'

'That's what we're trying to find out.'

Karen gave a little shake of her head. In apparent disappointment rather than grief.

'I always knew he had it in him.'

'Who?' asked Layton.

'Russell.'

Kennard flicked his chin up. 'Why's that?'

'The chip on his shoulder. The footy star who almost made it,' she said mockingly. 'The golden boy. And it was all taken away from him. Then add in that gallery of hers failing. I mean, paintings, for Christ's sake. How do you make money out of that? You can't eat paintings when you're hungry, can you?'

Karen paused for a moment, glancing towards the hallway beyond, then seemed to shake herself from her reverie. A look of distrust of them personally, or authority in general, crossed her face, arrowing her eyebrows.

'Is that all, Detective?' she asked. The distant sun was dipping towards the horizon, the second sun in the northwest sustaining its warm, terrifying glow.

The back door opened, feet big and small shuffling across the lino as Alvin returned with the kids. Up close, Kennard could see that the painting did him justice, the brushstrokes matching the lines on his face, the sternness of worry, a haunted expression in his eyes like the world was crushing him from the inside out.

'Finished?' asked Karen, directing this at her kids.

'Yes,' came the reply from the oldest.

'I don't think so,' she retorted. 'Chicken coops need to be cleaned, don't they?'

And in response to a command and clout that Kennard could only dream of, the three kids turned on their heels and left, without a scowl or a cross word.

He swapped a glance with Layton. With both parents together, it was time.

'When did you last see Tracey?' asked Layton.

There was a glance again between wife and husband, like before. Getting their stories straight. A secret language.

Karen spoke up. 'As I told you before, we weren't close. I'd see her in town, but last time we spoke was about eight months ago.'

'And you?' asked Kennard to Alvin.

'Same.'

'Did you ever go into the shop?'

'I don't need tat,' said Karen, looking around. Kennard followed her gaze. The kitchen was neat and tidy, but the lino floor was grubby and curled at the edges, the worktops scuffed and worn. Much like the outside of the house it was slowly falling into disrepair, a lack of money biting hard.

Layton stepped in. 'We have information that you were speaking to your sister on Monday afternoon.'

Again, a flicked glance from wife to husband. An order

to remain vigilant. Kennard kept his eyes on Alvin. There was a size to him that was unnerving, as if he could pick Kennard up and throw him out the window if he dared ask the wrong question.

Layton continued. 'And not only speaking to her but arguing with her.'

Karen's lips curled into a snarl. 'Okay, I spoke to her on Monday.'

'Our witness says it was more than that.'

'She took a photo of my husband,' said Karen, pointing at Alvin, who watched on mutely. 'Without his consent.'

'And what gave you such great concern about that?' asked Kennard.

'It's illegal. I don't know why she was taking them. Trying to cause more trouble with the government, probably.'

'*Were* they taken without consent?' asked Kennard, looking at Alvin.

'No,' said Alvin, as slow and laborious as his movements.

Karen snarled again. 'It still wasn't right.'

'Are you aware of why she was taking them?' asked Layton.

'Because she thought she could do anything she wanted to,' spat Karen. 'I told her to give them back. That was it. She was always causing us trouble. Getting the government on our backs. Making us jump through more hoops than a fucking show dog. Bitter. 'Cause she couldn't have kids of her own.'

'How did you know that?' asked Layton.

'Just how she would look at us. In passing. My sister

could hide most things, but the one thing she couldn't hide was her jealousy. Fuck, God bless her and all that, but it's just another death. I wasn't close to her when she was alive so I dunno why it would be different now she's dead. Now if you don't mind, Detective, we need to get the animals counted and locked inside for the evening. And then get some sleep. It'll be a long night ahead.'

Kennard turned to leave, then stopped. 'You never asked what she was doing with the photos.'

'Do I want to know?' said Karen, Alvin locked to her hip.

'She was painting them.'

'Painting them? Painting my husband?' stuttered Karen.

'Yeah. Portraits. Pretty good, in fact. We found a few in the shop. Of your husband and other men. She might even have shown you. Eventually.'

Twenty-Nine

They set off back to the station, a ute passing the other way loaded to the brim with furniture. There was a chance that they were looters, but Kennard and Layton didn't have time to pull them over and check, even though the vehicle was pulling sixty in a fifty zone.

'Not much sisterly love on show,' said Kennard.

'I'm with her,' said Layton.

Kennard turned towards his partner as she kept her eyes on the road.

'In that I don't get on with my sister,' she added.

'Why, have you been painting her husband?'

'Not enough pink in Sydney for that. Irish skin. Burns at even the mention of the sun. But I wasn't ready for how blasé she would be about it. I mean, if your sister was murdered twenty minutes from where you live . . .'

'Could put it down to shock.'

'We could, but it was one day after they had a face-to-face argument.'

'I can see why she might have exploded,' said Kennard. 'Would you want your sworn enemy taking photos of your

183

spouse? She said she thought Tracey was going to send them off to the government and get them into more trouble. She was angry about the photos, about the complaints about the farm. She snapped.'

'Or Alvin did.'

There was a silence in the car, the gentle whoosh of traffic passing in the other direction, cars and vans parked on lawns and driveways being loaded, the night closing in, the vicious red sky only growing more so.

'But I still think Russell is our guy,' said Layton. 'The lack of alibi, the original lie. The shit between Karen and Tracey has been rumbling on for years. No reason to snap now.'

On returning to the police station Kennard tried calling Bairstow to get an update on Caldicott, but couldn't get through. A comms blackout, he guessed, hopefully temporary. He did get a sense of the progress of the bushfire, eavesdropping on Sergeant Reinhold's address to his troops. The news wasn't good. Yarra Road had gone. Tugnasy was under immediate threat. Several fire breaks had failed, the wind casting a barrage of sparks across them to take root on the far side. There was despair in Reinhold's voice. He might not act it, but he cared. Caldicott was also mentioned. One half of the road had been lost – which half Kennard couldn't determine from what Reinhold was saying. In his mind he watched number 148 burn and tensed his jaw in frustration.

'Detective Kennard?'

Startled from his thoughts, he turned to find himself confronted by Winnie and Harald Thompson. He wondered if they had overheard the latest news as well. Maybe their own house had gone. If so, it hadn't dampened their smiles. It was a shame that something like this had to happen to this pleasant old couple. In many ways they reminded him of his parents – they'd navigated a hard life's work and all they wanted to do was enjoy their retirement without having their home burn to a crisp.

'How can I help?' asked Kennard.

'They let some of us go back and collect some items. Some of us lower down the hill,' said Harald.

'I heard.'

'Just a few things for overnight. Plus a few valuables. Which was naughty, but we have something for you.'

Harald waved for him to follow. Out of politeness more than anything, Kennard did. He had seen up close how near the fire had been to their house. That they had been allowed back might mean that the Hilmeyer house was okay, and that Kennard might be permitted to collect some valuables of his own.

Layton joined him in following the old couple over to the school, peeling off and heading inside as they reached it.

'How did the bowls match go?' asked Kennard as he, Harald and Winnie weaved between the parked cars.

'We were late,' said Winnie.

Kennard got ready for a bollocking.

'But fortunately it was called off. The other team didn't show up.'

No shit, with a raging bushfire approaching, thought Kennard.

'So, we get the walkover win,' said Harald with a toothy smile.

'Bowls really is ruthless,' said Kennard.

'No prisoners,' said Winnie, the cheeky smile offering more than a hint of malice.

At the far side of the schoolyard a white Nissan Micra was parked neatly on the basketball court. Kennard still wasn't sure what the old couple wanted. A simple 'thank you for your service' didn't necessitate this trek. Especially as he could see that both were struggling.

Reaching the car, Winnie popped the boot open.

'There you go,' she said.

Kennard looked in. For a crazy moment he wondered if there might be another body inside, that the old couple had murdered Tracey and were going to parade another victim in front of him like a pair of geriatric serial killers. But inside the boot was a long strip of clear plastic dotted with LED lights.

'We found this lying by the side of the road outside our house,' said Harald.

'Not right outside,' said Winnie. 'On the upper edge of our property.'

'Very good,' said Kennard, 'but I don't—'

'I picked it up a couple of nights ago.'

'Tuesday night,' confirmed Winnie.

'The news mentioned that you think Tracey Hilmeyer was killed a couple of nights ago.'

'That's true as far as—'

'I'd put it in the garage and forgotten about it. I thought it might be useful.'

Dragging a pair of gloves from his pocket, Kennard lifted the object. It was light. Not plastic, as he had assumed, but fibreglass, dotted with LEDs. He had no idea what it was, but his best guess would be that it was part of a bin lorry; a set of warning lights that had scraped the high kerb and detached. As much as he wanted to toss it in the bin, he didn't dare to in front of the old couple.

Leaving Winnie and Harald and depositing the strip of lights into his own boot, Kennard entered the school. It was after 8pm and the natural sun had disappeared for the day. But this would be no ordinary twilight, the fire offering the same sodium-powered glow that he had often witnessed over Sydney from afar, only here the streetlights were aflame rather than alight.

He found Layton in the kitchen where they were serving soup to an ever-swelling mass of people. Most of the beds had been taken, the hard brick reflecting a wall of chattering noise. The overall atmosphere was strained, tinged with worry, as people knuckled down to spend the night here. There was a chance that this wasn't even the first time for some of them, he supposed. These massive, uncontrollable bushfires were becoming a yearly problem for many.

Eyeing the crowd and keeping his back to the wall, Kennard sat down at one of the long tables opposite Layton. Her bowl of soup steamed in front of her.

'You must be hungry too,' she said as she dipped a chunk of bread into the soup. Potato and leek. One of Kennard's favourites. But not today.

'Not really.'

'Never know when you'll get the next chance.'

Kennard looked at the mix of people gathered in the hall and felt the air of melancholy among them; unrest at being stuck here, away from their homes and their own beds, helpless and adrift.

'What is it?' asked Layton, spooning more soup into her mouth.

Kennard looked around. There were eyes cast their way, but no one close enough to overhear. 'Russell's out there. Free.'

'We'll get him, Kennard. But right now, all we can do is track him. We've warned Bairstow. He'll stop Russell from accessing his house.'

'I understand, but . . .'

'I know you see me as an anchor holding you down,' said Layton, blowing on another spoonful of soup, 'but we don't need to put ourselves under any more time pressure, do we? Once we can prove that Russell doesn't have an alibi, or we find a witness or murder weapon, then we can question and charge him, and it'll be airtight.'

Kennard looked at Layton as she ate her soup. There it was again, the Paint-By-Numbers within her. Everything by the book. But this time he could see her point. There was a raging bushfire hellbent on destroying the murder scene and any further evidence. She could do nothing about that. There was a main suspect who had changed his alibi. An alibi that they were trying to verify, which would take time. She could do nothing about that. But she could manage the person who might just destroy the case. Him.

Kennard felt he should give her the satisfaction of being right but was saved by his phone buzzing in his pocket. He took it out and read the text.

'You better finish that soup quick,' he said. 'We might have just found our Devon.'

Thirty

In the end, Kennard finished the soup, Layton leaving it behind as she gathered her things. He tipped the rest of the bowl into his mouth and fired the last of the bread roll in after it. He was still chewing as he reached the car.

With Layton getting the jump on him again and claiming the driver's seat, Kennard read the information that had come through.

Devon King was a thrice-married man in his late forties who owned a courier business with fingers in property and shipping. He had been tracked down through a booking made for a party in an upmarket club in Mount Druitt. There were no details on what the party was for, but it had been privately catered and HQ had confirmed that extra security had been brought in.

Winmalee was twenty-five minutes from Rislake, straight down the highway and off Hawkesbury Road. It was a town that Kennard had never been to. His first impression was that it was one large suburb: expensive in nature, the roads smooth, the asphalt looking as if it had been laid fresh just yesterday, the lines clear and precise. Along the main road the houses were generously spaced apart, with large gardens dominated by larger trees obscuring what was going on behind them, a shield against the outside world.

The satnav guided them off the main road and down a series of tightening avenues before they reached the end of a cul-de-sac. From there a winding narrow driveway bound snugly by trees took them to a two-storey wooden slatted dwelling, a large porch and balcony extending out the front in the style of a house in one of the Southern states of America. The garden verged on untidy, a large red Christmas bush threatening to take over. It certainly wasn't a cheap house. Kennard guessed it cost at least twice as much as his own. This was another little foible he had noticed when he'd hit his thirties. Whereas when he was younger money had been measured in terms relative to the price of a pitcher or schooner, now it was measured in relation to house prices and mortgages. A steady descent into being boring.

Layton parked on the hill leading up to the front door, where a slight man with a strong jaw and a shaved head which hid a rapidly receding hairline was waiting for them. His expression was not welcoming, and he remained inside as he scanned their approach, his eyes lingering on the background as if expecting further visitors. As if they were just the advance party.

'Mr King, I'm Detective Sergeant Kennard. This is Detective Sergeant Layton,' said Kennard, holding his hand out as he made the last few steps up the steep driveway.

Devon King didn't extend his hand. 'Badges?'

Kennard and Layton complied. Devon King examined their badges until he was satisfied at last that they were who they said they were.

'How can I help?' he asked.

'May we come in?'

'Depends what you're here for.'

'Some answers,' said Kennard.

'To what questions?' King stood ready to slam the door shut. He either didn't care that he looked suspicious, or something was happening inside that he didn't want them to interrupt. The report had noted that he had two children, both girls, aged five and seven, so given that it was just past nine in the evening they were likely tucked in bed.

'Do you know a Mr Russell Hilmeyer?' asked Layton as Kennard peered into the hallway. It was decorated stylishly, modern and pristine. Recently cleaned.

There was a quick shake of the head. Kennard pulled his eyes away from the hallway and back to King. The rate of his blinking had become fevered; either he was rattled by the question or by their presence.

'Are you sure, Mr King?'

The blinking stopped, King fighting to regain his composure but gripping the doorframe tighter, his fingertips white with the strain. A coping mechanism. Kennard was well used to those.

'I'm sure,' said King.

'Did you throw a party at Napoleon's on North Street in Mount Druitt recently?' asked Layton.

King's eyes flicked to the ground, then back.

'I did. Nearly two weeks ago. Why? Did something happen?'

'You tell us. There was no fight? No argument?'

Layton bore the brunt of King's icy glare. 'It wasn't a fight. It was a disagreement. It was sorted.'

'We have information that Russell Hilmeyer was involved.'

King's tongue darted between his lips, nervous. 'He wasn't *involved*.'

'I thought you didn't know him,' said Layton.

King took a deep breath. 'I do now. I didn't then. I meet a lot of people in my line of work.'

'Which is?'

'Couriering.'

'You must do well for yourself,' said Layton, nodding to the expensive and chunky watch on his wrist.

'Enough to support my family.'

'And how well do you know Russell?' asked Kennard, silencing his mobile, which had started to chirp.

'Just from that disagreement.'

'And you never saw or contacted him after the party?'

The frantic blinking returned. 'I owed him for stepping in. He didn't have to, but he did. So, I passed him some work.'

'What kind of work?'

'Security work.'

'You'll need to be more specific, Mr King,' said Layton.

King huffed. 'If I needed to get something from point A to point B.'

'Like a bagman?'

193

'No, not like a bagman. A courier,' said King, defensive.

'Muscle work?'

'Muscle . . . ? No, Detective.'

'When did he last work for you?' asked Layton, firing the questions at King, trying to put him on the back foot.

'Two days ago.'

'Tuesday?'

'Yeah.'

'When?'

'Would have been at night. Just a simple pickup and drop-off. I liked him. I like him.'

'Why is that?'

'He's honest. Calls a spade a fucking shovel. A rare quality.'

Kennard could see why King might think that. But straightforward, honest characters didn't lie about alibis.

'From where to where?' asked Kennard.

'Excuse me?'

'The pickup and drop-off. From where to where?'

'Oh,' said King, glancing over their shoulders and down the garden as he thought. 'From Meadowbank to Liverpool. In the city.'

'And you saw him that night?'

'I did.'

Kennard looked King dead in the eyes. 'We'll need you to provide a statement to that effect.'

King frowned. 'Really?'

'Really, Mr King.'

King took a deep breath, then exhaled. 'Okay, I was with Russell for part of Tuesday night.'

'But not all of it?' asked Layton.

'No.'

'What part?'

'Early in the evening. Around eight to nine. Then he had to leave.'

'For what?'

'To do the job.'

'Couriering?' said Kennard, trying to imbue sarcasm into the single word.

'Yeah.'

'What was he couriering?'

King clenched his jaw and Kennard glanced at Layton. 'Stuff.'

'What kind of stuff?'

'I don't make a habit of relaying my business practices publicly, Detectives.'

'That's not a very satisfactory answer, Mr King,' said Layton.

Devon King smiled smugly. 'It's the only one I have.'

They were interrupted by a cry from upstairs. A kid awake. King looked at them both, eager for them to be gone. Kennard had one more question.

'Was this couriering done alone?'

King paused, then shook his head. 'No. He'd have gone with Chris.'

'Chris?'

'Christophe Stoltz.'

Thirty-One

Kennard got back into the passenger's seat. They had let Devon King go to tend to his crying child, but only after he had given up Stoltz's phone number.

As Layton navigated the dark, twisting road back to the highway, the light from their headlights enclosed by the overhanging trees, Kennard tried Stoltz's number. Three times. Straight to voicemail every time.

As they pulled back onto Hawkesbury, he was of a mind to go back to King's house and force an address out of him. King had insisted that all he knew was that Stoltz had mentioned Parramatta, but whether he lived there, he didn't know. These people were his employees, not his friends, and in his line of work, payment wasn't made via TFNs, bank accounts or official means. Kennard put a call into HQ and asked them to find an address for a Christophe Stoltz. Given the unusual name, he hoped it would be an easy task.

'Fancy a trip to Parramatta?' asked Layton.

Kennard wondered if this was a dig at him. She must have caught his glare out of the corner of her eye, as she clarified: 'To look for Stoltz.'

Kennard growled. 'With no address we'd have no idea where to even start. Let's go back to Rislake and dig into Mr King. See what we can find. You don't get a house like that in his line of work without either cutting corners or flouting the law.'

There was no need for a satnav or sign to indicate the turnoff for Rislake. The town was almost glowing with the new lights that hung over it to the northwest, the sudden gloom of the smoke overhead providing a stark physical barrier between firelight and twilight.

It was late but the police station was busy, every officer recalled from leave in preparation for a long night, civilian volunteers rushing around and merely getting in the way.

Sergeant Reinhold was in his office flouting convention – and the law – by puffing away on an e-cigarette, the little red dot punctuating his half-waved greeting. He looked stressed.

'What's wrong?' asked Layton, noticeably avoiding the vapour coming from Reinhold's e-cig.

'We lost Babington.'

Kennard froze, dizzy. Casualties were unavoidable he supposed, but he had hoped to limit it to one.

'Who was Babington?'

Reinhold frowned and took another puff. 'Babington. The street.'

'So, Babington isn't a . . .' started Kennard.

'A person? No,' said the sergeant, taking another deep puff. 'Bairstow was confident that the fire had been contained, but there was a sudden gust and a burnover.'

'Meaning?'

'The fire jumped the gap. Nearly took out four men.'

Despite Kennard's feeling of relief, he had a sudden realization of how close things had come to disaster – how close they still could come.

'We're closing in on a big Red. Full evacuation.'

'What about Caldicott?'

Reinhold snorted. 'Sealed off. I've called in everyone, even retirees.'

Kennard nodded. All hands to the pump. He would try to speak to Bairstow, or hopefully his replacement GC. Start off on a fresh foot. Nodding to Reinhold, he redirected himself to a free desk in the main office, the Leave-Shit-On-It desk, and shoved the mass of dried-out pens, old files and broken staplers to the side. Layton found a spot in the corner across the room right by the printers. They were the two spots no one wanted, Layton having to deal with the noise, and Kennard with the constant footfall.

She shouted across to him. 'You call the GC. I'll start looking into King's business dealings.'

Much to Kennard's frustration, Bairstow remained at the helm. For his part, Bairstow was equally irritated at Kennard for trying to put a fly in his fiery soup. Caldicott was classed as a no-go zone, and he had no spare hands to babysit visitors. It was after 10pm and some of the volunteers had to leave as they had work in the morning or families to get back to. He reminded Kennard that while he only had his arse to cover in there, as GC he had fifty-plus firefighters. The advice still stood: he would phone when Caldicott was safe, and he had someone to accompany Kennard around the scene. Then and only then.

Kennard dropped his mobile onto the table.

Layton called over to him. 'No luck?'

'No. Another polite invitation to rack off. You?'

'Yep, come over.'

Kennard made his way across, avoiding a constable who was merrily chatting to a colleague while walking backwards. No one had even asked who they were, everyone too busy dealing with their own shit to care.

Layton pointed at the screen as Kennard hovered over her shoulder. On the monitor was a cascade of newspaper reports and business magazines, one profiling Devon King, who was leaning against a random building and looking overly smug.

'These are all to do with his business. King's Shipping Company, or KSC. KSC is legit, all paid up according to both the ATO and the Customs and Border Force. It's solely owned by Mr King so there aren't any shady investors on the scene . . .'

'But?'

'The turnover is small, as are the profits. Too small to explain that house in Winmalee, that's for sure.'

'A poor year?'

'It's never been strong, according to the records. But KSC is mentioned in relation to some dodgy property deals. In one, a dead person was listed as the principal buyer. In another, the seller was quoted as feeling pressured into the sale. They believe they were hounded out by an aggressive and sustained blacklisting campaign.'

'So, could he have got his money from those deals? A dead relative? A lottery win? Rich wife?' asked Kennard.

'I'll look into it but there's a police report from two years ago which mentions a Devon King. In a case regarding debt collection. The target said they believed Mr King was behind it, but there wasn't any evidence. I'm gonna follow it up. See if it was a one-off.'

'What did you make of him?' asked Kennard.

'He wasn't happy to see us, that's for sure. Wanted us out of there as soon as. Granted he had kids sleeping upstairs but he was gripping the doorframe like a life raft, like he was trying to keep himself focused on saying the right things. Plus, initially he lied about knowing Russell.'

'Maybe he didn't put it together. He did say that he didn't know Russell's surname.'

'He was with him only two days ago. Russell is an unusual enough name that he'd probably remember it. And this couriering . . .'

'What about it?' asked Kennard.

'Given that police report, I want to know if it's debt collection under a fancy name.'

Thirty-Two

As Kennard stood up straight and cracked his back, a message came through. He had been right. The address of the only Christophe Stoltz within the Sydney confines had been easy to find.

The local cops had sent a team out to bring Stoltz in but they'd found no one home. His neighbours hadn't seen him since Wednesday morning. Which wasn't unusual apparently. He was a man who kept strange hours. The local department had posted a stakeout and would call if he returned. A trace had been put on his number should he use his phone, but Kennard hoped they hadn't scared him off.

They split up the next tasks. Layton agreed to check out the police report into Devon King and Kennard called Incident Control for an update on Russell's whereabouts.

'Good evening. Temporary Incident Control unit, Rislake.'

It was Lenka. He found her voice and presence calming, like a rock in the middle of a stormy sea he could look to and know it was there, above the water, guiding him.

'It's me.'

'Hello, Detective Kennard.' Despite the long shift and pressure of the ongoing situation there was a chirpiness in her voice. Kennard focused on business.

'Lenka, can you tell me if Russell Hilmeyer is still on shift?'

'His shift ended an hour ago. I left a message.'

Kennard looked at his phone. One missed call. One message. His stomach tightened. 'So, we don't know where he is? At present?'

'Afraid not. I last have him here at the school. Once he takes off his PASS locator, I'm as blind as a fruit bat.'

'Thanks anyway, Lenka.'

'Sorry I can't be of more help.'

'Are you on all night?' It sounded like more of a pickup line than he had hoped.

'As long as they keep paying me.'

There was a pause. Kennard didn't know how to end the call.

Lenka helped him out. 'If that's all, Detective, I need to keep the line free. For emergencies.'

'Of course, thanks again.'

He looked at the digital clock on the wall. 23.02. Creeping up on midnight, nearing a new day. He should call it quits and try to get some sleep himself. He wanted to be ready should they get a lead on Christophe Stoltz. But Russell running rogue was less than ideal.

Leaving the desk in a worse state than it had been, he made for the door.

'Where are you off to?' asked Layton, her hand covering her mobile phone.

202

'Out. Stretch my legs,' said Kennard.

Layton paused for a moment. 'Need some company?'

Kennard didn't know if he would. Not yet. It depended on whether he bumped into Russell. The off chance was no reason to drag both of them away from making progress.

'Call me if something comes up.'

'And remember to do the same,' she replied before returning to her phone.

It was a five-minute walk to the school, including the quick detour along the top of the main street. The crowd had mostly decamped from the pavement to the grassy verge lined with cherry blossom trees that separated the two sides of the road. In September and October, the trees would shed their petals like confetti at a wedding reception but right now the area looked like an oasis of calm, a desert island the townspeople had chosen to escape from the chaos and stare at the inferno in the distance, stray embers shooting up like fireworks before fizzling out to meld with the pitch-black cloud high above. It was like a giant bonfire on Halloween night, burning wild and out of control. Lower down and in the wedge of darkness on the north side of town Kennard could make out the faint flashing blue lights of the fire engines and support vehicles. Out there were people battling back the fire while everyone else watched and prayed. The feeling of helplessness clung to him like a black mark tattooed on his forehead. He fought against it, steeling the muscles in his arms. He reminded himself that he couldn't do anything useful out there, so he had to be content with doing something of use here. Figuring out Tracey's murder. Getting the person behind bars. Finding Russell Hilmeyer.

The school was lit up like a disco, but the grounds were hushed as if a curfew had been implemented to allow those in the gym to get some sleep. It had been a long and tense day, with the promise of another one tomorrow.

Kennard headed straight to the canteen but there was no food aside from some stale bread rolls in a large wicker basket. He chewed on one as he looked around. He felt more at ease here, among this crowd, their melancholy defusing any anxiety. These people were much too fearful to be confrontational, adrift from their homes, some trying for fitful sleep, others perched on camp beds, alert and on guard, or slumped at the tables unwilling to be stirred into action.

Asking around, he learned that Russell – 'that poor man' – had been seen hanging around the school about an hour ago, with Joel. Kennard decided on a tour of the grounds. The impromptu car park was as subdued as the hall, a low hush across the land, cigarette and vape smoke drifting from cars that dotted the playing fields, people sharing a drink as they watched the distant light show that might have been burning everything they owned to the ground. Kennard couldn't begrudge them that. He felt like a drink himself.

Twenty minutes of weaving in and out of the generous mix of vehicles and there was no sign of Russell. The worst-case scenario was that he was, by now, far away from Rislake. But up until now his actions hadn't suggested he was going to run, stubbornly reporting for duty, finishing his full shift.

Kennard took a seat on his own by the steel-wire boundary fence and called home. Ann might be pissed about him waking her up, but he reasoned that she might also be worried. Maybe. She was used to him being out at odd hours, his work the mistress she was forced to put up with.

She picked up on the second ring, and her slurred speech confirmed that he had woken her.

'Alex?'

'Yeah. Sorry for—'

'Where are you?'

'Rislake.'

A slight pause. 'Where that bushfire is? What are you doing there?'

'A case.'

'Will you be back?'

'Not tonight.'

'Oh.' She paused again. 'Are you sure you're okay? You aren't pushing yourself?'

'I'm fine. It's under control.'

'Are you sure?' She didn't hide the doubt in her voice.

'It's tough. But refreshing.' And it was. To be on a case, to be working it through. He had missed it. 'How was bridge?'

He wondered if he remained the villain of the piece but held himself.

'Same. Win some, lose some.'

'Am I forgiven?'

'In time. Rhonda might take a little longer.'

'I mean you.'

205

'As soon as you forgive yourself.'

As ever, Ann could boil everything down into a few words, nothing wasted. 'Be careful out there,' she continued.

'I will.' He didn't tell her about his trip to the frontline. There was nothing she could do about it, and it would only worry her.

'I'm going to sleep. Call you tomorrow.'

'Goodnight,' said Kennard, but she was gone. She was right: until he forgave himself, any forgiveness she could offer would only plaster over the cracks. She had always known the right thing to say to him, from his late nights to his foul mood when stuck on a case. At least he had spoken to her, the lifeline that gave him renewed hope. They had been harsh, honest words but her voice was enough. It always had been.

The conversation had left his tongue dry, swollen in his mouth, exacerbated by the intense exertion of the day. It cried out for something wet. So, leaving the temporary car park, he headed for the old workhouse bar perched at the top of Main Street, the location a godsend for any drunks that lived at the bottom of the hill who could let gravity guide them home.

He called Layton to let her know where he was heading and that she might have to text him. He got an immediate response.

'I'll meet you there.'

'You sure?'

'Yeah. Dying for a schooner, to be honest.'

The roar from inside the Imperial made him pause. It

meant it was doing good business. And that it would be packed. Back in Sydney, Kennard had been partial to an occasional Friday afternoon tear-up with the team. Up here in the mountains, he had maintained a distance so he wouldn't have to discuss the past.

Waiting for Layton was an option. But it was only a pub after all. Taking a deep breath, he entered. As the noise had indicated, it was heaving, betraying all the hallmarks of a lock-in: a raucous crowd, plenty to drink and people wanting to wash their cares away. They probably thought that no one was coming to stop them, the emergency forces otherwise occupied. Instigating the unnecessary pretence that he was there on business, Kennard asked the barman if Russell Hilmeyer had been in. The barman shook his head and insisted that he wouldn't serve any firefighters. While the fire raged, they went as dry as the land that was burning. After it was out, they were welcome to come in and drink the place under. If it was still standing, of course.

Carrying two ice-cold pints, Kennard suffered the jostle of the crowd as he made his way to a perch at the side of the room. There was music blaring from a jukebox that itself struggled against the din. He found that he could barely hear himself think. Which was good. He didn't want to think. Not for the next half hour at least. He regretted inviting Layton now. He longed for the peace and quiet you could only find amid the white noise of other people's conversations.

Turning, he faced a wall that was wallpapered in old posters of bands and local festivals. He was almost half-way through a refreshingly noisy pint when there was a tap on his shoulder that made him jump, almost knocking the rest of the glass over.

Layton stared at him. Kennard felt his heart pound in his chest, as loud as the conversations nearby.

'Caught me off-guard,' he said.

He could see that she was desperate to say something, that they both recognized the fear in the air.

'This mine?' she asked, pointing to the untouched glass, letting the situation drop.

'I didn't put you down as a beer drinker,' said Kennard.

'You seem to have labelled me before I even arrived,' she said, taking a big gulp.

It was a charge that he couldn't deny.

'Quiet pub you've chosen.'

'Busy enough so I can disappear.'

'Hide, you mean.'

Kennard studied her expression, trying to work out if she was taking a shot at him. But she was right. Sitting up against the wall, he was just another band poster watching over everything.

'No chucking tables tonight?' said Layton, taking another long gulp.

Kennard nearly coughed up his mouthful. 'How did you hear about that?'

'My mum goes to the same club. Your name came up,' said Layton absently, focusing on the schooner.

'It was an accident. I stood up too quick. Forgot how low the table was.'

'The story I heard was that you chucked it. And that you were angry.'

'I was clumsy. I got distracted and messed up the hand. I was annoyed at myself for not concentrating and so I got up to clear my head and . . .'

'Barely missed taking Rhonda Friest's head off,' smiled Layton.

'Don't believe everything an obviously biased witness says,' said Kennard with a smile of his own.

Layton put her pint down. She looked at him.

'What is it?' he asked.

'Was it clumsy with DS Uptill last week too?'

Kennard had wondered when this would come up. He had lost control with Uptill, but he had been lured into it. 'That was a misunderstanding. Let's just say he knows how to push my buttons.'

'You let him.'

'He does it on purpose.'

'Of course he does. He rips on me about my asthma, Sancho about his weight, DePaul about the footy. He's a cunt, but he's a cunt to everybody, not just you. Be honest,' said Layton. 'Have you been having any flashbacks, trouble sleeping?'

'Over flipping a bridge table?' asked Kennard, trying to deflect.

'It's not just that and you know it.'

Kennard felt his anger rise like bile. This was supposed to be a relaxing interlude in his day. He didn't need Parramatta raising its ugly head here too.

'What's that got to do with you? Did Haskell want you to check up on the nutjob?'

'We're partners. I want to know you're okay.'

209

Kennard was trying to figure out whether this concern was in fact nosiness. His anger didn't allow him to differentiate.

'I'm fine,' he said in a tone that did nothing to disguise the fact that he wasn't.

'If you need to talk ...'

'I've done plenty of talking in the last six months. It hasn't helped.'

Their spiralling conversation was interrupted by Layton's phone. Like the bell signalling the end of the round. She pressed it hard against her ear as Kennard helped himself to a large glug of beer. It tasted warm and bitter now, the joy gone.

Layton ended her call and looked straight at Kennard.

'We got an update from Tech,' she said. 'A ping from Russell's phone on Tuesday night.'

'Does it put him in Meadowbank or Liverpool?' asked Kennard.

Layton shook her head. 'Neither. The ping came from Caldicott.'

'Fuck.'

'Too right. I think we should bring him in for questioning. Now.'

'Despite what Haskell said?'

Layton nodded. 'His alibi is outstanding and now we can place him in the area when his wife was murdered.'

'We have to find him first.'

Thirty-Three

January 20 – 23.14 – Wind direction NE – Surface speed 18km/h

16 hours since North Rislake evacuation

South Rislake status = Amber (Prepare for possible evacuation)

They started with the people in the pub, jovial faces quickly turning sour as he and Layton went from table to table, pissing on everyone's parade.

Against the clock and despite Kennard's reluctance, they split up. Kennard found himself alone among the crowd. They passed by in a blur, his questions half-heartedly mumbled and ignored, people assuming by his mangled attempts that he was similarly drunk. By the beer-soaked pool table he tried to avoid a large guy in his thirties with a tan so deep it probably coloured his internal organs. The sway in his stance indicated that he'd had a gutful of piss.

'Oi, you Kennard?' he asked, flanked by two women, all three sporting expressions of thunder.

Kennard wasn't given a chance to answer. One of the women cut in, mascara laid on thick around her eyes like she had been punched.

'The bastard who caused our house to burn down?' She pressed up close to Kennard, her breath sticky with beer.

Kennard tried to back off but there was no room behind; he was walled in. His fingers tensed, his whole body freezing up like he was turning to stone. The options were stark: curl up in a ball or bully his way out and deal with the consequences later.

'If you could get out of our way, please,' said Layton, suddenly beside him, speaking calmly and clearly.

'We heard one of you lot told them not to fight it,' said the other woman, a skinny finger topped with a brightly painted nail jabbing at Kennard's chest.

'I'm sure that—' started Layton.

'Floral Drive,' said the woman.

'Talk to Reinhold.'

'That fat bastard? Be more use asking a dog to teach maths.'

The mascara woman cut in. 'I heard that it was a shitbag cop called Kennard that told them to focus on Caldicott and let Floral Drive burn.'

Which Kennard thought might have been true, but he didn't need to get into a fight right now. Jack Reacher he wasn't, but he did wonder who had put his name out there as the culprit. There were a few contenders.

'Who gave you that information?' he asked, forcing the words out.

'Are you him?' asked the mascara woman.

Kennard considered his next course of action, his senses in overdrive, their faces blurred, too many contrasting smells, the imaginary fist squeezing the air from his lungs. He could take a stand and admit who he was and suffer the consequences, or he could lie like a coward.

'You need to get out of our way. Right now!' ordered Layton, the group confronting them growing, a dozen faces now glaring at them, sizing them up.

Though his heart was pounding, Kennard devised a plan. A middle ground.

'Your information's wrong. Who gave you it?'

The mascara woman looked to her friend. 'Some of the guys.'

Kennard tried to find strength, raising his chin to meet them. 'Did you get their names? We don't need any incendiary rumours out there at the minute.'

'We're not dobbing them in,' said the man, resolute.

'Was it Russell Hilmeyer?'

'We're not naming names, copper,' said the woman with the painted nails.

Kennard felt a hand on his arm. Layton. Her eyes flicked towards the back exit.

'Bairstow?' asked Kennard, terrified but trying not to show it, letting Layton lead them around the edge of the scrum to the exit.

The air in the beer garden wasn't all that different to inside, heavy with heat and the stench of beer, the only addition being the residual pong of cigarette butts, one still smouldering in an ashtray nearby. Another spot fire to deal with.

He scanned around for an exit but instead found something else.

In the far corner sat Russell Hilmeyer and Joel Anselmo, the table in front of them littered with empties, the orange glow of the heaters surrounding the garden giving the momentary impression that the bushfire was upon them.

Behind Kennard the angry crowd had followed them outside. He looked at Layton, worry masking her face too.

'Over there,' she said, pointing to the exit with one hand, taking a shot of salbutamol from the inhaler with the other. Preparing to run.

Now was the time to go. Make their escape, get support and come back for Russell. It was not an opportune time to make an arrest. But Kennard didn't want to delay it. In Parramatta, delay had been deadly.

'Fuck,' said Kennard, stepping towards Russell and Joel but glancing over his shoulder, more people joining the angry mob by the minute. This was a bad idea, he told himself.

Layton caught up with him as he started to address Russell.

'Mr Hilmeyer, I'd like you to come with us.'

Russell looked at him and then Layton.

'What is this?'

'We need to ask you some questions.'

'About what?'

'You know what, Russell.'

The anger in Russell's face matched the anger in Joel's.

'Let the man mourn in peace,' said Joel.

'I'm afraid we need you at the station now,' said Kennard, looking to Layton for support.

The crowd closed in, menace in their eyes, two against twenty, surrounding them. Kennard felt the fluttering in his chest rise.

'Leave the poor man alone,' said someone in the crowd. They were now within a couple of metres, the heat of their breath on his neck, jostling to get into position to strike the first blow so the others could follow. Though no one really wanted to be first. The indecision felt like the only thing saving them both from a beating.

'Okay, Detectives Kennard and Layton,' said Russell loudly, angering the crowd further by revealing that the devil cop Kennard was indeed in their midst. Someone had put his name out there. Probably not with the intention of getting him beaten up, but certainly with the intention of damaging his reputation.

Kennard turned around to placate the mob. He only got halfway before hands were on him, the shove followed by a yell of 'fucking arsehole cop'. Putting his hands out to stop himself from falling over, they only found the edge of the table, upending it, seemingly his forte at present. As it kicked up, the table knocked into Russell, spilling the empties in a terrible crash.

Layton stepped into the breach, her hand on the firearm at her side.

'Everyone back up *now*!'

As Kennard regained his balance, black spots flashed

in front of his eyes. His heart raced like it was going to explode from his chest. In Parramatta, he had found the exit. But not here.

Layton talked over her shoulder at him.

'You okay?'

He wasn't but he didn't reply. What had fallen from Russell's hand in the melee had wiped all thoughts of Parramatta from his head. He focused on the two small plastic bottles, Codoxamol scrawled on the label. The same drug they'd found in Tracey's car.

Standing up straight, he made eye contact with Russell, who looked both angry and guilty.

'You hurt?' asked Layton.

'No.'

'Then get the cuffs on him and let's get out of here.'

Kennard squared up to Russell, whose eyes were flitting between him and the exit, on his toes as if about to run.

'Don't do anything stupid, Russell.'

He watched the idea ruminate but quickly vanish, Russell squeezing his eyes shut in surrender. Kennard didn't hesitate, bringing out his cuffs.

'There's no need for—' said Joel.

But Kennard wasn't buying it. He knew that Russell, dodgy knee and all, could still outrun him.

'Turn around.'

Russell did so, letting Kennard put the cuffs on him. With his back to the crowd, Kennard's safety was in Layton's hands, the mob throwing insults like confetti. But insults he could cope with.

With Russell secured, Kennard went to lead him out of the garden. Joel began to follow.

'No. You stay here,' said Kennard, his eyes on Joel and the surge of people around him, begging his legs not to turn to jelly as he made his exit onto the street.

The crowd followed, Layton still controlling them as best she could and covering their escape. His saviour. He didn't want to consider what might have happened if she hadn't been there.

Only once they had Russell booked and sitting in one of the interview rooms did Kennard finally relax, his hands trembling as he sat slumped at his temporary desk. Flashbacks to Parramatta ebbed and flowed in his mind. He tried to recall some of the breathing techniques that the psychiatrists had taught him, but his mind drew a blank.

'That was close,' said Layton, sitting opposite him. 'You looked a little ...' She waggled her hand to emphasize what she was about to say, 'jittery back there.'

Kennard didn't respond. Didn't know how to respond.

'It reminded you of Rhian Thorpe, didn't it?'

That name. The one he had blanked out. Or tried to. He found it difficult to decide if her tone was comforting or belittling and struggled to control his anger. His discomfort had been obvious. No use in denying it.

'Does it happen a lot?' she continued.

'Only when there's a mob after me,' said Kennard with a smile forced onto his face.

'Public Enemy Number One.'

'I get their point,' said Kennard. 'The fire fucked a lot of lives up and now they have someone to blame.'

'Think Bairstow told them?'

'Him, Russell, Joel, anyone. I'm getting used to not being flavour of the month. But thanks for having my back there. For taking the lead.'

'If it was up to me, I'd have arrested the gutless wonder that shoved you.'

'We got the one we wanted. That's enough. Let's question him.'

Layton shook her head. 'He's had a skinful, Kennard. And he'll need a lawyer. If you know one around here up this late, I'm all ears. If not, we have him. Let him stew a while.'

They were good points. Russell wasn't going anywhere. Some decent kip would give them the edge when it came to interviewing him. But Kennard knew that he wouldn't be getting any.

Thirty-Four

17.5 hours since North Rislake evacuation

South Rislake status = Amber (Prepare for possible evacuation)

He was right. He spent an hour staring at the late shift dealing with panicked phone calls, irate residents and a couple of drunks who would need to sober up quick if the wind blew disaster in the station's direction.

At some point he must have dozed, as Layton woke him up.

'Russell has waived representation.'

'Really?'

Layton shrugged. It didn't make sense to her either. Either he was confident that he was innocent, confident that they couldn't prove his guilt, or too cheap to hire a lawyer.

219

Grabbing a cup of grainy coffee, Kennard followed Layton into the interview room. After going through procedure, she kicked off the questioning.

'We need to ask you some questions, Mr Hilmeyer, about your wife. Her murder.'

Kennard watched Russell flinch at the mention of his wife's fate.

'Run us through Tuesday night again.'

'I was working.'

'For Devon King?'

'Yeah.'

'Doing a job of a type that you still won't say?' said Layton, leading Russell down the path she wanted.

'It was private business.'

'This is a murder investigation, Mr Hilmeyer. There's no such thing as private business. But we've spoken to Mr King. He claims you were working as a courier.'

'I was.'

'I don't think that's true, Mr Hilmeyer. We think you were debt collecting, doing muscle work. Is that the type of business Mr King is involved in?'

Russell stayed quiet, his cuffed hands clasped tightly together.

Layton continued. 'Mr King has informed us that he can only provide you with an alibi for part of the night. Early evening to be exact. We have been given the name of a person who can provide you with a full alibi, but we cannot locate him.'

Russell frowned. 'That's your job.'

'It's to your benefit that we do.'

'Yeah, I get that, but I only know his name. Christophe Stoltz. We've worked together a couple of times, that's all. We aren't best friends. Do you two know much about each other?'

'We're not the ones being questioned, Mr Hilmeyer,' said Kennard, his anger bubbling. 'When were you last in contact with your wife?'

'Tuesday morning. I left her watching television.'

Kennard flicked a glance towards Layton, who stepped in. 'We have received information from our Tech team that a ping from your mobile phone can be traced to your residence on Tuesday night.'

Worry finally caught up with Russell, shading his face. 'Uh, I can explain that.'

'We're all ears,' said Kennard, folding his arms and leaning back in his chair.

'I didn't have my phone.'

Kennard glanced at Layton. He wasn't buying it. From her expression, neither was she.

Russell continued. 'Tracey's was broken. She'd dropped it. So, I gave her mine. She needed it in case Tony Steyn gave her more shifts. We needed the money.'

'And you didn't need a phone?'

'I knew where I had to be on Tuesday and Wednesday.'

'The information we have is that it only pinged once. On Tuesday evening.'

'Maybe she didn't use it, or . . .'

'Or what, Mr Hilmeyer?'

'Or she was so out of it that she could barely make it to the bathroom never mind use a phone. It's not pretty but it's the truth. The tablets sometimes knocked her for six. Plus, you searched me when you booked me, didn't you? Did I have a phone then?'

'So where is it?' asked Layton.

'Wherever Tracey last left it. In the house.'

'I've been through the house,' said Kennard. 'Upstairs and down. I didn't see a mobile phone.'

Russell shrugged. 'I don't know what to tell you, Detective.'

'Tell us the truth.'

'It is the truth.'

'You could have been in the house, Mr Hilmeyer,' said Layton. 'You don't have an alibi. Your phone was there.'

'I *do* have an alibi. You just haven't tracked Chris down.'

'All we have is your word that you were at a location you won't divulge, doing something you won't divulge. Which means that you could have very well been at 148 Caldicott with her. Do you see how it looks?'

Russell shook his head. 'I was miles away. In Meadowbank or Liverpool to be precise. The first I knew of . . . Trace's death was when I saw you with her, Detective. By your reasoning *you* could have killed her.'

'But I've got a verifiable alibi for Tuesday night, Mr Hilmeyer.'

'Chris will give you my alibi. I can't tell you any more.'

'You can. You can tell us what you were doing on Tuesday.'

'I can't.'

'Because it incriminates you?'

'I just can't, okay?'

Kennard could see that they were getting nowhere with this, so tried a different tack.

'Since we last spoke, we've got some more information back from Forensics.'

'Oh?' said Russell, sitting up in his seat. 'About how Trace was murdered? The murder weapon? Fingerprints? DNA?'

Kennard held his hand up.

'Tracey was pregnant.'

Kennard meant this as a big hook out of left field, something that would buckle Russell's knees and hopefully cause him to spill what had happened on Tuesday night. It looked to have worked: Russell rocked back in his chair, his head cast back, eyes blank, as if stunned.

'I take it this comes as a surprise to you, Mr Hilmeyer?'

The lack of a response told Kennard everything. He pressed on.

'Why does it come as a surprise to you, Mr Hilmeyer?'

'How long was she—?'

'Was it your baby, Russell?'

'My baby?' said Russell, the initial shock morphing into rage, a swollen torrent of contempt rushing to the surface. 'Fuckin' oath it was my baby. Why would you—?'

'We have information suggesting Tracey had problems conceiving.'

'How . . . ?'

'From speaking to your doctor.'

'Is he allowed to tell you that?' said Russell.

'Is it true?'

Russell took a deep breath. Exhaling slowly, his head lolling forward, allowing his shoulders to sag.

'We tried for years. Nothing.' He raised his head. There was an unbound sadness in his eyes. Beaten. 'So, she was actually pregnant? Finally?' He shook his head, eyes squeezed shut.

It was the same bittersweet tone that Kennard had encountered the first time he had met Russell, slumped by the police barricade. He glanced at Layton. Russell had started sobbing; the confession was coming, he could sense it.

'Do you think . . . ' said Russell, his tears dying down, letting loose a wet sniff. 'Do you think she might have told the real father? If it wasn't mine? What if she told him and he didn't want it? He got angry and killed her?'

'You might have got angry when she told you it wasn't yours,' said Layton. 'There've been anger issues in the marriage before, haven't there?'

Russell's eyes flicked between the two of them. Another deep breath. 'Sometimes. The last year, the last few years, were hard, no getting away from it. But I loved her. I still love her.'

'Were you ever violent with your wife, Mr Hilmeyer?' asked Layton.

'We were violent with each other.'

'In what way?'

'Words mostly.'

'So sometimes it became physical?'

'A few drunken arguments.'

'Which turned violent?'

224

INTO THE FLAMES

'You're trying to twist my words, Detective.'

'I'm just looking for the truth. If you hit her, just tell me.'

'No, I didn't hit her. Sometimes she would get so fed up that she would swing for me. Most of the time I could block her punches. But it would leave bruises on her arms and hands. Then I guess she could tell whatever story she wanted.'

'So, you're saying she lied to people?'

'I don't know. Losing the gallery knocked her.'

'So what happened on Tuesday night? When you killed her?' asked Kennard.

'*I didn't kill her*,' shouted Russell, eyes fixed on Kennard. Neither backed down.

'So, who did?' asked Layton.

Russell turned towards her, allowing Kennard to blink, his eyes dry from the heat and the pressure. 'I don't know. That's your job. Find out who killed my Trace.'

It was an impassioned plea, but one that did not strike a chord with Kennard. Or, from the dispassionate look on her face, with Layton.

Kennard looked at her and nodded over his shoulder. They got up to leave the room.

'You didn't tell me how she was murdered?' said Russell.

Kennard turned back. 'You're right,' he said. 'I didn't.'

Thirty-Five

Kennard stood outside the interview room with Layton.

'Nothing concrete,' she said. 'Are you buying the tears?'

'He's holding out on something. Let's hit him with these,' said Kennard, holding out the small white bottle of Codoxamol.

'Where did that come from?'

'Russell Hilmeyer's pocket. In the pub. When the table spilled.'

A fresh cup of crap coffee in hand, they re-entered the room.

Russell was alert in his chair, eyes wide. 'Are you going to tell me how Trace died?'

'We're not at liberty to divulge that,' said Layton.

'You can't . . .'

'Can't what, Mr Hilmeyer?'

'Can't not tell me.'

'I'm afraid we can. It's an ongoing investigation.'

'But if you want to talk, we can talk about these,' said Kennard, putting the Codoxamol carefully on the table.

Russell closed his eyes and breathed deeply, looking guilty to his core.

'What can you tell us about these, Mr Hilmeyer? This is pretty strong stuff. We know Tracey was taking it too. Life had got on top of her, there's no shame in it.' Russell's jaw twitched. He was eager to speak. Kennard kept pressing. 'Everyone needs support sometimes.'

'They're for my knee,' Russell said, through gritted teeth. 'It's always there. The pain. The reminder of what I could have had. Of what I could have been.'

He looked at the table and shook his head. Ashamed of the crutch that he had. The painkillers he needed to cope with life.

'What do you mean?' asked Kennard. He glanced at Layton and wondered if that had been a confession in a roundabout way.

'Just that I couldn't live up to my promise of giving her the life she wanted. We were close for a while. She had the gallery. I had, well, not much, but enough so that we could live.'

'And after she lost the gallery, she blamed you for it all going wrong?'

Russell shook his head. 'No, I don't think so. She was just disappointed. Staring every day at what could have been. Life, it grinds you down. Like this town. You can throw a lick of paint on it but it's still the same shit-heap in the mountains. Besides, Tracey wouldn't use Codo. They're too strong.'

'You said she was high a lot of the time.'

'Not high, just confused.'

227

'We found the same bottles in her car.'

Russell looked confused. 'You did?'

Kennard pressed on. 'Where did you get them, Russell?'

'The doctor.'

'That's not the truth, is it? Never mind that these have expired,' said Kennard, holding up the bottle. 'Did Tracey supply you, or did you supply Tracey?'

Russell looked at Kennard, sighing and shaking his head. 'He said he could get them cheap.'

Kennard looked at Layton. 'Who said? Devon King? Kingsley Musa?'

'I don't want to . . .'

'Who supplied them, Mr Hilmeyer?'

'There wasn't one single supplier. Just the right price. Hash, anti-anxiety, antidepressants, uppers sometimes.'

'Who supplied the pills, Mr Hilmeyer?' Kennard asked again, more forcefully this time, looking to break through Russell's reluctance.

'A friend of mine. In Sydney.'

'Does this friend have a name?'

'He does. He also has a bad temper. And bad associates.'

'It doesn't look good that you aren't telling us.'

'It doesn't look good getting beaten up either.'

'We can protect you.'

Russell laughed loudly, sarcastically.

Layton jumped in. 'Where did the money come from? For this Codo?'

Russell glanced down, then back up to meet her stare. 'It just did.'

'We heard that you've been missing some shifts recently.

That you were asking around for money for a project. What project was that?'

Russell rubbed his face. He looked pressured. As if the answers to a million different questions were swirling around his head. 'That? It was a stupid idea, that's all.'

'What was?'

'The farm idea.'

Kennard and Layton waited for him to continue.

'I thought that if Alvin and Karen could make a go of it, then maybe I could too. I'm a good worker. Ask anyone. And you don't need have to have qualifications to be a farmer, just dedication. But I needed the money to start.'

'You were thinking of rearing animals? On Tracey's land?' asked Kennard.

Russell nodded. 'But I was keeping it quiet.'

'Why?'

'For one, in case they laughed.'

'And why would they laugh?'

'I was scared that people would just say that I was being stupid. But I know I could make it work.'

'Okay. What were the other reasons you kept it quiet?'

Russell squeezed his eyes tight. 'In case Karen tried something.'

'Like what?' asked Layton, frowning. 'Telling her sister?'

'No,' said Russell. 'If anything, that would have only spurred Trace on. I mean she might try something like poisoning the ground. They've loaded shit onto Trace's land before and let it rot. Animal carcasses, waste, old machinery, like it's their personal dumping ground. I think the plan was to keep it rotten enough so that Trace couldn't sell it. Not that it matters now anyway.'

'What do you mean?'

'With Trace gone, Karen will get the farm. She'll own it all.' Russell sniffed a laugh rife with bitterness. 'Trace would have hated that. Karen will inherit the land and the house. So, bang goes any financial trouble they might have had. She gets everything and, given this change in wind, it looks like I'll be homeless.'

Thirty-Six

Russell slumped after that outburst, his energy gone. The realization that he was going to lose everything – his wife, his house, his town. All in one day.

Kennard looked at Layton, who called the interview to a close. He went to the toilet, then joined her at her temporary desk. He could feel his energy levels flagging too. A long day, stressful to the extreme.

'What do you think?' he asked. 'He looked shocked that Tracey was on Codo.'

'If it's true. He might be fobbing us off.'

'And this quest to become a farmer?'

'The land was Tracey's so with some capital it's

231

possible. But the accusations that Karen was dumping stuff?'

'We know Tracey made some welfare complaints in the past few years, so it could be feasible. Anything on the whereabouts of Christophe Stoltz?'

Layton nodded towards the computer screen. 'No sighting as yet.'

There was a pause.

'What do we do now?' asked Layton.

'My advice?' said Kennard. 'Get some rest. It might be a long day tomorrow. We'll see what crops up by morning.'

Kennard tried to take his own advice and get some sleep. Again, he couldn't, the backseat of his Passat particularly uncomfortable, his days of sleeping in it at festivals or outside bars long gone. By five in the morning, he had made his way back to the station again and snaffled a spot on a wooden bench behind the reception desk.

After another hour of being unable to doze off, hunger caused him to raid the vending machine by the main door for a packet of prawn cocktail crisps and two chocolate bars. He headed outside, smoothing back his ruffled hair in the dark reflection of the window. He looked how he felt. Like shit.

He sat on the step and stared at the ominous pulse in the distance. Rislake was waking up to twin balls of fire trying to inch over the horizon and a welcome chill in the early morning air. He hoped it would last.

Thirty-Seven

January 21 – 06.04 – Wind direction NE – Surface speed 20km/h

23 hours since North Rislake evacuation

South Rislake status = Amber/Red (Evacuation imminent)

Kennard had finished the crisps and was halfway through the first chocolate bar when his phone rang. Layton.

'Where are you?'

'Enjoying the sunrise.'

'That's nice,' she said sarcastically. 'Might want to get back in here, though. Parramatta picked up Stoltz.'

Inside, he found her at her desk. In the same clothes, with the same weary look on her face. The loyal bloodhound. The life of a detective wasn't all car chases and heart-racing thrills, except for those rare moments when you had to process murder scenes in the middle of a bushfire.

'Get any sleep?' he asked.

'About as much as you, it looks like.'

Kennard sighed. It was too early in the morning to even attempt a joke.

Layton continued. 'He was picked up coming back to his apartment about an hour ago.'

'An hour? Why didn't they tell us?'

Layton held up her phone. 'They did. Comms blackout. Message only came through now.'

'So, are we going to question him?' asked Kennard. Parramatta station would be a quick sixty minutes at this time of the morning.

'They already have.'

'Who?'

'Applegate and Lam.'

Ken Applegate and April Lam. A pair of DSs Kennard knew well. Experienced enough to smell bullshit.

'Okay, so what did Stoltz tell us?'

'See for yourself.'

Layton clicked a button and video and audio feed from the interview room started to play on the screen. It was the usual greyscale, fuzzy rubbish but clear enough for Kennard to make out a guy in his late twenties with a heavy build, his black – or dark grey – T-shirt almost bursting at the seams.

The monotone voice of Ken Applegate was running through the standard preamble; names, ranks, time and place.

'Get to the good stuff,' Kennard said.

Layton forwarded the video to just before the

four-minute mark. Stoltz's voice came through the speakers, more high-pitched than his build implied.

'. . . coffee would be good.'

Ken Applegate's very hairy hand pushed a photo across the table.

'For the record, I've passed Mr Stoltz a photograph. Do you know this person, Mr Stoltz?'

Stoltz tilted his head forward and seemed to study the photo. He looked up.

'Yeah.'

'Who is it?'

'Guy called Russell.'

'You have a surname?'

'Stoltz,' said Stoltz with a grin. It lasted only a brief second. He had misread the room. 'Hilmeyer, I think he said.'

'How do you know him?' asked April Lam, in her languid style.

'Seen him around.'

'Can you tell us where you have seen him around?'

Stoltz shrugged, playing for time. Wondering what the police had. Kennard recognized the tactic. Provide as little information as possible. There was no concern in his answers or posture. He had clearly been questioned under caution before.

'We've been told that you two worked together.'

There was a slight tilt of Stoltz's head, enough for the DS to keep pressing.

'For a guy called Devon King.'

There was more than a slight tilt of the head this time. Stoltz glanced off to the side at Applegate. Worried now. Secrets being revealed.

'I might have done some work with the guy.'

'With Russell?'

'Yeah.'

'When?'

'About ten days ago, then again last Thursday ... and this Tuesday.'

'When on Tuesday?' asked Lam.

'Why you asking?'

'That's our concern.'

Stoltz paused. 'Evening.'

'Times?'

Stoltz shrugged his shoulders. 'I'd say from seven 'til midnight. Maybe a bit after.'

'Doing what?'

'Couriering.'

This was obviously the default position should they be questioned.

'Couriering what?'

'Am I under arrest?'

At this, April Lam looked at Ken Applegate.

Stoltz settled back in his chair, relaxing into it. 'If you're asking me if I know this guy and where he was on Tuesday night then, yeah, he was with me. We couriered a package from Meadowbank to Liverpool. Don't know what it was and don't care.' He flicked his eyes to the interviewing officers. 'We done?'

They were. Lam ended the interview.

'So, Russell has an alibi for Tuesday night,' said Layton, stopping the video.

'His second alibi,' reminded Kennard. Stoltz's vagueness

and his relative comfort in the interview frustrated him. Lam and Applegate had asked the right questions but didn't have any leverage.

'Is he still in custody?' asked Kennard.

'No. There was nothing to hold him on. So, what now? Rule Russell out?'

'I don't think we can rule him out. Stoltz might be lying.'

'Which we can't prove.'

'For now.'

Layton sighed. 'You might not like it, Kennard – I might not like it – but the man has an alibi.'

Kennard didn't buy her plea. 'Let's hold him. For now.'

Thirty-Eight

'For now' only lasted a couple of minutes, the duration of a phone call from an incensed DSS Haskell.

'I thought I told you not to arrest him!'

Kennard spoke up. 'We didn't. We took him in for questioning.'

'Don't play semantics with me, DS Kennard.'

'It was my call—'

'Our call,' interrupted Layton.

'I don't care who made the call. A wrong call is a wrong call.'

'We had reason to believe—' started Kennard.

'Tell me those reasons,' said Haskell.

Kennard explained about the phone, the pregnancy, the painkillers.

'So, circumstantial at best. No witnesses to Russell Hilmeyer being there at the time of the murder. No insurance motive, no demonstrable reason to kill his wife.'

'His phone pinged in the area on Tuesday night,' said Layton.

'He gave you a plausible explanation for the phone.'

'But she was pregnant. And if it wasn't his, he might have been angry enough to do something stupid.'

Though Kennard and Layton fought their corner, Haskell was right; everything they'd found was still circumstantial. Kennard knew it. And so did his boss.

'I don't want to hear any more. Russell Hilmeyer has an alibi. We have nothing to hold him on. I have an irate Fire Commissioner and union rep on the phone wanting to know why we're obstructing firefighters from tackling this blaze. No doubt the press will latch onto it too. Release him immediately. And apologize to him. The man's just lost his wife, for Christ's sake. And after this all dies down, I'll be expecting a report. From both of you.'

Haskell hung up. Kennard stared at his partner, both of them drawing in a breath, recovering from the bollocking.

'That settles that,' said Layton.

'Does it?' Kennard didn't think that it settled anything, but it wasn't an order he could flout without inviting more trouble.

'She's right, Kennard,' said Layton. 'I can't say I'd build a house with the soundness of the alibi, but what else do we really have?'

Kennard gritted his teeth. He wanted to throw his phone across the room. Haskell was being sensible. Layton was being sensible. And worse, they were right.

'Both Stoltz and Hilmeyer won't say what exactly they were couriering for Devon King,' he said eventually. 'Russell might not be guilty of his wife's murder, but it's pretty clear he is guilty of something.'

'Look, I agree with you,' said Layton. 'But right now, unless it's murder, I don't think Haskell wants to hear it.'

Russell Hilmeyer looked as badly rested as Kennard felt, but he had the excuse of a hangover and the death of his wife. Despite that, Kennard was finding it hard to feel any sympathy for him, his suspicion lodged deep in his gut, refusing to budge.

He confronted Russell just outside the station, the morning chill waning, allowing the heat to return even though the sun was still masked in a smoky haze.

'Where are you off to now?' he asked.

'I didn't know that I had to inform you of my movements.'

'Only because we've had a hard time pinning them down.'

The edges of a grin appeared on Russell's face, though his tone carried more sympathy than malice. 'I'm sorry for you, Detective. I hope you do find the right person. For Tracey's sake. For my sake.'

Kennard bit his tongue.

'But if you really want to know, I'm going back out there.' Russell pointed towards the widening front of smoke and flame in the distance. 'It's my job. You do yours and I'll do mine.'

As Russell Hilmeyer left the police station a free man, Kennard felt Layton tap his arm.

'Let it go,' she whispered. 'We have enough to do.'

Kennard turned away from her. He wanted to punch something right now. Something that wouldn't get him into trouble. In the end, the already dented ashtray out the front bore the brunt of his frustration.

'Better?'

He shrugged. Nothing but locking Tracey's killer up would make him feel better.

'We'll keep chipping away,' said Layton. 'There are other angles we need to check.'

As he watched Russell slope away, Kennard tried to will himself not to focus on him. He knew he needed to keep an open mind.

'Kennard?'

He pulled his eyes back to Layton.

'We need to check out Tracey's sister, Karen. She has a motive given the animal cruelty complaints and the joint ownership of the farm. Plus, given the argument the neighbours heard on Tuesday night, the argument Tony Steyn witnessed and the fact that the house on Caldicott wasn't broken into, we have to accept the possibility, even probability, that Tracey knew her killer. Which means Karen is in the frame.'

'I'll check out the complaints,' said Kennard. It would at least get his mind off the stink of failure for a while.

'And Kennard?'

'What?'

'Don't go and do something stupid.'

'There's nothing stupid about catching a killer.'

'There is if you catch the wrong one.'

Thirty-Nine

A quick search located the government department concerned with the treatment of animals, the DPI, the Department of Primary Industries, which to Kennard sounded like a front for something more sinister. Its primary industry was death after all. The webpage explained that their work covered Fishing, Hunting, Animals, Forestry as well as Climate and Emergencies, which felt appropriate given that Rislake was presently burning to the ground. There was also a section on Animal Welfare and complaints.

Amusingly, for Kennard at least, the government webpage immediately passed the buck onto other agencies, stating that the officers of their department did not have the powers to enforce complaints in this area.

One of the three agencies he was directed to contact was the NSW Police, but a search of the internal systems found nothing of use. The other two avenues were the RSPCA and the Animal Welfare League: both groups reliant on donations and volunteers. It seemed that the welfare of animals was down at the bottom of the list of government priorities, fobbed off to agencies who relied on charities to get the job done.

Kennard called the RSPCA. The automated message informed him that the office wasn't open, so he hung up and tried the Animal Welfare League. He got straight through.

'Yeah, mate?'

The greeting wasn't trained, the accent ocker through and through, rough and curt but not, in this case, confrontational.

'I'm Detective Kennard based out of ...' Kennard was about to say Glebe – old habits die hard – but he stopped himself. '... Katoomba.'

'A copper, eh? Finally, these early starts pay off! What can we do for ya?'

The tone perked up. This man, in his twenties if Kennard had to guess, seemed genuinely happy, as if sensing something dramatic about to happen.

'I'm looking for some info on a complaint.'

'Got any de'ails?'

'The subject of the complaint would have been Karen Lautahahi.'

'Okay ... 'Strine?'

'Yeah, Aussie. Fijian surname though.'

'Bingo! I have a complaint made against a Karen and Alvin Lautahahi.'

'Made by?'

'Can you confirm their address? Plus, I need your badge number and date of birth.'

'Why?'

243

'Security. We get all sorta bogans phone up and try and find out who's been dobbing them in.'

'Right.'

Kennard gave him the details. Stating his date of birth out loud made him feel old. The 80s was Chernobyl and *Challenger*. It was Bob Hawke and Malcom Fraser, First Nation Rights and the Berlin Wall. There was more frantic typing in the background.

'So, can you tell me?' asked Kennard.

'Keep your hair on, grandad.' It was the first sign of impatience, but was said without malice. 'Just confirming creds with your buddies.'

Kennard had no idea how long that would take. Too long.

'Do I ring you back?' he asked, getting impatient himself.

'Nah, these checks are usually quick.'

There was a pause.

'You up at the bushfire, then?' asked the operator. Kennard was looking for answers, not small talk, but guessed that he was bored or lonely, probably stuck in an office alone, firing balls of paper at a rubbish bin.

'How did you know?'

'Got the address here, haven't I?'

'Yeah,' said Kennard, wondering who he needed to speak to next. It was 6.31am now, according to the clock on the wall.

'How bad is it? I was in the middle of one about three years ago out in Wollemi. Me and some mates chased through the middle in my mate's ute. It was crazy. The flames, the heat, the sparks. And worse . . . the beer went flat.' He laughed.

'I've never experienced anything like it,' said Kennard, praying for someone in HQ to get their arse in gear and get a confirmation back to this guy.

'One-time thing,' said the operator. 'Wouldn't try that shit again. Ah, goodo.'

'What is it?'

'You've got the nod. Detective Sergeant Alex Kennard, born . . . blah, blah, blah, a long time ago. What do you need to know, Detective?'

'Everything about the report.'

'I have two. First complaint was lodged in April last year. A TF-4 regarding animal welfare on a farm in Poolmaroo run by Karen and Alvin Lautahahi.'

'What was done with it?'

'Uh . . . it was classed as urgent, so an inspector was sent out the following day. Seems like it wasn't technically an urgent case. We get that oft'n. People so worked up about the state of the animals that they over-egg it. To be honest, mate, it's what you have to do to get anyone off their arse and out investigating. Just in case you need it sometime.'

'Thanks,' said Kennard. 'What was the outcome?'

The guy whistled a mindless tune as he typed. 'There's a comment about the general wear and tear of the farm. Buildings and gates needing to be repaired, a pen to be enlarged, a couple of fences to neighbouring land made more secure. Some questionable practices as to the welfare of the animals.' The operator paused. Then laughed.

'What is it?' asked Kennard.

'Got a note at the end. The woman, Karen Lautahahi, attempted to assault the inspector. Not surprised.'

'Why's that?'

'It was Dazzler Durke. He probably tried to hit on her, fucking slimebag. Anyway, it was checked again in August, and it passed.'

'Would it have cost a lot? To sort out those issues?'

'Yeah, I'd say. Time and money. Two things we're all short of.'

Kennard thought it was probably an unwelcome expense for a farm that was scraping by.

'And the second complaint?'

'December. Just before Christmas.'

'From the same complainant?'

'Yeah. A Tracey Hilmeyer of 148 Caldicott Road, Rislake, in the good old NS of W.'

Much as Kennard expected. Both complaints were made by Tracey, both having more to do with the feud with her sister than the welfare of the animals.

'Another TF-4. Another urgent welfare complaint. Recommendations were made along much the same lines but focusing more on fences onto adjoining land. It's due to be followed up in May. Anything else?'

'No, that's all. Thanks—'

'You need anything else from here, ask for Kev-o. I'm on 'til lunch.'

Kev-o seemed keen to keep the conversation going, but Kennard had business to attend to. To find out what these complaints meant to the family and the farm. The real cost. The real impact. It was obvious that there was

no love lost between the sisters, but this particular spite-
fulness had financial implications. And could have been
a real motive.

'Will do, Kev-o. Thanks.'

Kennard hung up before the young man could say anything else.

Forty

January 21 – 06.49 – Wind direction NE – Surface speed 19km/h

24 hours since North Rislake evacuation

South Rislake status = Amber/Red (Evacuation imminent)

Kennard left the window down in the car, the fading chill of the morning air keeping him awake. He should have rested more last night. He needed to pace himself. He was not a young man anymore, as several people, including Kev-o, apparently liked to keep pointing out.

Layton was sitting beside him, her fingers discordantly tapping on the dashboard, not used to being a passenger.

He drove parallel to the glow from the other side of town, the sun peeking over the horizon to compete with its temporary rival.

As he pulled up at the farm in Poolmaroo, he could see there was already movement. Alvin was letting the animals out of the shed at the front and into a small enclosure with patchy grass, shouting at them to move in his soft and almost lulling Pacific Islander-affected Australian. As they got out of the car, Alvin quickly disappeared off behind the sheds after the animals.

The oldest kid was peeking out the front door.

'Is your mum in?' asked Kennard as they approached.

The kid bolted, letting the screen door shut with a rattle behind him.

Kennard knocked on it. Karen appeared at the door dressed in worn dungarees. The washed-out look on her face disappeared immediately, replaced by anxiety.

'You two again?'

'Can we come in?'

'As long as you don't mind getting an earful from a bunch of sleep-deprived kids.'

Kennard followed her inside. The youngest child was lying on the battered old sofa crying her eyes out. The one who had bolted from the door was now playing in the back hallway with a makeshift plane bolted together from pieces of wood. The middle child was absent.

'Rough night?' asked Kennard, as he met Karen in the kitchen clearing away the breakfast dishes. Cardboard boxes were stacked by the door. Packed and ready to leave in a hurry.

'Nightmares about the fire.'

'Yeah, poor kids,' said Layton.

'No. I was the one having nightmares. One change in the wind ...' said Karen, before dropping the subject, bringing some plates to the sink. 'Anyway, what are you doing back here? I don't know anything else about my sister that might help.'

'We wanted to talk to you about some animal welfare complaints.'

The plates dropped with a crash into the soapy water. She turned slowly. The sourness in her expression had the power to curdle milk.

'Why? That shit's all sorted. We've had that lot here twice. Did everything they asked. Repaired the fences and sheds. Installed gates that met their regulations. It cost us a lot of money. Money we don't have. And our reputation. Having those lot out here snooping around. Accusations that hurt our livelihood.'

'Hurt their livelihood too,' said Kennard.

Karen flicked her tongue over her teeth, the edge of her lip curled upwards, the sneer fading away just as quickly as it arrived.

'I barely touched him. Now, I know they have to come out and tick their boxes and all that sheep dung, so I'm not getting at them. It's the person who made the calls that knots my gut.'

'And you know who that was?'

'I can guess,' said Karen coldly, throwing the remains of a half-eaten breakfast into a black bucket.

'Did you confront them?' asked Layton.

'Yeah, too bloody right I did.'

'And what did they say?'

'You mean, my sister?'

Layton said nothing.

'She didn't deny it. She had the gall to tell me that

someone needed to look after the place. As if we aren't. She hasn't lifted a finger to help out in nearly fifteen years! Anyway, I don't have to worry about more complaints now she's dead.' Karen lifted the bucket up to leave. 'You got any more questions?'

'I'd like to ask your husband a couple,' said Kennard.

Karen's nostrils flared. 'You can try. He dislikes you lot even more than I do. I'll call him.'

With that Karen kicked open the back door and exited in a hurry, as if wanting to get to Alvin before Kennard and Layton did.

'There's no need. I'll find—' Kennard called after her, listening to her yell out for her husband.

As he stepped onto the bare patch of earth that was their backyard, he found himself surrounded by chickens, Karen layering the remains of the breakfast over the ground behind her for them to peck at and forcing him and Layton to step carefully.

'Best you both stay here,' Karen said. 'Don't want you wandering off and disappearing. Don't need more plods here.'

Wading his way through the gobbling mass of birds, Kennard aimed for the barn that he had seen Alvin duck behind earlier.

A few steps ahead of him Karen was still calling out for her husband. Kennard could sense something in the increasing pitch of her voice, desperation or annoyance that Alvin wasn't responding.

As he crossed the driveway towards the barns, Karen paused in front of them, bucket in hand.

'We can find our way around, Mrs Lautahahi,' said Layton.

Karen was now blocking them from going any further. 'You'd need a warrant for that for starters, Detective. But more than that, I don't want you lot spooking the animals. They don't take kindly to strangers.'

'Is there something that you don't want us to see?'

'What is it, *wati*?' Alvin appeared from a small alley between the two barns, spade in hand. He looked at his wife first and then at Kennard, suspicion rolling off him as freely as the sweat. It was still early in the morning, but Alvin had clearly been toiling away.

'The detectives have some questions for you,' said Karen, moving to stand beside her husband.

'Done a full day's work already, Mr Lautahahi?' asked Kennard.

'It's Alvin.' Alvin's face remained stony, only the deep brown eyes moving, flicking towards his wife, as if wordlessly asking her what was going on.

When she didn't say anything, he continued, 'There's always lots to do. It is a farm, Detective, and not good farming land. For animals anyway.' He kept his sentences short, like witnesses were coached to do on the stand. Keep replies brief and to the point. Allow no wiggle room.

'And what are you up to this morning?'

Alvin's eyes again flicked towards his wife, a slight panic in them. Kennard could see that he didn't want to make a mistake. Maybe he had made a mistake back when the inspectors had come around. Said something that he shouldn't have which cost them dearly, and now he had been coached to be ultra-cautious with authority.

'Work. The animals. We have to take them indoors at night because of the fire. They get scared. During the day we have to watch them.'

'A full-time job,' said Kennard. 'How many do you have?'

'Twenty-two cattle, thirty-four sheep, seventy-five chickens and two goats.'

'And three children,' added Karen, drawing a nod from her husband.

'What did you think of your wife's sister, Tracey?' asked Kennard.

'He didn't know her as—' said Karen.

'Please let him answer, Mrs Lautahahi,' said Layton.

Alvin's eyes ran off to the mid-distance as if trying to remember. Or forget. 'Tracey was . . .' He backed away a little.

'Mr Lautahahi . . . Alvin?'

Alvin took another step back, his youthful, full-bodied face creased into wrinkles, struggling with something. Maybe something he had done.

'Where are you going, Alvin?' asked Kennard.

'You're upsetting him,' cried Tracey, grabbing for her husband's arm, trying to catch up with him. Alvin had turned his back and moved off through the space between the sheds, purpose in his stride.

Kennard was left to follow again.

Forty-One

Alvin stopped at the other side of the sheds. Kennard stopped too, Layton beside him. His attention was drawn to the patch of scrub ground behind the sheds, old machinery rusting slowly, empty fertilizer bags stabbed onto an upturned fork, discarded tyres and some red jerrycans. There was a black patch of earth that looked recently burnt and an area of disturbed soil. No direct sunlight reached it due to the sheds and the overhanging scrub, so he assumed it wasn't a vegetable patch.

'A stray ember?' asked Kennard, pointing to the burnt patch.

Alvin turned. He looked confused. As if it was the first time he had seen it.

'I didn't mean to do it,' said Alvin, his doleful eyes searching his wife's face for affirmation.

Kennard felt his whole body tense, his heart suddenly pounding in his chest, getting ready for action. How was he going to subdue Alvin? And Karen? The whole world closed in, two on two.

'Did you kill her?' asked Layton, Alvin's words putting

her on edge too. Her focus remained on the big guy, her hand edging to her side and her firearm, slow and steady, though Kennard could see it tremble slightly in anticipation.

Alvin shook his head. Once only, hard, as if he had been struck. 'Kill her? No.' He dropped his head. 'I took her money,' he said, looking towards his wife. Karen was staring open-mouthed at him. 'It was only thirty bucks and we needed to pay for the feed and—'

'You should have told me!' she barked.

'I wanted to but—'

'We don't take money from her. Not after what she's done.'

Karen took a step towards her husband. He flinched a little as she did.

'She only wanted a photo, *wati*. It was only a photo.'

Karen shook her head. 'I told you not to get involved with her,' she said, turning to Kennard and Layton. 'She's like a tiger snake. Sleek and pretty but you don't want to get too close.'

'That could be said about you too, Mrs Lautahahi,' said Kennard.

'Only when threatened,' sneered Karen.

'And did Tracey threaten you? With the complaints, with the photos of your husband? What did you do when you found out about the photo?'

'*Do*? Nothing.'

'You did go to the souvenir shop.'

'Yeah, but I didn't kill her. Why would we kill her?'

'Because of the photo. Because of the complaints. Not

JAMES DELARGY

just the first one, which cost you money and your reputation, but the second. You felt like she was spiting you.'

'Spiting us? No. We're used to it. She was always spiting us, as you put it.' Karen reached her hand up to her husband's broad shoulder to calm him. 'You know she even had a lodger move in with us at one stage. Into her half of the house. Russell said they needed the money, but Tracey didn't care what we thought or that we did all the maintenance on the place. She didn't even care who the lodger was or that she had allowed a complete stranger into a house with three kids. Her own nieces and nephew. *That* was spiteful. It was dangerous.'

'Did anything happen?'

'No, we made sure of that,' said Karen, openly hostile now. 'He moved out within two months. The kids and the animals drove him mad.'

It was certainly a shitty thing for Tracey to do, if true. But Kennard wondered if Karen was putting her hatred of Tracey out there in the open to mask what she did.

'And your sister never rented it out again?'

'No. But I think she meant it as a statement, you know? That even though she wasn't living here, she was still in control.'

Another, much younger voice interrupted them. 'Mum, Ke'ana is trying to put a coat hanger into the plug socket again.' Kennard turned to see the middle kid peeking out from the alley, hugging the wall of the barn for safety.

Karen broke off contact with Alvin and quickly made her way towards the house. Kennard glanced at Layton, who followed her, leaving Kennard alone with Alvin.

His mobile buzzed. He considered ignoring it, but last time he had missed Lenka's call. It might even have been Ann, awake and wanting to say good morning.

It wasn't Ann, but HQ. He answered.

It was the English woman again. She informed him that they'd run the tests on the gym equipment taken from the Hilmeyer house. All clean aside from sweat residue belonging to both Tracey and Russell Hilmeyer. No murder weapon amongst them. It was a blow. And she had another lined up. Checks on the souvenir shop found no hint that it was being used as a front to sell drugs of any description. There were a couple of reports regarding shoplifting but those had been two and four years ago respectively and bore no relation to the case. Tourists wanting a shitty souvenir without being out of pocket.

'Thanks, Constable.' He hung up before having to say a name. Another busted line of enquiry. The day already felt like an uphill battle.

Kennard shoved the phone back into his pocket. He looked up. Alvin was gone, a single stray chook pecking at the ground.

The photo, the money, the complaints and the fact that Tracey had rented half of the house to a stranger gave Karen and Alvin plenty of motive. And if they had gotten wind that Tracey was going to sell her half to feed her habit like Russell had said, it would have been a major issue for them, since they obviously didn't have the money to buy her half and were using Tracey's land to feed their own animals. Which had led to the complaints and having to erect better fencing and gates between the fields. But was that enough to kill? Or had the photo sent Karen over the top? Had she felt threatened that Tracey might steal her man? Karen's temper was well, and officially, documented. And Alvin couldn't be ruled out – strong, single-minded and willing to protect his family.

Tracey had left behind a mass of questions. Like so many dead bodies, whose last acts on earth were to leave conundrums for the living to solve.

Kennard sat down on a stack of used bricks and rubbed his face. Sweat trickled down his forehead, the temperature increasing as the wind swept the hot air towards them. A richer scent lingered on the breeze, deeper than the sweet, pleasant smell of burning eucalyptus. It reminded him of charcoal. Maybe the twist in the wind was causing the fire to burn a section it had already charred. It reminded him of the barbie last week.

Forty-Two

Katoomba – One week ago

It was a chance to try out the new barbie that he had installed himself, the brickwork done via a YouTube instruction manual, the grill sitting proudly on top with enough space to cook ten steaks and various accoutrements.

Most of the team were there. Hoskins with his kin, Sancho and Crookshank on a boys' outing, their families ditched for the day. Sarah DePaul was with her new boy-friend, a man who looked nervous to be around this many cops, as if this was some kind of elaborate sting operation to catch him having one too many beers.

A few people had failed to show. Georgina Layton had cried off with a personal matter that Kennard hadn't questioned. He hadn't expected her to come. She was all snappy dressing and onward progression. Letting her hair down might have revealed her fun side. And a fun side was not how you progressed in the force.

That was certainly what DSS Una Haskell seemed to espouse. She was another non-attendee, no reason given. Kennard guessed she didn't want to get down and dirty with her underlings for fear of being seen as human.

Last to show was the man Kennard expected would turn up last, Simon Uptill. Uptill had a way of making himself the centre of everything, believing he was God's gift. He had been the one least pleased by Kennard's arrival in Katoomba. A cop from the city swanning in to challenge him for his spot as head honcho by mere virtue of past achievements. As such, he revelled in any attempt to shoot Kennard down, trying to make the newcomer's life a misery. He needn't have bothered. Kennard was adept enough at that himself.

He continued to slowly cook the meat, half-concentrating on the conversation around him. Until the topic of the recent Mendelsohn exposé came up.

The exposé had come out in the *Morning Herald* the week before. Teresa Mendelsohn, a reporter of some renown – awards, TV and column inches – had alleged that a few days before, she had been led by an unnamed source to a container in a rundown dock on the north bank of the Parramatta River. Inside, she claimed, with photographic evidence to back it up, were the remnants of a massive shipment of illegal drugs that had been recently smuggled into the country. Which would have been a massive story in itself, but Mendelsohn, in her typical abrasive style, had gone on to claim that the police – or at least, some members of the police – had been aware of this shipment and had looked the other way. More than that, she alleged that members of the force had given their blessing to it. Not only were the police failing to do their duty in protecting the public, but they were actively profiting off insider knowledge of lucrative crimes.

It had been a bombshell report that had rippled across countless broadsheets and TV channels, gripping the public's attention.

The NSW Police Commissioner had stated that the allegations would be looked into and if something was uncovered, they would perform a full and transparent investigation. Mendelsohn wanted answers immediately. So did many others. She called for a full public inquiry, saying this was at the very least a case of failed policing and at worst an example of serious corruption and profiteering. Even if it turned out that the police were only looking the other way, it was still a scandal. And, as Mendelsohn was quick to point out in subsequent interviews, if it had happened once, who was to say how many times it had happened before? She had tossed the grenade into the room and waited to document the aftermath.

At first Kennard merely listened to the conversation batting back and forth, focusing on the food.

'I think it's clear-cut,' said Uptill, tipping a bottle of beer into his mouth. He had quickly relaxed into his setting, leaning back on the fold-up seat with his arms stretched over the two beside him.

'I don't think we can say that yet,' said Ann, glancing over at Kennard. Though the Sydney police had kicked him out, she knew that he still felt a loyalty to them. Thirteen years' worth.

Kennard drew his eyes away quickly and nudged the sausages further to the right, down the temperature scale. They were almost done. The burgers too. The corn on the cob would need a few more minutes. Ann had insisted on having it as the token vegetable. Making the meat healthier by its sheer presence.

He had read the piece in the *Herald* and had tuned into the hour-long interview on Channel 9 about it. Both the case and Mendelsohn herself were compelling, but Kennard had questions about the tip-off and the evidence she had produced.

Uptill leaned forward as if about to deliver the meaning of life. Up himself as usual. 'It's all there. Black and white.'

'So why isn't anyone doing anything about it?' asked DePaul's new squeeze tentatively.

Uptill shrugged his shoulders. A your-guess-is-as-good-as-mine shrug.

'They need to corroborate the evidence,' said Kennard, unable to resist grabbing the bait.

'She isn't going to just lay it all out on TV, is she, Kenny?' said Uptill. 'There are book deals and podcasts and—'

'The only concrete evidence is that the building was indeed being used to smuggle in contraband. But when and who was using it hasn't been explained. So far, she's just made some vague references to police and backhanders.'

'It has your old boss worried.'

'Everything has him worried.' For all his loyalty, Kennard didn't think much of Gosforth. He was a weak man who had weaselled his way up to the rank of Commissioner.

'How do you explain the lack of cameras in and around the building? Removed apparently. There used to be regular police patrols in the area but those were suddenly stopped six months ago.'

'And you think that's on purpose?'

'It looks suspicious.'

'And you don't think it's possible the place might have been chosen by the smugglers *after* the patrols were stopped, not before? Criminals are more likely to take advantage of situations rather than actively create them. You've done some policework in your life, surely? Or at least so I'm told,' said Kennard, the sizzle from the grill matching his growing temper.

'Mate, in the past it was common, wasn't it? Efforts made to ensure a lack of eyes at a scene.'

'Wood Royal was nearly twenty-five years ago.'

'Still happened, though, didn't it?' Uptill left his eyebrows raised. 'You might even have been around then, Kenny?'

This brought a snigger from DePaul and Hoskins. Sancho even punched Uptill playfully on the arm, smiling.

Kennard hadn't been around and Uptill knew it. The Wood Royal Commission had taken place between 1995 and 1997. It was an NSW-wide commission, but Sydney had been the main focus. It had resulted in a finding of corruption among a group of detectives who were receiving backhanders, called 'the laugh', every week from drug traffickers and local criminals. It led to the resignation of the commissioner at the time. And proved what a lot of people had thought. You can't trust the cops. It continued to be a solid stick to wield to this day.

Kennard refocused on the corn. He turned the first piece. It was burnt on one side. That was okay. He would claim it.

'How long until the food's ready?' asked Ann. The worry lines that had appeared in the last few months and which Kennard blamed himself for were pronounced. This was her attempting to divert the oncoming argument.

Kennard's finger slid down the inside of his thumb. It was greasy with sweat. He couldn't resist hitting back. 'Uptill, even you know that, most of the time, we're working on the back foot, trying to piece together people and events after the fact.'

'Which puts some of your *ex*-colleagues in a great position to keep ahead of their own investigations,' said Uptill.

Kennard knew he shouldn't let it, but Uptill was getting to him. He didn't like the entire force being tarred with one brush. In every organization there were people who took advantage. The point wasn't to condemn the whole lot but to weed out the bad apples.

'You're commenting on shit you don't know, Uptill.'

'So, what do you know, Kennard?'

'Nothing.'

'You lot never do.'

There was silence apart from the sizzle of the corn as it burned.

'Quick to cover up, quick to shoot,' said Uptill. 'Or *not* in your case. What's another dead bogan, eh, Kennard?'

Forty-Three

January 21 – 08.28 – Wind direction NE – Surface speed 15km/h

25.5 hours since North Rislake evacuation

South Rislake status = Amber/Red (Evacuation imminent)

Kennard was still taking a breather by the barn when his phone buzzed. The number was Lenka's.

'Nice of you to call,' said Kennard.

'Had a free second. You want an update?' she asked.

'Hit me.'

'The crews are being pushed back. The fire has taken Angel Hills and is threatening Watkins, the next street along. Luckily the wind hasn't increased in knots yet, but a new direction means new fuel in its path.'

'I've caught the plastic in the air,' said Kennard. 'Nearly choked me.'

'They reckon it was a large prefab shed out the back of

Watermain. They expect the wind to push in strong later this morning. Has everyone on edge. There's also something else.' Lenka spoke in a whisper. 'But this didn't come from me, okay? They'll want to clear the report.'

'Sure.'

'The team investigating where the fire originated found a canister near what they believe is the origin of the blaze. Northwest of town. Preliminary indications, from what I overheard, are that an accelerant, likely petrol, was used to start it.'

'Arson?'

'Looks like it. But you didn't hear it from me.'

'Understood. And thanks.'

'Anytime.'

Kennard caught up with Layton outside the back door of the farmhouse, the chooks pecking at their feet.

'False alarm,' she said.

'What was?'

'The plug socket drama.'

'Well, I have real news. Our fire might not have been natural or accidental,' said Kennard as they stepped further into the yard, out of earshot.

'It happens,' said Layton. 'Some no-mark wanting to cause chaos.'

'Yeah, could be.'

'You don't think so?'

'All along we've assumed the bushfire to be a freak occurrence. Natural, unfortunate. Just another obstacle to us finding the killer.'

'But what if it was deliberately set to try to torch the

scene and Tracey's body?' said Layton, finishing his thought.

Kennard nodded. 'They've found a canister with the remains of petrol northwest of town, so though the fire didn't originate at the crime scene, it wouldn't have taken long to reach it. And if it was an accident, why didn't the person who started it come forward?'

'They didn't want to get into trouble?' offered Layton.

'But risk the town, risk killing people?'

Layton nodded. 'Confirmation would be good.'

Not wanting to get Lenka in hot water, Kennard got another operator to make the call. He could hear the sigh as Bairstow realized who it was. Kennard was definitely off the man's Christmas card list.

'The answer is no. The wind has decided to be a mutt. Any chance you had on getting back to that house is on hold.'

'That's not what I'm after.'

There was a pause. In the background Kennard could hear the roar of a hose hitting distant timber. 'What do you want, then? I'm busy.'

'Confirmation on the origins of the blaze.'

Silence.

'That it was deliberate,' added Kennard.

'Where did you hear that?'

'I'm a detective. People talk. Look, if the rumour's swirling around, how long do you think it'll be 'til the press gets wind of it?'

'Is that a threat, Detective Kennard?'

'Not if you don't want it to be. It would be good if the police were in the loop as well.'

There was a grunt in reply. A quick calculation. 'We discovered a canister just off a bush service road about ten kilometres northwest of town. No one uses that road except for us the odd time and maybe some hunters.'

'And it was the source of the fire?'

'All indications are that some accelerant was released from it.'

'Not accidentally?'

'Given that it was sprayed over about half a mile, it doesn't seem likely.'

'Anything more you can tell me about it?'

'It's a standard jerrycan, red, no other apparent markings. We'll have it checked for fingerprints, but it was pretty beat up.'

'Let me know if you get—'

The phone was hung up. But Kennard didn't care. The nature of the can had got him thinking.

'I can hear the whirring from here,' said Layton. 'Spill.'

'Bairstow mentioned a red jerrycan. Like the ones out back,' said Kennard, nodding to the barn.

Layton frowned. 'Probably a million of them around the country, Kennard.'

'But only a few that belong to people who would benefit from Tracey Hilmeyer's death.'

'But put their own farm – and lives – in danger?'

'You've seen the boxes inside. They're getting prepped to leave. We checked into any insurance Tracey and Russell had on their house. What about Karen and Alvin?' said Kennard, looking around. Alvin was still missing, Karen inside the farmhouse.

'Why not start the fire closer to here, then?'

'So that it didn't look too obvious. They might have reckoned that a big enough fire would torch everything.'

Layton glanced towards the farmhouse again. 'But they must have realized that it would threaten the whole town.'

'What better way to cover your tracks? Torch the whole town and everybody makes a claim. Much easier to hide a motive in a haystack. Especially if it's burnt to a crisp.'

Forty-Four

Tracey – Before

December – Last year

Karen had always been difficult, or complicated, depending on who you asked. They had been close once. Growing up in Fevertree with a mutual enemy – the kids in school and their vicious nicknames. Back then the 'Deadwells' had stuck together.

Tracey had looked out for her younger sister, waiting for her at lunchtimes and after class so they could check in with each other; everything okay, no tears, no tantrums.

But Tracey had evolved. She had grown into a young woman who was wanted and desired. Karen had not, her face never losing its puppy fat, her figure squat and mis-aligned like she had been moulded in a hall of mirrors. Tracey's rise in status as Russell's girlfriend had benefited both of them but had caused them to drift apart. Tracey married young, moving into her dream house on the hill and pursing her art, while Karen was stuck at the family farm, looking after her two elderly parents while the place crumbled around her – no social life, no partner and no hope.

But time had swung its sword and the last decade had changed all that too. Their parents had died, and the handbrake had been taken off. Karen had met Alvin, a giant of a man who scowled at Tracey every time they passed each other in the street on his way to Lunnock's store for some supplies of feed, as if poised to attack. God knows the stories Karen had told about her. Probably the worst. While Alvin scowled, she and Karen chose a different approach, barely acknowledging each other's existence when they happened to run into each other. As if the other was merely a ghost from their past they could ignore. Poisoning their relationship with neglect. Which was even more powerful than outright hatred. At least hatred required emotion.

Phoning the Animal Welfare League was petty. As was putting the lodger into her half of the house. But she had needed the money. It was the only way to get the gallery back, the empty storefront opposite the souvenir shop, goading her daily. That and the fact that she had been kicked out, but nothing else had moved in, her art and dreams deemed less worthwhile than an empty space.

Karen and Alvin could start up elsewhere, on more fertile land. The farm would be smaller, but the only reason it was sizeable in the first place was that they were using her share of the land as well as their own. So, it was only fair that she should benefit from it as well. Not that Karen saw it that way. Tracey was the witch trying to tear her life apart.

It had led to words. It had led to threats. And eventually it had led to violence.

Forty-Five

Kennard felt the tension, heavy on his lungs. Karen was somewhere inside the house and Alvin was somewhere out here. Both wandering free – both, no doubt, with access to firearms, given it was a working farm.

'It's all circumstantial,' said Layton. Though even she looked on edge, as perturbed as he was. 'You know that. A circumstantial motive of getting full ownership of the farm and land upon Tracey's death. There's no direct evidence linking them to anything.'

'There are the jerrycans. And there's something else,' said Kennard. 'Come with me.'

The yard felt too exposed all of a sudden, with sight-lines from the road to the house to the outbuildings. He imagined Karen taking aim with a rifle as he rapidly moved into the narrow alley between the barns, the un-plastered breezeblocks brushing his shirt, surprisingly cool, undisturbed by the sun for twenty-three hours a day.

'What is it?'

Reaching the end of the alleyway, Kennard pointed out the scorched earth and disturbed soil.

'What about it?' frowned Layton.

'Recently done.'

'So?'

'I want to dig it up.'

'Why?'

'To see what's under it.'

'What are you expecting? It isn't unusual. My uncle—'

'It was the look on Alvin's face this morning. It was the fact that he backed off towards that patch of land when I put pressure on. It's the dynamic between them. It's like Karen is afraid of him saying something. I think they have buried something under there. Like a murder weapon.'

'These are all just hunches, Alex.'

'I know.'

'And my uncle burned shit all the time. Leaves, animals, even a shed one time. Easier than tearing it down. There's probably an innocent explanation.'

'And if there is, there is. There's no harm in checking all the angles.'

'Do you think they could really have done it?' asked Layton. Their voices echoed off the brick, too loud for Kennard's liking.

'If they were desperate, yes. They knew Russell was out of town, they knew that Tracey was likely to be alone.'

'We'd need a warrant, which might be a struggle based on what we have.'

'I know.'

Layton looked at him, despair in her eyes. 'It's not going to stop you, is it?'

'We're only going to look around. If they're innocent, they have nothing to hide.'

'Doesn't mean that they want us snooping all over their property.'

'Then you better get Haskell to pull some strings,' said Kennard, smiling.

As he kept an eye out, he listened to a hushed Layton on the phone asking Haskell to persuade the assistant commissioner to pressure any judges or magistrates that might be favourable to this urgent request. She was given a name that Kennard didn't catch and she spoke calmly and clearly to the voice on the other end, pressing the right buttons, noting that the request was to do with the recent murder of a young woman in a town that was currently all over the news, that the police were under pressure to work quickly and that it would help if all branches of law enforcement did the same to foster a thorough investigation. Kennard could see that she was destined for better things and that he might be in trouble if she ever achieved them.

'Cogs are turning. How do you want to do this?' she asked, covering the mouthpiece with her hand.

'You keep Karen and the kids occupied and I'll—' said Kennard.

'Hang on, why am I keeping the kids occupied?'

He was saved by the voice over the phone. Layton returned to the call, ending it with a calmly delivered 'Thank you'.

Kennard turned to her. 'Well?'

'We have our warrant. And backup on the way. But

we've been warned not to cause a grieving sibling any undue stress.'

'Their place is in the path of a devastating bushfire. And they might be trying to cover up a brutal murder. I'm not sure we could put them under any more stress if we tried.'

Layton stared at him. 'Okay, let's do this.'

She made for the farmhouse, the chooks scattering as she ran past, an off-yellow dust rising with each footstep.

When she reached it, Kennard turned and headed for the disturbed patch of soil. It was larger than he had realized, a good eight feet by ten – enough to bury a whole car, never mind a murder weapon.

The dark soil was rapidly drying in the heat, forming hardened crumbs, something sour in the air.

The voice behind him was cold and questioning.

'Detective?'

Kennard nearly stumbled, turning to meet its owner. Alvin was leaning against the barn smoking a roll-up cigarette, a soil-stained shovel resting against the brick, a red jerrycan at his feet.

Kennard was at a loss for words. He kept his eyes on the shovel for now. Alvin was big enough to cause serious damage with it.

'What's happening?' asked Alvin, moving away from the side of the barn. The shovel stayed propped up against the wall but still within reach.

Kennard pointed at the soil. 'What's under here, Mr Lautahahi?'

Alvin's forward momentum ceased. His eyes drifted to the disturbed ground. His smooth face creased into fatty lines under his eyes, and he glanced towards where his house stood, obscured by the barns.

'It's just us, Alvin. Your wife isn't coming to help. What's under there? Is it a murder weapon?'

On hearing this, Alvin's brow hardened.

'No murder weapon.'

'Then what?' asked Kennard, keeping up the pressure.

'We just needed to hide—'

'Get away from my husband!'

Karen, with the youngest kid in her arms and the other two in tow, appeared from the gap between the barns. Layton was following her. The look she shot Kennard was loaded with apology. Kennard didn't blame her. Karen had proven herself to be someone that was hard to stop.

'We told you everything we know. What are you still doing snooping around?' Karen asked, the angry words spilling from her mouth. 'This is harassment.'

'You said we needed a warrant,' said Kennard. 'We got one.'

'So this one here says,' she said, indicating Layton.

Kennard pointed to the disturbed soil. 'We have reason to suspect that you have buried something underneath here that is of relevance to the ongoing case regarding your sister.' He didn't want to say the word 'murder' in front of the kids. They looked agitated enough as it was.

'What?' Karen began to laugh. Kennard glanced at Alvin. He wasn't laughing, instead remaining stern and focused.

'In fact, before you arrived, I think your husband was about to confess.'

Alvin shook his head, staring at his wife.

'Confess to what?' asked Karen.

'Do you want me to say it?' asked Kennard, pointing at her kids.

'I do.'

'Confess that he had hidden something. Likely the murder weapon involved in the death of Tracey Hilmeyer.'

Alvin opened his mouth but was interrupted again by Karen. This time with a laugh that echoed off the concrete walls of the farm.

'Buried . . . ? That's what you think? You want a confession?' she said, her eyebrow raised.

Kennard didn't answer. He didn't know what game Karen was trying to play. He glanced at Layton, who seemed just as confused.

Karen spoke to Layton. 'Take my kids into the house and I'll give your partner the confession.'

Layton looked at Kennard. Leaving him meant two against one. But he had his handgun if needed. He nodded.

The kids began to cry, arguing that they didn't want to go, but Karen tempered them with the announcement that if they went inside, the nice police officer would get them all an icy pole from the freezer. Any flavour they wanted. So, with a final glance back, Layton led the kids between the barns and away. Kennard was alone with two possible murderers.

'So, confession time,' said Karen.

Kennard watched them both closely in case they tried anything, though it was hard to see what they could do. He had the advantage. Or so he thought. The last time he had been one against two it had gone tragically wrong.

'Are you sure?' asked Alvin, his soft voice hardening, stepping forward with the shovel.

'Our detective is sure he wants to know.'

Kennard felt the hairs raise on his neck. Karen and Alvin were planning something, he just couldn't determine what. He licked his lips, the cracked dryness rough on his tongue, helping keep him on edge.

Alvin stepped towards the far barn.

'Where are you going?' asked Kennard, fighting the urge to reach for his gun.

'To get your confession,' said Karen.

Kennard was stuck between the two of them. 'Slowly.'

Alvin nodded. Kennard watched as he grabbed something from just inside the back door. He only needed one hand. Kennard pictured everything from a bloodied hammer to a crowbar to a shotgun.

'Here's your confession, Detective,' Karen sneered.

In one powerful hand Alvin dragged the bound hooves of a recently sheared sheep, its head lolled back. Not resisting. Very much dead.

'What's this?' asked Kennard.

'It is a sheep, Detective,' said Alvin coldly.

'I know. Why are you showing me a dead sheep?'

'Because, Sherlock, that's what's buried under there,' said Karen.

'I don't understand.'

'That's bloody obvious.'

'Our animals have been dying,' said Alvin, taking a deep breath.

'Poisoned,' said Karen.

'Poisoned? How do you know?' asked Kennard.

'Look at it,' said Karen, as Alvin carted the limp body forward. Kennard didn't know what he was meant to be seeing.

'The eyes, Detective,' said Alvin. 'Yellow.'

'Jaundice,' said Karen. 'Probably anaemic too.'

'Copper poisoning,' said Alvin bluntly.

'And it's not the feed,' said Karen, ready with her answer as if she'd had to defend herself on this topic before. 'We don't give 'em much, we just let them wander.'

'Why didn't you inform the authorities?' asked Kennard.

Karen's sharp, bitter laugh returned. 'Really? We've had enough run-ins with the authorities this last year. Don't want to give them another reason to shut down the farm for good. So, we burn them and bury them,' said Karen, pointing at the scorched earth.

Kennard glanced at the jerrycan by the shed. That would explain its presence. But could the couple be desperate enough to start a larger fire? To cover a multitude of sins?

'So why do you think they were poisoned?'

Alvin looked to his wife. She spoke. 'We allow the sheep to use Tracey's land. Those arsehole inspectors made us close off access but it's good land gone to waste. Tracey knew we used it. She dobbed us in because of it but I'm not going to let it just sit there spinning wild.'

'But they've been dying,' said Alvin.

'And you think Tracey did it?'

'Not Tracey,' said Karen. 'She wouldn't lift a finger. Not even to a Pommie batsman. But she might ask Russell to lay some tainted feed out.'

'And he would do it?'

'I dunno. I think he had eyes on the land too. Since recently. Furniss in the store said he was asking lots of questions, what equipment he needed, auctions, vaccinations, diseases to look out for and that.'

After that, Karen and Alvin stayed quiet. Waiting on what Kennard would do. Their explanation sounded plausible, at least for the patch of disturbed soil and jerrycan. But this was a murder investigation. He needed to make sure.

'We'll have to dig it up,' said Kennard.

Alvin offered no plea against. Karen only offered him some advice.

'Wear a mask.'

Forty-Six

'I'm going to need you both to leave,' said Kennard.

'The cops couldn't get us to leave earlier; we aren't leaving now,' Karen replied.

Alvin cast the dead sheep back inside the barn and walked back over towards them both. Kennard backed off, wary of Alvin's lumbered but intent approach.

'This is a crime scene,' he insisted.

'*You* say it's a crime scene, Detective. It isn't,' said Karen, now joined by her husband.

'I need you both back inside the house. Now!' Kennard aimed for authoritative but wasn't sure he made it. He fumbled for his phone, his hands greasy with sweat.

'We have a farm to take care of,' said Karen. 'You can't threaten our livelihoods.'

'Like you threatened your sister?'

'I didn't threaten her.'

Just then Layton appeared from the gap between the barns, all eyes shifting to her. She studied the scene, her hand moving for her weapon.

'The kids want their parents.'

It was the right button at the right time. Given the choice between arguing with him or seeing to their children, Karen and Alvin immediately retreated to the farmhouse, followed by Kennard and Layton.

'What was that about?' asked Layton as they crossed the yard.

'They claim they're burning and burying dead sheep. Poisoned sheep.'

Layton narrowed her eyes in confusion, but it quickly dawned on her what he meant. 'It's plausible.'

'Your uncle . . . ?'

'My uncle.'

They followed Karen and Alvin inside, the kids huddled around the couch in the main room, their mouths smeared in different fluorescent colours.

'I want someone in to check it out for definite. I'm not saying there's a murder weapon under there . . .' He tailed off.

'. . . but it would be a good cover story. Bury it under a pile of dead animals,' said Layton. 'You called it in yet?'

Kennard looked at her.

She sighed. 'I'm not your skivvy, Kennard.'

'I wouldn't even dream of thinking that. I'll call it in. You keep an eye on them.'

Kennard walked into the hallway. As he went to put a call in to HQ to request a forensics team be sent to the farm, his eyes fell on a glass ornament that was placed high up on a shelf, on show for guests but out of reach of younger kids.

He absently picked it up. It was heavy, a solid glass

ornament weighted at the base, where the blue that ran through the whole piece was at its darkest. Within it was a gold spiral like a pair of ribbons dancing. It was cheap yet pretty, but that wasn't why it had caught his eye. Russell Hilmeyer had told him that Tracey was sure that a blue and gold ornament had been stolen from their house. He turned it over and looked at the bottom. It was engraved: *To my darling wife, Ginny. Love, Stephen.* Karen and Tracey's parents. From husband to wife. A family heirloom. Something that might be worth stealing from a sister.

The line clicked in his ear. HQ. He made the request for an FSG team to be sent out to the farm ASAP.

He returned to the kitchen. The kids were enraptured by the TV as Alvin watched over them, pacing behind the couch. Kennard kept one eye on him as Karen sat at the table with Layton.

'I've told you there's nothing here,' said Karen, as exasperated as she had been outside, but the volume of her voice lowered.

'Then we'll find that out,' said Layton. 'How does it feel to own the house and farm?'

'Feel, Detective? My sister's dead.'

'I'm sure it's a shock,' said Layton.

'Death always is,' said Karen, her hands twisted together, white around the knuckles. Fighting to stay calm. To not get emotional. Or angry. 'But we didn't have anything to do with it. And as for the house, luck evens itself out.'

'How do you mean?'

'It should have been mine from the start. I was the one who had to live with them after Tracey moved out.'

'Your parents?'

'Yeah.'

'So, it wasn't a happy situation?'

Karen shook her head. 'What could I do? They were pretty crook most of their last few years.'

'And Tracey didn't help?'

'Out of sight, out of mind. Too busy to come by. Pursuing her art. But she still got half the house and the land,' said Karen, vitriol staining every word. 'Nothing in this house, nothing on this land should have been hers.'

'It isn't now,' said Kennard, watching Alvin as he reached under the couch, breathing out hard when all he brought out was what looked to be a plastic alpaca, giving it to one of the kids.

'And yet she's still fucking up my life.'

Kennard watched Karen's jaw tense, nostrils flaring wide. Anger at her sister.

'When did Ginny and Stephen pass?'

Karen bristled when she heard their names.

'Why do you ...? Ten years ago. A car crash. Dad shouldn't have even been driving.'

Kennard recalled the story Reinhold had told. The violent meeting with the semi on the highway coming down from Hartley.

'I guess the ornament in the hallway was something they passed down to you.'

Karen baulked at that. 'It ... they always intended for me to have it.'

'How's that?'

'It meant more to me than it did to my sister.'

'Russell mentioned that an ornament had disappeared from their house recently. That Tracey was upset about it.'

'I don't know anything about that.' The sudden aversion of her eyes told Kennard that she did.

'Were you in 148 Caldicott recently, Karen?'

'No,' said Karen, still refusing to look at them, gazing into the main room at her kids.

'Were you just there to steal the ornament?' asked Kennard.

'She gave it to me.'

'Tracey?'

'Yeah.'

'Given the animosity between you two, that seems out of character.'

'She did,' insisted Karen.

'Did you go in and take it, Karen?' asked Kennard.

Karen looked down at the table, her finger inching along the straight crack in the wood as if with enough effort she might be able to squeeze her whole body through.

'Did you take that ornament, Karen?'

Karen stayed silent.

'Karen, did—?'

'I don't have to talk to you,' said Karen suddenly. 'I want a lawyer.'

Forty-Seven

Tracey – Before

January

It was a strange dream. Because her sister was in it. Karen rarely visited her dreams. About as rarely as she visited in person. In this dream Tracey was in a house that looked vaguely like hers, save for the pictures on the wall being of horses, cattle and sheep, dull pieces that looked shop-bought, nothing imaginative in them, the kind of thing that she would expect the older kids in school to come out with. Four legs because it should have four legs, black noses, two eyes and a tail. Accurate rather than expressive. Her own house had her art on the walls. The closest she had to a gallery at present. Pieces that she could admire. Alone.

Karen was standing over her, concern or curiosity in her expression. As if Tracey was on her deathbed and her sister was itching for her to pass.

'Geddout.' The words seemed heavy in her throat, almost as if stuck there.

Karen didn't move. She just kept watching.

'Gedd . . .' The words faded. Karen wasn't budging, and Tracey wondered if her sister was simply another painting too, or if this was even her house. Was it the farmhouse? The pictures on the wall didn't match her parents' place either. No shelves full of bric-a-brac. No varnished wood panels.

'You okay, sis?'

The last word was hissed, the words like a memory recalled through hooded eyes, the edges blurred. Tracey breathed out hard. It was a dream after all. After the lodger and the complaints made to Animal Welfare there was no way Karen was coming around to say hello.

But Tracey felt warm. Too warm. As if there was an open fire in the room. It put her on edge. Karen was still there, holding a wavy blue object that glowed in her hand. High above her. Ready to crash down onto Tracey's skull.

Forty-Eight

As soon as Karen asked for a lawyer, Kennard ushered Layton into the hallway. In the background, Karen remained at the table, not raising her head. Alvin had joined her, standing at her shoulder, watchful. Kennard studied them both together, watching for a flicked glance that would spur them into action.

'What ornament are you talking about?' whispered Layton. 'And why has—?'

With his eyes still on Karen and Alvin, Kennard pointed towards the blue and gold glass design on the shelf.

'I think that's the ornament Tracey told Russell had

gone missing from their house. The one he didn't report because he didn't want the cops around.'

Layton nodded, processing the information. 'Do you think Karen stole it?'

'I think it's likely. It's clear that Tracey wasn't going to give her sister anything without a fight.'

'What if they did fight?'

Kennard nodded. He was thinking the same thing.

'So, after the first successful heist, Karen went back for something else,' said Layton. 'Maybe she was planning on slowly bleeding the place dry. But Tracey caught her. The ensuing argument got out of hand and Karen killed her. Are Forensics on their way?'

'Yeah. Just the traffic to deal with.'

'I suggest we make a start ourselves,' said Layton. 'Who knows how long we have.' Dragging an evidence bag and pair of latex gloves from her pocket, she delicately placed the heavy ornament inside and sealed it. 'House first and then the sheds.'

Staying together was the smart move, two against two. In normal circumstances. But there was a rising heat in the air that almost curled the hairs on Kennard's arm.

'You take the house and Karen,' he said. 'I'll take the sheds and Alvin. Best to keep them apart.'

'Why do you get the sheds?'

'You can have them,' said Kennard. 'Dead animals and all.'

Layton paused for a brief moment. 'You're on sheds. And, Alex?'

Kennard turned towards her. 'Yeah?'

'Keep your radio close. Any trouble, call me.'

'You too.'

The shed nearest the road was the older of the two, the brickwork crumbling at the edges, the plaster cracked in a thousand places. The inspectors had passed it a few months ago but soon it would fail, giving the couple yet another bill to pay. If the farm was still around by then. Inside, the floor space of concrete, hay and animal dung was fenced off with wooden pallets roped together into makeshift pens. It was mid-morning and already like an oven, the heat of the day and of the distant blaze turning the tin roof into a hotplate. Kennard parked Alvin at the entrance and told him not to move.

'What are you looking for?' asked Alvin.

'I'm not sure yet,' said Kennard, moving from pen to pen, poking around the dirt and crusted fleece, the aroma that of gathered dung baking slowly.

He checked between the wooden slats of the pallets and in any nook and cranny in the walls that might provide enough space to stash a weapon. Keeping the murder weapon around would be stupid. But people did stupid things in times of stress. And excess heat. It frazzled the brain into overlooking simple acts of self-preservation.

Ten minutes and he had finished the search of the shed. It felt perfunctory but the sweat that dripped off him told him that he had put in a decent shift. The forensics team would do a more thorough job, while probably cursing him from here to Dubbo.

The rear shed was crisper and cleaner. Whereas the first was used solely to house the animals, the second was divided into two sections, one for the animals, but with permanent metal grates rather than pallets as dividers, and a second part that contained a range of machinery and farming utensils, troughs and buckets, stacks of feed and nutrient support in plastic bags lined up against the far wall.

An old set of dresser drawers was chock-full of tools and scrap metal, the wood chipped and smeared with oil and paint that had been daubed onto the animals to identify who they belonged to, these smit marks crucial when they could escape to pretty much anywhere beyond these fences.

With his gloves on, and keeping one eye on Alvin, who lurked by the door, Kennard searched through each drawer. They held any number of items that could have been a murder weapon: screwdrivers and hammers, various mechanical constructions that looked to have been sheared from old vehicles, a gearstick, rear lights, three car batteries, rusted shears and a battered tick sprayer. It looked as though nothing was thrown away on the farm in case it might come in useful at some point in the future.

He opened the top drawer. Whereas the other ones spilled over with random items, this one was neatly arranged, the bottom carpeted in fresh newspaper. It contained a box of tools which were polished and meticulously laid out, obviously Alvin's pride and joy. As Kennard opened it up, he glanced over at Alvin, who was on his toes peering over.

'Don't move,' warned Kennard as he looked inside.

The set of spanners, screwdrivers and drill bits practically gleamed. They looked almost unused, aside from a few minute scratches on the faces. He studied them closely, looking for the tiniest speck of blood, but could find nothing – not with the naked eye at least.

As he pushed the stiff drawer back in, the whole dresser shook on the uneven floor. Something clattered to the floor with a loud, metallic clang.

Kennard glanced at Alvin again. The big man's eyes seemed to swell from his head in worry.

'Don't,' warned Kennard as he knelt down to peek under the dresser. In the middle of a sea of scrap metal and dented hubcaps was a shiny spanner.

Gently he eased the sheet of scrap metal out, the mass rattling along the ragged concrete as he did. In the light Kennard could see a noticeable dark stain along one side of the spanner, the outer edge cleaned, but not well enough. The need to hoard had caught husband and wife out.

There was a rustling close by. Kennard turned to find a large shadow over him. Using the noise of the metal sheet as a distraction, Alvin had snuck closer and was now towering over Kennard. The detective felt the air stall in his lungs, at the mercy of Alvin's feet and anything else he wanted to throw at him.

All Kennard could think of to do was roll painfully across the dusty surface and struggle to his feet, breathing out hard.

At this, Alvin turned the angle of his body towards the door.

'Don't move, Mr Lautahahi.' Kennard took a dry gulp and prepared himself to chase Alvin down and tackle him. Which would be difficult. He tapped the button on his radio, touching the edge of his firearm, ready should he need it.

'Layton, I found something.'

His eyes remaining on a nervous Alvin, he eased his phone from his pocket and took snaps of the location and position in which the spanner had been found. He wanted to bag it up as soon as possible, afraid that any delay would reveal it as a mirage in this heat.

'What?' came the crackled reply over the radio.

Alvin crooked his head back towards the house. Time was of the essence. Picking the spanner up in his gloved fingers – Kensington Mech imprinted into the metal – Kennard eased it gently into an evidence bag.

Holding it out in front of him in his non-dominant hand – allowing him access to his handgun, just in case – he addressed Alvin.

'We're going back inside.'

Alvin didn't respond.

'I said—'

Alvin stepped forward. 'That isn't mine.'

'Mr Lautahahi, I told you—'

'That isn't mine.'

'You can explain that later,' said Kennard, feeling dizzy in the heat, with the pressure. Alvin paused for a moment before he turned and walked. Kennard wanted to know what the other man was thinking. He looked stoic but his photo in the souvenir shop had been just as expressionless, like it was a mask he wore. He expected that at any second Alvin might run. If he did, there would be no way of stopping him other than the gun. He was built like two front rows mashed together like clay.

The chooks darted out of their path as they made it through the yard to the back door and inside.

Alvin strode to the far side of the kitchen, Kennard wary that there could be a knife in any of the drawers, a gun on top of any of the cupboards.

'Keep your hands where I can see them,' he ordered, sweat forming on his fingers.

'What's going on?' asked Karen, sitting at the table as Layton searched the kitchen. Her eyes darted towards the evidence bag Kennard held. He tried to gauge her reaction. Shock, it seemed, her eyes blinking furiously. But it might have been fear.

'Where did you find that?' asked Karen.

Kennard didn't answer.

'I told him I didn't know anything about it,' said Alvin, sidling up to his wife, again drawn to her like a magnet. Kennard wanted to split them up. As soon as possible.

'We're going to find Tracey's blood on this, aren't we?' said Kennard.

'That's . . . we had nothing to do with her murder,' said Karen, a little too loud, drawing the attention of her kids in the living room.

'We know that you had a disagreement with her,' said Layton. 'The day before she died.'

'Yeah, a disagreement. We had lots of disagreements.'

'We know that you were pissed off about the house, the lodger, the land going to waste, the calls to Animal Welfare. The photos and that ornament,' said Kennard.

'That was mine.'

'Which you broke into Tracey's house to take.'

'Which she had taken from me,' said Karen, striking her fist on the table, her puffy face turning a darker shade of red. Alvin rocked on his feet in the corner, anxious, ready to move on command.

'It doesn't mean that you had to kill her,' said Layton.

Karen let out a sob but there were no tears. Her anger did not allow for that. 'I didn't kill my sister.'

'Did your husband do it?' asked Kennard.

'No, Detective,' said Alvin, his voice booming around the small kitchen.

'What about *her* husband?' asked Karen. 'And she must have pissed other people off too. The people she got her drugs off. She was always hiking up the rent here, for her half of the house. She knew that we had to pay, that we couldn't afford not to pay. I thought that she was doing it out of spite but maybe she just needed the money.'

Karen was desperate now, her speech coming in short machine-gun bursts like her breath. The heat was intense, and the blistering accusations were doing nothing to cool the atmosphere down. But despite her insistence and all of the alternative motives she had offered, the murder weapon had been found hidden on her property. They had been caught out. Kennard could see it in the husband and wife's anxious expressions, their confusion over what to do next, Karen glancing up at Alvin as if searching for a way out.

'You were paying rent? To Tracey?' asked Layton.

Karen nodded. 'For the house. To stop her renting it to a stranger. She wanted too much for the land.'

Kennard recognized what his partner was hinting at. Another motive to get rid of Tracey. A landlord bleeding their tenants dry. Tenants who had no choice but to pay. It might also help explain where Tracey was getting money for her supply. Maybe she had increased the rent and hadn't told Russell about the extra income. Not all marriages were like his and Ann's, joint mortgages and joint bank accounts. Some were a little more secretive. Some had bank accounts in the Cayman Islands and clandestine trips to holiday resorts. Some had a little extra cash hidden away. Should push come to shove.

Forty-Nine

There was a crackle on the radio attached to his trouser pocket. A message. Their backup and the forensics team were five minutes out. So, Kennard and Layton spent the next five minutes explaining to Karen and Alvin what was about to happen. That they were going to be arrested.

Karen's hands balled into fists. Kennard stood back and watched Layton do the same. They didn't want to handcuff her in front of her kids unless it was necessary.

'You can't do this!' Karen cried out, standing up from the table. 'That,' she said, pointing at the evidence bag, 'it's not ours.'

'It was found on your farm, Mrs Lautahahi,' said Layton.

'We don't know anything about it.'

It was what Kennard expected. It had been their story all along. And they had a tight, strong bond that might be hard to crack.

Karen's eyes darted towards her husband. As if giving the order to strike.

'We don't want to have to restrain you,' said Layton.

'You can try,' sneered Karen.

'Think about your kids, Karen,' said Kennard.

Karen's jaw tensed. 'What about my kids?'

'You don't want them to see you—'

'Getting arrested for something we didn't do? They may as well get used to the authorities coming in and doing anything they want. Without reason. You better take care of them, or else,' said Karen, seething.

'We'll have a suitably qualified officer look after them,' said Layton.

'What about my animals?' asked Alvin.

That was a different matter. For this, Kennard had no one to call. Not with the bushfire soaking up all the resources.

'They'll be taken care of.'

'How? They need to be put inside later. Kept together in one place so they can be moved if the fire arrives.'

Kennard couldn't promise anything. He didn't want to promise anything. Plus, there was no way that the animals would be allowed inside those sheds until they had been checked over by what was probably now a very weary forensics team.

'That isn't something to concern yourself with,' said Layton.

'It is. It's our life, our livelihood. We don't want it to be lost.' Alvin flicked his chin up. 'There is enough death in the air.' His brown eyes focused on them. Death *was* in the air, both the threat and the actuality.

The back door opening broke the tension as a couple of local officers entered, filling the kitchen and finally outnumbering their suspects.

A family liaison officer had sped up the road from Penrith with the blues and twos blaring to look after the kids. It was explained to them that Mummy and Daddy had to go away for a few hours for a chat and that they were heading off on an adventure for the afternoon.

The children were concerned, but the idea of an adventure won them over. More than it did their parents, who hugged their kids and told them they loved them while staring down the local cops with a look of pure hatred.

Karen was still smouldering with rage when Layton finally arrested her, out of sight of her children. She resisted the cuffs for a brief second before giving in. Kennard prepared for Alvin to offer the same resistance, his massive hands held out, a sternness on his face that warned that none of this would be forgotten.

The kids were driven away in a police van, giddy, unaware of what was really happening. They were gone before their mum and dad were brought outside and placed into two separate cars.

Kennard turned and looked at the farmhouse and barns. They had found what looked to be the murder weapon. Karen and Alvin had motive, access and opportunity. He had been wrong about Russell Hilmeyer, so he needed to be sure to get it right this time. Because lately he had been getting decisions very wrong.

Fifty

Katoomba – One week ago

'Quick to cover up, quick to shoot,' said Uptill. 'Or *not* in your case. What's another dead bogan, eh, Kennard?'

With that, Kennard snapped. The meat cooking on the grill, the sunny day, the beer, none of it mattered any longer. None of it even existed. There was only him and the gutless decision he had made. Before he realized it, he was standing over Uptill.

Then it was a blur. Like he had blacked out. A punch had been thrown. Not even a good punch. Thrown with his weaker hand. The tray of burgers he had been balancing in his favoured hand went flying. So did Uptill, out and over the back of the chair, as much caught out by the action itself as by the force behind it.

Someone tugged on Kennard's arm. He turned to see that Ann had grabbed his shoulder. In front of him Sancho was crouching down to help Uptill back to his feet, as if his colleague had fallen in the line of duty.

Kennard's muscles twitched ready for the retaliation, but Uptill was either all foam and no beer or aiming for the high ground and taking this on the chin – or chest as it ended up.

The inquest was immediate. Ann apologized to everyone for Kennard's actions as if he was a bub that had spewed all over someone's good clothes. It was agreed that the barbie was over, Uptill ushered out by Sancho and Crookshank, Hoskins rounding up his kids with a whistle. Leaving only Kennard. In his garden. In the silence.

The burgers were still there the next morning, dry and shrivelled up on the ground, half pecked at by birds, the rest of the meat and buns spoiled and in the bin. He'd spent the rest of the morning angrily scraping the crap off the grill.

Left alone, he churned over in his mind what he had done. What had he been trying to achieve? What had his subconscious wanted to prove?

Had he wanted to stand up for the force? That might have been noble if it were true. But striking Uptill had been a cowardly act.

The pall had spread to Monday. Side-eyed and sidelined by the entire station, word spreading like the wildfire that no one knew then was coming. Haskell had called him into the office to tear him a new one. Uptill hadn't outright snitched but had stated his grievances loudly enough so they could be easily heard through the thin walls. Kennard explained what had happened. In broad terms, cutting out most of the detail. Haskell had listened, stock still in her chair. When he finished, she gave him a warning.

Formally. There was to be no repeat, no further black marks against him.

Ann finally spoke to him on Tuesday, to suggest that he make an appointment to see a counsellor.

He understood her position. That he had been in the wrong. Provoked, but in the wrong. But he also believed that he had done enough talking. Talking hadn't helped, so instead he opted for the solution identified long ago by Ces and Lisa: get back on the horse.

Fifty-One

January 21 – 10.01 – Wind direction NW – Surface speed 18km/h

27 hours since North Rislake evacuation

South Rislake status = Amber/Red (Evacuation imminent)

There had been a discussion – and a disagreement between himself and Layton – about whether their suspects should be taken to Katoomba for questioning. Kennard won the argument so Karen and Alvin were taken to town instead, with the understanding that if the bushfire closed in further, they would be transferred.

He got together with Layton in the backyard, surrounded by chickens curious more about the next feeding time than the absence of their owners, to discuss what came next. Questioning Karen and Alvin was high on the list, but they first needed to be processed through the system and have lawyers arranged.

The black cloud reaching far overhead was like a curled fist preparing to strike as the forensics team suddenly appeared en masse, flooding into the yard. Kennard recognized the team leader, Eric Henia, with Andrews shuffling along in tow. Kennard had worked with Henia a few times on some cases out of Glebe. He was efficient bordering on rapid, perfect for this situation. Kennard had seen him process and release an entire one-bedroom flat in three days.

After a quick greeting Kennard gave them space to set up. With the FSG/SOCO mix on scene there was nothing else he could do but step back and let them work, which made him feel at a bit of a loose end. He hunted out Layton and found her chatting to one of the FSG team, a tall, handsome guy in his mid-twenties who was rocking a thick, dark moustache.

She touched his forearm before letting him turn away and slip into a protective scene suit.

'What's happening there?' asked Kennard.

Layton swung around sharply. 'Nothing,' she said, embarrassed.

'Young love?'

'I'd presumed you would have forgotten what that was,' she said with a smile.

'I keep myself strictly business.'

'So do I. During business hours,' she said, laughing, open and heartfelt. It was obvious that she liked the FSG guy. A lot by the looks of things. Kennard couldn't imagine sleeping with someone who was around dead bodies and crimes scenes all day, every day. Imagining where their hands had been.

'Decision time,' he said. 'Process or picking through?'

'I'll process our suspects.'

'You don't want to stay with lover-boy?' smiled Kennard.

'Space in a relationship is important.'

'Especially when that space is filled with sheep carcasses?'

'Exactly.'

Layton left for the car. Kennard immediately sought out a weary-looking Eric Henia.

He found him in the farmhouse kitchen, five of his team, including Layton's boyfriend and Lyle Andrews, standing around the table. Eric was dividing the property into plots with the help of the tablet in his hand. Each of these paper-suited minions had their own smaller team and area they would be concentrating on. There was a collective slump in their shoulders. This was a day that would never end.

'Can I help?' asked Kennard.

'Stop dragging us out to sites,' said Eric. He had the reputation of being someone who enjoyed a laugh. Today was not one of those days.

'Believe me, I don't want to be here any more than you.'

Eric grunted. 'You want to help?' he asked. 'Go get a suit and grab a shovel.'

Kennard did as ordered. He wrestled himself into the paper suit – much lighter than the bunker gear and only half as sweaty – and met Eric around the back of the barns.

The disturbed soil had been taped off, standard procedure, but in reality, it was little more than decoration.

Four people in white suits identical to his own were already at work and had even struck paydirt, dragging the soil-covered corpse of a sheep from the hole. The stench found Kennard's nose. He shut his eyes tight and tried not to retch. Alvin hadn't bothered with quicklime to help with the smell. Something else they couldn't afford perhaps.

Sliding his spade into the dirt, Kennard very quickly uncovered another corpse, which the team dragged away from the shallow, firm grave and lined up alongside the others on a plastic sheet.

After twenty minutes of this punishment, sweat stinging his eyes, his skin clammy and crying out for air, he approached Eric, who was pacing around the sheet studying the dozen corpses.

'What have you got?' asked Kennard.

'The precursory sift has brought up nothing but dead sheep.'

'And how did they die?'

'I'd have to open them up and run some tests, but if I had to guess, I'd say poisoning.'

'That's what the suspects said.'

'I don't think they were lying, then.'

'Deliberate?'

'From the appearance of the corpses, I'd say yes. Raised levels of copper. Animal Health should have been notified but burning and burying's the cheaper option.'

Karen had mentioned she thought Russell would have been capable of poisoning their animals. This might well have been true, but Kennard wondered what Russell would get out of it. Would he do it solely to please Tracey? But to what end? A simple case of spite, ruining her sister's life and business? The farm being ruined might affect Russell's stunted attempt to become a farmer, but it could have opened up the opportunity for the house and land to be sold as one, providing Tracey with half the proceeds and allowing her to purchase more drugs or set up another gallery. If she was desperate enough, she wouldn't have cared that poisoning the land meant risking the value. Money in her hand was all she would have cared about.

His thoughts were interrupted by Eric, who was gathering up some equipment to move to the next marked location.

'I suggest we concentrate on the barns and the house. With whatever time we have left,' said Eric, nodding over his shoulder at the oncoming glow, the smoke sweeping low now, blotting out the sun and creating an artificial dusk over the farm, dark enough for a couple of searchlights to have been rigged up to guide the crew.

In the distance there was a faint boom. They both turned in the direction of the sound.

'Another propane tank,' said Eric, resigned.

'Have they given you a time limit?' asked Kennard.

'My call,' said Eric. 'But I'm not going to put my team in danger.'

'Anything worth noting on the spanner?'

'The luminol confirmed the presence of blood. There seemed to have been an attempt to clean it, but a sloppy one. The blood was already dry.'

'How long would that have taken?'

'Not long given the heat. Not counting this,' said Eric, waving his hand at the blast of fire-blasted air that stung Kennard's eyes. 'I'd say thirty minutes.'

'And the house?'

'Nothing yet. Nothing to indicate that anything of that level of violence took place, nothing to indicate that the victim was ever here.'

Kennard nodded. Something more than the simple presence of the murder weapon would have provided some clarity, but it was what it was.

'Let me know when you're done,' he said.

'Not long,' said Eric. 'Then I'll pull what we have together. Unless you drag us somewhere else.'

It was a playful comment but there was no smile on his face.

Fifty-Two

Kennard drove back towards the police station, passing a beleaguered officer who remained at his post in the middle of the jam, getting honked and yelled at by motorists ignoring his directions. The rule of law was fading but Kennard couldn't let it collapse completely.

Through the smoke hovering around the station, he could see cars squeezed into every available space. A short, sharp shower of embers like a million burning matches carried on the wind rolled across the asphalt in front of him. The last thing they needed was an outbreak of spot fires on the south side of town as well. A main front was powerful and deadly, but more predictable and manageable than a series of little blazes that would only multiply.

Ignoring the yelled questions from the press hanging around outside the gates, he entered the station. Inside, the extra bodies were immediately apparent, the building abuzz. Sergeant Reinhold was holding a meeting in his office, and the room was packed wall to wall with officers. Despite the ringing phones and tortured whirr of over-worked printers, Kennard overheard him bellowing out instructions, wanting his officers to prepare residents and onlookers to pull out. The time was coming. They could fight it all they wanted, but nature always won in the end.

He found Layton loitering outside the two interview rooms built directly opposite each other along one of the back corridors. The fluorescent light embedded in the ceiling was on its last legs, the glow dull and foreboding. Two people were with her. Kennard immediately recognized them. Ernie Sancho had smartened up since the barbie, his jacket and ironed trousers making him look like he was dressed for an interview, his nose striped with the strangled red veins of an avid drinker. Sarah DePaul was with him, a subtle shade of lilac lipstick framing her small mouth and matching the colour of her blouse. They offered nothing but a glare as they headed for the main office before Kennard reached them.

'Given up already?' asked Layton.

'Eric will let me know what he finds. Nothing more than the possible weapon at present. What are they doing here?' asked Kennard, tilting his head at the retreating Sancho and DePaul.

'Haskell's call. She phoned for an update. Said that because this thing keeps growing tentacles, she was sending a couple of extra hands. More if we go to full-scale evacuation stage.'

Kennard twisted his mouth, the anger flickering. It was unlike Haskell to phone for updates. Either she was panicking, or interfering. It seemed like a critique of his handling of the case. Specifically, an implication that he couldn't handle it. She hadn't intervened on any of the other cases he had taken on in his first six months. Though they had been nothing of this magnitude.

'Ernie and Sarah are going to liaise with HQ.'

Kennard interrupted. 'Did you ask for them?' He was unable to prevent the accusing tone in his voice.

Layton stared at him. 'Ernie and Sarah? No.'

Kennard tried to read if she was telling the truth. He wasn't sure. The nail of his index finger scratched the inside of his thumb. It wasn't soothing.

'It's good they're here, isn't it?' she asked. 'They can keep on top of things while we question these two.'

She was right, but still Kennard wondered if Sancho and DePaul had been called in as additional spies.

'Kennard?'

'What?'

'You okay?'

'Yeah,' he said. 'We'll focus on Alvin. As solid as he looks, I think he'll crack quicker than Karen. More than anything, I want to know why they kept the weapon around.'

'Do you think that maybe he didn't know? That she put it there?'

'Let's find out.'

Layton put her hand up. 'The lawyers are asking for more time with their clients before we interview them.'

'They have as long as it takes me to get some coffee,' said Kennard.

Fifty-Three

January 21 – 10.24 – Wind direction NW – Surface speed 21km/h

27.5 hours since North Rislake evacuation

South Rislake status = Amber/Red (Evacuation imminent)

Layton entered first and took the seat closest to the recording unit. Kennard sat down beside her. Across the table were a focused-looking Alvin and a lawyer sporting a heavy stubble that could have been either an intentional fashion choice or the result of being called into action at the last minute. His suit was cheap, and he looked barely out of his twenties. That was the problem with Legal Aid. It was a lucky dip. And not everyone got lucky.

Layton ran through the usual housekeeping, getting Alvin to state his name, date of birth and address and making him aware that anything he said could be used against him in a court of law. Kennard had heard it a million times, but the words always forced his gut to tighten, in anticipation that the case might be solved. This was despite the overwhelming number of occasions when it hadn't been, when the suspect or interviewee had no relevant details or comment to make. But there was always that chance. The drug that kept you coming back for more.

Layton opened proceedings, the reserved Alvin aiming a deep, heavy, unblinking stare at the two detectives.

'How long have you been married, Mr Lautahahi?'

Alvin glanced at his lawyer before answering, already suspicious of the question. 'Nine years.'

'How did you two meet?'

'I was here on holiday. I met Karen. We liked each other.'

'Was it a quick marriage?'

At this point the stubbled lawyer intervened. 'I don't see the relevance in this line of—'

Alvin answered anyway. 'It was quick. It was love.'

'Was?' asked Layton.

'Is. I have been asked these questions many times before, Detective.'

'By whom?'

'Immigration. By people who don't understand love, or have fallen out of it.'

There was a temper bubbling just under the surface, Alvin's anger at where he was, at questions he had been asked many times before. His worry about his children.

'So, tell me why the spanner was hidden in your barn?' asked Layton.

The young lawyer put his hand up immediately to prevent any sudden answer, eager as a whippet to be involved. He whispered into his client's ear.

Alvin turned back towards Layton and shook his head. 'I do not know.'

'But you agree it was hidden?'

The lawyer put his hand up and whispered to Alvin again. This time he answered on behalf of his client. 'Any answer to your question could prejudice my client.'

Kennard responded. 'The fact that we found what looks to be the weapon used in the murder of Tracey Hilmeyer stashed on your client's property prejudices your client.'

That brought a momentary silence to the room. Layton picked up the line of questioning.

'How can you explain the item's presence on your property?'

'I cannot.'

'You didn't put it there?'

'No.'

'Did your wife?'

Alvin opened his mouth to speak but again the lawyer quickly whispered in his ear before he could respond. 'No comment.'

'Could she have done it without your knowledge? From what we can determine, your wife had more motive for murder than you did, Mr Lautahahi.'

Alvin's nostrils flared at the accusation, his neck tendons strained. He shook his head. 'My wife would not do this.'

'It looks bad for one or both of you,' said Layton. 'We have the weapon. We have the financial motive with the house and farm reverting to your wife's name upon Tracey Hilmeyer's death. All of the land you ever wanted, the chance to make a real go of the farm.'

The lawyer tried to interrupt but Alvin answered. 'We did not do this.'

'We know from her own words that she and her sister didn't get along. They argued. They fought. Especially the night before her brutal murder.'

'They did not fight,' said Alvin.

'We have a witness,' said Layton.

'I was there.'

Kennard caught Layton's eye. Tony Steyn hadn't mentioned Alvin being there.

'I made sure they didn't fight,' added Alvin.

'Our witness didn't—'

'I was in the storeroom.'

'Why?'

'I – we – wanted my photo back. My wife was worried it was more than a photo.'

'That you were having an affair.'

'Yes.'

'But you weren't?'

'No.'

'And the money?'

'That was a mistake. My eyes and hands being greedy. But it was not a fight. We did not do this.'

'Then who did?' asked Layton. 'Can you account for your whereabouts on Tuesday night?'

'I was at home. With my wife.'

'Did anyone call? Stop by? Did anyone else see you?'

'Would the children be able to verify this, Mr Lautahahi?' asked Kennard.

This stopped Alvin in his tracks, any anger blunted. Involving his kids in this was not something that he wanted to do.

'They were in bed.'

'So, they cannot confirm that you were there? Or that your wife was there?'

'No.'

Kennard leaned across the table. He was probing for an answer that he could latch onto. An anomaly. A contradiction. He had taken the lead from Layton. A different voice. A different angle.

'How well did you know Tracey Hilmeyer?'

'I had met her.'

'Where?'

'In that shop.'

'How often?'

'One time last summer, one time in October.'

'Why?'

'I wanted her to not send any more inspectors.'

'You knew it was her?'

Alvin nodded.

'How did she react?' asked Layton.

Alvin shook his head. 'She said it wasn't her. But it was. We knew.'

'And that made you angry.'

'That's something—' offered the lawyer, but Alvin was not for staying quiet.

'It was something that we didn't need, Detective,' he

said, gaze focused on her, voice stern. 'I also met her before Christmas.'

'Why?'

'I wanted her to give up her half of the house. I told her we would pay her back as fast as possible.'

'And Tracey didn't go for that?'

'She wanted to think about it. She asked if we were okay. She offered money. A few bucks. For Christmas presents for the kids.'

'Out of nowhere?'

Alvin shrugged. 'I took it. To pay for feed.'

'Which your wife didn't like?'

'No.'

'Because she wanted a photo with that money?' said Layton.

Alvin nodded.

'Naked?'

Alvin shook his head vigorously. 'No.'

'What did you think of her?'

Alvin's lawyer raised his hand, but Alvin answered anyway. 'We call them *vuca gata*. A rotten snake. She uses family as a weapon.'

'So, you hated her?'

'No. I have too much to do to hate her.' Kennard sensed that Alvin was trying to contain his anger, that his words didn't match his true feelings.

'Even after everything she tried to do? The farm, the lodger, the complaints?'

Alvin's jaw tensed. Hard. Squaring up as if to fight. 'No, Detective.'

'And your wife? What did she think of her sister?'

The lawyer interrupted. 'My client can't be expected to know everything his wife is thinking.'

Kennard shook his head. Another smart-arse lawyer.

'Have you ever been to Russell and Tracey Hilmeyer's house?' he asked.

'No.'

'Are you sure?'

'I am. I had no reason to be there.'

'Has your wife ever been?'

'She was her sister.'

Kennard took that as a yes. He fired out the next few questions.

'Have you ever considered killing Tracey Hilmeyer?'

'No.'

'Ever talked about it? You and your wife?'

'No.'

'Has it ever crossed your mind?'

'No.'

'Have you killed before?'

There was a pause. Alvin turned and looked at his lawyer, who was watching all this unfold, intrigued, like a member of the public who had won a competition to sit in on a police interview rather than the person charged with protecting the suspect.

Alvin looked directly at Kennard when he replied. 'Yes.'

The room fell silent. Kennard wanted to ask a follow-up question but found the words stuck in his throat. Even Alvin's lawyer seemed to wake from his trance and stared at his client, mouth open, before turning to Kennard.

'I don't think my client should—'

Alvin continued regardless. 'Only sick animals,' he clarified.

'Was Tracey Hilmeyer a sick animal?' demanded Kennard.

'No. She was a human being. She did not deserve to be killed.'

'But she was killed all the same.'

'She was,' said Alvin, staring at him.

His lawyer took the opportunity to pipe up. 'I think this is a good time for a break.'

To Kennard it looked like the lawyer was the one who needed the break, a stunned look in his eyes. Maybe he'd realized he was in over his head. Kennard looked to Layton, who nodded. It was time to take a run at Karen.

Fifty-Four

They shuffled across the hallway to the other interview room. As soon as they opened the door, Karen jumped up from the chair as if on springs. It startled her lawyer, who dropped her notes onto the floor and muttered to herself as she tried to scoop them up.

'How are my kids? How is my husband?'

'Let's start with the interview first, shall we?' said Layton.

'No. Not before you tell me how they are,' Karen said, turning to her lawyer, a small woman of Indonesian descent who seemed to be overwhelmed by the sheer voracity and direct nature of the client towering over her. 'I'm not answering any questions until I know.'

She sat back down and folded her arms. Waiting.

Taking the lead, Layton reminded Karen that all she had a right to demand was a lawyer, and she now had one. Even if the lawyer looked like she wanted to be somewhere else entirely.

'Can you give my client any assurances regarding her concerns about her family?' the lawyer asked. She had a broad Sydney accent, and she was rifling through her notes as she spoke. For someone who appeared flustered, her voice held a certain practised confidence.

A heavy, tense pause settled between the two sides.

Kennard spoke up. 'I will get one of our team to check on the children.' He would put DePaul or Sancho on it. Keep them out of the way.

The lawyer looked to her client. Karen didn't look appeased but nodded once.

Layton covered the necessary prologue: name, date of birth and address. Then she launched straight in.

'Mrs Lautahahi, can you tell us where you were on Tuesday night?'

'I was at home.'

'All night?'

'All night.'

'Your husband stated that there is no one else who can corroborate that.'

Karen shrugged her shoulders. 'I guess not. We didn't think that it would need to be corroborated.'

'But it does.'

'That's your opinion,' said Karen, remaining obtuse, raging against the machine. 'We have three children, Detective. It's not like we can just leave them alone in the house.'

Layton jumped on this. 'Both of you don't need to be in the house, though, do you?'

'We both were at home.'

'Your husband has also stated, for the record, that you and your sister, Tracey, didn't get on.'

Karen laughed, shaking her head. 'That's not front-page news.'

'What put you over the edge? The photo of Alvin, thinking that she wanted to steal him from you?'

Karen frowned. 'What would you think if your sister suddenly took an unusual interest in your husband? She never had before. When Alvin told me about the photo, her having him pose, I thought . . .' Karen trailed off.

'What did you think, Mrs Lautahahi?' asked Layton.

Karen closed her eyes and tilted her head back. 'I thought that she was toying with him. Luring him in. Like she did with past boyfriends I had. Using the money to buy loyalty, I guess.'

'Was that the last straw?' asked Kennard. 'After increasing the rent, calling the inspectors, letting out half of your home to a stranger and putting your kids in danger. Did she threaten that she was going to do it again?'

Karen looked at Kennard and shook her head. She looked tense and exasperated, but still in control. Kennard decided to try to upset her present balance.

'Or was it the family ornament that did it? Did she gloat that she had it, so you went over to teach her a lesson, snapping like you snapped with that inspector? You went over, demanded the ornament, she refused, you lashed out and before you knew it, she was dead.'

Hearing the theory about what might have happened to her sister seemed to rattle Karen. As if she had never considered the full implications. She glanced at her lawyer, then shifted in the seat. 'That's . . . no, nothing like that, Detective.'

'Then what was it like? Tell us.'

'How many times . . . ? I wasn't there.'

'But you were there. To get the ornament back.'

Karen fidgeted in her seat. A seat designed to make the interviewee uncomfortable. Small, plastic, uneven. 'Not on Tuesday.'

'When?'

'Last Sunday.'

'The 16th?'

'Yes. When Alvin had the kids on a picnic.'

'And Tracey just handed it over?'

Karen looked to her lawyer again as if wanting her to object. Nothing was forthcoming.

'No. I took it. Russell wasn't home. Tracey was sleeping so I went and took what was mine. Okay?'

'So, you admit to breaking and entering?'

'I didn't break anything; the door was open.'

'Trespassing, then?'

Karen swallowed hard. The lawyer jumped in. 'My client is admitting to no offence.'

There was another stretch of silence before Karen spoke. 'I'm not heartless. I worried for my sister. For her health,' she said, her eyes narrowed.

Layton's frown matched Kennard's own. 'That doesn't sound like an accurate depiction of your relationship from all we've heard,' she said.

'It's still true.'

Layton changed tack. 'How do you account for the concealment of the spanner which we believe to be the murder weapon, in your barn?'

'I don't know where it came from.'

'But it was found on your property, Mrs Lautahahi. If it wasn't you or your husband, then who put it there?'

Karen paused for a long while. Thinking. Desperate to escape the box she was in. Fighting for survival. Something that was also currently going on barely a few streets away, but on a massive scale.

The lawyer jumped in, finally breaking the silence. 'My client has stated it wasn't her. That should be all—'

'There was someone,' said Karen, brows furrowed. 'Helping Alvin with the sheds. On Wednesday. Showed up out of the blue.'

Kennard sat forward in his chair. Trying to tell if this was a lie.

'Who?' asked Layton.

'This guy called Joel.'

Kennard looked at Layton. Her mouth was open, but she was struggling to form a follow-up question. He stepped in.

'And you're saying this Joel was in the shed where we found the spanner?'

'I think so. With Alvin. I was getting the kids ready for the day. For school.'

Kennard paused the interview and returned to the other room with Layton to speak with Alvin. His scruffy young lawyer was reluctant to let them question his client again before he had done some preparation work, but Kennard ignored the plea.

'Your wife has told us that someone visited the farm on Wednesday.'

Alvin paused for just a second before answering. 'Yeah, that's true.'

'Who, Mr Lautahahi?'

Alvin rolled his eyes up in thought. 'A guy called Joel.'

'Last name?'

'I don't know. I have seen him with Tracey. In her car. Driving out of town.'

Kennard glanced at Layton. Joel Anselmo had given no indication that he was that close to Tracey Hilmeyer.

'When did he visit?' asked Layton.

'Early in the morning. Very early.'

'Did he say why he was there?'

'I think he was looking for work. Tracey probably told him about us. I was trying to bolt a panel that had slipped off the side of the shed and he asked if I needed a hand. I did need a hand. So, he helped.'

'What shed?' asked Kennard, finding the edge of his seat, his heart pounding.

'The good shed.'

'The one we discovered the spanner in?'

'Yeah.'

'Was he ever alone inside the shed?'

Alvin looked towards the side of the room. 'Yeah. I left to get some chalk to mark out the holes I needed.'

'How long was he alone for?' asked Kennard, firing the questions at Alvin.

'Maybe two minutes.'

'And you couldn't see him?'

'No.'

That sold it for Kennard. He looked at Layton and

could see that she felt the same. There was no good reason for Joel Anselmo to be at the Lautahahi's farm, other than to plant the murder weapon. Everyone in town knew that Tracey and Karen didn't get along with each other and he would have realized that he couldn't pin Tracey's murder on Russell as he was in Sydney working.

They had to find Joel Anselmo.

Fifty-Five

They broke off the interview abruptly, leaving Alvin and his lawyer sitting stunned in the room. Kennard was straight onto Incident Control. He hoped for Lenka and got her, finding himself staring at his reflection in a dark computer screen and fixing his hair as if he were face to face with her.

'Lenka.'

'DS Kennard, I presume.'

'The very same.'

'How can I help you today?'

'Can you give me a location for Joel Anselmo?'

'Yeah. No worries.' There was a few seconds' pause. 'Currently have him at the corner of Durdon and Greaves. You might have another problem, though.'

'What problem?'

'The wind change. That house on Caldicott is back on the danger list. The teams are on the move towards the area. Joel too.'

'Shit. Thanks, Lenka. Can you get Bairstow to ring me immediately?'

'Will do.'

'And let me know right away if Joel's status changes, will you?'

'Will do.'

Kennard hung up. Though he wanted to get out there immediately, they had to get their ducks in a row first.

'I've got a location,' he said to Layton at the other desk.

'Goodo. Look here.' She pointed at her screen.

'What is it?' asked Kennard, darting across the room.

Layton summarized what he was reading. 'Mr Anselmo received a minor conviction for selling hash and knock-off painkillers just outside of Geven two years ago. He was found with three hundred and twenty grams of hash. Over the trafficable limit of three hundred which pushed him into the indictable band.'

'Did he go to prison?'

'No. Because it was borderline and a first offence, he got a Community Corrections Order and a fine instead. According to the records he hasn't reoffended, but the skinny is he's still connected. Suspicions he's dealing in stronger stuff. Small-time, though. Out of his car.'

'Stronger stuff like?'

Layton flicked down the screen. 'Shit! Codoxamol and Febridol.'

Exactly the same types of opioids that they had found in Tracey's Mazda. That, along with the conviction for selling, left Kennard with no doubt that Joel Anselmo had been the one supplying Tracey Hilmeyer. Alvin Lautahahi had mentioned that he had spotted Joel and Tracey in Joel's car. So how well had they known each other?

Fifty-Six

Tracey – Before

August – Last year

Joel was persistent. Stocky and hard as a bullet, his shaved head only compounded the similarity. He was always lurking around when she least expected it, but the need for his stuff overwhelmed any disgust she felt, even if the price she was paying was beginning to spin out of control.

The drugs had entered her life long before Joel Anselmo had come along. Weed was easily sourced no matter where on the planet you were. She expected that even Vatican City had a contact. Opioids were different. They were tricky, more controlled, harder for dealers to pass over without getting their knuckles rapped.

So, at the start, Joel had been a godsend. He dealt hash, that was known. But she was after something else.

He was intense as always, flitting around like a dog desperate for attention. He was even set like a bulldog, cheeks crushed up into his eyes, puffy like a batch of Botox gone wrong. Whispers had reached her ears about him before. That his persistence could border on obsession, restraining orders filed by one girl in Geven and another in Katoomba. But deflecting unwanted attention was a skill she had developed over the years – a necessary one.

She reckoned his desperation would make him easy to manipulate and that it would be just as easy to guilt-trip him with the fact that she was his best friend's wife. And it had worked. It had kept him at arm's length. But as time had gone on, he had started expecting more. Like with the Codo and Febridol, his tolerance levels were building, and he was beginning to itch for something extra. Her ways of cooling his desire were waning, and so they found themselves locked together in this dance.

She had spotted Joel on the main drag, passing her window as she waited for the next load of tour buses. She darted outside to stop him. 'Joel?'

At first, he froze, glancing around as if she had shone a spotlight on him.

'Can I speak to you?'

'Okay.'

'Inside?'

At this, Joel glanced in the window, scoping out the land. He remained hesitant, like a cat that was unsure whether to cross a boundary line, but in the end, curiosity won out and he followed her inside the shop. His eyes wandered up and down the length of her. Taking it all in.

'I'm looking for you to hook me up.'

'Whatever weed you need—'

'Not weed. Opioids.'

Joel began to back off, towards the door. 'Look, I dunno—'

'Just some Codo.'

Again Joel glanced behind him, as if expecting a cop to suddenly materialize behind him. 'I don't know if I should.'

'I can pay.'

She could see the twitch in his eyes, the understanding that he shouldn't be doing this.

'Look, Trace, I don't think Russ would be happy.'

'He doesn't need to know.'

Still Joel looked unsure. So, she put her hand on his shoulder. It tensed immediately, as firm as a block of wood.

'You'd be doing me a huge favour,' she said, flashing a smile at him.

'Look, I'll see what I can do. No promises. And no telling Russ. Okay?'

She put a finger to her lips. Joel offered a faint smile, his resolve broken. Not that it had taken much. He had scampered out of the shop as if she had lit his tail on fire.

It had been two days before she spotted the hideous spoiler that made his car look like a shopping trolley.

She threw the CLOSED sign on the door and retreated out back. Five minutes later there was a knock on the gates, Joel glancing around before entering. He kept his hands firmly in his pockets, elbows poking out and head tilted to the side, while his eyes performed the same slow wander over her body that seemed to happen involuntarily whenever he saw her. 'Got anywhere private?' he asked.

'We're walled in,' she said, frowning.

'I don't like to conduct business outside.'

She stared at him. He was dressed to impress, but the bold shirt and cut-off puffer jacket did nothing for her. He was just flashing his wealth. Like her tourists.

'Come inside,' she acquiesced, and led him through the shop and behind the counter curtain out of sight of anyone nosy enough to stare in through the front window. Up close, his aftershave was strong. Recently applied, too, given the harsh red burn under his rounded jaw.

'You sure about these?' he asked, hands still wedged in his pockets, reluctant to reveal the goods.

'It's not my first rodeo, Joel,' she lied, twisting her voice into the alluring tone that had won Russell over all those years ago.

His hands came out of his pockets holding little white plastic tubs that he shook like maracas.

'You want this to be a regular thing?' he asked.

'If you can get them.'

He smiled, raising his eyebrows. 'I can get them.'

Tracey handed over the money. Lots of colour in exchange for plain white bottles. Unmarked. Anonymous.

Joel turned to leave but stopped.

'Not a word to Russell, eh?'

Tracey put her lips together, drawing a zip across them.

What she'd come to realise was that drugs weren't all bad – not that this would ever be stated on any government leaflet. They were the button that switched off the lights. Transporting her to another world where the edges were sanded down. Usage was generally restricted to her days off, though lately it had begun to creep. That was the thing about addiction. It was fucking cunning. It promised the earth but only stole time. It became the entire world, the only thing she looked forward to, and even that sliver of paradise became harder to attain, the weed at lunch nothing but a sticking plaster.

The meetings in the shop soon turned into meetings at the disued brickyard, then Jipps's Lane and the old look-out that had washed away with the heavy rains three years ago. He was always there first, aftershave and mouthwash hanging around him like a fog. They always met in her car, not his. She insisted. For some reason she felt that if she got into Joel's car, she wouldn't be getting out again. It was just a feeling she had. There was that cold look he fostered in public that made him seem dangerous, his words tinged with desire and frustration, a gaze that almost tried to cage her as his own. With her he tried to act sweet, but she got the sense he could turn at any moment.

As the stuff kept coming in, though, she struggled to find the money to pay. She was always short, spinning him lies to keep him feeding her habit for the cheap knock-off Codo from China. Recently expired, not that she cared. Lately she had been forcing customers out of the shop, using the trick of being too engaging. Hanging off their shoulder looking eager for a sale. And if that failed, she would over-charge them, less interested in what they looked like than what they could produce from their wallets. And that was the thing about tourists. They didn't have a fucking clue about

what things actually cost, especially the smaller items –
South Australian opals, the silver jewellery marketed as
Indigenous but made by Sally Gunter and her sister on
Cromach Street. People will pay for shiny or what they
believe is authentic. The extra cash helped ward off Joel
for a little longer. She was still short every time, but she
was managing. The next day was the next day and finding
the cash to pay for what she needed could wait until then.

'Got the dough?' he asked when they had parked on
the lane that once ended in the Farnoo lookout, his tone
upbeat.

'Bit short.' She had managed to scrape some cash together by cutting down on what she ate. By telling Russell
that she needed a few bucks for work on the Mazda, a new
subscription to a streaming service that she would never
sign up to.

Joel looked at her with pity. She hated pity. Hated that
she needed it.

'We can't keep doing this, Trace.'

'I know. I promise. Next time.'

'You always promise,' he said harshly, his friendly per-
sona cracking a little.

'Look, it's tough right now.'

'It's tough for all of us, Trace. We all have responsibilities.'

That was when the big lie came out of nowhere.

'I've got a relative. They're on their way out.'

'Oh.' These were the moments when Joel looked most
attractive, his bulldog expression softening, the stiffness
in his jaw released. The times he wasn't trying to get into
her knickers.

'Yeah, it's tough,' she lied.

'What relative?'

'You don't know them. From back home in Queensland.'

But the relative that Tracey was thinking of was very much around here, and she began to wonder if indeed her sister should maybe die. Her death *would* free up the land. It was a thought that she didn't want to entertain, one she tried to push away, though it wouldn't leave, as hard as she tried. Karen and Alvin out of the way, the land hers, sold to fund a gallery she could get back up and running. She knew that they were struggling from the many times that she'd driven by the place, checking that they weren't doing anything with her side of the farm. She would see the run-down house and barns, the broken slates and the decay, the kids running around the yard, playing happy families despite the poverty. It made her sick to her stomach. As if the roles had been switched and Karen had ended up with the three kids that Tracey wanted.

So she continued to feed Joel stories. About her family. About her parents. About the farm and Karen kicking her off it. Lies about how her sister was trying to get full control of the land and the farmhouse.

'How do you know that?' Joel was staring at her, in thrall by just being near her.

'I know my sister. You must have seen all the government folks up there.'

'Yeah, but I thought they were just having a nosey.'

'That's what she wants us to think. Don't you think it's suspect that it keeps going?'

'Never thought about it.'

'They'd have closed it years ago if . . .'

'If?' He was hanging on her every word.

'If she wasn't dobbing on people.'

'You think so?' Joel was frowning, all his facial features seeming to crush into one singularity like a black hole.

'I do.'

'She can't sell your land!' Joel slammed his hand on the dashboard.

His show of anger startled Tracey and she found herself inching away from him.

'There's not much I can do.'

'There's always something.'

She stared into his eyes, his hard glare meaning business. She wondered how far she could push him. What she could make him do. He had already admitted to her that he'd had a few run-ins with the cops before, tales that he recounted with pride and in so much detail that she knew they were true. Intimidation of ex-boyfriends of women he was seeing. Of women who'd eventually grown tired of him but who she now knew he didn't let go. She should have run, but as much as he had his claws in her, she needed him. Or at least, she could use him. Could he drive Karen and Alvin off the farm? But how? The idea of poison had taken root. Animals get sick all the time out here, don't they? And there were always accidents catching people unawares. And that was the thing about accidents. No one could foresee them.

Fifty-Seven

Kennard had an idea. 'Can we bring up his car registration? If it's parked in town, we might be able to have a snoop around it. I'm sure we could find grounds for a proper search.'

Layton brought it up onscreen. 'A silver Holden Barina. Registration XCA-39B.'

A small firework exploded in Kennard's head.

'An old silver Barina? I've seen it. Parked at the school. Distinctive. Like a shopping trolley. As Alvin said: pimped to the extreme.'

As Kennard dashed through the makeshift car park with Layton in tow, the air caught in his throat causing him to cough. The unmistakable cloying smell of burning plastic. Something big was burning. Another ingredient in the massive soup of destruction. But that was merely irritating. What was worrying was that the smell had reached his nose in the first place. It indicated a shift in the wind direction. Northwest. Pushing back towards Rislake. Giving the bushfire a chance to reach out and grab onto some valuable kindling.

By one of the fifty-metre lines on the footy field he spotted a boxy silver Holden, unlike any Barina he had ever seen. It might have been twenty years old, but it had clearly been given a number of facelifts, pimped up in a cut-rate manner, an oversized wing arching over the rear of the vehicle like a scorpion's tail, a low spoiler hanging off the front like something better suited to a snowplough, headlights that looked as mean as a cat's eyes. It was undeniably ugly. If anything deserved to burn up in the fire, it was this monstrosity.

Through the window he could see that the inside was rather less modified than the exterior, retaining the basic brown knobbed gearstick, the original analogue dashboard and handbrake. The only things to have been upgraded were the steering wheel, which had what looked to be a Lamborghini crest glued to the centre, and a row of switches where the CD player used to be.

There was nothing overly suspicious – no bottles of pills strewn on the seat, no murder weapon – but he wanted to take the car apart, panel by panel. Usually, he felt a little shame at ordering the destruction of a perfectly good object or vehicle, but in this case, it would be doing the world a favour.

Taking a breath, a wave of dizziness suddenly hit him hard, swiftly followed by a coughing jag, the choking smell of plastic overwhelming him. It felt like he was hacking his lungs up, and he put his hands on his knees to catch his breath, coming face to face with the strips of underglow lights fitted beneath the doorframes. He sucked in as deep a gob of air as he dared and moved to the other side, where Layton was peering in through the window.

'What is it?' she asked as he bent down again.

'The missing lights,' he said, holding in a cough.

'What about them?'

'Call Eric. Or your boyfriend. I just have to get something.'

Fighting the stars in front of his eyes, he retrieved the fibreglass strip from the boot of his car and returned to the Holden.

'Where did you get that?' asked Layton.

'Matches, doesn't it?'

'Seems to,' said Layton. 'Where did you find it?

'I didn't. Winnie and Harald did.'

'The neighbours?'

'They found it on Wednesday morning outside their house. Which means that Joel was parked near the Hilmeyer house not long before then. The car that Winnie and Harald heard speeding off late on Tuesday evening must have been his. In his haste, he left behind a strip of these lights.'

'Why was he there?'

'That's the question.'

'The obvious answer is that he was dropping off a supply to Tracey. Possibly timed to coincide with Russell being away,' said Layton.

'But why would he kill her?'

'A fight over payment? A fight about the pregnancy?'

'It's an unusual match.' Joel Anselmo was short, with pug-like features that were almost a match for his horrendous car.

'But not impossible. As her dealer, he probably exerted an element of control.'

Kennard needed Forensics to scour the Hilmeyer house again, for Joel's DNA this time, and then do a search of his car for Tracey's DNA. One thing was for sure, he wasn't going to be getting a Christmas card from Eric Henia this year.

'Anything from Bairstow?' he asked, coughing again. He needed to hear from the GC but wasn't hopeful. The change in wind direction would surely have him on edge. A reminder that the advancing fire wanted to destroy everything – their scene, their evidence, even their suspect. It was a fire that took precedence over Tracey's murder, that much was clear.

'Nothing yet. We need Haskell's help,' said Layton.

Kennard had been resisting it, itching to go solo, to prove himself. But Layton was right. He swallowed his pride and phoned the DSS.

'Kennard? What trouble are you bringing me this time?' Haskell, as ever, sounded serious. As if every second of her time was so precious, he was wasting it by leaving even the smallest gap between his words.

'We have a probable murder weapon.'

'Found at the Lautahahi farm. I know this, DS Kennard.'

'We also have witness testimony that Joel Anselmo was at the farm on Wednesday morning with the opportunity to plant the weapon,' Kennard continued before Haskell could say anything more. 'The Lautahahis' claim that he turned up out of the blue pretending to be a good

341

Samaritan. He had no other reason to be there than to plant the murder weapon after he'd brutally killed Tracey. Russell was out of town and Joel couldn't pin it on him, but he knew that the sisters didn't get along, so it was the next best option.'

'And risk getting caught?'

Layton jumped in. 'Maybe his plan was to sneak in, but an early-rising Mr Lautahahi beat him to the punch and so he was forced to gain access by pretending to help.'

Kennard went on, 'We have further evidence that Mr Anselmo was at, or close to, the scene of the crime on the night of the murder. We believe that he was supplying the victim with illegal prescription drugs and other substances.'

'And your evidence is?'

'Joel received a Corrections Order for supplying hash and there's a strong rumour that he deals in opioids and expired painkillers of the same type as those found in Tracey Hilmeyer's vehicle. We also have a statement from Alvin that he had spotted Joel in Tracey's car previously. And a statement from Russell and Tracey's neighbours about a loud car speeding away on Tuesday night and a set of strip lights recovered by them the morning after that matches a missing part on Joel Anselmo's vehicle. That places him at the scene on the night of the murder.'

'Where is the suspect currently?'

'Dealing with the ongoing bushfire situation. We'd like to arrest him,' said Kennard.

There was a long pause. Kennard wondered if the comms had dropped.

'DSS Haskell?'

'Still here. I'm thinking.'

This was the longest he had known Haskell to deliberate for. She usually trusted her judgement implicitly and was known for making snap decisions, so it was obvious to Kennard that it was him she didn't trust in this equation.

'Does DS Layton agree?' Her tone was stiff, braced to argue. Seeking a second opinion. Not fully trusting his when push came to shove.

'I agree,' said Layton, looking at the phone rather than Kennard, as if embarrassed. For him.

'So, you want me to clear it with the GC in command?' asked Haskell.

'Probably best,' said Kennard. 'We don't exactly see eye to eye.'

'That doesn't seem to be unusual for you, DS Kennard. Do you need more support down there?'

Kennard railed at the note of condescension in her voice – she was treating him like a rookie. He just about managed to hold his tongue.

'We can get the local sergeant involved,' he said.

'Are you sure?'

'I think our suspect might be less likely to flee from faces he knows if it comes to it.'

'All right. Do it. I'll get on to the GC to tell you when it's safe.'

'Ask for—'

But Haskell had already hung up. Kennard followed her lead and wasted no time before phoning the local station and getting patched through to Reinhold.

'We need to arrest Joel Anselmo.'

Reinhold spluttered his response. 'Another firefighter? Have you cleared—?'

It was Kennard's turn to cut someone off. 'It's being cleared as we speak. We need two of your guys with us in case he tries to run.'

'I need everyone I can get. With the wind change, people are getting twisted knickers.'

'Just get me two solid bodies. And a total blackout on comms about this. Our suspect can't know that we're coming to get him.'

The answer to this was a frustrated mumble before Kennard hung up the phone. His ear was burning. His mum would have warned him that someone was talking about him. Which was probably true in this case, and with less than friendly words.

Immediately, Layton's phone rang. Kennard tried to eavesdrop on the conversation, anxious to get going.

'Bairstow?' he mimed at her.

Layton hung up.

'No. Haskell has got the go-ahead for the car and Joel's house. She's sending people there now, including a FSG team from Sydney.'

'Already?'

'Already,' said Layton.

That was one positive thing to say about Haskell: she sure worked fast.

Fifty-Eight

Tracey – Before

January

The ultimatum was expected. Overdue, really. It finally came a week after New Year, when they were parked out the back of the old railway station at Phail mine, twenty minutes from town, the platform overgrown, the station building rattling as each train roared past without stopping.

'I'll need the cash. All of it,' said Joel. He looked antsy, sweat rolling off his angled head.

'Another week?' she asked, fluttering her eyelashes.

'No, not another week, Trace. There's been too many "another week"s. I need it.'

'Come on, Joel, you know I'm good for it.'

Joel shook his head. His brow furrowed, casting a shadow over his eyes.

'I don't think you understand, Trace,' he half-snarled,

345

turning his face away, staring out the window, the tendons bulging in his neck. This, above everything else, unnerved Tracey. Joel always looked at her, studied her, so in love with her that he was prepared to wait. His turning away from her signalled that her hold over him was waning. 'I *need* it.'

Tracey didn't have the money. None of it. Nothing to even fob him off with this time. The week's skim from the shop had been poor – bad weather, low footfall. She had reached her last resort. She grabbed his head and pulled it around to face her. She leaned in and kissed him – on the lips, putting her full weight into it to try to mask the fact that she didn't want to. His lips were dry and thin, like kissing cardboard. He let it continue for a few seconds before pulling back and glancing around.

His frown had disappeared, replaced by fear. 'What if someone sees us?'

'There won't be a train for another twenty minutes. We're just two people having a lunchtime pash.' She was banking on this being enough to buy another week's stay of execution. She was barely hanging on.

Joel stared at her, trying to read her face as she tried to do the same to his. He looked confused, caught between anger and finally getting what he had been angling for all along. He leaned in for another kiss, taking the lead, his lips chaffing, their teeth clashing as his tongue pressed into her mouth like he was rooting around for gold.

Now, a week and a half later, Tracey knew the kiss had been a bad idea. It had unleashed a part of Joel that she hadn't seen before. He had gotten a taste and now he wanted more, the seal of Pandora's Box broken. His fear of being seen together at a disused railway station had quickly vanished and he had since taken to cruising by the house when he knew Russell was away. She had found out first-hand that the rumours were true – there were two sides to Joel: the sweet, caring side and the obsessive, unbridled side. That side had stalked two former girlfriends, had left first flowers and then aggressive notes and broken bottles outside their doors. That part of Joel had flirted with the limits of various restraining orders until the threat of jail had finally stopped him.

'Trace?'

The sound of his voice made her shiver. The effect of the weed wore off in seconds, her heavy eyes lifting, alert to danger. She rose to follow the noise of the raps, insistent on the plastic outer panel like a woodpecker. *Peck, peck, peck.*

'Who is it?' she asked, though of course she knew who it was at her door. The back door, thankfully; he was still fearful enough to retain some element of secrecy.

'It's Joel. I need to talk to you.'

'What do you want?'

'You know what I want.'

She did. She made it to the door and pressed against it. She knew it was unlocked but if she attempted to lock it now, he would hear the click. And she was a little frightened of what he would do if she rejected him outright.

'A bit crook here, Joel. The cold or flu, I dunno. I'm a mess right now.' She wasn't kidding about that. The sweat on her skin was very real, but it wasn't from illness or withdrawal. She was scared of her unannounced visitor. All the way up here. When she was alone.

'I can help. Bring you—'

'I don't want to see anyone, Joel. Not today.'

'Just let me in.'

'I . . . You don't want to get sick.'

'That's my choice.'

But it wasn't his choice. It was hers.

'Tomorrow,' she said.

'It needs to be tonight, Trace.'

'I'm not in the mood for—'

'I need something. A promise isn't enough. Not anymore.'

'What if Russ comes back?'

'He won't be back. You know it, I know it.'

Joel had been waiting. For Russell to be out of town for the night. To have her alone and vulnerable.

She sniffed, trying to sell the illness. It wasn't hard, fear forcing her to the edge of tears, her nose beginning to run.

'You're suffering. Let me help.'

'It's better on my own – dark room, eyes closed.'

'Right.' There was a long pause. She hoped that was it. But Joel wasn't finished. 'I need the money, Trace.'

'Another few days, I promise. My uncle's about to croak—'

'They're putting the squeeze on.'

Joel had been candid about that. About how he was on the hook to his suppliers, a sob story about how dealing was only meant to have been a temporary thing, but the money proved too good. Filtering whatever was needed up from Sydney. Benzos, coke, weed, Codo, Feb. Even H when it was asked for. Paying his dues. Earning well. But things had begun to fall apart lately. Tracey had understood the subtext. She was the reason it was unravelling.

'I know, and I'm sorry.'

'Trace, it's no joke. It's time.' His voice was getting louder, enough that Winnie and Harald would catch everything. If they let slip that Joel had been here, it might send Russell over the edge.

She didn't answer. She didn't know what to say.

'I need to know that this is real, Trace. I love you.'

Tracey held her breath. Joel's profession of love wasn't unexpected. It had been apparent in his devotion, his desire to see her and help her. It meant that the time had come. A lie and she would have to do something she didn't want to. The truth . . . the truth might be worse.

Fifty-Nine

Inside the school building the fluorescent lights helped provide a contrast to just how dark it was outside. It was like being at night school, only there were no teachers, just a bunch of students who didn't know what test they might have to pass.

Lenka was at her desk, on a call, delivering the latest report to whoever was on the other end of the line with an air of assured authority, impassioned yet calm. Bad news was still news, and it had to be delivered clearly and concisely. Kennard imagined her as the captain going down with the ship but shook that image away. He hoped it wouldn't come to that.

The number of operators on the morning shift had increased to five, their caffeine intake betrayed by the pile of paper cups stacked on a spare desk in the corner beside a grubby instant coffee maker.

As he and Layton approached Lenka, Kennard could see that the influx of caffeine, constant pressure and extended shifts was taking its toll on her. There was a quiver in her hands and a slightly washed-out expression on her face. Not even liberal cups of coffee could quench this kind of exhaustion, the dark liquid almost seeming to have drained into the circles around her eyes.

'Still on shift?' he asked with a sympathetic smile. 'Who did you piss off?' This close he caught a whiff of her perfume. Given that she had been sitting in a sticky room for over twenty-four hours, she smelled good. Kennard had no such protection and found himself very aware of it.

'As long as they keep paying me, I'll keep answering calls,' she replied, taking another shaky sip from her mug. She looked around the room at the other operators. 'But I'm guessing this isn't a social visit.'

'Not entirely,' said Kennard. They hadn't heard from Bairstow, Haskell's wonders running dry. 'We still need Bairstow. Can you get in touch with him?'

'Reception's spotty.'

'So that's a no?'

Lenka shook her head. 'Not at present.'

'Still got eyes on Mr Anselmo?' asked Layton.

Lenka pointed to a blue dot on the screen. 'There's your man. Still at the front. Been a tough few hours.'

'How come?'

351

'The wind change is blowing embers around town, increasing the number of spot fires. Means that resources are being stretched even thinner to cover evacuations and warnings.'

'That's why the yard's so empty of vehicles?' guessed Layton.

'Exactly.'

'What's it like out there?' Kennard asked.

'Hell on earth, I've been told. And that's from a twenty-five-year veteran. He said that the embers were sparking everything, and that with the swirling wind it's getting harder to predict what might catch next. Rislake is essentially now one massive fire area with a pyro-cumulonimbus cloud hanging over it.'

'And that means?'

'That it's generating its own lightning. And, of course, lightning starts more fires. He didn't hold out much hope for the town unless the wind dropped or somehow reversed.'

'You're kidding me? Lightning?' said Kennard. He didn't need more reasons not to go to the north side.

Lenka shook her head. 'Here. This was filmed an hour ago. Out in Versaille.'

Onscreen a camera feed quivered, a phone held up in the wind to the dark mass above. Rain was falling on the lens in hard, heavy drops.

'It's raining,' said Kennard. 'That's good, isn't it?'

But Lenka didn't look happy. Above the column of smoke from the wildfire was a cloud, the top flattened into the shape of an anvil. Huge and terrifying in size.

'The cloud you see above the smoke is caused by water vapour condensing on the ash. You know the famous photos of the mushroom cloud over Hiroshima?'

'Yeah,' said Kennard. It was an image he had seen many times. The giant plume towering over the city like a marker of death.

'People think that's the radiation cloud. It's not. It's the pyro cloud after. And that's not the real problem. The rain is,' said Lenka.

'How?'

'It creates cold air, a downdraft that can carry embers further along the ground, igniting spot fires. It also leads to this.'

Onscreen there was a loud crack and then a violent spear of lightning, disappearing somewhere behind the trees, the boom deafening over the speakers. Kennard felt his heart hammering in his chest, his arm twitching. He spied Layton watching him. As if she wanted to say something.

Lenka interrupted before she could. 'There's a chance of dry lightning. Maybe even a fire tornado.'

Kennard didn't want to ask what that meant. His imagination was working overdrive as it was.

'We need to go in,' he said, putting the words out there just so they couldn't be taken back.

Lenka shook her head, astonished. 'There's no one to support you.'

Kennard felt his stomach sink. 'No one?'

'No, it's the final push.'

Kennard looked at Layton. The trepidation he felt was

etched on her face. Abruptly, she turned and headed outside. Possibly to chunder.

'Are you really going in?' whispered Lenka.

'We have to,' he said.

'Then load up with full gear.'

'We will.'

'Take breathing equipment too. If you get caught in the middle of it, you'll scorch your lungs and suffocate in your own fluids.'

'Thanks for the pep talk.'

'It's the best I can do after four hours' sleep in forty-eight.'

They exchanged tired smiles as Kennard got ready to leave.

'Head towards Kinsey Road, just west of the old firehouse. He's still there.'

'Call me if he moves.'

'I'll try, but don't be surprised if you can't get a signal out there. The fire's been tearing through lines and masts like paper. We're struggling even with basic comms.'

Kennard nodded and left to catch up with Layton. If she wasn't throwing up, she was hopefully prepping the two local constables who were joining them as backup on this mission to hell.

But she was on the phone, her voice low. Possibly a personal call. To her boyfriend or someone else. A 'goodbye just in case' call. He knew he should do the same for Ann, but he was too pumped up. He just wanted to get on with it. They had been distracted by Karen and Alvin for too long. Played by Joel. Of course the Lautahahis wouldn't have risked their family to murder Tracey. And burning

354

the house on Caldicott down would only have put their own livelihood under threat. It was too big a risk, burning down what they had painstakingly built.

Even with the heavy drifting smoke blocking out a significant portion of the sun's power, Kennard began to sweat. He cracked open a bottle of water and downed it, though he hated the taste of water and had done ever since childhood, fastidiously sticking to fizzy drinks, tea and then beer. Water was for emergencies only.

His eyes were drawn to the pyro cloud in the distance. The one he was about to head straight for.

'Do you want me to stop DS Kennard? Take DePaul instead?' Layton's muttered words carried on the wind. They drew Kennard's attention. This wasn't a personal call. They were talking about him.

Layton hadn't noticed him standing nearby. After a pause, she answered whatever question she had been asked. 'In my opinion, yes. Classic signs of PTSD. He isn't sleeping well, he's irritable, nervous. Prone to—'

She went silent again, listening to the response. Nodding.

'The most prudent option would probably be to replace him, but like I said earlier—' Another pause for a response. She was clearly speaking to someone in authority. Someone superior. Someone who liked interrupting. DSS Una Haskell. 'If you do it, do it now. We need to move.'

Kennard butted in. 'We *do* need to move.'

Layton nearly dropped the phone, startled.

'Kennard!'

'Who's that?' he asked, nodding at the phone.

Layton paused, glancing at it and ending the call. 'Home.'

'You'd make a shit bridge player,' said Kennard. 'So, who has PTSD? Who is it that you want to replace?'

Layton glanced away for a moment before focusing back on him.

'DSS Haskell was asking.'

'Asking what?'

'If you were okay. If you could go back in there.'

'And why wouldn't I be?'

'Because you *are* suffering from PTSD, Kennard. It's plain to see. I've studied it, I'm writing . . .' She trailed off, turning away.

'Finish your sentence, DS Layton. You're writing . . .'

'A thesis.'

'On PTSD in officers?'

'Yeah.'

'So, when the chance came up to be partnered with me you thought you'd observe a real-life nutcase?'

'It's not like that.'

'It sounds exactly like that. You volunteered, or you were volunteered, because Haskell thinks I'm a liability. She wants you checking up on me.'

'I volunteered. I want to help.'

'By spying on me?'

'Haskell wanted you taken off the case. But she—'

'She preferred me to come to the same conclusion on my own. Ask to leave. Or fuck up badly enough that she'd have an obvious reason to get rid of me.'

Layton was silent.

'I'm guessing that's the truth or close enough to it,' said Kennard, spitting the words out through gritted teeth.

'The truth? The truth is that you have PTSD, Kennard. You can rage against me and against everyone but *that's* the truth. You need help.'

'And you're that help? Pretending to be my partner.'

'I am your partner.'

'And my psychiatrist too, apparently.' Kennard was furious now. The betrayal was choking him, his blood boiling. He thought that they had started developing a rapport, but he had just been Layton's subject all along.

'We'll get into this later. Now we have a job to do.'

'So, you've decided that I'm fit to risk my life but not fit enough be a detective. Is that it?'

'I told Haskell that you were. That you could cope with going back in. That I would take the heat if something goes wrong.'

Kennard studied Layton closely, trying to read the truth. 'Why?'

'Because you're a fighter. Mostly against your own better judgement, but you're a good detective. I don't think you're a liability.'

'Do they give out medals for not being a liability?'

There was a moment's silence, the tension simmering.

Layton broke it. 'No, but they do for apprehending murderers.'

Sixty

28.5 hours since North Rislake evacuation

South Rislake status = Red (Evacuation procedures commence)

Pyro-cumulonimbus warning in place

As they suited up in the bunker gear, there was an air of uneasiness among the four of them that wasn't helped by the unwavering gloom and the scattered explosions in the distance. The extra layer to Layton's discomfort was obvious. She had been caught spying on him. Dobbing him in to their boss. No matter the reason, no matter the truth behind the reason, she was still a snitch.

Kennard's own nervousness came from what might lie ahead. Whether, as Haskell doubted, he could handle it. It was impossible to tell what they would face in there. The pyro cloud video hadn't helped his confidence levels.

One more weapon in nature's arsenal. They would be stepping into an arena where the conditions were unstable and dangerous, and where their suspect would have the upper hand through sheer experience. All they had was the element of surprise.

Lenka had made one last attempt to call ahead and warn Bairstow that they were heading out to speak to Mr Anselmo. That they were planning to arrest him had been left out of the communique in case word got to Joel in some form. Or to Russell, who might piece together why his friend was being sought so desperately by the cops and do something rash.

Transport was another issue. All the PCs were in use. The tankers and support trucks too. All hands were literally to the pump. That left Kennard's own car. A Volkswagen Passat. Not exactly the ideal vehicle for facing an inferno.

Even getting into the car was tough, the bulky clothing pressing up against the steering wheel. As he shoved the seat back to afford some space, he was met with a howl of disapproval from the cop wedged in behind him. His name was Morrow. He lived on a farm southwest of Rislake. One that wasn't threatened by this bushfire. The other cop was a local, Cockburn, a serious-looking man with eyes the colour of granite staring back at Kennard from under his white helmet.

Kennard turned in his seat as best he could to give them a rundown of what they might face, drawing on his experience from the day before.

'When we get there, don't attempt anything heroic. DS

Layton and I will approach the suspect while you maintain the perimeter. Should he break the perimeter, then you can try to intercept him. But don't put yourselves at unnecessary risk.'

He meant this for himself and Layton as well. What they were about to do was brave – which Layton could stick in her report – bordering on stupid – which Layton might also stick in her report – but they could still manage the risks. Speech over, he pulled out of the yard and passed across the top of Main Street. Where once he could have made out the crossroads at the bottom, plain as day, now the scene was shrouded, a grey pall cast over the picturesque view. The gloom had affected the people too. The sliver of a thrill that had been present yesterday had today been replaced by full-blown panic, as the furious car horns, waving fists and backed-up traffic testified. When the fire had been confined to the north of town, it had been their neighbours' problem. Now it was everyone's.

As he turned to descend one of the side streets, the windshield caught a shower of sparks that drifted through the heated air and scraped along the asphalt. Having shifted back on itself, the wind was increasing in force, insistent on taking the town.

Kennard picked up the pace, houses flashing past, homes with love poured into them, spruced up with an array of hanging baskets and quirky floral arrangements, the neutral colours suggesting coordination, nothing too garish, designed to accentuate the whole rather than the individual. The street was very familiar to him with its off-straight kerbing, as if whoever had laid it had been hungover from the night before. It made him look twice, as it had done all those years ago as a teenager, as though his eyes were playing tricks on him, the shimmer of heat and the misaligned kerbs creating a road that danced and twisted in the haze.

Halfway down the hill, he slowed as he approached the rented house from his childhood summers with its narrowing porch that funnelled towards the front gate. Kennard could remember exploding out that front door, jumping off those very steps to the pavement. The cherry red had gone, the current sea blue more demure and in keeping with the rest of the street. He could remember being very happy there, his only responsibility to be home for dinner, his biggest worry being small, biting insects, larger kids and whether his pocket money would stretch to a Violet Crumble.

As Kennard drove past, he wished he could stop and take some photos to show his parents. They might have even helped jog his mum's memory, which had been fading slowly over the last six months – the onset of dementia. Thankfully it had been very mild so far, but like a stone rolled down a hill, it was only going to pick up speed.

Near the bottom of the street, they passed a pair of police cars parked clumsily by the side of the road, dark shadowy figures helping an old couple out of a house and into one of the vehicles. The evacuation of the south side of Rislake had begun. As Kennard slowed the car, he could see a flicker of orange flame rising up from behind the adjacent house, and another blazing a hole in what was once a neatly tended flowerbed.

At least Layton wasn't complaining about his leisurely pace as he made the gully at the bottom of the hill, the smoke briefly clearing as they crossed the wide, low bridge to the other side of town. Kennard didn't dare look at his passengers in case their terror made him chicken out. This was it. If the south side of town felt ominous, it was nothing compared to the deadly threat posed by the north side. The car rose once again into the band of smoke, the murky gloom closing in on them fast. The fumes were thick and black, the headlights failing to pierce them and merely highlighting just how dark it was. They passed a few vehicles still parked at the side of the road, abandoned by their owners just as their houses had been. A brilliant shower of embers crossed the path of the car like a thousand sparklers discarded into the wind. They struck the windshield and shattered into even tinier pieces, each searching for a place to start another fire. Only one or two would have to be successful for the results to be disastrous.

Kennard's headlights caught a swirl of thicker smoke that clouded the road ahead. As they were swallowed up in it Layton tried to guide him via the map on her phone, but the signal was becoming intermittent, their dot pausing then jerking along Sinton Road, which curved to the right as it climbed parallel to Caldicott only a few streets across.

Last time he had been out here there had been a marked difference. Back then, the wind had been carrying the smoke and the flames across the outer edge of the town, which had allowed him a view of the houses on the hill from a distance. Now the smoke felt like it was wrapped around them like a blindfold. Kennard tried to stay alert.

They would be approaching the top soon and he didn't want to be crushed by a tanker blindly rushing down the hill. His Passat wasn't built to take on a thirteen-ton fire truck head on.

Suddenly a wall of noise hit them. It was the sound of destruction, cracking, snapping and popping, the angry howl of the town being ripped apart. How could anything survive this? Was he going to reach the top of the hill and find nothing but a burnt-out shell and a series of charred skeletons? These thoughts, the ever-present roar of destruction and the loaded silence in the car made him want to say something. Just to confirm to himself that this was really happening. Only the searing heat reminded him it was, the sweat that ran down his face trapped by his goggles, pooling underneath his eyes, eliciting a sting that blurred his vision and made the world outside look even more surreal.

The silence was interrupted by a melodic ring. Out of his peripheral vision he watched Layton swipe her finger over her phone screen. It glowed, lighting her face like some Halloween storyteller, flashlight under her chin ready to tell a spooky story.

Kennard wondered if it was Lenka telling him that Joel had been dispatched back to the school. He hoped so. He could turn the car right around and get the hell out of there.

'It's Joel Anselmo's house,' said Layton.

Kennard glanced across at her. 'Put it on speaker.'

Layton did. They listened as the raid got underway, hearing the sound of a door being busted in and a cry of 'Police!' ringing loudly over the speaker. As Kennard eased through the smoke, he wished they could extend to a video feed but knew the comms situation wouldn't allow it.

'What does it look like in there?' he asked over the two-way.

Uptill answered. Even the sound of his voice made Kennard angry. 'Untidy. Nah, wait, I'll rephrase that. There's shit everywhere. Definitely a bachelor, that's for sure.' The way he said it made it sound as if he was glad not to be one any longer, presumably another new girl-friend half his age had arrived in his life, ready to sweep up his mess.

'Anything striking you as odd?' asked Layton, as loud shouts of 'Clear!' sounded in the background.

They listened to Uptill's laboured breathing as he passed from room to room. 'No drug paraphernalia immediately visible. I'll have the guys check for any hidey-holes but on the surface the house looks clean of narcotics. But still dirty if you get my drift. The garage is ten times worse. Body parts all over the place.'

'Body parts?' asked Kennard.

'Yeah, chill, Kenny,' said Uptill, dripping with conde-scension. 'Car parts.'

That was to be expected. It was how Joel could *afford* all these car modifications that was of interest.

'Anything else?'

'Tools ... two motorbikes in ... oil ... jerrycans,' said Uptill, the connection breaking up.

'The jerrycans. What colour?'

'Couple red, one green.'

Kennard looked to Layton. Again, there were millions of red jerrycans out there, but the link tingled.

'He could have started the fire,' said Kennard.

'Who better than a firefighter,' added Layton. 'He'd have a good idea about trajectory, speed, the direction it might take.'

'Why are you asking . . . jerrycans?' interrupted Uptill.

'Just let us know what you uncover.'

'How's it . . . there?' asked Uptill.

'Like Hell,' said Kennard.

'Wrong place, wrong time . . . story of . . . life,' said Uptill, accompanied by a broken-up chuckle.

Kennard gritted his teeth. He was left with a horrible feeling of being bested. It made him want to drive all the way out to Geven and punch Uptill. A proper blow this time. But he was still paying for two disastrous choices without adding any more.

Or was it already three? After all, he had been the one to insist that the Hilmeyer house was saved from the flames, so if there was blame to be thrown around for the bushfire not being under control, he had to take some.

He itched to be right about this case. Missteps had been made, but the one uniting factor was him. *He* had been wrong. About Russell. About Karen and Alvin. Even about his partner, Layton. She might have been a Paint-By-Numbers cop, but she was efficient, determined and smart. It was he who had led them down the wrong path, *he* who had penned a narrative and stuck to it. It was as if he had lost his knack as a detective completely. Top-class sports stars got the yips all the time. Was Parramatta that for him? He had certainly frozen at the crucial moment, not spotting the danger in time, reacting too slowly. And if it had happened once, couldn't it happen again?

In fact, in some ways it already was. Doubting himself when he should be trusting his instincts. The same disease that had infected his mind and body over the last six months. The counsellors had told him that the most important thing was to find a way to come to terms with it. But it was hard to come to terms with the possibility that he could no longer do a job he had been doing for over thirteen years. Nothing worked like it did when he was younger. Much like the bands of relationships stretched over time, his own nerves and neurons had been stretched until they could no longer be trusted to fire when needed.

Uptill's voice returned over the speaker. Cocky.

'Bingo!'

'What is it?' asked Layton.

'We ... set of Kensing ... spanners.'

Kennard looked at Layton, cursing the ever-worsening signal.

'Please confirm,' yelled Layton into the receiver.

'... Kensington Mech spanners ... found ...' Dead air filled the car before Uptill's voice broke through, insistent. 'One missing.'

'Are you sure?'

'Confirmed.'

'Thanks,' said Layton, closing the call.

Kensington Mech. The same brand as the spanner found in the Lautahahis' barn. The pieces were coming together now. They could link Joel to the suspected murder weapon, to the location where it was found and, given his car was on Caldicott that night, to the probable scene of the murder itself.

Kennard felt his adrenaline spike, his heart thumping. He pressed his foot onto the accelerator, plunging onwards through the smoke. They had to find Joel. Now.

The hill seemed to stretch on for ever. On a typical day, in the broad sunlight approaching noon, he would have been able to see the houses in the distance and judge just how far they had to go, but in the smoke, there was no chance of preparation. What you came upon, you came upon. Another volley of arrow-like embers crossed their path, settling on trees and bushes beyond the road, finding plant pots and gutters to set fire to.

Another arduous minute later, a flashing blue light broke the pattern of their dull yellow headlights reflecting off the smoke and the glowing orange in the distance. The beacon that signalled they had arrived.

Kennard got as close as he dared, pulling onto someone's lawn, off the pavement and the road so that he didn't block access for any vehicles.

He turned to Cockburn and Morrow in the back. 'Remember to maintain the perimeter. We'll go in and get him.'

There were rushed nods underneath the helmets. They didn't want to be here but didn't want to back down either. Kennard wished them all the strength in the world. He turned to Layton.

'Ready?'

367

She took a deep whooshing shot from her inhaler. 'Ready.'

Kennard swung his door open. He'd braced himself for the heat but the sheer weight and oppressiveness of it was suffocating. He couldn't back away, and there was nowhere he could turn that would lessen its intensity. The noise, too, was just as overpowering, like a workhouse pub only multiplied to the nth degree, so much so that, rather than attempting to be heard, he just pointed at his fellow passengers to signal that they should follow him.

Underneath his feet the lawn was already singed, bone dry and set to ignite, the house that he had parked in front of intact but under threat, the paint bubbling and peeling off the wood, the bushes surrounding it quivering in the breeze as if frightened to death.

Kennard couldn't worry about this house, though. Couldn't worry about the Hilmeyer house either. He had to find Bairstow, or Mirza at least, so he scanned the crowd for an orange helmet among those near to the cordon of pumpers and tankers. It was hard in the gloom and the constant flux of bodies, and as he drew closer, he could make out the ropes of water being aimed at what lay immediately in front of them. It was a majestic and terrifying sight. The largest bonfire that he had ever witnessed up close. Two houses, side by side and fully alight. Ground and upper floors in unison, flames tonguing the façades of the buildings, coaxing them to catch alight, determined to destroy. Timber cracked and spat over the roar of the flames and the crash of the water, lives and properties destroyed with nothing the firefighters could do other than try to prevent the blaze from spreading. And with the swirling wind, they were fighting a losing battle.

Kennard's heart rate peaked. People passed by almost unseen in the gloom. Something or someone bumped him, knocking him to the ground, sticky asphalt pulling on his gloves. He tried to blink the smoke from his eyes and found that he couldn't. Panic started to form like a crust, stiffening his bones.

'Are you okay?'

Layton was standing over him. All he could see were her eyes, full of concern, or was it fear?

Kennard was unable to answer.

'Get up,' she said, her hand out to help him.

Kennard looked at it. His legs felt weak. *He* felt weak. Back here, surrounded by the unknown.

'You can do this,' she said, encouragement in her breathy tone, obviously struggling as well, her lungs tightening in the dense smoke.

'I can ...' he started, levering himself off the ground, bristling against her help given her recent betrayal.

As he stood clumsily and looked around, Kennard could see that no one was paying attention to them, the new arrivals; they had their own jobs to attend to. He looked for a familiar face, but they were all covered by masks that were singed almost black. Only the terrible whites of their eyes were showing – windows of determination, fear and exhaustion in equal measure. Who knew how long some of them had been out here, risking life and limb for a town and people they might not even know?

About twenty metres away Kennard spotted what he

JAMES DELARGY

was looking for. An orange helmet. Pushing past a couple of firefighters who were rushing towards the front, he led his small, fearful team to the truck. The orange helmet belonged to Bairstow. He was in deep conversation with another orange helmet. Mirza.

'If it's gonna blow, get them out of there,' said Bairstow to his deputy as Kennard tried to make his presence known.

Mirza glanced at Kennard before rushing off.

'Five minutes, then pack up and get back here,' shouted Bairstow after her. He then switched his attention to Kennard, narrowing his eyes.

'What are you doing here?' he said as he pressed the button on his radio. 'Two to one-six-four. Spotfire threatening property.'

'We need Joel Anselmo. Now,' said Kennard.

Bairstow paused. He glanced over Kennard's shoulder at the band of scared soldiers behind him. 'What's the issue?'

'You don't need to know,' said Kennard.

'If you're dragging one of my more experienced men away, then—'

'It's to do with an ongoing case. We need to speak to Mr Anselmo urgently.' Kennard didn't want to say any more.

Bairstow glared at him before pressing a button on his radio. 'I need a position report for Anselmo. There are—'

Kennard flicked out his hand and knocked Bairstow's finger off the button. Bairstow's fist curled. He looked as if he wanted to punch Kennard out. He probably could have.

'We don't want him to know that we're looking for him.'

Bairstow knitted his brow, hit by the realization that whatever this was, it must be serious. He pressed the button again. 'Just get me a position report for Anselmo.'

A white helmet rushed up, panting. 'Sir, fourteen has developed an issue with one of the lines.'

'Fixable?'

'Need to shut it down for ten minutes.'

'Fuck! Have nineteen cover.'

The white helmet rushed off again. Bairstow turned to the map that was cast on the tablet in front of him. Kennard felt his impatience growing, even though he knew that Joel had shown no signs of running. Instead, he had dutifully fought the fire. It was, Kennard thought, the ultimate cover. Why would anyone believe that he had murdered Tracey if he had stuck around?

The radio finally crackled, and a message came through.

'Joel Ansel . . . Sixteen. West . . . Caldicott and Ballaroo.'

'I suppose you want directions,' said Bairstow, shaking his head and turning his tablet around. 'I don't have anyone to support you and I don't want you anywhere near Ballaroo, so go back down the hill, first right, then circle back up just after the substation. Watch out for any downed lines. Don't need you frying up and becoming another spot fire I have to deal with.'

Bairstow's hard eyes made it clear he was being serious. He didn't want Kennard fucking things up for him again.

Kennard led his team back to the car, squeezing inside. As ordered by Bairstow, they moved down the hill and away from the fire before slowly winding across, past the substation, which was smoking but intact, and back up the hill straight into the thick smoke again. A pair of flashing blues signalled that they had arrived. He launched the car onto the pavement and got out to face the heat once again. The location might have changed, but the scene was much the same: houses alight, a snapped powerline on the ground, the pole ablaze, standing like a tall and lonely beacon against the darkness.

Reaching the fire trucks, he turned to Cockburn and Morrow. 'Stay here. You know what he looks like, but he might be hard to recognize in the bunker gear. If you think you see him, detain him, then call me. Otherwise stay put. If he tries to run, he'll likely head this way.'

'What's the plan?' asked Layton.

'I don't know,' admitted Kennard. 'Let's find him first.'

Sixty-One

January 21 – 11.48 – Wind direction NW – Surface speed 30km/h

29 hours since North Rislake evacuation

South Rislake status = Red (Evacuation procedures commence)

Pyro-cumulonimbus warning in place

Their first port of call was the plethora of people amassed around the assembled vehicles, their hurried interruptions met with cold looks and confrontational responses that made Kennard tense up every time. Those they couldn't stop, they approached from behind, trying to make out the surnames scrawled onto the panels on the backs of their helmets through the thick smoke that clung to everything.

After circling the vehicles without success, they intercepted a group of firefighters returning to the trucks. Kennard stepped back, allowing Layton to stop them, staring in through their masks to try to identify Joel among them. She turned and shook her head.

Kennard removed the mobile from his pocket. Lenka would be able to tell him exactly where Joel was amongst this crowd. Or she would have been able to, if communications hadn't been down. He didn't even have an emergency signal; the north side of town was cut off entirely, the world here quite literally dark.

'He must be further in,' shouted Layton over the din.

They had to go deeper.

They advanced up the centre of the road for as much safety as that could provide. The asphalt was tacky underneath Kennard's feet and lifted with each step, like he was walking through glue. Meanwhile, bright orange spot fires scarred his vision, leaving glowing after impressions when he closed his eyes.

There was a tug on his arm.

'Over there,' shouted Layton, pointing at a few people silhouetted by distant flames and the flashing lights of the trucks obscured by the slight bend in the road.

As he nodded there was a distant boom like a bass drum being struck, hard. They both jumped. Maybe the tank that Bairstow had warned the white helmet about earlier.

They made for the nearest truck and the nearest firefighter. He was leaning against it, head down as if catching his breath. Kennard approached cautiously. They made it within five metres before the head came up. The eyes beneath the helmet blinked as if believing Kennard and Layton to be some sort of mirage.

It wasn't Joel; this firefighter was tall with a long face covered by a hood and mask.

'Have you seen Joel Anselmo?' shouted Layton.

The man didn't answer, his gaze flitting between the two of them.

'Joel Anselmo?' she repeated.

'What crew you with?' asked the firefighter.

Kennard almost picked a random number, but this was no time for guesswork.

'Police,' he said. 'Now, have you seen him?'

'He was on Sixteen, line two.'

'Was?' asked Layton.

'Far as I know. This is Twenty-three.'

'Where's Sixteen?'

'About forty metres that way,' said the firefighter, pointing further up the road into the dense smoke.

Kennard and Layton set off immediately, rounding the first tanker. The second was parked behind it, the front wheels on the pavement and the hoses stretched around the side of a colourful bungalow that was surrounded by fire on two sides. The flames flicked out at it, trying to take hold, but the building was standing firm. As were the three pairs of firefighters manning the hoses. From this distance it was impossible to tell if one of the six was Joel. Kennard followed the rubber-lined hoses, water pumping through each at high pressure, Layton close on his heels. Moving down the alley by the side of the bungalow they passed a trampoline that had buckled in the heat. As Kennard was about to step around the back, he was stopped.

'What are you doing here?'

An officer in a white helmet and orange stripe glared at both of them.

'Police. We're looking for Joel Anselmo.'

'What do you want him for?'

'That's for us to know,' said Layton.

'You shouldn't be here.'

'You have your job, we have ours,' said Kennard. 'Where is he?'

The officer frowned at them. This seemed to be the standard reaction. Disbelief. Kennard supposed it was an unusual situation, two cops wandering around in the middle of a bushfire. It took a little extra comprehension.

The officer unclipped the radio from his breast pocket and pressed a button.

'It's Tommo. Can you give me a location update on two-six-seven-one?'

He depressed the button.

The wait was excruciating. Kennard could feel his sweaty palms cramping with anticipation. He wanted to arrest Joel, but he also wanted out of there. They could wait for Joel back at the school; he had to come out sometime. Fighting the urge to run he tried to stay focused. They needed to collar Joel now in case he didn't survive this inferno. Get him, secure him, get out. It was as close to a plan as he had.

The officer, Tommo, brought the radio speaker up close to his ear.

'Roger. Thanks.'

He clipped it back into his pocket.

'Across the road,' said Tommo, pointing at the house opposite. 'He's on a half-hour rotation. Probably resting.'

Kennard and Layton set off in the direction he'd indicated, moving between the tankers, not taking their eyes off the house. It was a family home, a pair of kids' bikes left abandoned in the rush to get away, the front windows reflecting the glow of terror opposite like cat's eyes. It was next in line should the bungalow fall.

Kennard had hoped to arrest Joel either on the hose or assisting. Using the advantage of surprise and their prey being otherwise occupied. Now they only had surprise. And only if they could get to Joel without him spotting them first.

They climbed onto the porch, Kennard careful with his steps even though any creaks would be lost in the roar of the flames. They stood on either side of the front door. He felt for his gun as he pulled the screen door open, and Layton reached out and tried the handle of the front door. It was locked. Security conscious, even though the bushfire wouldn't care.

The rear was next. Kennard took the left side, Layton the right. He encountered a scatter of junk, an old bedframe, an empty rain barrel and an exercise bike that had been forcibly folded in half. He peeked around the corner. A backyard with a rattan table and chairs next to a foldup umbrella that was both cheap and flammable. In the far corner was a swing set that faced away from the house and stood over a small man-made pond and water feature that dominated the back third of the garden.

They made it to the back door and repeated the same order of checks, Kennard on screen door, Layton on main. The back door was locked too. So, Joel wasn't inside, but

Tommo had said that he was resting. Kennard turned back towards the swing set in the far corner.

He pointed at the high back of the seat and Layton nodded. They spread out, Kennard again resting his hand on his firearm, the dry grass crunching under his feet like fresh snow, sweat stinging his eyes. His movements felt restricted in the bunker gear, his arms and legs stiff and unwieldy. He recognized the sensation. He had experienced the same crippling anxiety when facing Rhian Thorpe and the gun. He swallowed hard, his throat parched, the heat and tension causing his head to pound, beating out a rhythm of anxiety and fear. But they had Joel surrounded. They had him. There was nowhere to go.

As they reached the back of the seat together, they paused. Kennard raised three fingers. His hand shook as he counted down, his fingers disappearing back into his fist. On zero, they darted around the sides of the swing seat.

'Joel Anselmo, we are here to—'

Kennard stopped. The seat was empty apart from a small, orange box, a tiny red LED light flicking on and off. He hadn't seen one before, but immediately knew what it was. Joel's PASS locator. He had removed it. Which meant that he could be anywhere.

Sixty-Two

Kennard lagged behind as he followed Layton back around to the front of the house. His lungs felt tight, a mix of the heat and the struggle to suck air through the fine mesh of his mask. He was saving the breathing equipment just in case, having no idea how much oxygen it held.

The choice was to return to the car and get Cockburn and Morrow, or to carry on looking. Kennard glanced up at the street sign he was leaning on to catch his breath. They were on the corner of Versaille and Caldicott. Which meant that the Hilmeyer house was close by.

He started to jog up the road, fighting the incline and forcing oxygen into his lungs. Layton jogged alongside him, struggling too in the dense air, asking him in gasps where they were going. He didn't have the spare breath to say.

As they climbed the rise, the noise decreased. Not quite to a whisper – the roar of the fire was too pervasive for that – but towards an eerie and growing silence. It was now truly dark, only the faint glows of destroyed fences, buildings and outhouses acting as beacons. The burnt grass, trees, buildings and asphalt left the air noxious and choking. Everything on the far side of the road smouldered, defeated. It didn't bode well for 148 Caldicott. Bairstow hadn't mentioned if it had burnt down, though he had other things on his mind, Kennard supposed.

As they made their way up the street towards the Hilmeyer house, he spotted the shell of a burnt-out car sitting surrounded by four bare walls in a destroyed garage. The house adjoining it, too, was in ruins, one wall collapsed in, nothing behind the shattered windows but gutted rooms, as if thick black paint had been dropped from the sky to douse everything.

Kennard switched his focus back to the road. Through the smog the top of the hill approached. He wondered what state he would find the Hilmeyer place in.

The house came into view, still standing, charred but unbroken. The same house he had been in just yesterday, where he had discovered Tracey Hilmeyer's body, where he had risked his life. Today, however, there were no tankers, no crews, no people attending it. There were no flames either, just cloying smoke drifting from elsewhere. Even the heat had tempered a little, the direct rush of the flames replaced by a residual burn, a reminder of what had passed. It was still undeniably hot, but nothing that he hadn't faced before. George Street in the summer – only this time dressed in a Kevlar suit.

The yellow police tape that had been strung around the entrance had melted to the front of the house, the section crossing the door signalling 'No Entry' completely gone. Kennard hoped that it had simply melted away as well, but he knew it was unlikely.

'You think he came back here?' asked Layton, taking a hit of her inhaler.

'I think so.'

'Why would he do that?'

'I don't know. Maybe to get rid of some evidence we might find now that the house has dodged the worst of the fire. Why else do people go back to the scenes of their crimes? Why else would he leave his PASS behind?'

'He could be starting another fire,' said Layton.

It would be the smart move, thought Kennard as they edged up to the front garden, the small picket fence collapsed, dried mud boot prints marking a well-worn path around to the back.

As they made their way to the front door, he took a dry, choking breath. He was about to enter the house again and, as likely as it was that Joel had returned to destroy evidence, he couldn't help but wonder if he was about to encounter another dead body. That the guilt had got too much for Joel.

He turned to Layton and whispered: 'Go around back. If I flush him out your direction, arrest him.'

'And if he's not here?'

'Then our problem just got worse.'

He watched Layton take a wide berth around the house, giving her enough time to make it into position. It occurred to him that he had no idea what was back there, what state it might be in. Just like he had no idea if the structure of the house had been compromised by the heat. He hadn't been given the all-clear to return by Bairstow, after all.

After sucking in a few more deep inhales to try to calm his breathing, he finally stepped inside. His eyes were immediately drawn to the bottom of the stairs. For a second, he pictured Tracey's body still there, the pool of blood ringing her crushed skull, but with a hard blink she was gone.

He took each step carefully, testing out the floorboards and listening for movement elsewhere in the house. He glanced upstairs at the landing. The darkness didn't allow him to see much, but enough to conclude that there was no body swinging from the rafters.

Another couple of tentative paces brought him to what remained of the pool of blood. It was dried solid, black now from the soot that had settled on it. Steeling himself, he poked his head around the doorframe into the living room. No Joel. In fact, nothing looked different aside from the dark coating of soot that altered the décor from homely to emo.

Past the living room and straight ahead was the kitchen, and now impatience was getting the better of him. Kennard became fearful that this was a wild goose chase, and that Joel was elsewhere, long gone. The squeak of a door caused him to freeze, as if it had generated the perfect frequency to immobilize his every muscle. It was followed by some shuffled footsteps. Kennard rushed to the kitchen, but it was empty. Layton's head was poking through the back door, scanning the room just as he was, glass showering the floor from windows destroyed in the heat.

She shook her head. Nothing. No Joel.

Kennard turned around. He entered the short hallway that led off between the kitchen and the living room, windowless and pitch black, the garage at the end. Using his fingers to orientate himself, he brushed against framed pictures that he couldn't make out in the darkness as he inched along. His chest grew tighter, hot air sucked through a mask that seemed to be clogged. Sweat rolled down his face, seeping through eyebrows that Ann was always at him to clip, way too bushy in her opinion, the eyebrows of an old man. At the end of the corridor the door to the garage came into view.

When he opened it, he saw that the space beyond remained intact, the toolboxes and the workbench seemingly untouched, cardboard boxes full of junk that he had missed first time around littering the near side, full of old plates and implements, toasters, microwaves; all broken and tossed out here to rot amid the toxic, overpowering smell of a box of cleaning products that had burst in the heat, bleaches, polishes and disinfectants all curdled into one foul mass.

There was only upstairs left, but as he turned to leave, he spotted the other door. Plain and unmarked, obscured by a stack of boxes. It led off the back of the garage, separate from the kitchen. Carefully, he approached the door and opened it, revealing a back room filled with old furniture, possibly stuff that was being thrown out by the people Russell did removal work for, stuff he thought he might be able to sell or repurpose – wardrobes, chests of drawers, filing cabinets.

There was one other thing of note in the room. Wrenching at the locked drawer of an old desk in the corner, was Joel Anselmo.

Sixty-Three

Kennard froze. Joel was facing away from him, pulling at the desk drawer as if it was stuck. He hadn't spotted Kennard, preoccupied with getting into the drawer, his breathing apparatus off and sitting on the desk. Suddenly he let out a loud grunt as the wood cracked and the drawer flew open. Paper, pens and stationery scattered across the floor. Joel dropped the offending handle and bent down to check the strewn contents. He was looking for something. Kennard wondered what it was. What was so important that it would bring him back here? It must have been something that connected him to the scene, to Tracey. Bottles of pills? A photo? A painting?

Whatever Joel was looking for clearly wasn't among the clutter, an audible 'Fuck!' floating around the room.

Kennard clenched his teeth and curled his hand around his firearm, then began to slowly close in. He wanted to shout for Layton to help but couldn't risk losing the element of surprise.

Then Joel turned, his jaw dropping like he had seen a ghost. He looked at the desk and then at Kennard.

Kennard put his left hand up. His right stayed on his gun. He tried to remain calm, but tension constricted his muscles, his whole body on high alert. His mind flashed back to Parramatta, Rhian Thorpe's face appearing where Joel's was. This time he was going to keep control. He had the gun, Joel didn't. There was no hostage to think of either. Everything was weighted in his favour, but as much as he tried to convince himself that he was in charge, he didn't feel it. Not yet. He wouldn't until Joel was handcuffed and in custody.

'Just take it easy, Joel.'

'I . . .' Joel started but didn't – or couldn't – continue the sentence. 'What are you doing here?'

'This is a crime scene,' said Kennard, hopefully loud enough to attract Layton's attention.

'I thought I saw some flames as I was passing. Came to check.'

'Why were you passing? And why did you take off your locator?'

'I needed some time away.'

'What did you think was in here, Joel?' said Kennard, flicking his eyes towards the broken desk.

'Nothing. It was a fire.'

'I don't see any smoke,' said Kennard.

'I put it out. I need to get back to work,' said Joel, stepping towards him.

Kennard backed off, allowing himself some space, the furniture acting as the crowd behind him, pushing him on. Baying Joel on. The door at the rear opened with a slam as Layton kicked it in. She positioned herself in the doorway, taking the discovery more in her stride than Kennard had. He stepped forward again, retaking the initiative.

'Mr Joel Anselmo, we are arresting you in connection with the murder of Tracey—'

'I didn't kill her!' Joel took a step backwards, bumping against a filing cabinet in the centre of the floor.

'You can explain all that at the interview,' said Kennard.

'I didn't kill her! I wouldn't . . . I couldn't hurt her.' The words were screeched, genuine emotion wound through them. 'I loved her.'

So impassioned were the words that Kennard suspected he was right. Somewhere in here they would find a photo, a painting, or evidence of their connection. But what had happened to sour it?

He flicked a glance towards Layton. She was ready, her hand on her firearm.

'Were you having an affair with Tracey, Joel?'

'Yes. No. It never got that far. Not yet. I was prepared to wait for her.'

'Wait for her to do what? Leave Russell?'

Joel shook his head but didn't answer.

'Is that what she told you?' asked Kennard. 'But then she backed out of the deal. She said she wasn't going to leave Russell and that she wasn't going to be with you. And you couldn't handle the rejection.'

'That's not it at all! She *was* going to leave him.'

Kennard pursed his lips, his heart pounding in his chest. Reminding him that Joel remained free. 'Just come with us, Mr Anselmo. You can tell us your side of the story.'

'There *is* no story. I didn't kill her.'

'You're only making things worse for yourself, Joel,' said Layton. 'We found the part that you lost here on Tuesday night.'

'What part?' Joel looked confused.

'The passenger's side strip lights from your car,' said Kennard.

Joel stared at the floor. Not denying it.

Kennard carried on. 'We know about the drugs too. The opioids, the expired painkillers.'

Joel swayed from foot to foot. It was the awkward, restless shuffle of someone who was scared, the murderous act that he had tried to conceal having caught up with him.

Kennard watched as Layton narrowed the angle on their suspect, slowly cornering him. Her eyes flicked towards Joel. Expecting Kennard to make the move. To reach out for him. But though Joel wasn't Rhian Thorpe, and he didn't have a gun, something held Kennard back.

'Where did you get the pills?' he asked, shuffling a step forward, inching towards Joel, just a little closer.

'I can't say.'

'Why not?'

'You know why not. It's not in my best interest.'

'You're being arrested for murder. That's not exactly in your best interest either.'

Joel looked at both of them.

'The pills you sold had expired,' said Kennard.

'I don't ask. I just sell.'

'Is that why you visited Tracey on Tuesday night? A delivery?'

Joel shook his head at this. 'I just wanted to see her.'

388

'So, you went to see her and then you killed her.'

'No. I didn't go in. We'd had a fight the week before.'

'Over what?'

Joel didn't answer.

'Did she tell you that she didn't want to see you again? That the affair was over?' asked Layton. 'You have previous for not taking no for an answer. For terrorizing ex-girlfriends.'

'That was . . . I wasn't terrorizing them.'

'That's not what the court orders say.'

'I told her that I could support her. If she left Russell.'

'And she didn't accept it. You let it brood over the weekend and then something snapped. Maybe you even tried one more time. When that didn't work, you bludgeoned her to death with a spanner,' said Kennard.

Joel was almost within reach now, backed up against a desk, trapped.

'No,' said Joel, shaking his head. 'You're making this shit up.'

'Why did you go to her sister's farm?'

'I was looking for Tracey. I was worried. She didn't answer the door—'

'So, you admit you were here? On Tuesday night.'

Joel clammed up for a moment. 'I wasn't inside or else I would . . .'

'Would what?'

'Have seen her.'

'You mean, her dead body. Her blood all over the floor. Her head bashed in.'

'Shut up!'

JAMES DELARGY

As Joel shook his head vigorously, Kennard stepped closer. So did Layton.

'She wasn't there, or at the shop, so I thought that she might have been at her sister's. She'd talked about the place a few times. About the aggro with her sister and the farm.'

'And you helped Alvin out?'

'In the shed, yeah.'

'Where you planted the murder weapon,' said Kennard, clenching his hand into a fist, feeling it slick with sweat.

'No. Just doing a good turn. I don't know anything about a murder weapon. I didn't kill Tracey.'

'We think you did, Mr Anselmo. Now turn around and put your hands on the wall.'

Kennard watched as Joel squeezed his eyes shut. Giving up. He reached out to grab him. To turn him and cuff him. To do what he hadn't done in Parramatta.

But then Joel turned. And started to run.

Sixty-Four

Kennard was caught on the back foot. Layton wasn't. She moved to block the exit.

But Joel wasn't the only thing moving. The frame of the doorway that Layton was guarding suddenly cracked and started to fold in on itself, the garage of the house giving in to the abuse it had taken.

'Layton!' shouted Kennard, pointing above her head.

As she looked up, Kennard moved, his feet feeling like lead, the suit like concrete. He willed his body to react as the doorframe collapsed, bringing the wall down with it.

Layton seemed immobilized, the world about to crash down on her.

Kennard hit her hard, hands out, pushing her out the back door, feeling something heavy slam into one dangling foot before they ended up in the blackened dirt that had been the Hilmeyer garden, ash puffing up around them like the denouement of a rubbish magic trick.

He winced in pain, his foot surely bruised but in one piece. Layton had her eyes squeezed shut.

'Are you okay?' he asked.

'Fine,' she gasped, fumbling the inhaler from her pocket. 'Landed on a rock. Knocked the wind outta me.'

'You okay to move?' asked Kennard, clambering to his feet, hands out to help her up.

Layton sat there. She looked as if she was gathering herself, almost sorrowful. 'Yeah. Sorry I didn't tell you about the updates to Haskell,' she said, taking another puff of the inhaler. 'It was a shitty thing to do.'

'We all do shitty things,' said Kennard, as she grabbed his hands. 'Let's just get this bastard.'

They turned to watch the shadow of Joel Anselmo disappear into the scorched undergrowth, the lack of light helping him to quickly fade into the background. Unlike the detectives, he was practised in moving swiftly in the heavy coat, boots and trousers.

They were about to start the chase when they were interrupted by a voice.

'You both okay?'

It was Russell Hilmeyer, stepping around the side of the garage. He pointed into the undergrowth. 'Was that Joel?'

Kennard didn't have time to answer, adrenaline taking over. He nodded briefly before charging as quickly as he could after the fleeing man, who was quickly becoming lost in the gloom, his choppy strides kicking up ash and charred branches.

Layton caught up with Kennard quickly. As did Russell.

'What are you two doing here?' Russell demanded, easily keeping pace with both of them despite the limp from his bad knee. 'Why are you chasing . . . ?'

Russell stopped talking then, and Kennard saw the realization dawn on his face.

'Why are *you* here?' he coughed out, trying to distract Russell as he clumsily vaulted over a fallen tree that had not survived the fiery onslaught.

'Tommo sent me to check on you. Did Joel kill Trace?' asked Russell, only his stern and focused eyes visible behind the goggles and mask.

Kennard didn't answer, just tried with all his might to keep up with Layton. In the distance the glow of the raging bushfire approached, Joel's outline now stark against it. Layton had her gun drawn but the distance and the terrain prevented a clean shot. Never mind the fact that there might have been firefighters on the other side.

As they got closer to the flames, Joel didn't divert his path. Underfoot, Kennard could feel the heat oozing through his soles, small patches of undergrowth still alight, acting like a primitive form of emergency floor lighting.

The air grew hotter with each step. Like yesterday morning when he had first discovered Tracey Hilmeyer, he once again found himself running towards a bushfire. There was little comfort in knowing that Russell and Layton were with him; he couldn't outrun the awareness that he was now chasing a desperate murderer. Every breath seemed too strained, the air from the tank too constricted. Panic threatened to overwhelm him, held back by only the thinnest membrane.

He pushed through the skeleton of a shrub, which exploded in a puff of charcoal, all moisture drained from it.

'Where's he heading?' panted Layton.

'If he makes it through there's a forest road out back,' said Russell.

'You mean through the fire?' asked Layton, wheezing hard.

Kennard put his hand out, stopping them both.

'Both of you, go back. Layton, find that road. In case he makes it through.'

Even with the words out there Kennard could not quite believe that he had uttered them. Could he really go on alone?

'I'm not leaving,' said Russell.

'This is a police matter.'

'This is my wife.'

Kennard turned to Layton. 'Grab whoever you can and get around back. Be safe.'

'Are you sure?' she said, struggling to get the words out.

'Not in the slightest,' said Kennard. 'But you can't go on.'

'I'm okay.' She put the inhaler to her mouth and pressed. Nothing. She tried again and got the same result. All out.

She looked at him. 'Shit.'

'Go,' said Kennard.

Layton nodded and took a direct route towards the back of the nearest house, the paintwork now daubed in black soot, the conservatory just a skeletal mess.

'You too, Russell.'

'I told you, I'm not leaving.'

Kennard could see that he wasn't going to budge. He couldn't blame him. If it had been Ann . . .

'Stick tight to me, then. And don't do anything stupid.'

'Like run towards a bushfire?'

He had a point. There was nothing sane about any of this.

Kennard and Russell carried on the pursuit, following Joel's silhouette deeper into the fire. Within a few minutes they had reached what looked to be the back edge of the wall of flames, the leaves on the trees still burning, dropping down on them like mini firebombs.

Kennard slumped to one knee, struggling for breath as he watched Russell carry on past him. He couldn't let Russell get to Joel first, afraid that one would kill the other out of necessity or sheer rage.

Coughing hard, he removed his mask and spat a lump of sooty phlegm onto the dry earth. He was gearing himself up to keep moving when footsteps hit the dust next to him. When he looked up, Russell was standing over him, his breathing apparatus strapped tight to his face. Russell helped him up and got him into his own mask, the fresh air welcome relief to his lungs. Into the darkness came a dazzle of stars as his body drank in the oxygen. The boost reached his muscles and on they continued, their pursuit helped by the lack of leaf cover and the dazzling orange light.

They stalked their prey deeper and deeper into the fire, licks of flame from the surrounding undergrowth clawing for them as they passed. Kennard tried to keep up but gradually fell a few steps behind, showered in the embers cast as Russell brushed against the lower branches of burning trees.

He wondered if Joel was on a mission to kill himself, the desperation at being caught proving too much. Cowardly thoughts of self-preservation crept into Kennard's head; if Joel did want to kill himself, that didn't mean Kennard had to follow him. Yet he carried on, determined to bring Tracey Hilmeyer's killer to justice.

The silhouette that was Joel disappeared completely in a cloud of sparks, vanishing from sight only to reappear a few seconds later, picking himself up after a fall before continuing his escape.

'We can catch him,' said Russell. Surrounded by fire, the darkness that had been prevalent was now tinted a bright orange, like the whole world had been dyed, the glare almost blinding. Russell's eyes were wide open, intense, driven. Kennard realized that as much as this was his own attempt at redemption, it had become Russell's too. For his wife. For his stunted footy career. It pushed Kennard on, reinforcing the knowledge that he couldn't let Russell get to Joel first and attempt to dispense his own justice. His friend had been having an affair with his wife. Or at least attempting to, according to Joel.

Kennard followed Russell as the flames enticed them in deeper, the heat stinging his palm through his glove as he grabbed onto a tree to keep his balance. The firefighter seemed to have no such trouble, in his element out here among the grasping hands of branches, probably reminiscent of the grasping hands of the football players he used to dodge, though his limp was becoming more pronounced with each step. Joel was almost within reach now, a wall of flame in front of them, the whole bush burning before their eyes. He stopped and turned to face his pursuers, a look of sheer panic in his eyes.

'Give it up, Joel. There's nowhere to go,' said Kennard, trying to take more air into his lungs but finding it increasingly hard to do so.

Joel glanced over his shoulder as if weighing up his chances. Minus the breathing apparatus he had left behind in the house, he was going to be in trouble soon, and he knew it.

'What did you do to Trace?' shouted Russell over the cracking of branches and the roar of the flames rapidly consuming all the oxygen around them.

'I didn't do anything,' gasped Joel.

'You're a lying, murdering bastard.'

'Why did you run? Why were you searching the house?' asked Kennard, keeping an eye on both men, trying to position himself between them and feeling the heat poke at his suit as if trying to eke a way inside to scorch his tender skin. This was Parramatta all over again, but this time he was surrounded on both sides, stuck in between two warring parties with a bushfire raging ever closer. A fog of dizziness formed in his head, his breathing suddenly shallow and sharp, worryingly so.

'He ran 'cause he's guilty,' answered Russell, taking a step towards his now former friend.

'Leave this to me, Russell,' said Kennard, pulling out his gun. It felt hot even through the gloves, heavy in his hands.

'I ran because I ran. I don't know,' said Joel.

'What were you looking for in the house? What did you think was there?' asked Kennard.

'You and her?' interrupted Russell. 'You were my mate.'

Kennard could see that Russell's anger was building alarmingly.

'We didn't do anything.'

'Fuckin' oath. She probably turned you down, you mongrel. And you couldn't take it,' yelled Russell.

'Leave it, Russell,' said Kennard, glancing at him while aiming his gun at Joel. 'Joel Anselmo, turn your back and get on your knees.'

Joel paused, then turned. Kennard waited for him to sprint into the fire, heart hammering. If he did, would Russell charge after him? And would Kennard do the same? *Could* he do the same?

Sixty-Five

January 21 – 12.02 – Wind direction NW – Surface speed 32km/h

29 hours since North Rislake evacuation

South Rislake status = Red (Evacuation procedures commence)

Pyro-cumulonimbus warning in place

Joel sank to his knees. His shoulders bobbed up and down. He might have been sobbing but Kennard couldn't hear over the rage of the bushfire.

He approached cautiously, sliding his gun into one of the outer pockets of his thick jacket and reaching for his cuffs. Each movement was slow but deliberate. He didn't want to make a mistake. Not now. The cuffs felt warm in his hands, as if warning him that handcuffing a suspect in the middle of a bushfire and rendering them helpless was a bad idea. But it was the only way. Both he and Russell could drag Joel out if needed. Sliding the cuffs over Joel's wrists in the bulky suit, he locked them into place. Done. His suspect captured.

'I didn't . . .' spluttered Joel, his shoulders still bobbing.

'Joel Anselmo, you will be charged—' started Kennard.

'You're lucky I didn't get you first.'

The voice was so close to Kennard that he almost fell. Russell was right beside him, at his shoulder.

'Get back, Russell. I have this under control.'

'I'm telling you, I didn't do it,' repeated Joel.

Kennard hauled him to his feet, his suspect's clothes black with ash from the earlier fall, his helmet stained. Marked as a murderer.

It was time to get out of there. Holding onto the cuffs, he steered Joel back towards Caldicott. He wanted to concentrate on his steps across the scorched earth, but he had questions that couldn't wait.

'You said you were at the house on Tuesday night, but you didn't go inside.'

'I didn't.'

'But why else would you be there in the first place? Was it to have it out with her? To confess your love?'

'I did love her.'

'You gutless mongrel!'

Russell exploded with rage, striking Joel hard in the gut and dropping him to his knees. As he was holding onto the cuffs, Kennard could do nothing about the punch, instead finding himself jerked forward as Joel fell.

He caught his breath. 'Do that again and I'll arrest you too, Russell.'

'Again?' spat Russell, looking as if he was just getting started.

Joel was coughing hard, struggling for air. Kennard glared at Russell. He didn't need his suspect incapacitated any further.

'Are you okay to move?' he asked Joel, aware that he had no idea how much air his own oxygen canister might hold.

'Don't consider his fucken' well-being,' said Russell. 'He didn't care anything about Trace's.'

'I did care. I loved her.'

'You fucken' ratbag,' said Russell, stepping forward only to collide with Kennard, who had moved to block his path. Kennard turned to Joel, who was still recovering from the gut shot.

'I told her I loved her.'

'And she rejected you?' he asked.

'I realized that she was using me. That she had always been using me.'

'How had she been using you?' Kennard pressed.

'She owed me money. A lot of money.'

'For the drugs?'

'Yeah. Money that I owe to other people. That's why I was searching the house. That's why I went to see her on Tuesday night. I thought that if I got the money from her then the people I owed money to wouldn't hurt me.'

'It's not them you have to be worried about,' spat Russell.

'Keep out of it, Russell,' warned Kennard, continuing the

march away from the flames. He focused on Joel. 'So, once you realized she wasn't going to pay you back, you hit her.'

'Hit her? I've never hit her,' said Joel. 'Never!'

'Fucken' liar!' screamed Russell, looming large beside them.

Joel continued. 'I left as angry with myself as much as I was with her. I must have scraped the kerb when I was leaving, tearing off the strip lights.'

'Or as you were driving away in a hurry after committing the murder,' said Kennard.

'No!'

'We found a set of spanners at your house. One is missing. It matches the one we found at the Lautahahi farm. The spanner we believe is the murder weapon.'

'I don't know—'

'Just admit it,' said Russell, following them both. Kennard remained wary of his presence, of Russell's proximity to Joel, of his own disadvantage, two against one.

'I'd already given her name to my supplier. I was out of options. I had to give them something. Tuesday night was my last attempt before . . .'

'Before what, Joel?'

'I don't know. Honestly.'

Kennard almost choked on the air pumping into his mask. There was nothing honest about Joel. He had lied and kept lying.

'So, you were searching the house looking for money?'

'I thought that there might be some cash. Somewhere.'

'And you didn't have time to look after you killed Tracey, did you?' said Kennard. 'You panicked and fled.

Then you went and started the fire. A fire that could destroy this entire town. Tear down property and even cost lives. The lives of your fellow firefighters.'

As he said this, Kennard turned to keep an eye on Russell. This revelation of Joel's utter cowardice and wickedness might send him over the top.

'No, I didn't. I swear,' pleaded Joel.

'You knew that I was out of town,' said Russell.

'You set the blaze and hoped that everything burned,' said Kennard. 'This isn't your hometown. You don't have a stake in anything here, so who cared if it burned? Then you went around on Wednesday morning before Tracey's body was discovered and planted the murder weapon at Tracey's sister's farm as a backup. You knew that Tracey and Karen didn't get on. She'd told you. You knew that we would look at Russell first, but it was a solid backup plan should it be needed.'

'Why don't we just shoot him?'

Kennard stopped. Russell was staring at him with eyes that begged Kennard to say yes.

'I'll back you up. I'll claim that there was a struggle and you had to do it.'

'I'll call for help,' said Joel, sobbing.

'No one will hear you. They won't even hear the shot,' said Russell. He was standing right in front of Kennard. Edging between him and his prisoner.

'That's not how this works,' said Kennard.

'I know how it works. He'll plead insanity or some other bullshit and get off. Or claim he's some racial minority being victimized.'

Kennard looked over Russell's shoulder as Joel began to back away. Towards the flames again. The flashback was vivid. The apartment block in Parramatta. His charge moving out of reach.

Not this time.

'Let me do my job,' said Kennard, shoving Russell to the side and moving towards Joel again.

There was a crackle from the radio hitched to his breast pocket. Faint words followed, hard to pick up between the static and the continued roar of the fire.

Kennard held his hand out for Joel to stay where he was. He didn't want to move too far and lose the signal. He could call his position in and get support to come to him. If only he knew where he was.

Joel continued to back off despite the warning. Kennard glanced at Russell and would have loved to have ordered him to make sure Joel stayed put, but he couldn't be sure that the grieving husband wouldn't just kill him where he stood.

'Repeat,' said Kennard into the radio receiver, holding it close to his mouth, feeling his cracked lips scrape across the hot plastic surface.

There was a hissed response that he couldn't make out.

'In the bush west of Caldicott,' said Kennard, hoping they could at least hear him and get their position.

There was a tap on his shoulder. Russell shook his head. 'East,' he mimed.

'Correction. East of Caldicott. I have the suspect, Joel Anselmo, in custody. Need backup.'

There was a loud pop as Joel stepped on a branch.

'Stay right there, Joel,' ordered Kennard.

The radio crackled into life again. Kennard put his hand over one blistered ear to try to make out the message. It was Layton.

'. . . you hear me?'

She didn't give Kennard time to answer.

'The spanner . . . farm . . . not the correct size.'

'What do you mean?'

'For Tracey's wound . . . too small . . . not the murder weapon. The blood . . . is Tracey's, however. Confirmed.' The signal cut out briefly. '. . . Stoltz arrested . . . assault on his girlfriend . . . recanted . . . Russell did the second job alone. Doesn't know where.'

The signal broke up again. Kennard looked at Joel, trying to process this information. The spanner found at the farm wasn't the murder weapon, but it matched one missing from Joel's toolbox. And it had been confirmed as having Tracey's blood on it. So, if it wasn't the murder weapon but had Tracey's blood on it, that meant . . .

Kennard understood. The spanner had been planted, as had the blood. And Joel was unlikely to have planted his own spanner and implicated himself. And Karen and Alvin had no reason to implicate themselves by stashing the spanner at their own farm. Which left only one option – Russell.

Karen and Alvin had noted that their animals had been spooked the last few nights. They had thought it was a predator of some sort, or the animals sensing the oncoming fire, but had found nothing. Of course, they would have been sensitive to these things given that their animals were being poisoned. But what if their animals had been spooked by Russell himself, sneaking onto the farm at night when he was supposed to be out of town on a job, planting the spanner, framing Joel or Karen or Alvin. Any one of them. He would have known the layout of the farm better than Joel would have, especially in the dark. He would likely know where to hide a spanner and know to direct a rash detective towards the sister of the victim.

Kennard's realization of his stupidity was framed by a flash of lightning from the dark sky above, the bolt arrowing to the ground not five hundred metres from him, cracking almost instantaneously. It was the loudest sound he had ever heard. As if the earth had rendered a giant fissure that would swallow him for not realizing the truth earlier.

He had been right from the start. Russell Hilmeyer had killed his wife. But he had allowed himself to be consumed by the chase. He stared into the trees, the charred shadows lining up in front of him like all the mistakes he had made. He had the wrong man in handcuffs. And a murderer who all but had thrown up enough smoke to conceal the truth forever.

Sixty-Six

Kennard turned around to face Russell. He had the wrong man in cuffs, and a murderer at large. As he desperately tried to process his options he heard a sickly familiar sound, almost obscured over the cracking of burning trees and popping of seeds germinating in the heat, and flinched reflexively. A gunshot. Joel slumped to the ashy ground, shock and confusion in his eyes and a bullet in his chest. He didn't get up.

Time seemed to freeze for an instant. Kennard turned towards the direction the sound had come from, his limbs feeling like they were moving through treacle, his thoughts scrambled. For a second he paused, then he reached for his own gun. It was gone. In a split second he realized why. It was pointed straight at him.

His own voice seemed tinny in his ears. 'What are you doing, Russell? I don't know what you think you heard—'

'Don't try that. We both know.'

Kennard swallowed. 'You don't have to make this worse.'

Russell smiled. 'Worse than it is?'

Thoughts crashed through Kennard's head. It was as if his life was passing before his eyes, but rather than some semi-remembered collage of blissful events, it was a complete car crash. Nothing made sense. His family skipped by in milliseconds, as did former cases, Rhian Thorpe, Gary Snook, Billy Dancey. Old partners and holidays abroad. They all swept past in a hurry as if making space for the end. This case. His supposed redemption.

Then it clicked. As if the mashed-up jumble had suddenly settled perfectly into place. Why Russell had killed Tracey.

'It was over the drugs, wasn't it?'

'What are you talking about?' There was a scoffing rasp to Russell's voice, but it was forced. Kennard knew he was on the right track.

'Joel said Tracey owed him money. He also said that he had given his supplier Tracey's name. Devon King was that supplier, wasn't he?'

Russell didn't answer, his head tilted to the side.

'And he hired you to collect the money. That was your job, after all. Debt collecting. Muscle work. We know from both you and Christophe Stoltz that you had two jobs that night. But Stoltz now says that he wasn't with you on the second job. That you did it on your own. Now I know why. Because you knew you were being sent to collect money from your own wife. But Devon didn't know that, did he? Didn't know you were headed to your own house. That's why you didn't take Stoltz along.'

Kennard was getting into his stride, his mind blanking out the weapon pointed at him. Blanking out that he was at Russell's mercy.

'What happened, Russell? There's no way you intended to kill her. If it was an accident, it was an accident. A judge might see that. They might get that it was a complicated situation and—'

Russell shook his head. 'Accidents don't happen, Detective. Someone is always to blame.'

'Trust our justice system.'

'People like me don't get justice. Our lives just get ruined, and everyone moves on.'

'Is this about your footy career?'

'Do you have any idea how it feels to be looked at as a failure because of a piece of bad luck? Because of something that you have no control over?'

'More than you think. It hurts. But there is a way out. Just tell me what happened, Russell.'

Sixty-Seven

Tracey – Before

Tuesday – Evening

She hadn't responded to Joel's profession of undying love. Her head was too fuzzy, her heart beating too hard to know how to play it right. He had hammered on the door a few more times, demanding she open up, before eventually he had stormed off. She had listened to his footsteps move away from the door, crunching across the gravel. She knew that she had led him on. Her need had grown out of control and now so had his. She wasn't prepared to give him what he wanted, and now he was angry, jilted, desperate.

She had listened to the sound of Joel's cobbled-together car leaving, the distinctive rattle it made on shifting up from second to third gear. But now the knocking had returned. She hadn't heard the car stop, but that didn't mean anything. It was hard to tell what was real and what wasn't anymore.

She wanted to peek out the window but couldn't face what she might see, so instead she sat down again, the television muted, anticipating Joel's return. She was frightened about what it meant. She hadn't paid him, and now she'd rejected him. A double whammy. Her fear had driven her to the garage to find something she could use to protect herself, one of Russell's spanners hidden up her sleeve. She would use it if she had to.

'Trace? You in?'

Not Joel. Russell. Her husband. Relief flowed through her. She hadn't expected him home tonight. As she weaved her way to the door, she allowed herself a giggle of release.

She opened the door. There was a look of confusion on his face as he pointed at the lock.

'Can't be too careful,' she said, her smile wide and easy.

'Don't think brown snakes know how to open doors, Trace. You're pretty safe there.'

'You never know.'

This caused him to frown again, studying her. 'You feeling okay? What have you taken?'

'What makes you think I've taken anything?'

Russell sighed loudly. A judgemental hiss that made her angry.

'Just a hunch,' he said.

'Maybe I have, maybe I haven't. Can't I just be happy to see you?'

He closed his eyes and took a breath. 'Sorry.'

'That's . . .' She couldn't finish the sentence. She was just happy it wasn't Joel. She considered telling him about his friend. About everything. Or most things. He would be angry, but he wouldn't let anything happen to her. Loyalty was written into their vows.

'Did you park out back?' she asked.

'Yep. Need an oil fill. Old girl's running dry. Both of them.'

'If that's a joke, it's not funny.'

'I know,' he said, puffing out his cheeks.

'Are you back for the night?' She hoped so. She slipped the spanner from her tracksuit sleeve onto the counter.

He looked at it. 'What was that for?'

'Thought I saw a redback earlier.'

'So, you were going to clobber it?'

'Maybe.'

Russell shook his head. There was a sadness in the movement. As if resigning himself to something.

'We need to talk, Trace.'

She stared at him. This was his serious voice. The one he adopted when talking about the house, her addiction, her sister's house and how they might go about forcing them out.

'Go on.'

'You owe some serious people money, Trace.'

Her husband looked straight at her. Tracey felt the blood rush from her head, her stomach fluttering. The pause had been too long to deny his accusation. But how the hell did he know?

Sixty-Eight

'She wasn't going for it, was she?' said Kennard. 'Joel said you had gambled big in the past. Owed a bit of money that Tracey had warned you about. So, I guess she thought that this was a ruse to cover your own losses. That you had fallen back into it. That there was no way that you – her own husband – would be sent to collect her debt.'

'It was nothing to do with that.'

'What was it, then?'

'She threatened to go to you lot.'

'And would she have?'

'I don't know. Trace was as stubborn as a mule.'

'And pregnant.'

Kennard could see the anger flare in Russell's eyes.

'It wasn't mine.'

Kennard pushed. 'How do you know?'

'I know. We'd tried for so long.'

'That doesn't mean—'

Russell interrupted. 'I wanted to know who the father was. She said she didn't know.'

'And that made you angry?'

The barrel of the gun dropped slightly. Kennard tried to inch closer to Russell. To the gun. But Russell jerked his head as he caught the movement, steadying his aim. Kennard stopped in his tracks.

'Did she end up telling you who the father was?' he asked.

'No. But once I found out about the drugs, I had my suspicions.'

'Your friend Joel.'

'Yeah. Joel,' said Russell, practically spitting the name.

'My guess is that you spotted his car parked close by that night. You recognized it and guessed why it was there. What was going on right under your nose.'

There was a pause before Russell said, 'I'd advise you to make your last words something more profound than that, Detective.'

'It wasn't his,' said Kennard.

Russell didn't react, holding the gun steady.

'He admitted that he wanted to,' said Kennard, 'but he was waiting. It might have been yours.'

'But it wasn't,' said Russell coldly.

Sixty-Nine

Tracey – Before

Tuesday – Evening

Her husband was still staring at her. She held his gaze, trying to read him, read his emotions.

'Was it Joel?' she asked.

'Was it Joel what?'

'That told you?'

'No. Why?'

Tracey wondered if they had passed each other. If Russell had been watching as Joel left. She could see that her husband was trying to remain calm. The vein bulging at his temple warned her that it was an ongoing battle.

'I've something to tell you as well,' she said. 'I'm pregnant.'

It was her husband's turn to be shocked. He took a moment to compose himself.

'Whose is it?' he asked sharply.

'What do you mean, "whose is it"? It's yours.'

'Mine?'

'Yeah.'

'It's not Devon's?'

Tracey sucked in her breath. Devon King. The tanned guy from the party in Mount Druitt. There had been something about him that warned her he was trouble. But that was exactly what she had been looking for. The baby could well be his. That night had been a blur. She had woken up undressed in a random hotel room. Alone. Her last memory was of getting into Devon's car the night before.

But how did her husband know about Devon? Was he spying on her? Had he been there? If so, why had he not stopped her? Or Devon? Anger and frustration boiled up in her, and she decided in an instant that the best form of defence was attack. Reaching for the table, she touched the warm metal of the spanner. With her other hand she slapped her husband. Russell rocked slightly but took the shot well, blinking, the tendons in his jaw mashing with rage.

'Don't, Trace.'

They stood in silence, glaring at each other.

Russell backed down. 'Look, I don't care, Trace. About the debt. About the baby. I'm not angry.'

Again, the raised vein in his temple told a different story. He took a break and went on. 'It's our baby. What happened, happened. But we need a way out of this. Ten grand is a lot of money.'

'You haven't said how you found out . . .' Tracey tilted

her head to the side as the answer came to her. 'You work for Devon King, don't you?'

'It's my job.'

To this she laughed. Loudly. Enough to feel her throat crack in the dry air. The baby's possible father asking the baby's probable stepfather to beat the money out of her. Fucking savage. 'So, you're here to hustle me?'

'It's not like that.'

'What's it like?'

'I've got a plan.'

'I'm all ears.'

'This is hard for me too, Trace.'

'Doesn't seem to be.'

'When Devon told me the address my mind was all over the place. I came alone. Ditched my partner. No one needs to know.'

'I know,' she said coldly, her stare boring into her husband, reminding him what he was doing. No matter how much he was trying to justify it.

'Trace, I'm trying to fucking help.'

She raised her eyebrows. He carried on.

'The plan is we pay the money back.'

'That's the plan? Pay back ten grand. How do you expect to do that?'

'We'll get it.'

'I don't see how—'

'We pay it, but we get to keep twenty per cent. My usual fee for a job.'

'So, we get to keep, what, two grand?'

'Yeah.'

'And lose eight. Great business sense there! And it still means that you're expecting me to pay for the stuff. Only you come good out of this.'

'But we don't lose as much. I've got a couple of grand saved up. It'll stall Devon for now. We'll make our losses back in a few months. It's good work.'

'And what do I do in the meantime? Come beg you for a handout? My big, strong husband? The derro arsehole who can't keep his wife happy for longer than two minutes. And I was happy for two minutes. When you walked in. Glad you weren't Joel. Now I'm not so sure.'

Russell's face hardened. The same way it always did when he was angry with her, when his knee hurt.

'It's your fault we're in this mess,' he said, his voice low. 'Why didn't you tell me?'

'And have you lecture me? Like this?'

'I could have helped.'

'By doing what? This was my way of dealing with everything,' she said, throwing her arms up. 'You wouldn't have helped. But Joel did.'

Russell clenched his jaw, his face turning red. He was furious, at her and at Joel, who was likely to find himself at the end of Russell's fist the next time they bumped into each other. That was okay, though – it might warn him off for good.

'It wouldn't have worked for ever, Trace.'

'I didn't need for ever. Just until I sold the farm and started the gallery again.'

'The gallery,' said Russell, shaking his head. 'Stop living in a fucking dream. We need to get—'

She slapped him again. A good shot, a crack that stung her palm and made her wince. She didn't see him grab the spanner from the counter. Or anything after that.

Seventy

Russell stopped, his hand shaking slightly. The death of his wife at his own hand was something he obviously still hadn't recovered from.

Kennard spoke softly, laying it all out, his breathing growing ever more laboured. The heat taking its toll, he guessed, weighing heavy on him. 'Tracey is dead. You've hit her harder than you meant to. You panic, trying to come to terms with it. But you rebound quickly. You know that she hasn't got a shift in the shop for a couple of days. You know no one is likely to come looking for her immediately. You know that Joel has tools at his place, spanners that you could swap, to implicate him in Tracey's murder. Staying over Wednesday night gives you the perfect opportunity. But you didn't think the size would matter. Just that a spanner of the same make would do. You come back, rub Joel's spanner in your wife's wound, even getting some of her grey matter on it. A disgusting job, but you manage it.'

Kennard looked up to gauge Russell's reaction. To see how far he was pushing him. To see if he was right.

'But that wasn't enough. To cover your tracks even more you decided it would be better if the house burnt up, if Tracey burnt up along with it. So, you go out that night and plant the fake murder weapon at Karen's house. You know your way around the farm, and you know that she has as much motive as you do to kill her sister to get the land and the house that she badly needs. You clouded the whole scene. The husband is always first in the queue of suspects, but lengthen that queue or muddy the motive enough and you can fade into the background.'

Kennard was on a roll now. It was all coming to him. Russell wasn't stopping him, instead listening to it all unwind, allowing him this brief moment of glory before it ended with a gunshot.

'So, you start the fire. The winds are looking good for the next few days, perfect if something catches hold. I'm guessing a douse and drive. Tying the jerrycan to the back and letting it slosh petrol everywhere. Maybe lighting it halfway along and then outrunning it. Hoping that the house goes up and takes Tracey's body and any DNA with it. After everything has calmed down, the cops will find the wreckage and assume she fell down the stairs in her drug-fuelled haste to escape the inferno. A tragic accident. More heartbreak for the local hero to bear. The fire investigators have picked up a red jerrycan from where they believe the blaze started. I'm guessing that if we check CCTV from one of the local gas stations, we'll find evidence of you filling up a similar can.'

Kennard didn't hear the choked laugh over the noise of

421

the flames surrounding them, but he could see Russell's shoulders jerk.

'We all fill up cans for emergencies around here, Detective. You and I both know that. I doubt you can match DNA from that can to me.'

'We'll work on it.'

'You won't be working on anything,' said Russell, aiming a glare at Kennard that was ice-cold despite the all-encompassing heat.

Kennard could only watch as his finger squeezed the trigger.

Seventy-One

January 21 – 12.23 – Wind direction NW – Surface speed 35km/h

29.5 hours since North Rislake evacuation

South Rislake status = Red (Evacuation procedures commence)

Pyro-cumulonimbus warning in place

There was no shot. Russell stared at the gun. He tried again. Still no shot. It had jammed. Possibly the extreme temperatures coupled with the extra heat from the bullet that had killed Joel had warped the internal mechanism.

Kennard let out a shaky breath, trying to collect himself. 'Am I right?' he asked, glancing around, trying to buy time. Trying to increase Russell's confusion.

Russell pulled the trigger again. Same result. No shot.

'Maybe she had found something with Joel. You had let her down too many times. Either that or you couldn't get it up. The pregnancy shows that there was nothing wrong with her reproductive system. It was all you,' Kennard continued, faster now, trying to wind Russell up into making a mistake.

'He was just taking advantage of her. Like a weasel,' hissed Russell.

He raised the gun again and pulled the trigger, three or four times, desperation taking over. They were all jams. Kennard felt his heart fluttering, his own breaths rasping now, struggling for air.

'So, what was it? What made you kill her? Desperate to be the big man again? The big, bad debt collector?'

Russell's composure cracked. 'I didn't want to be a laughing stock. A failure. Do you know how that feels?'

'I do,' said Kennard, the image of Rhian Thorpe at the forefront of his mind. 'The only reason I'm up here at all is because I let a boy die. So, I do know how it feels to make the wrong choice. But if you drop the gun, we can sort everything out. I promise.'

Russell fell silent. Kennard pressed his feet into the earth to suppress the urge to back away. He looked at the gun. It was still a little out of reach. But there was a chance.

He steadied himself and tried to draw in another deep breath, but nerves seemed to have caused his lungs to shrink. All around them the smoke had grown thicker, as if night was rapidly closing in even though the afternoon had barely begun. Maybe the wind direction had changed again, sending the smoke towards them. If so, he hadn't felt it. Though it was hard to feel anything through the heavy clothing, mask and goggles. Something was definitely wrong, however. His lungs weren't getting enough air.

This realization caused his anxiety to spike again. It felt like he was trapped in a bubble, his focus drifting away, all his former failures suddenly coming back to haunt him. He tried to catch another breath, but all he could taste was fear.

'Struggling?' asked Russell. There wasn't concern in his voice so much as glee.

Kennard blinked hard, trying to snap out of it. It didn't work. He could feel heat course through his body, his limbs heavy, exhaustion taking over.

'I nicked your air line earlier. I was wondering how long it would take for you to feel it. Luckily you spent a long time demonstrating how smart you are.'

Kennard heard the words, but it took a few seconds to grasp them entirely. He thought back to when Russell had helped him up off his knees and on with the mask. Plenty of time to tamper with his equipment. Especially for somebody who was familiar with it.

'They'll look . . .' said Kennard, but couldn't muster the breath for more words.

'I'm sure they will, but it will take them a while to find you. Especially as we're not east of Caldicott as you told them on the radio. We're west. I lied. Just to keep them off our tails a little while longer. Give us some breathing space.'

Russell laughed loudly at the joke, basking in the plentiful oxygen from his pack.

'We know the truth.'

There was another laugh. At Kennard's desperation.

'That won't help *you*, though, will it? And how will your colleagues prove it? The actual murder weapon is long gone. That arsehole Devon isn't going to blab about his business, and neither is Stoltz. He'll retract any story with enough pressure. Me and Devon will come to an understanding. I know about the port being used to smuggle shipments into the country now after the last one was busted by that reporter, Meddlesome, or whatever her name was.'

'It won't last.'

'It will. He owes me for saving his skin in that fight. Now he can repay me. Get me out of the country. Get some distance from this.'

Kennard squeezed his eyes shut again. This was no good. The mask had to come off. The air looked thick and dense and no doubt hot enough to scald his lungs, but it had to be better than no air at all.

But what then? He could run, but he was likely to simply be shot in the back if the gun began to work, and even if it didn't, he wouldn't make it very far before Russell caught and overpowered him. More talking wasn't going to help. He had thought he was being smart in buying time for backup to arrive, but they could be anywhere now, having been given the wrong directions. By him. Trusting Russell, the killer, once again.

There was only one choice. He had to stand his ground here. Face up to Russell. Bring him to justice.

Another tortured breath made his mind up for him. Ripping the mask off, he inhaled deeply. The air was mostly smoke and fumes, charged with the scent of destruction, burning foliage, heavy and clogging. He coughed hard, doubled over, forcing out soot and phlegm and taking another breath, dragging in some oxygen from closer to the ground. He felt dizzy, his mind slow and his muscles slower. Russell and the gun were somewhere above him. There had been no shot yet, the plodding cow waiting dumbly for the bolt to the back of the head. He could only pray the gun was still jammed or Russell was expecting him to just collapse and die. But he wasn't going to.

Tensing all of the muscles in his limbs and blanking out the danger, he charged.

Only after the first long stride did he look up. Through the blur of slow motion and lack of oxygen he could see Russell raise the gun and prepare to shoot.

This time the gunshot came, and not even the roar of the fire or the tight balaclava could muffle the sound of the report. Something ripped into his body, twisting it to the side. The pain arrived instantly. But it wasn't enough to halt his forward motion.

He smashed into Russell. Low, as planned. Right into his dodgy knee. Kennard's shoulder jarred as it met bone, eliciting another burst of pain, greater than he'd expected, as if he had broken his collarbone in the collision.

His target fell. Chopped down like a tree in a firebreak to stop it causing more harm.

Kennard too hit the deck, ash puffing up around him, choking his breath. The earth felt hot underneath his body, even through the bunker gear. He looked at his arm. It hung limply, the pain severe, blood flowing from a hole in his jacket. Trying to ignore it, he summoned his remaining energy and began to crawl forward on his one good arm to try to get on top of Russell and subdue him. He'd only made it a couple of inches when a foot shot out and kicked him in the injured limb. Kennard cried out in anguish, his mind no longer dulled with lack of oxygen but with agony. His arm felt like it was on fire, as if flames were searing directly through the wound and right into his bones.

Looking up, he watched Russell clamber to his feet only to fall back to the earth in an explosion of ash. His cry of pain gave Kennard another burst of energy. Russell's old injury returning. The bane of his life. Evening things up a little.

The pursuit began. Kennard crawled after Russell, who in turn scrambled away, his hands sweeping through the blackened undergrowth. Searching for the gun which had been lost in the tackle. Kennard joined the search, the ash stirred up by their hands turning into a blinding mist.

Suddenly Russell's torso jerked to the right as he grabbed at something. With no time to waste Kennard made it to a crouch and pounced. His good hand grabbed the gun. His bad arm curled in, his elbow smashing directly into Russell's face, sending his mask up into the bridge of his nose, forcing his head against the packed, dry earth.

Kennard rolled to the side, wrestling the gun away from the dazed Russell. Blinking the pain away, he pointed the gun at him, now just a blur among the floating ash.

'Enough, Russell.'

It was all he could manage with the lack of oxygen and a mouth that tasted like a workhouse pub's ashtray.

He tried for a breath. There was nothing. The deep, hacking cough doubled him over again, his lungs hurting as badly as his arm, tight and closed as if Russell had crushed them in his fist.

His blurred vision caught Russell backing away, using his one good leg to propel himself. The gun had gone but he still had the most important piece of equipment: a working oxygen tank. He just needed to get far enough away and wait it out. He could even use the blown-out knee to his advantage when spinning his story, explaining why he hadn't been able to drag Kennard to safety. The brave detective who had been shot by a desperate and guilty Joel. Kennard couldn't allow that. He pushed on, staggering forward to try to rip the breathing equipment from Russell's face, but his target merely backed off further. Kennard's fear rose, his lungs empty. The desperate fear of being unable to breathe overwhelmed him. He collapsed to the earth, crawling after Russell, gasping out with each excruciatingly painful movement. Two pathetic figures sliding across the ash and detritus trying to survive in the middle of a bushfire. Kennard had no air in his lungs now, but he kept going. Following. Chasing. Not going to give up. Not this time.

A sudden rush of wind passed over him, followed by heavy thudding sounds, as though his heart were pumping the last of its precious oxygen through him. Then came the shadows, riding in like the four horsemen of the Apocalypse. They grabbed him. Lifted him. About to carry him away from his prize for good. But he saw the horsemen grab his prey too. Taken together. Neither of them destined to win.

Though his fugue, Kennard was able to see that instead of being dressed in the traditional black, these horsemen wore fluorescent jackets and bunker gear. It was the last confusing step for his consciousness. He could feel it wane. They have him. They have Russell. He was safe to go now.

So, he went.

Seventy-Two

January 22 – 11.21 – Wind direction E – Surface speed 5km/h

52.5 hours since North Rislake evacuation

Rislake status = Green/Yellow (Remain vigilant. Residents may return)

Wherever this was, it was too bright. Like a summer's day once again, not a cloud in the sky and the sun beating down oppressively onto him. But there wasn't just the one sun. There were four, dotted in the four corners of the sky. A sky that was a pale blue, clear of smoke. He took a breath to make sure he wasn't dreaming. The pain confirmed that he was very much awake. Air struggled into his lungs, his throat bone-dry.

He tried to lift his arms. The gnawing ache in one was overtaken by the stabbing pain in the other. If this was heaven, God or whoever was in charge were short on morphine.

His good hand came up to his nose. Tubes trailed from his nostrils, a cannula bandaged into place at his elbow and connected to a drip.

Heaven was beginning to look a lot like a hospital.

'He's awake.'

A face filled his vision. Clear, not masked by smoke. Ann, his wife, was looking down at him and smiling wider than he had seen in six long months, her red hair falling down from behind her ears like curtains, the orange freckles that he had fallen in love with dotting her nose.

'How long was . . . ?'

He stopped there and coughed, his chest heavy. He felt like he was swallowing razorblades.

'You breathed in a lot of ash,' said Ann. 'The doctors say you're okay, though. Or will be in a couple of days. Your arm will take a few months but there's no permanent damage.'

'What happened?'

'How much do you remember?'

'Nothing after the firefighters picked me up.'

'They picked you *both* up.'

Kennard crooked his head to the side to make out the source of the voice. It was Layton. She was standing in the corner of the room.

'How did they find us?'

'They told me that they couldn't find any trace of you, Russell or Joel east of Caldicott. I couldn't understand why they were searching east when I knew you had gone west.'

'Russell lied,' said Kennard.

'I got them to redirect the search and they found you both. Which I believe makes it two to one. To me.'

'What does?'

'Saving you,' said Layton with a smile.

Kennard returned it. Weakly. 'And Joel?'

Layton shook her head. 'Dead.'

'Russell admitted everything,' said Kennard, keeping his sentences short for the benefit of his throat. 'Killed Tracey in an argument. Planted the weapon. Started the fire.'

'He hasn't talked yet, but he will,' said Layton.

'You have him?'

'On another ward. Guarded. His knee's wrecked. Ligaments gone again.'

'Footy career over,' said Kennard with a smile.

'On hold for the next twenty years at least,' said Layton.

'And the fire?'

'It's finally under control. They saved most of the town. The north side will recover. And no lives were lost in the fire.'

Which Kennard supposed was officially true. He had another question.

'Karen and Alvin?'

'Released. Their farm suffered pretty extensive smoke damage but nothing else. They'll get ownership of Tracey's half of the land and the house after everything is signed and stamped.'

Layton stepped forward, thrusting a phone at his face.

'What does it say?' he asked, the words blurry up close.

Layton took back the phone and read out the headline and the article beneath it.

433

'Killer Caught in Bushfire Murder Plot. Brave police and firefighters teamed up to capture a murderer in the midst of a bushfire which threatened the picturesque tourist hotspot of Rislake yesterday. DS Alex Kennard, the detective who led the hunt for and capture of the suspect, has been praised for his bravery.'

Kennard smiled. He wanted to stay awake but found his eyes closing of their own accord. He was exhausted. Every muscle in his body seemed drained of energy. For the first time in a long, long time he felt at peace.

Acknowledgements

Well, it's been a while, folks!

Assuming of course you have read the other two books. If not, hello! And welcome.

Straight off I have to say that this has been a blast to write, despite the terrifying subject matter of bushfires and the destruction they wreak. In the book I tried to get across the power and devastating qualities of bushfires, how they can uproot a community and destroy livelihoods, and I hope I have in some small way.

Geography plays a big part in all of my writing, and Rislake itself is based on a town in the Blue Mountains that I visited in 2019 and which provided some of the inspiration for this novel. Some of you will probably have a good idea of where: a beautiful town that I kind of fell in love with when I was there, unique, undulating and spectacular, and which I have reshaped and reimagined into the town central to this book. As ever, I thank Australia as a whole for always being so vivid in my imagination and a pleasure to write about every time.

I've got lots of people to thank at Simon & Schuster

for their dedication and perseverance with this book. To Katherine for editing and making the book much, much better; Victoria and Georgina – who quite eerily is almost an exact namesake for one of the main characters even though the book was written before I met her – for their copy-editing and making sense of my numerous mistakes. Everyone else behind the scenes also deserves a big thank you; for the cover design, marketing, promotion and everything that I would have absolutely no idea how to do, so thank you all for your hard work.

A shout out to my wonderful agent, Marilia, who as ever provides me with a first edit, great advice and direction, and is a champion for all my work no matter how many manuscripts I try to snow her under with.

I'm lucky to be part of a wonderful network of writers, from the Criminal Minds group to those further afield, who provide support and plenty of distraction. There are too many of them to name but they know who they are. Hopefully. I'll remind them next time I see them.

My wife is my first reader, who I can guarantee will provide me with her honest opinion on what works and what doesn't and who is there for me through thick and thin. I often take it for granted just how much she does for my soul and I shouldn't. I resolve to improve on that and this book is dedicated to her. For everything. I've got to thank my parents and my family who brought me up to love reading books and inventing things to do on long, rainy days, though I probably also have the Irish climate to thank for that.

Finally, a thanks to all the readers and booksellers out

there who support us and give us their time and dedication. Without them we are just shouting into the wind.

That's about it, and I hope to be back on the page soon in WA, NSW or wherever the story takes me.

All the best!
James